HARRY

THE TARGET

Laurie Dicker

Dicker Books

Dicker Books
PO Box 1304, Buderim, Qld, Australia, 4556

www.dicker-books.com

First published by Dicker Books, 2020

This is a work of fiction. Characters, institutions and organisations mentioned in this novel are either the product of the author's imagination or, if real, used fictitiously without any intent to describe actual conduct.

ISBN: 978 0 6488954 0 4

Prepublication Data Service
National Library of Australia
Dicker, Laurie
Harry The Target
Editor: Rosemary Allan
Cover design: Marnie Hinton
Proof: Lorraine Wendt

Crime mystery fiction—Australia

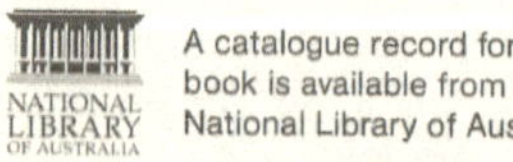

A catalogue record for this book is available from the National Library of Australia

Dedicated to

Marjie

for her support, encouragement

and inspiration.

Chapter 1
Thursday

It's New Year. One minute past midnight, 1948. Detective Senior Constable Harry Taylor was standing near the window in the converted shed that he rented for ten shillings a week from his Uncle Joseph. His uncle owned an impressive terrace house facing Hugo Street in Redfern. Harry was watching and listening to the fireworks explode over the city. A spectacular light display shot dancing flashes of colour onto the stark grey walls of his flat. Explosions from the nearby fireworks were deafening. Harry's spirits were lifted by the cheering from the nearby hotel and railway station. The city was alive with the spirit of the celebrations. Joy, excitement and love was in the air.

Earlier that evening Harry had been at his friend Tony Jacobs' house for a barbecue. He'd come home early. He was still feeling the after-effects of malaria he'd picked up in WWII while serving behind enemy lines in New Guinea and Borneo. He'd been in the special commando Z Force, four years ago. Tony, the head of the Scientific Investigations Bureau, was a wonderful host, but Harry had not been up for the small talk and heavy drinking from some of his police friends. He was tired from the long hours investigating the murder of a well-known criminal at Pyrmont two weeks ago. He wanted a quiet night at home.

Boom! The window next to Harry's head exploded in a shower of glass. He went down, flat on the floor. He was hit. Blood oozed from wounds on his face, neck and shoulders.

Cutting through the noise of the fireworks, he heard the full -throttle roar of a motorbike in the lane next to his flat.

Harry switched automatically to his army training: if hit, go down. Lie still. Count to thirty. If you're still breathing you're not dead; but the enemy thinks you are and moves on.

Harry was about to sit up when he heard a loud banging on the door. He froze. Should he play dead or prepare for the next assault?

"Harry? Harry? Are you okay? What happened? It's Uncle Joe. We're coming in."

Harry lifted his head. "Uncle Joe, be careful. There's broken glass on the floor. Wait till I get up. I'll check the damage."

Uncle Joe; dressed in short pyjamas and leather slippers, opened the door cautiously. He breathed heavily with anxiety, his face was flushed, his eyes flicked back and forth nervously. His dishevelled grey hair made him look anything but the stereotypical image of a professional city accountant.

Before Joe could utter a word, Aunty Mary; hair in rollers, brunch coat hanging loosely around her body, feet in pink fluffy slippers, pushed past him to get to Harry.

"Oh my God. My poor boy. What happened?" Mary kneeled beside Harry but jumped up quickly to find a shard of glass dangling from her leg. She pulled it out and wiped the blood away with the bottom of her nightie.

"Wait a moment, Aunty. I'm okay. I'll get up and sit in the chair."

Harry sat up slowly but felt weak. He paused for a moment and, using the leg of the table for support, pulled himself up. He reached for a tea-towel on the table to stem the bleeding from a face wound.

"My God, Harry," said Joe, as he came further into the room to assess the damage. "What happened? This place is a mess."

Harry looked at the window before replying. "It was a shotgun blast. Look at the way the window shattered. Someone tried to kill me."

"Did you see who did it, Harry?" asked Mary as she ran her fingers gently through his hair to remove pieces of glass.

Harry pointed to the window. "Just before the blast I noticed a shadowy figure go past outside, but I didn't have time to react before the window exploded beside my head."

Joe walked over to the window. "How the hell did you survive when the gun was so close to the window?"

Harry turned and studied the damage. "Uncle Joe, I can only put it down to my good luck and his bad management. Look at the window. It's colonial in style with four panes of glass. The shooter obviously rushed his shot when he saw me turning around. It looks as if the timber joints in the middle absorbed most of the blast. You can see how those centre joints are smashed and pushed to one side. It appears that the shooter was also at an angle to the window when he pulled the trigger."

Harry staggered to the window and pushed out some shards of glass. He pointed in the direction of the shot. "When shotgun pellets hit glass they lose some momentum. And being side on, the friction on impact changes their direction. But he still got me; and it feels like I copped some pellets and splinters of glass."

"Joe, get the car now. Come on. Get going. Hurry, hurry. We're taking Harry to the hospital," screamed Mary, as if Joe was upstairs in the house.

"No, Aunty. I'm alright," interrupted Harry. "I just need to get cleaned up here. I need to get after that shooter."

"Did you see who it was, Harry?" asked Joe.

"No. It all happened so quickly; and he was in the dark. I heard a motorbike roar away; so he won't be anywhere around here by now." Harry tried to get up but fell back onto the chair as shock set in.

"Joe. For God's sake, get the bloody car now," shouted Mary, wiping away some of the blood to check out Harry's wounds. She used her former training and experience as a nurse to check the cuts to his face, neck, shoulders and upper back. Pieces of glass and pellets were embedded in his neck and face and had cut through his shirt. Harry looked in a bad way. She needed to get him to hospital quickly. He was suffering from shock and loss of blood.

Joe brought his prized 1938 Riley sedan to the back gate. He and Mary helped Harry into the front seat.

"Take him straight to St Vincent's Hospital at Darlinghurst, Joe. That will be the nearest," shouted Mary as she jumped into the back seat.

"No," said Joe. "The New Year's revellers at Kings Cross will be all over the road up that way. I'll go straight to Royal Prince Alfred on Missenden Road instead; much quicker. They won't have as many drunks and crash victims to deal with in the emergency unit."

***

Joe screeched to a halt under the emergency sign. Mary rushed in to get help. A young triage nurse in her starched blue tunic, white cap and cream lisle stockings came to assess Harry. She quickly called for a gurney to take him inside.

"Get this man into surgery," she shouted as she pushed the gurney along the corridor. "Get Doctor Smithers and Doctor White now. This is an emergency. Come on. Move it. Move. Move."

Another nurse ran into a room at the end of the corridor shouting for the two doctors. They came out and disappeared into the surgical theatre where they had taken Harry.

Joe went outside to move his car. Mary collapsed onto a hard chair in the corridor, looking somewhat bedraggled. Rollers and strands of hair were dangling over her face and her brunch coat was stained with blood; but she couldn't care less. She and Joe had no children and they looked on Harry as their own when he stayed in the shed at the back of their house. There was no way she could face Harry's parents if she had done nothing to help him.

Joe, still in his pyjamas and slippers, returned and stood beside Mary to await the results of Harry's examination. Another nurse, seeing their distress, escorted them to a waiting room, poured cups of tea and placed some arrowroot biscuits on a saucer.

Joe started to think. Will Harry survive? Will he be crippled for life? Who wants to kill him? Does it have anything to do with his current investigations? Was it the result of mistaken identity? Was it some idiot, drunk with New Year celebrations, firing a shotgun randomly to let off steam? Will he still be able to work as a policeman or will he have to return to Goonaburra to work on the farm to help his aging father? So many questions. So few answers.

Chapter 2
Thursday

Uncle Joe came out of the waiting room and, on seeing a nurse, called out, "Excuse me, Miss. That man who you took into the operating theatre is a detective and someone tried to kill him. Please call the police and let them know. They'll want to get on to it straight away."

"I'll get on to it as soon as I take this plasma into the theatre," replied the nurse, all prim and proper in her neat uniform.

"Come on, Mary," said Joe as he walked back into the waiting room. "Let's go home and get cleaned up. There's nothing we can do here until they finish with Harry in the theatre."

Mary stomped her foot and pointed her finger angrily at Joe. "There's no way I'm leaving here until I know he's okay. You can go if you like, but I'm staying right here."

The nurse came back. "I've rung the police. Someone from the Newtown station will be here as soon as they can. Now you two go home. Harry will be in theatre for some time. You'll have plenty of time to go home and have breakfast before you can see him."

Mary thumped the coffee table. "Don't tell me what to do, young lady. I'm staying here until I know that he is safe and well."

Joe moved quickly to Mary's side, put his arm around her shoulder and lifted her face. "Darling, don't blame the young nurse. She and the others are doing everything to get Harry well and there's nothing we can do to help." He lifted her gently to her feet. "Now, we're going home to get tidied up, have some breakfast and get back here when nurse lets us know Harry is out of theatre."

"Thank you, Mr and Mrs Taylor. We will look after Harry. Give me your number and I will call you at home if there is a change." The nurse showed them to the door.

As Joe and Mary drove onto Missenden Road, a police wagon with lights flashing, turned sharply into the hospital entrance. Sergeant Stan Drummond and Constable Alby Green rushed up the steps. The triage nurse, Penny Alexander, met them in the corridor.

The sergeant stepped forward, overshadowing the petite Penny. "We have been told that you have a policeman here who has been shot. We need to see him now."

Penny stretched herself to the full extent of her five foot three inches, looked up at the sergeant and sternly replied. "The policeman is in surgery and will remain there without interruption until the theatre doctors and I decide otherwise. Now, how might I be of help to you?"

"I don't think you understand, miss. A policeman has been shot and we need to get out there and catch the perpetrator. To do that, we need to speak to him. So, show us the way to theatre now."

"My name is Nurse Alexander and I am the triage nurse on duty tonight. I will decide who goes where in this unit, and I'm telling you that you will not be able to see him until he is fit and well enough to see you."

"That's not good enough, Nurse Alexander. We will go into that theatre when we..."

"You'll do no such thing," interrupted Penny. "Turn around and get into that reception area and I'll tell you as much as I know. If you try to enter that theatre I'll have you removed from the premises. Is that clear?"

The policemen followed Penny to the reception room but remained standing. She explained the extent of Harry's wounds and what would happen in theatre. She stated that the weapon was a shot gun as revealed by the pellets. She described Joe and Mary and their efforts in getting Harry to the hospital. Stan noted their phone number and address in his book.

"I anticipate that the officer will be in theatre for at least three hours and then in recovery for some time after that," explained Penny. "If you leave the phone number of your station, I will call you when he's in a fit state to be interviewed. Goodbye officers. I have to go. There are many casualties here tonight and I don't have time to stand around talking any more with you."

The officers left, mumbling to themselves.

Harry was lying on his stomach, unconscious on the operating table. Arthur Smithers worked on one side while Don White attended to the other. They were both experienced trauma surgeons who maintained an unflustered approach to their work, while other staff were running around like chooks with their heads cut off.

"How's it going on your side, Don?" asked Arthur.

"Not too bad. The deeper wounds are mostly on your side which must have been closer to the window when the shot was fired. I've closed off some of the worst ones here at the back of the neck and shoulder."

Arthur pointed at Harry's neck. "He's bloody lucky. Two slivers of glass penetrated on this side, but missed an artery by a fraction of an inch." He tied off the stitches below the ear.

Don shifted his attention from the neck to the deep cut into the shoulder blade. "Thankfully, the cuts missed his major arteries on this side; although the overall impact has put him into shock. We'll have to keep him sedated for some time yet. I'll give him a shot of epinephrine to reduce the impact and increase his blood pressure."

Arthur turned Harry's head and finished stitching a deep wound along the jaw line and pointed to another wound. "He was lucky with this one here. It hit his temple and sliced upwards across his eye brow just missing his eyeball. That could have been very nasty."

Nurse Lucy Withers hovered in the background, attending to needles, threads, swabs, forceps and the other piece of equipment required by the doctors. They were a well-oiled team. She wiped the doctors' brows. It was a hot humid night and the closed theatre let in no fresh air. The large ceiling fans were working overtime, but to little effect. "When you have closed the worst wounds let me know and I'll get some mugs of tea."

Don nodded as he closed off another wound. "He's lost some blood, but not enough to warrant a transfusion; and the plasma is taking effect now. The good news is that he is very fit in what I call a case-hardened sort of way. It'll certainly help his recovery. He's a very lucky man."

At that moment the door opened and in came a man dressed in police uniform, closely followed by Penny Alexander screaming at him. "Get out, get out of there. How dare you go in there against my orders. This is a sterile clinical operating theatre. Get out now."

Arthur Smithers put down his forceps, thread and needle and walked towards the intruder. "Get out of this theatre now. Who told you that you could come in here?"

"I am Chief Superintendent Twain from the New South Wales Police. The man on that table is one of my officers and he has been shot. I need to talk to him now. We have to get out there and catch the person responsible."

Arthur Smithers was six foot six inches tall, fourteen stone and as fit as a mallee bull on steroids. He played for many years in the front row of the Sydney University first grade rugby union team and never took a backward step. Now, he stepped towards the superintendent, jabbing his fingers into his chest, pushing him out through the door. In the corridor outside he shoved the Superintendent down into a chair.

"I don't care if you're Jesus Christ or God Almighty. You don't come into my operating theatre unless I say so."

Don White strode out fuming as he swept past Twain. "You fucking idiot. You have now contaminated that room. We will have to change and scrub up again and shift to another theatre. We have a corridor full of patients in emergency waiting for us to finish here. That man in there could die because you have delayed our chances of saving him. If he dies on the table in there, I'm going to hold you responsible."

Arthur shouted. "Nurse, call security to get this prick out of here. If he comes back, I'll castrate the bastard and throw his balls into the garden for the crows to eat."

Allan Twain got up, brushed down his neatly starched uniform, and strode towards the door.

Penny Alexander followed and called out. "Sir, wait a moment please."

Allan Twain half-turned with a look that hovered between disgust, anger and embarrassment. "What?"

Penny pointed. "Please come into the reception room for a moment. Let me explain."

Penny poured a mug of tea and handed it to Allan. "This is an emergency unit. This is New Year's Eve. We are short-staffed, and as you can see in the corridors, we have many casualties needing attention. We will be lucky to finish this lot before dinner tonight. Those two doctors are working their arses off to save your detective and will probably be on duty for over twenty-four hours with him and the others here. With luck, and their skills, he will survive. But he won't be ready to be interviewed for some time."

Allan Twain pulled at his collar and wiped his brow with his sleeve. "But I need to get on with this investigation. The killer is getting away. I need to move now."

Penny picked up a pen and pad. "Give me your phone number and I will let you know when you can see him. Is that understood?"

"I suppose that's all I can expect," he replied as he stood up, wrote the number on Penny's pad and walked out, leaving his mug of tea untouched.

When the doctors completed their final tie-offs, Harry was wheeled into the recovery room for the remainder of the day.

Chapter 3
Friday

Harry woke to find himself in a hospital bed and overlooking a lane. It was early morning and the air felt like a hot, wet blanket; typical in January after an overnight thunderstorm. He could see the steam rising from the bitumen. He kicked off the sheet. His head was throbbing. When he tried to stand, he remembered being brought to the hospital by Uncle Joe and Aunty Mary. The door opened.

"Good morning, Detective," said the nurse. "Now hold on a moment. Take it easy. You have a lot of injuries. Let me help you. We don't want any of those wounds opening up."

"Call me Harry, nurse," he said as he slowly stretched, feeling the stings as the stitches strained to hold together. "Where am I?"

"My name is Janet Simpson, Harry. I'll be looking after you today. You are in the Royal Prince Alfred Hospital. You came in last night in a bad way. Someone tried to shoot you. You were operated on last night and you are now in the ward. We have got you in a room by yourself. The police department have a guard outside your room."

"My head, neck and shoulders feel so sore. Tell me the truth. How bad is it?"

Janet eased Harry back onto the edge of the bed. "Let me explain, Harry. You are an extremely lucky man. Doctor Smithers and Doctor White worked on you through the night and did a marvellous job. You were lucky they were on last night. They are the best in their field of trauma surgery. You were also lucky that the window took most of the shot before it hit you. Luck was again on your side because the splinters of glass missed all of your vital organs and arteries. You should get someone to go and place a bet on the horses for you today."

Janet placed her hands under Harry's armpits and gently turned him while she described each of his wounds. He was impressed by the confident way she went about her explanation. He felt he was in safe hands. Although he felt very sore, he realised his wounds were mostly superficial rather than deep and life threatening. He felt relieved that there was probably not going to be much permanent damage other than a few scars and lots of bruising. "Thanks for that, Janet. That makes me feel a lot better. Could you help me to the toilet?"

Janet took him by the arm and led him out to the corridor where a smart young constable snapped to attention.

Harry tapped him on the arm. "Relax, sunshine. I'm Harry Taylor, and I presume you are here to guard me. Is that right?"

"Yes. I'm Constable Jack Travers from Newtown Police, and I'm on duty here until midday."

"Well, Jack," replied Harry with a grin, feeling a little more relaxed, "you'll have to help me go to the toilet and, because I'm injured, you'll have to hold the old fella for me when I go."

"What did you say?" gulped Jack.

Harry coughed out a weak laugh, happy that he was still alive and relieved he was capable of walking and talking. He patted the constable on the shoulder. "Don't worry, Jack, I'll get Nurse Simpson to do it for me. She'll know what to do. You stay outside and keep the others away. Don't let anyone in while we're in there."

"That was naughty of you, Harry." said Janet as she helped him onto the toilet.

"Don't worry, Janet. He seems a decent bloke, and he'll come across a lot worse than me before much longer in this police force. You haven't got your eye on him, have you?"

Janet gave him a gentle smack on the bottom as he sat. "Call out when you are finished."

When Harry got back into bed and Janet had left, the impact of what happened last night cut through the early morning mental fog. This was serious. Forget about the injuries; someone had tried to murder him. He had been in many fire fights in the jungles of Borneo and New Guinea, working behind enemy lines with Z Force against the Japanese. In those situations, however, he knew who the enemy was and where they were coming from. It was extremely dangerous, but he could plan for the attacks. In this situation, he didn't know the enemy or from which direction they would attack next.

The questions Harry asked himself were many. Who could be trusted? Why would anyone want to kill me? Did it have anything to do with my recent investigations into the murders of those young women out at Goonaburra? Was it a random hit that has nothing to do with me personally? Was it mistaken identity? Who could hate me so much to murder me? Was it connected to my current investigations into the death of Knuckles Elliott, the small-time criminal, at Pyrmont? If so, why did they want to stop my investigation? Who was so involved to want to take that action? Who had the most to lose? Do I need to follow the money trail?

Harry was known for his clear analytical thinking. After tossing all the possibilities around in his mind he eliminated the least likely causes of his attack. Some people in Goonaburra were unhappy with his investigations and would have liked to punch in his head, but he was certain it had nothing to do with that case. He was also convinced it was not a random attack or an accident caused by some drunken fool letting off steam in the local neighbourhood on New Year's Eve.

In the end, it came down to his recent investigations being the most likely compost heap from which this attempt on his life germinated and grew. He decided to revisit everything that had happened in the last few weeks.

***

Before Christmas, 'Knuckles' Elliot, a miserable low-life criminal was shot and killed in broad daylight at Pyrmont. His body was found under a tree in Fig Lane Park; two nine millimetre shots to his head. It was a professional hit. Chief Superintendent Allan Twain called in Harry to investigate.

"I'm short-staffed, Harry. I am sending you a new young detective, Constable Jock Burns, to assist. I can't give you any more officers. He should be there shortly. It's obviously a gangland killing so it shouldn't be too difficult to find the culprit."

Harry drove to Fig Lane Park. He noticed a roped-off area surrounding a body covered by a tarpaulin. A local constable, guarding the site, was talking to another young man in a suit, tie and hat.

The other man strode stiffly towards Harry as if he was on army parade. He confidently thrust out his hand. "Good morning, Detective. I'm Jock Burns. I've heard a lot about you and, can I say, I'm pleased to be working with you on this case."

Harry sized him up and was impressed with what he saw. Jock was about five-foot-ten and super fit in a rock-hard-granite sort of way. He reminded Harry of a regimental sergeant major from the Royal Scots' battalion he'd met in Singapore immediately after the war. He was alert and keen to go. The stiff regimentation could be knocked out of him later. "G'day, Jock. I'm Harry. Pleased to have you on board. We should make a good team. Now let's get busy."

The uniformed officer turned. "Good morning, Harry," said Senior Constable Mark Lindsey. "Great to see you again. I answered the call today and I've been here waiting for you to arrive."

"G'day, Mark. What can you tell me?"

"We got a phone call at the station that there had been a shooting, so I rushed here. Knuckles was already dead. There was nothing I could do for him. I secured the site and went across the road to see the bloke who called it in."

Harry looked at the surrounding buildings. "Where does this bloke live?"

"Across the other side of the park in that terrace house over in Upper Fig Street; that one with the flower box near the front door. His name is 'Chook' Fowler."

"Jock, get over there and interview Mr Fowler, and call into all the other terraces to see if anyone else saw this shooting. Mark, you go across the street to the phone box and call Tony Jacobs at the Scientific Investigation Bureau. Tell him to get his forensics team out here as soon as possible."

Harry started in the roped-off area. He lifted the tarp to examine the body. It was slumped awkwardly, face up. He easily identified Knuckles. The distinctive tattoos of snakes and skulls down both arms, on his neck and on his hands were clear evidence. Harry had booked him for minor offences in the past.

Harry turned Knuckles' head to get a better look at the wounds. The first entry hole was central to the lower forehead and slightly larger than a nine-millimetre bullet. Harry surmised that it might have been a hollow-pointed slug, which probably meant that it spread on impact and, together with the sonic blast, would have made mincemeat of the brain. The fact that there was no exit hole tended to support that theory. A second shot had hit Knuckles in the mouth and exited below the ear. He had no other injuries.

Harry could see stippling, discolouration and a darkened edge around the forehead wound that he took to mean the shot came from very close range. The fact that there were no other injuries suggested either Knuckles came voluntarily with his assassin, or that they had met in the park. He had not been beaten up elsewhere and carried to that site. He probably knew and trusted his killer. This had all the hallmarks of a clean, ruthless professional murder.

Mark returned to help Harry search for any other evidence. They covered the area around the body and out into the laneway, but found nothing of significance.

When Jock returned, he reported that Chook Fowler had seen the whole event. The killer had got out of a black two-door Ford coupé; about a 1937 model. He wore a rain jacket with a hood so Chook couldn't see his face. He shook hands with the victim and then pulled out a gun and shot two rounds to the head. He ran back to the car and drove off, turning right into Bulwarra Road. Chook said the killer was a big man with a slight limp. Some other neighbours heard the shots and saw the car drive away but didn't see the killer.

After the forensic team arrived, Harry drove Jock back to the Central Street Police Station to show him Knuckles' police record and to discuss tactics. He showed Jock where Knuckles fitted into the big crime scene in Sydney.

He displayed mug shots of the four main crime bosses in Sydney. The first was 'Whispers' Durante who owned hotels, nightclubs and illegal casinos, operating mostly out of Woolloomooloo. He'd got his nickname after a knife attack to his throat before the war. 'Squeaky' Walsh, an ex-jockey, ran brothels and SP betting from his headquarters in Palmer Street, Darlinghurst. Rosie Travener ran brothels and the drug trade in The Rocks area. Tony 'The Greek' controlled SP betting and race fixing in town from his mansion in Marrickville. All of them were involved in the drug trade.

Under them were a number of nasty men who did the dirty work. Tom Lebovich was the standover man for both Whispers and Rosie. 'Bluey' Ricketts looked after Tony the Greek. Ben 'Bomber' Earl did break-ins and bank heists but also collected debts for Squeaky. Tony Pantano and 'Shooter' McGill were well-known hit men who worked for any of the big boys when required.

Harry explained to Jock that Knuckles was small-time but had recently tried to set up his own drug network, operating out of a number of hotels in the city. There was no way the crime bosses were going to let that happen; and that was most likely the reason why he was shot.

The next day Harry received a report of a burned out vehicle in the side street next to Harold Park Raceway. He and Jock drove there to find that it fitted the description of the Ford coupé used by the killer. They interviewed some stable hands who worked at the raceway. One of them said he looked up to see a car on fire and saw a man with a slight limp walk away around the corner. The man had removed his rain jacket as he walked away. The man's description fitted that of Tom Lebovich. Tom had a slight limp, the result of a failed attempt from a rival to kneecap him five years ago.

Following further investigations over the next week, Harry and Jock went to Darlinghurst, where they arrested Lebovich and brought him back to Central Street Station for questioning. He refused to answer any questions and demanded a phone call to his lawyer. Twenty minutes later the phone in the interview room rang.

"Harry, this is Charlie Rockwell from Criminal Investigation Branch. I understand you are holding Tom Lebovich in regard to that shooting at Pyrmont."

"Yes, Charlie. That's correct. We have reason to believe he was involved with the murder. Constable Jock Burns and myself are investigating."

"Well, I have to inform you that you two are no longer on the case. This matter will now be taken over by us in CIB. There are other matters involved with Lebovich that I don't intend to go into here. We will handle this matter now. Thanks for your good work but you will now leave it to us."

"But the chief super put us on this case," explained Harry.

"Listen to my words carefully, Harry. You are no longer on the case. Have the desk sergeant hold Lebovich and we will be in there shortly to take over."

Harry went to Allan Twain's office. "Sir, could you please explain why you took us off the case when we had the main suspect here in the room and about to lay charges?"

"It has nothing to do with your work, Harry. Some of the big crime bosses from Melbourne are trying to break into the Sydney scene and the locals are not happy with that. We suspect that Knuckles' murder was a result of that, and it's why I have asked the CIB boys to take over this case. It's part of a wider examination of this Melbourne matter."

"Why can't we be part of that team? We've done the hard work."

"Because I want you two for other things. My decision is final. Now leave, because I have an important meeting with the commissioner." Twain got up and left the room.

Two days later, Jack Tomlinson, the desk sergeant from Central Street, informed Harry that Tom Lebovich had been released because there was insufficient evidence to proceed to court.

Harry and Jock were given the task of investigating the disappearance of a teenager who failed to return home from a trip to Luna Park.

***

Nurse Janet came into the room to check Harry's wounds and dressings. She could see the stress on his face. "What's the matter, Harry? Which part is hurting most? Let me have a look at it."

"No, Janet. It's not the wounds. I'll get over them okay. It's just something I have to deal with in my own good time and I don't want you worrying about me."

"Doctor Smithers has asked me to give you a sedative. He wants you resting for the remainder of the day. No visitors. And that's an order. So, let's go to the toilet and then back to bed."

"And if I say no?" said Harry with a grin.

"Then I'll throw you over my shoulder, toss you on the bed and put you in a step-over toe-hold. After that I'll probably get angry and break your leg. Do you get the message?"

"Okay, okay, I hear you loud and clear. I believe you could do just that. I give in. Take me to the toilet and then tuck me in. Do I get a kiss, Mummy?"

"You'll get a smack across the bottom if you don't behave. Now get moving."

Chapter 4
Saturday

The view from Harry's bedroom window was clear. The morning was bright; hardly a breath of air. Harry thought it would be a perfect day for the beach but he was locked up in this hospital room. Nurse Simpson came in.

"Good morning, Harry. I went off duty at lunchtime yesterday, so tell me; how was yesterday afternoon, and how did you sleep last night? How do you feel this bright and beautiful morning?"

"I couldn't go to sleep last night because I was thinking about you," he replied with a cheeky grin.

"You're definitely too sick to go home. I think you need a psychiatrist. I'll arrange for one later today," was her reply as she busied herself around the bed, straightening the sheets and checking the daily reports.

With blood stained patches on his face, neck and shoulders Harry stood up, walked towards her, took her by the shoulders and said, "Janet, with your help, I'll get cleaned up and dressed and then I'll be out of here."

Janet edged him back to the bed. "You'll do no such thing. You're not leaving here until the doctor says so, and by the look of you, that will be some time yet. Now let's get you to the bathroom so that you might look half-decent for your visitors. And if you don't cooperate, I'll order the constable outside to hold you while I wash your bottom."

Harry shuffled to the door. "I thought we got rid of the Gestapo three years ago."

He felt a slight sting as the towel flicked his ankle. "Come on, soldier. Left, right, left, right, left...left...left. Come on, pick up those feet." The two of them laughed as they ambled down the corridor to the bathroom. It was such a relief after the trauma of the last couple of days.

At ten-thirty, Doctor Peterson, the hospital's resident physician, came to see Harry. After reading the notes from the other doctors and nurses he turned to Harry. "You're a very lucky man, Harry. The wounds are nowhere as bad as we initially thought. You have cuts from the glass and minor wounds from the pellets, but none are life-threatening. Most of them will leave nothing much more than minor scars. There is still much bruising, but that will disappear in the next week or two."

"Thanks, Doc. Well that means I can get out of here today and go home."

"No, Harry. There is a risk of severe infection in those wounds, and until that danger has passed, you'll remain here. I'll let you know when you can be released."

"But Doc, I'm in more danger here from the beatings I'm getting from Nurse Simpson. You've got to let me out of here."

Doctor Peterson laughed out loud. "Mate, Nurse Simpson has been placed here specially to make certain that you don't leave. So don't argue. Believe me. I did once and I got the rounds of the staff room right and proper. I'll see you again this afternoon."

As Doctor Peterson left, Janet came in to inform Harry that a journalist was outside wanting an interview about the shooting.

Harry sighed. "It's going to happen sooner or later, so let's get it over and done with. Let him in, but tell him he's got no more than five minutes."

"Hi, Detective, I'm James Bolton from the *Daily Mirror*. We met about six months ago, when you were investigating the murders of those young women at Goonaburra."

"How could I forget, James? You weren't very kind to me then, so I hope you have matured a little, now that you're working in the big time in the city." Harry pulled up the sheet.

"Sorry about that, Harry. I had a job to do then and I did what I was told."

"No, James, be truthful. You were hell-bent on getting a job with a big city newspaper. Now you've got that, start getting some balance and maturity into your stories or you won't get any cooperation from this police force. I'll promise you that. You're not working in a small country town any more. If you want to be a serious crime writer in this big city you'll have to convince both the police and the criminals that you're fair dinkum. It's all about trust, James."

James sat on the guest chair nervously twisting his pen between thumb and first finger. "What can you tell me about the shooting, Harry?"

Harry sipped a glass of water. "Very little, James. I didn't see the shooter."

"Do you think that you were the intended target, or was this a mistaken identity or accident?"

"I don't know. I've been in hospital since then, so I've had no chance to get out there to find out."

Janet came in and walked smartly to Harry's side. "Is everything alright, Detective? Is there anything you need? In two minutes I'll be back with your medication." She eyed James Bolton up and down before leaving.

"James," said Harry. "I can't help you any more at this stage. However, now that you are working in the big-time reporting, you'll be making contacts with both the police and criminals. But I'll give you some sound advice. If you make a mistake today, someone could die tomorrow. I want you to keep your ear to the ground and let me know if you hear anything; even rumours. Now, you must go before Nurse Simpson comes back and reprimands you for overstaying your time."

"Thanks, Harry, I'll keep in touch." James left as Janet returned.

Five minutes later there was a knock at the door and in walked Jock Burns who, in his broad Scottish accent, said, "Well, you look a right and proper numpty and clawbaw."

"And what the bloody hell might that mean? Speak bloody English," demanded Harry.

"It means you look like a right wanker. Do you understand that?"

Harry burst out laughing. "I think you and I will get on just fine, Jock. What's that in your hand?"

Jock handed him a parcel wrapped in brown paper. "It's pieces of my granma's black pudding, shortbread and gingerbread. She's the best cook in the world. Get that into you and you'll be up on your feet in no time. You look a bloody mess, Harry. Tell me about it."

Harry took his time to explain everything that happened from the time he'd left Tony Jacob's house on New Year's Eve. Jock had a thousand questions, for which Harry had no answers. In particular, he wanted to know if the attempt on Harry's life had anything to do with their investigation of the murder of Knuckles Elliott, and why they were taken off the case.

"What do you think, Jock?" asked Harry.

"I don't know, Harry, but something's not right. We had the main suspect and then we were kicked off the case. It's got the smell of my grandfather's socks about it. I don't like it."

Harry sat up on the side of the bed. "Is anyone talking about it?"

"This morning, someone in Central Street Station said that it all had something to do with the influx of Melbourne criminals into Sydney. They are trying to move in on the territory of the big boys here. The local boys don't like it."

"But that doesn't seem to explain the attempt to get rid of me. I've done some work lately that involved the increase in drugs in the city, but I wasn't especially involved in anything to do with this Melbourne mob. There has got to be another explanation."

"Well, Harry, I'll keep my ear to the ground. I'm still trying to find that kid who went missing after he left Luna Park. There are no clues yet."

Nurse Janet walked in. Jock stood up and watched her move around the room.

"Meet Nurse Simpson, Jock. I want her to join the police force; and when she does I won't need you any more. So, you best go now and solve that case."

"Okay, I get the message. Is she the one writing your sick-leave passes to keep you in here?"

"Now listen to me, Constable," said Janet coming around the bed. "If you go on like this, I'll have you removed and you'll never see Harry again. Is that clear?"

Jock snapped to attention, clicked his heels, saluted, turned and marched out the door with a broad grin.

Janet straightened the bedclothes. "Now, there's a young man with a bit of spirit, Harry. I like him."

"Well you can't have him. He's on my team and I want his mind on the job; not distracted by some flighty young thing who flutters her eyelashes every time he's here."

Janet was distracted by another person coming through the door. "Excuse me, sir, but who are you and what do you want? Have you got permission from the office to be here?"

"I'm Chief Superintendent Twain, and I don't need your's or anyone else's permission to be here. Now leave this room. I want to speak with Constable Taylor, alone."

"And I'm Nurse Simpson, and this is my ward, and I'll decide when it's time to leave this room. Is that clear?"

Harry interrupted. "It's okay, Nurse. This is my boss. He and I need to talk about the shooting. Thanks."

"Is he the same person who burst into the operating theatre when they were working on you? If so, I'll leave. I'll come back when he leaves." Janet strode out the door without so much as a backward glance.

"Impudent young so-and-so," snorted Twain. "I don't know what they're teaching young women these days. Since women got involved in the workforce during the war, they think they can do and say anything. They should get back in the kitchen and the bedroom where they belong."

"Well, I'd have her on my team any day. Now, did you come to inquire about my health or to inform me that you've caught the shooter?" asked Harry.

"Tell me what the doctors have said."

Harry outlined the nature of his injuries. "I anticipate that I will be out of here tomorrow and back on duty by Monday."

"No you won't," replied the chief. "You will remain on sick leave until further notice. I don't want you anywhere near this case until the shooter has been caught. That's an order."

"But I need to be out there to chase up a few leads. I was the one who was shot, not you. I have a personal stake in this investigation, and I'm going out there to catch the bastard who did this to me."

Allan Twain moved towards the bed thrusting his open hand towards Harry. "I've put the boys from the CIB onto this case. Joe Cross, Bob Crow, Charlie Rockwell and Fred Sherman will take over this investigation. They are the best in the Force. They'll find the shooter. You can bet on that."

"But I was the one who was shot; I need to be included," shouted Harry, becoming more frustrated.

"You'll do no such thing. You'll stay here until you've recovered and then you'll go on leave until I decide otherwise. That's an order." Twain turned and walked out.

Harry got out of bed and shuffled to the door to be met by Janet Simpson. "And where do you think you're going?" she asked.

"I'm going out there to strangle that bastard."

Janet saw the fury on Harry's face. She took his arm. "Now, why don't you and I go for a slow walk around the corridor and you can tell me all about it. Don't worry about him. If he comes back into this hospital I'll deal with him. So, calm down and let's go."

As they got back to the room, Tony Jacobs came into the room with a bunch of flowers.

Janet was helping Harry into the chair. "Not another one. The whole police force has been in here today. Why aren't you lot out there catching criminals? Why do we taxpayers keep supporting you when you can't even catch a fly?"

Harry patted her on the shoulder. "It's okay, Janet. This bloke's alright. He's one of the good guys. But he could have brought a bottle of whisky instead of flowers. He probably nicked those out of his neighbour's garden."

"Hello, Janet. I'm Tony Jacobs from the Scientific Investigation Bureau. I'm the one who has to clean up after Harry makes a mess. Thank goodness they've got you to look after him because nobody else would do it."

"I'll leave you two alone," said Janet as she walked out.

"I've come to tell you Harry that there is nothing surprising in the evidence from your place. It was a single 12-gauge shot. It hit the window at a 45 degree angle. You were lucky that most of the shot hit the timber joints first. There were scuff marks outside your window but no clear footprints. There was a skid mark outside your gate that resembled a take-off mark from the bike, but nothing clear."

"Thanks, Tony. I should have stayed at your place, got drunk and slept it off on the couch."

"Put it this way, Harry. You got shot this time, but you're alive. If you had stayed they would have chased you down, and the next time you might not have been so lucky. I hear they've put the big boys on this case. Is that right?"

"Yes," replied Harry trying to get up. "Twain was in here a while ago. He's put Joe, Charlie, Bob and Fred onto it."

"Hell. That's the most firepower in the country. Anything could happen with those four in charge. Stay away from it, Harry. They normally get their man. You've worked with them; you know. So sit back and relax."

"Okay, Tony. I'll think about it, but won't make any promises."

Tony snorted with doubt in his mind. "Yes. I know what that means, Harry. You haven't listened and you'll do it your way."

As Janet came back in, Tony added, "Nurse, chain this bastard to the bed until I give the all-clear. Don't let him out of here. He'll do himself and others injuries if you let him out."

"Okay, you two have had enough. Time for Harry to get cleaned up. Go on, Sergeant, out of here now."

"See you, Harry. Thanks, Nurse." Tony walked out knowing that Harry would take no notice of what he said.

Chapter 5
Saturday

As Janet helped Harry back from the bathroom they were confronted by four huge men standing in his room.

The oldest looked at Janet. "Okay, darling, you can leave him with us now. We'll look after him. Make certain we're not disturbed. Now, off you go."

Janet glared back. "I'll have you know that I'm not your darling. Only my family and boyfriend call me that. Might I ask who you are and what you are doing in this room?"

"Whatever you say girlie. I'm Detective Senior Sergeant Sherman and the others here are Detective Sergeants Cross, Rockwell and Crow. We're here to investigate the attack on Detective Taylor. Now leave the room and close the door behind you."

Harry turned. "It's okay, Janet. I know these officers. I'll be alright." Janet helped Harry to the bed and took her time straightening the bedclothes, adding a note to the daily chart and filling his glass with water before leaving.

Fred Sherman had a face that looked like a long-dead banksia flower head: hard, dried, twisted and ugly. It had been in too many rugby scrums and fights over the years. If his long-dead mother returned to earth today, she would not recognise him. He was the toughest man in the police force but was loved and glorified by senior officers, politicians, public and media. He was the man who cleaned-up the big criminals. He had received a number of bravery awards for his encounters with the worst of them. Although he was getting on in years, he was still as tough as a slab of basalt. He was a hardened, fifteen stone man who had earned his nickname of 'Sherman Tank', or more commonly, 'The Tank'.

Joe Cross, by contrast, was in his late thirties. He was good looking, had red wavy hair and was super fit. Before the war he won a medal at the Australian Pentathlon Championships. But he, like Fred, was tough and unforgiving and had also won a number of bravery awards. He was the up-and-coming man at the CIB.

Bob Crow and Charlie Rockwell were in their fifties and had been long enough in the CIB to establish strong connections with well-known criminals, politicians, lawyers, and police forces in other states and overseas. They were not as nimble-footed as Joe, but they made up for it in their knowledge and contacts in the real world of crime. The four of them were a formidable team of crime-fighters. Harry could not have had a more experienced team on his case. Shooting a policeman was at the top of the list for action by the Force. All other cases were taken off the table until they caught the person responsible.

"G'day, Harry," said Fred, settling back into the only guest chair in the room. "You look a bloody mess mate. Tell us about it."

"G'day, Fred. G'day, boys. Thanks for dropping in. I hear that you four have been put on my case."

Joe Cross had been pacing the room looking at everything in the room as well as out the window. "Yes, Harry. Twain wants us to get on and catch this bastard, so anything you can tell us will help."

"Well, Joe, I can't tell you much because I didn't see the killer. It was midnight and dark outside. I saw a shadowy figure go past the window but, as I turned, he shot me and took off. I heard a motorbike take off in the lane outside my place."

Charlie Rockwell leaned forward off the back wall. "What have the doctors said?"

Harry outlined the extent of his injuries. "I hope to be on my feet in two days and back at work. I want to work with you lot to find this bastard before he gets another chance to kill me or someone else."

Fred snorted, coughed and blew his nose on an old handkerchief. "No Harry. That's not what's going to happen. Twain has already told you that you're off the case. You're on leave. We don't want you being the target while we're investigating. We don't want them taking pot-shots at us because you're there. You stay here with your pretty nurse and let us get on with it. We're not as good looking as that little sheila, and we don't have the skills or the time to nurse you out there on the street. You'll just be a distraction, so stay out of it. Is that clear?"

Harry threw back the sheet and sat on the edge of the bed. "I'll think about that but I won't make any promises."

Bob Crow stepped forward. "Have you got a death-wish, Harry? There's some bastard out there trying to kill you. You don't know who he is, but he knows you and where you live. He can take you out at any time. Now listen to Fred. Leave it to us and stay out of it."

Harry brushed off Bob's comment with a wave of his hand past his left ear. He turned to Fred. "Tell me Fred. Who do you think would want to kill me?"

"We don't know yet, Harry. We've only just been given this case. We need to test out a few angles."

Harry was getting more anxious. "Has this got anything to do with me being taken off the Tom Lebovich case?"

"No. That had nothing to do with it."

"Then why was I taken off?"

Fred undid the top button on his shirt and wiped the side of his forehead on his sleeve. "I can't discuss the details Harry, but it has to do with another investigation we are on and Tom Lebovich is assisting us with others matters. It is at a vital stage and we needed him there."

Harry thrust both hands forward. "But we had a lay-down-misère case against him."

Joe walked around beside Fred. "Harry, we checked out your case against Lebovich. The bloke who claimed to have identified him behind Harold Park is so short-sighted that his wife has to give directions when he's driving, because he can't see past the car in front of him. Besides, there are three other blokes who will swear on the Bible they were playing poker with Tom Lebovich at that time in the back room of the Empire Hotel. You didn't have a case. We had to release him."

"Tell me, Fred," said Harry turning to face the leader, "who do you think is involved?"

Fred stood up to stretch his legs, arthritic pain kicking into his knee joints. "I don't know, Harry. We're only just starting. But if you want my opinion, I believe it has something to do with that mob from Melbourne who are trying to break into the big scene here in Sydney."

"But why would the Melbourne mob be interested in me? I've had nothing to do with them."

Charlie broke in. "While you were investigating the murder of Knuckles Elliot, you were digging into the background of some of his mates and associates. Some of them are helping the Melbourne boys get set up in suburban hotels. You were getting too close to them and they were worried you might put a dampener on their intentions. Those boys from down south are very nasty and they won't take no for an answer. They want you out of the way."

Fred walked towards the door. "Listen here, Harry. Stay out of it. Leave it to us. When you're back on your feet, let me know and I'll book you into a great hotel in Newcastle, on the beach. My mate Curly runs it. He and I played footie together years back. He'll give you a good time in more ways than one; and it won't cost you a penny. I'll give him a call. Stay there as long as you like."

Fred waved to the others. "Come on, you lot. Give him the whisky, Charlie."

Charlie passed Harry a brown paper bag containing a bottle of aged, single malt, twelve-year-old Scotch whisky. "See you, mate. Look after yourself."

The four officers walked out as Janet came in to check on Harry.

"Harry, I know those officers are working with you but there is something about them that gives me the shivers. I'm pleased they're gone."

"You don't have to worry about them Janet, unless you're a big- time criminal. If you are, then watch out because they can get very nasty. They are the top cops in this state. They deal with the worst criminals and put them away. I'm glad they are working on my case."

Janet pulled back the sheet. "I want you back in that bed. You've had lots of visitors today and it's doing nothing for your healing. I want you resting."

"Okay, boss. Whatever you say." Harry slipped under the sheet.

Half an hour later as he was dozing off, Uncle Joe and Aunty Mary walked in.

"Sorry to disturb you, Harry," said Joe. "We just dropped by to see how you are. We would have come this morning, but Mary had to do the shopping."

Mary rushed past Joe to get to Harry's bedside to check on him. "How are you, my dear boy? You don't look well with all those cuts and bruises. They obviously aren't looking after you well enough in here. You're coming home with us. I'll look after you."

Harry held her hand. "Aunty, stop worrying. They are doing a marvellous job on me. The cuts and bruises are mostly skin-deep and are not dangerous. It looks much worse than it is. I'll be perfectly okay in a few days."

Janet came back in. "Hello, Mr and Mrs Taylor. It's good to see you again. Harry's a little tired because half the police force has been in here today. They all think they own the place, so it's good to have someone as nice as you two."

Mary looked at Janet but said nothing. Joe responded. "Nurse, can you give us an up-to-date report on Harry? When can we take him home?"

"I'm sorry, but he's not ready to go yet. The doctor has ordered him to stay here until there is no longer any danger of serious infection. He needs time to get over the shock and for his wounds to heal." Janet left to give them some privacy.

Mary turned to Harry. "Now listen to me, young man. I've made up the bed in the spare room and you're coming home with us when the good doctor lets you out."

Harry put his hand on Mary's knee. "Thank you, Aunty. I know I can always depend on you but, on this occasion, I won't be staying with you. It's too dangerous."

Mary waved her hands in front of her face. "What nonsense. Nobody is going to hurt us. We have security on our doors."

"Aunty, these people are not burglars. They're killers. They're armed and dangerous. Those locks on your doors won't stand up to the firepower they have. It'll take them five seconds to get into your place."

"Well, you can't stay in the shed. That's no protection any more. We'll just have to put some big padlocks on our place."

"No, Aunty, I'll find somewhere else to stay. And I'll get someone in to fix the window and clean the shed."

"That won't be necessary, Harry," interrupted Joe. "One of my clients is a carpenter and he'll be there on Monday to fix it. He owes me a favour. Don't you worry about it."

"Well, where are you going to live when you get out of here?" asked Mary, anxiously twisting her handkerchief around her finger. "Harry, I want you to get out of the police force. It's too dangerous."

"Aunty, stop worrying. The CIB are on this case. They are the best. They will find the shooter and deal with him in no time at all. Wait until I find a place to live and I'll let you know then. I don't want anyone else to know. Now you must go so that I can get some rest, or the nurse will thrash me."

"Come on, Mary," said Joe. "Let's go and give the poor man some peace. We'll try to come tomorrow after church."

"Bye bye, darling," said Mary as she left with Joe.

Janet came back in. "Now, here's your medicine. Take that. Your dinner's coming in now. After you've eaten that, I'm switching off the light and you're going to get some rest. No more visitors. I'll tell the constable outside. That's an order. You've had a long day."

Chapter 6
Sunday

It was early morning. The view outside Harry's window was dull and uninviting. This was going to be a hot, humid, oppressive day with no sea breeze for relief. The low cloud cover prevented the sun from penetrating the glass. After a good sleep Harry felt much better, although the deeper wounds still hurt as he stood up and stretched. As he walked out to go to the toilet he saw Jack, the constable, guarding him for the night. He was half-asleep in his chair in the corridor. Harry kicked the leg of the chair.

"Good morning, Constable. Did you have to shoot any intruders during the night?"

"Good morning, Sir. Sorry about that. I must have dozed off. It's so damn boring here; it's hard not to go to sleep. I would have been happier if someone had tried to kidnap you. At least that would have kept me awake. I finished reading the paper by ten o'clock last night and had nothing to do from then on except to watch a nurse come past about every hour."

Harry noticed the Saturday edition of *The Sydney Morning Herald* next to the chair. "May I borrow that paper for a while?"

"Sure, Sir. Take it with you. I'm finished."

As Harry sat on the toilet he scanned the pages for places to rent. He wanted a room, a shed or a garage, reasonably close to the centre of the city, near a railway station, but one that wasn't exposed to the passing public. The city was too expensive so he looked at suburbs further out like Marrickville, Campsie, Erskineville, Punchbowl and Bankstown. The most promising appeared to be a garage off Douglas Lane at Stanmore. He returned to his room.

In the cupboard he found his clothes that had been taken home by Aunty Mary; cleaned, ironed and returned. He folded them neatly into a small bundle, put them together with his shoes and socks over his arm and covered them with a towel.

"Jack," said Harry as he came from his room, "I'm going to the washroom to have a good sponge down in the basin. The doctor told me it will relax my muscles and speed up my recovery. I'll be at least half an hour. Why don't you duck down to the kitchen and get yourself some breakfast while I'm in there. It'll give you a chance for a break."

"Thanks, Harry. I might just do that. If anyone comes to your room then there'll be nobody there to guard."

Harry walked to the bathroom. The constable walked in the opposite direction.

After a quick wipe down at the basin, Harry got dressed, leaving the gown and towels on the floor. He opened the door slowly to check if anybody was in the corridor. When all was clear he walked away, down the stairs and out a fire exit door onto the laneway. He passed a doctor who was more interested in not spilling his mug of tea as he hurried back to his surgery.

Harry walked out onto Missenden Road, holding the newspaper against his face on the hospital side. He sat on the bench at the bus stop. Fifteen minutes later a bus arrived with its destination shown as Central Station. Harry hopped on and bought a ticket.

"Cripes, mate," said the conductor putting the money into his bag, "what's the other bloke like? You look like youse done twelve rounds in the ring with Vic Patrick."

Harry moved to the nearest seat. "No worries, mate. I just ran into a brick wall."

Harry got off the bus at Railway Square next to the big Marcus Clarke department store and walked to the station. He caught the next train going west and got off at Redfern. There were a few odd looks from other passengers, but Harry ignored them as he tried to look as if there was nothing out of the normal. From there he walked to the shed behind Uncle Joseph's house.

The window was still in need of repair but everything else was spotless. It was obvious that Aunty Mary had been in. She had even washed and ironed his clothes and cleaned the plates and cutlery that had sat in the sink for the last three days. Harry took his time packing his belongings into two suitcases and his old kitbag. He went out to check his pride and joy; a 1940 Vauxhall Caleche, two-door coupé with a canvas top parked in the laneway.

Unfortunately, the shooter had stabbed one of the front tyres to make sure that Harry couldn't follow him. Harry jacked up the car and changed the tyre with the spare attached to the back of the boot lid. He pushed his belongings into the small boot and onto the back seat before walking to the back door of Uncle Joe's house. From the kitchen, Mary saw him and opened the door.

"My God, son, what are you doing here at this time of morning? Joe and I couldn't sleep so I got up to get a cup of tea for us. Come in, come in."

Harry gave her a big hug and a kiss. "It's okay. Aunty. I've just come to pick up my gear. I have to find another place to stay. I can't put you good people in danger with me being in the shed out the back. I have to find a place where nobody knows me so that I can work out this mess."

"Harry, darling, you'll be safe here in the spare room. You can't go out there on your own."

"Stop worrying, Aunty. I'm going out now to get another place to rent. I found some places advertised in the paper. I'll look at them this morning. I can't tell you or anyone else where I'll be because I will be working undercover for a while. I'm officially on leave, so if anyone asks, tell them that I've gone back home to Goonaburra to recuperate on the farm."

"Oh Harry, what am I going to do with you? You're here, there and everywhere, and you're always into other people's troubles. And just look at you. What a horrible mess. You can't go out working in that condition."

Uncle Joseph came down the stairs. "I thought I heard voices. What's going on? G'day, Harry. What's up?"

"G'day, Uncle. Don't worry. I'm just picking up my gear because I'm going to rent somewhere else where nobody knows me. It's got to do with my work. I'll keep in touch, but nobody must know where I am."

"I don't understand, Harry, but you must do what you believe is for the best."

Mary waved a wooden spoon angrily at her husband. "But Joseph, he must stay here where he is safe."

Joseph moved to her side, put his arms around her shoulder and kissed her on the forehead. "Mary, I have absolute trust in Harry. He's not a boy any more. He's a grown man who has proved during the war that he can handle himself in the worst of conditions. He knows what he has to do, so let him go with our best wishes and blessings." Turning to Harry he said, "Keep in touch my boy to let us know that you're alright."

Harry gave them both a big hug, walked out the door and drove off.

Passing Stanmore station, Harry turned into Douglas Street and pulled up outside a neat, well-maintained terrace house with a wrought iron balcony. The brass knocker made a deep hollow sound, too loud for this time in the morning. An attractive slim, young woman opened the door. She was dressed in a neat white linen, three-quarters-length dress, white shoes and pillbox hat with a short net wrapped around the brim.

Harry bowed slightly. "Excuse me, madam, I apologise for coming at this time on a Sunday morning, but I was wondering if the unit you had to rent was still available. I saw your advertisement in *The Herald* yesterday."

"Whatever happened to your face?"

"It looks worse than it is. I had a car accident on Friday. The impact broke the window and the glass shattered into my face. The doctors have said I will be okay in a few days."

"What do you do for a living, Mr. What's your name?"

"My apologies again; so rude of me. My name is Harry Forsythe. I'm an insurance inspector. I have to travel around checking out possible false claims against my company."

"And who do you work for, Harry? May I call you Harry? I'm Eileen Matthews." She put out her hand to shake Harry's.

"Certainly. I work for Prudential."

"The flat I advertised yesterday is still available, but you have to understand that it is only a converted garage and it comes off Douglas Lane behind my house. You don't enter through this house."

"Would you mind if I looked at it, Eileen?"

"I was about to go to church up Percival Road, but I can give you ten minutes. Drive around to the lane and I'll meet you at the back."

Eileen pointed out the features. "I had this garage converted after my husband Robert was killed in the North Africa campaign."

The brick garage was well constructed, with a lined plaster board interior. A kitchen bench with a stove and sink had been added to one side, and a shower and toilet installed at the back. The remaining space had a single bed, a kitchen table with two chairs, an old lounge chair and a tallboy that fitted neatly at the end of the bed. An old radio stood in the corner.

Eileen added. "I don't drive and I need the extra income. If you're interested, the rent is fifteen shillings a week, payable a month in advance."

Harry reached into his pocket for his money. "Mrs Matthews, thank you very much. This will be ideal; and here is three pounds for the first month. May I move in today?"

"Certainly. Now, I must be off to church, or I'll be late."

"Hop into the front seat. I'll drive you there." Harry opened the car door and closed the door to the garage.

Harry dropped Eileen at the Catholic church and returned to unload his gear.

Chapter 7
Sunday

Harry unpacked his clothes into the tallboy. He looked under the sink and found an electric jug that he filled with water and boiled. He found a half-filled Bushells tea caddy with kookaburras and kangaroos painted on the side. He put three heaped spoonfuls into the large yellow ceramic teapot. There was no milk or sugar or anything to eat, but he savoured the hot black tea while he sat in the lounge chair. He went over in his mind his present situation and what he planned to do next. There were a thousand questions and no answers.

Who was the shooter? Why was he the target? What was the reason for the attack? Was the shooter acting independently or was he a hired killer? Was it an accident? Was it mistaken identity? Who had the most to gain by his death? Which of his recent cases involved someone so bitter that they would want to kill him? Was it someone brought in from outside on contract to do the job? Could it be the Melbourne mob? Why would they want to target him when he had nothing to do with them?

While Harry had no answers he was sure about some things. No one was to know where he was now living. Despite his injuries, he would immediately start investigating this crime. In army terms, his injuries were just minor flesh wounds; so just get on with it.

Clearly, this attack involved the top end of the crime scene. People don't shoot police officers for minor traffic offences, taking drugs or break and enters. This had to be the big time. Harry knew the Mr Bigs would stop at nothing to protect their turf. This was more dangerous than working with Z Force behind enemy lines against the Japanese because, in this situation, he didn't know the enemy. Because Twain had put him on extended sick leave until further notice, he would have to work independently.

He couldn't be seen interfering with the investigation by Fred, Joe, Charlie and Bob from the CIB. In his present state, they certainly wouldn't want him to be on their team. That meant he wouldn't have access to the police department resources. At times, he would have to work undercover without head-office approval.

Harry decided to restrict contact with fellow officers to a few trusted friends. How many could keep a secret? He had to eliminate those who would not want involvement in an operation that didn't have approval from the top. His life would depend on the loyalty and discretion of a few friends. Harry thought of the many good officers he trusted, but eliminated those he did not want involved in these circumstances. Tony Jacobs, head of the Scientific Investigation Bureau, was the first to come to mind as one he could trust.

Although Harry had been working with Jock Burns for only a short time, he admired the young man. Jock was his type of man: strong in body, mind and spirit and with a good sense of humour. Harry was confident that, if there was to be a fight, Jock would be able to handle himself with the best of them. Jock was still a bit raw around the edges, but he was one who would give his all for Harry if the going got rough.

Father Captain Ambrose, the Catholic Chaplain at Ingleburn army camp, was a close friend. Harry and Ambrose had worked together at the Intelligence Unit at Port Moresby towards the end of the war. Ambrose was someone to whom Harry could go if he needed an honest, confidential, down-to-earth opinion on any matter. However he knew that he would get a thorough bollocking for not going to church recently. He also knew that, after a roughing up by Ambrose, they would do their best with a bottle of fine Scotch that Harry always took as repentance and payment for good advice.

Harry locked the garage, walked out onto Douglas Lane and walked the few blocks to Stanmore Station. He found a telephone booth, dropped some pennies into the coin box and dialled Tony Jacobs' number.

"Hello, Tony. This is Harry."

"G'day, Harry. How are you, mate? What's it like in hospital?"

Harry shifted the phone to the other ear to avoid it rubbing on some stitches. "I walked out of there this morning."

"What?" gasped Tony. "You did what? Are you telling me that you walked out without permission? Where the hell are you now?"

"Just hold your horses, Tony. I needed to get out and find who took a pot-shot at me. I can't tell you where I am. I've moved from Redfern to avoid being a target again."

"But I heard that Twain put you on sick leave until further notice. Is that right?"

A young boy stood outside the telephone box, staring up at Harry. He called out to his mother to come and look at the ugly man.

Harry turned his back on the boy. "Yes, Tony, but I can't just lie there and do nothing. I need to be out there doing my own investigation. I'm running out of pennies. Can I come around this afternoon to talk about this?"

"Yes. Sure, mate. Is one o'clock okay?"

"Thanks, Tony. I'll see you then."

Harry rang the home number that Jock Burns gave him when they first worked together. A woman with a strong Scottish accent answered the phone. Harry asked to speak to Jock.

"I'm Jock's mother. Jock is out at the moment. Could I take a message?"

"Thank you, Mrs Burns. It's Harry Taylor speaking. Would you please ask Jock to be at Tony Jacobs' place at one o'clock this afternoon? It's urgent."

Harry gave Mrs Burns Tony's address at Coogee.

Tony lived in a side street off Coogee Bay Road. Harry turned the corner and parked. Tony's house was an imposing, neat white Victorian mansion that had been handed down to Tony's wife, Vickie, after the death of her parents. A jacaranda tree framed the arched entrance which, with the colourful beds of flowering petunias and marigolds, invited guests into a warm and friendly home. As Harry opened the wrought iron gate, Jock roared to a halt on his 1940, 250cc Waratah motorbike.

"Where did you get that heap of rubbish, Jock?" asked Harry with a smile.

Jock tilted the bike onto its stand. "My brother sold it to me when he bought himself a new Vincent. It's nothing flash but it gets me around cheaply. Gee, Tony's place is a bit grand, isn't it? Where would he get enough money to buy a place like this?"

Tony escorted them through the house to the back patio where Vickie offered them lime cordial and cheese savouries. She fussed over Harry, demanding to know all about the shooting and his injuries.

After ten minutes, Tony interrupted. "Vickie, darling, could you go check on the kids? Harry, Jock and I need to talk police business."

When Vickie left, Harry sat forward. "Thanks for seeing us, Tony. I want to explain my present situation and what I propose to do from here on."

"Before you go on, Harry, I'll give you a clear piece of advice. Get out of here. Go back to that hospital. Apologise to the doctors and nurses who are taking shit now because you left on their watch. Stay there until they say you can go home. Look at you. You are a walking medical cot case."

Jock moved nervously side to side like a boxer about to get into the ring. "Tony's got a good point there, Harry. Why don't you take his advice and leave the nasty work to us until you get back on your feet?"

Harry spread his open hands. "Well, that's not going to happen. I'll apologise to the doctors and nurses in good time, but now I have a job to do. I need to get the bastard who tried to kill me."

Tony took a sip of his drink. "You're a sitting duck, Harry. He knows you but you don't know him. Leave it to the CIB boys. If anyone can get him, they will. They are the top team in this country."

"The killer even knows where you live, Harry," said Jock.

"I'm not living there any more, Jock. I've moved to a new place and I'm not telling anyone until we get this bloke."

Tony stood up and got a bottle of beer and three glasses. "You can't get involved, Harry. You're on sick leave. Twain will have your guts for garters if you show your head anywhere near this case. Butt out and leave it to the CIB."

"What the hell can you do, Harry?" interrupted Jock. "You can't be seen anywhere around police stations or headquarters, or working with any of us, or having anything to do with this investigation. If Twain doesn't get at you, the CIB team will. They won't want you interfering in their work. They're just as likely to shoot you to get you out of the way. They'd call it 'collateral damage'. For God's sake, Harry, stay out of it. Go take a holiday."

Harry explained his escape from hospital and his change of address without telling them where it was. "Because I'm officially on sick leave, I'll be freer to move around in civilian clothes in my own car and go where I want without interference from Central. I don't have to report to anyone. If anyone from the Force sees me, I'll tell them that I'm going shopping. It's quite simple, really. It's none of their business where I go on sick leave. I'm a free man."

Tony sighed. "Oh, Harry, if it was only so simple. The criminals don't care whether you're in uniform, a suit or in your fishing gear. They'll shoot you no matter what. The more you stick your nose out of the door, the sooner they'll find you."

"Listen carefully," said Harry. "I hear you clearly, but I can't sit around waiting for others to do my hard work. And let's be clear; I'm not asking you to stand beside me while I'm looking for this bastard. It's best if I work alone. I can blend into the woodwork best if I'm on my own. But there will be times I might need help with information from files or what's happening officially with this case."

"How can we help?" asked Jock.

"Would you two be willing to look up files and keep me up to date from time to time? If I leave a message for you it will be under the name of Forsythe. That's the name I'm using at my new flat. When you see that name, you'll know it's me and I'll be calling you back; probably at your place."

Tony opened another bottle of beer and filled the glasses. "I think you're stark raving mad, Harry, but you know you can count on me when you need to. And by the way, I know some good undertakers who often pick up bodies from us after we have done our examinations. I'll get your family a good discount for you."

"You're all heart, Tony. And can you put some of your petunias on my coffin?"

The sudden outburst of laughter broke the tension. Jock got up and tapped Harry on the back. "I'll get the undertaker to put a Scotch thistle between your legs. You'll need something nice there to tickle your fancy."

For the next hour, the three of them sat there drinking beer and nibbling on arrowroot biscuits and cheese while they discussed various police and criminal personalities and the current state of play in the big crime scene in the city.

Harry got up to go. "You know, I can't thank you two enough. This is not going to be easy and it might all end up in disaster, but I have to give it a go and I know I can depend on you to be there when I want you. Thanks again. I must get back to my flat."

"Cheers, Harry," Jock called out. "Keep your guard up, mate.

Harry drove back to Stanmore.

***

There was a faint tap on the side door of the flat. Harry cautiously moved the curtain to see Eileen outside. He opened the door.

"I don't want to intrude, Harry but I realised that I hadn't left any milk or sugar for you. It's Sunday, so you wouldn't have had a chance to get yourself some food. I've brought down some cold corned beef and veggies that were leftovers from my lunch. I'll leave it on the table for you."

"That's so kind of you,, Eileen. You are very thoughtful. I'll enjoy that very much. Thank you."

Eileen placed the food on the table and left with a smile.

Chapter 8
Monday

A shaft of early morning sunlight cut through the gap between the curtain and the window frame. Harry moved the pillow to block it from his eyes. Ten minutes later the anxiety got to him. He had to get up and get started. Lying in bed would achieve nothing. He had things to do. He put on the jug to boil while he had a shower. He decided not to shave. The stubble, stitches and scars were a good distraction; and besides, it was still too sore. If he dressed in his old army slouch hat, unironed khaki trousers and shirt and scuffed army boots, nobody would suspect him of being a detective on duty.

After a cup of tea he locked the shed and walked to the railway station. He called into the Greek café and ordered fried eggs and bacon on toast. After breakfast he crossed the road to the station. A young boy, standing outside the entrance with a bundle of newspapers under his arm, called out. "Payyer. Get yer payyer. Big news. Detective disappears. Get yer payyer."

Harry turned, paid the boy two pennies and took a copy of the *Daily Mirror*. The headline was in bold print.

Detective Disappears

Top police investigating

Under the main heading was a photo of Harry. It was one taken by James Bolton at the Goonaburra police station last year after the murders of two young women.

The article read:

The Daily Mirror crime reporter, James Bolton, visited the Royal Prince Alfred Hospital on Missenden Road last night to check on Detective Senior Constable Harry Taylor, a victim of an attempted murder in the early hours of New Year's Day. As reported in the Daily Mirror last week, the detective was the victim of a shotgun blast and is lucky to be alive.

James Bolton arrived to find the hospital in crisis.

Detective Taylor, who had been under police protection, was missing. His injuries were so serious that he had not been allowed to leave the hospital. Everything points to the detective being taken by force from the building.

How could this happen in a public hospital?

Someone has to be called to account.

The policeman guarding Detective Taylor had gone to the toilet and returned to find him missing. Hospital authorities have confirmed that nobody matching the detective's description went past the nurses' desk or the front door. This appears to be a carefully planned kidnapping. How many people knew he was in that hospital? How did they get access unnoticed? How did they get out unseen?

Sources close to police headquarters have confirmed that, since Thursday, there has been a major investigation involving the top detectives from the Criminal Investigation Branch searching for the perpetrator of this ugly crime.

But what have they achieved? Not only have they not found the shooter responsible for the detective's injuries but they have now let him be taken from a public hospital from under police guard.

Detective Taylor is a war hero, having served with distinction behind enemy lines against the Japanese in the islands north of Australia. He was the detective who solved the case of the murder of two young women at Goonaburra last year. He is an up-and-coming member of our police force in this state.

How could the police bungle a simple act of guarding one of our finest policemen? All attempts to try to talk to the senior officers of the department have failed. What have they got to hide? Why won't they tell the public what is going on?

Commissioner, you have a lot to answer.

Harry sat on a bench outside the station to read the rest of the article. He pulled his hat forward and down to cover his face even though his present appearance had little resemblance to the figure in the photo. He was gobsmacked. Young James Bolton was at it again, but this time Harry was not the target. He sat back, took a deep breath and thought about what he should do next. He couldn't let head office run around in a panic not knowing what really did happen, even though he knew he would be abused and possibly demoted for doing what he did.

He walked to the telephone booth and asked the operator to put him through to Central Street headquarters.

"Sergeant Tomlinson here. How might I help?"

"Hello, Jack. This is Harry Taylor. I'm..."

"Bloody hell, Harry," interrupted Jack. "Where are you? There's so much shit hitting the fan in here it's dribbling down the walls. For God's sake, get in here now or mine and everyone else's job will be on the line. I've never seen the chief super and commissioner so angry."

"That won't be possible, Jack," replied Harry in a calm, measured tone. "I'm on sick leave. The chief super ordered me to take it, so I'm going away on a holiday."

"Harry, every newspaper reporter is outside the front door wanting interviews with the commissioner and Twain. They are not going away until they get answers. Please come in here and put everyone's minds at rest."

"Sorry, Jack, but I can't do that. I'm on leave."

"Then hold on and I'll put you through to the chief super."

"But Jack, I don't need to talk to..."

"Hello, hello, this is Chief Superintendent Twain here. To whom am I talking?"

Harry gulped, touched his finger to his hat, wiped his brow with the back of his hand, and paused momentarily before answering. "It's Harry Taylor here, sir. Did you wish to speak to me?"

"Of course I bloody well want to speak to you," he shouted. "Where are you?"

"I'm on leave, sir. You remember? You sent me on leave two days ago."

"Don't try your bloody smart-arse tricks with me, Detective or I'll kick you from here to Timbuktu. Now tell me where you are."

"I'm in a safe place."

"Where is this safe place?"

"That's for me to know and you to find out, sir."

"Get in here now. That's an order."

Harry paused before answering. He could hear the super's heavy breathing on the other end of the line. "I have moved. I no longer live at Redfern, and I have no intention of telling you or anyone else where I am. I won't be coming into head office. There is no way that I'll put myself in a position where the shooter can get another shot at me. Do you understand? Anything you want to say to me you can do so on this phone."

"What the bloody hell happened at that hospital?" screamed the chief super.

"Just calm yourself down, sir. Don't blame the constable on duty. He's a good officer and it wasn't his fault. Don't blame the hospital. The doctors and nurses in that hospital are first class. What they did for me was outstanding. The decision to leave that hospital was mine and mine alone. Nobody else was involved. I wasn't kidnapped as written in the papers this morning. I am safe and well. So go out there and call off the dogs from the papers."

"But they are not going to believe that unless they see and talk to you. Get back here now."

"Sir, I'm not a bloody fool. If the shooter has any common sense he will be sure that, at some time, I'll be going to your office. He only has to sit across from the entrance to Central Street to wait for me to come along. After that he can follow me anywhere and finish me off."

"Get in here and we'll give you real protection."

"You failed once and I'm not going to be a guinea pig again. I'll look after my own protection. At least I can trust myself."

"Don't be so insolent."

Harry changed the direction of the discussion. "Sir, I have never seen anyone as professional as you in dealing with the press. You'll have to do it, sir because I'm not coming in. I need to stay out of the limelight while ever the killer is still running loose."

"I'm ordering you to get back in here now."

"You can order a ham sandwich from the cafeteria, or order anything or anyone else as much as you like but you're not going to order me anywhere. I'm not going to set myself up as an easy target for the shooter, there or anywhere else. Just tell the press I'm okay and I have gone on holidays to see my sick uncle in Adelaide. Goodbye, sir." Harry put the phone back on the hook.

Harry walked along the street to the butcher where he bought steak and sausages, and then to the general store where he bought some essential supplies to last him for the next few days.

Back at his unit he sorted the groceries into the cupboard and refrigerator. He found a frying pan, chopped some onion and tomato, and when that had caramelised, he put in the steak to cook slowly. He opened a bottle of beer that he bought at a hotel on the way home.

He felt more at ease now that he had informed Twain of his circumstances. He smiled to himself as he imagined Twain putting on his best jacket, brushing it and his hat to remove any flecks of dust, fluff or dandruff, and standing in front of a mirror to make certain that he would look perfect for the photos that will appear in the newspapers tomorrow morning.

Twain will have the angry press in the palm of his hand with assurances that Harry is still under police protection, and that his disappearance from the hospital was a planned move to distract the shooter. He will tell them that Harry was interstate in a safe house known only to him. He will assure them that an arrest is imminent because his best detectives are on the case; the same ones who were involved in bringing in many of the worst criminals in the history of the state.

Harry smiled as he imagined himself standing in disguise at the back of the press pack outside headquarters, watching the charade unfold.

Harry cleaned up after finishing his early lunch. He suddenly realised that the day's events were catching up on him so he kicked off his boots and lay on the bed for a rest.

Chapter 9
Tuesday

Harry rose early, showered and dressed. He heated a pan on the stove and dropped in three big beef sausages which, when cooked, were smothered with tomato sauce and eaten with delight. With his finger Harry wiped the edge of the plate with his finger to get the remains of the sauce and gravy. He was ready to face another day.

There were lots of questions. Who had the answers? He wasn't having an affair with someone's wife. He hadn't stolen money or anything else. He had not been involved in a fight with anyone who might invite retaliation. If he was the victim of a shooting, it must surely involve the top echelon of criminals.

He thought back to his last big case at Goonaburra. He knew that he had upset the powers to be in the Church, the courts and the police force on many occasions, but those incidents didn't warrant an assassination. Despite the religious and racial bigotry he had faced he could not think of anyone involved in that case who would want him killed.

He thought of all the cases he had worked on before and after Goonaburra, and came up with a blank. He and Jock had brought in Tom Lebovich and charged him for the murder of Knuckles Elliott, but that case had been taken over by the CIB; and Lebovich was released. There should have been no repercussions on Harry. There was a chance, however, that the big boys who used Lebovich to do their dirty work might have been involved.

It was well known that the big operators paid protection money to ensure they could continue running illegal casinos, pushing drugs, SP betting and prostitution. Some politicians, judges and police turned a blind eye to those activities. Maybe they saw Harry as someone they couldn't bribe and one who wanted to clean up corruption and play by the book.

As Harry sipped the last of his tea he remembered a former detective sergeant in the CIB with whom he had worked in 1939 and

1940. Buster Stacey retired early in 1945 and was now living in a terrace house in Bourke Street, Darlinghurst. He decided to pay Buster a visit.

Buster was an old, rough, barnacle of a man who was born at the end of last century, fought in France in the First World War and joined the police force in 1920. He served his time in country towns before becoming a detective at Parramatta in 1932, and later at Liverpool. He was appointed to the CIB in 1939 and served in that unit until his retirement in 1945. He was only fifty-three but was riddled with arthritis and had retired on a medical pension. His wife had died two years ago.

On the way to see Buster, Harry's car started to play up. It spluttered, coughed and stopped on three occasions. Each time it happened Harry got out, cleaned the plugs, points and battery connections. He even opened the carburettor and blew away any fine particles that might have blocked the fuel line. There were no more stops, but Harry knew that the car needed a good service.

Harry walked up the steps to the door of the terrace house. The walls were stained by leaks from rusted pipes. The small front balcony had an old wooden recliner in need of a paint job and there was a stack of old boxes in the corner. As he banged on the door knocker he was greeted by the sound of a small dog yapping in defence of the property.

"Shut up, Spot. Come here. Sit down," came the deep-throated voice from inside. "Wait a minute. I'm not as fast these days. Just be patient. I'm coming."

"Take your time, Buster," called Harry. "It's Harry Taylor."

As the door opened, a small fox-terrier dog rushed out and sniffed around Harry's ankles. Harry bent down slowly and allowed the dog to sniff the back of his hand.

"Spot, get inside. Get up on your couch," shouted Buster.

The man in front of Harry looked in his eighties. He was bent low over two walking sticks. The grimace on his face reflected the pain in his body. Harry took him by the arm and helped him back to his lounge chair.

"G'day, Buster, I'm sorry to come in on you like this, mate, but there have been a few things happening and I thought I'd like to come and get some good advice from someone I can trust."

Buster pushed himself back in his chair with difficulty. "Yeah, Harry. I've seen in the papers that you've been in a bit of strife but I don't take much notice of it these days. This morning's paper had that poseur

Twain puffing out his chest in front of the cameras. I never did trust that bugger. Too much up himself for my liking."

Harry stood up. Spot leapt off the couch to check on him. "Buster, before we have a talk, could I use your phone? On the way over here today my car started to play up. I need to get my mechanic to look at it for me."

"Yeah sure, Harry. The phone's on the wall in the kitchen."

Harry got put through to Stumpy Baxter's garage at Redfern. He explained the nature of the problem and his need to have wheels in the next few days.

"Stumpy, it'll be after knock off time when I get there, so I'll leave the car this afternoon in the lane off Hugo Street, outside where I used to live; behind Uncle Joe's place. I don't want to drive it any further. Could you walk around the corner in the morning and pick it up?"

"Okay, Harry. Leave the keys in the glove box. I'll put it back there tomorrow when I finish. See you, mate."

Harry walked back to the lounge room. "Buster, you probably know what happened to me the other day. Don't believe what you read in the papers. I have moved house and nobody knows where I'm living. The killer's still out there and I have to be careful, but I came here to seek your advice on a few things."

Buster took a sip from a glass of water on the coffee table. "Mate, I don't see how I could be of any help. I'm out of it now. I rarely see the blokes from the old team. They're all too busy doing their own thing. One or two drop in on occasions. They don't want to talk to old geezers like me any more."

Harry sat forward. "Whatever is going on must be part of the big crime scene. You were in this game for a long time, and I've always respected how you went about your job. That's more than I can say about some others. How do you see the situation going these days? Who would possibly want me out of the way?"

Buster came out with a deep racking cough, spat phlegm into a dirty handkerchief and wiped his mouth on the back of his hand and forearm. Harry could see by the half-filled ashtrays and the stale smell of tobacco in the air that Buster had not given up smoking. Buster wiped his eyes with his forefingers before answering.

"Well, let's look at what we've got. Whispers Durante is still number one at Woolloomooloo. He controls the casinos, prostitutes and drugs in that area. Squeaky Walsh runs the brothels and SP betting around here. Rosie, bless her soul, is the boss of The Rocks area; and Lord help anyone who tries to cut in. Tony the Greek is the main man in the betting ring; and he deals in drugs as well."

"But I don't see why any of them would try to eliminate me," said Harry. "I know I arrested Tom Lebovich for that job on Knuckles Elliott, but the CIB boys took over and he got off."

"Harry, I wouldn't trust any of them. The big four are not going to do the dirty work. If they want to get rid of you, they'll get one of their henchmen to do it. Or, they'll make an offer for anyone to take it on for a price. Men like Lebovich, Pantano, Bluey Ricketts, McGill and Benny Bomber Earl are all nasty men. They will do anything for money. They are not like ordinary men. They have no personal feelings for you or anyone else."

"I don't have a beef with any of them," said Harry.

"Pay them plenty of money and they'll do the job and go home to their wives and kids, the same as if they were a bank teller, or plumber. If they don't want the job, there are plenty of others who will do it for the money and a chance to get into the big time."

"But I still can't see why I'm the target."

Buster coughed again. "Well, the Melbourne gangs are moving into the hotels in the suburbs. I hear that they're setting up gambling rooms upstairs and have prostitutes in the bedrooms. They started in Liverpool and Parramatta but have now expanded into Newtown and Pyrmont. They are very good at paying off the local politicians in those areas. They're getting too close to the Sydney operations, and the locals don't like it."

"That still doesn't explain the attack on me," said Harry.

"Get real, Harry. You and I both worked in the CIB. There are a lot of really top cops working in that branch, but we both know that there were some who were on the take. It would only take one of them to suggest that you were protecting the Melbourne mob and you would become the target."

Harry stood and walked to the window. He turned to face Buster. "Since I came back from that job in Goonaburra, I've nabbed Bomber Earl for receiving stolen goods, and I did Pantano for possession of drugs, but they got off with a fine from a friendly judge."

"The Sydney boys might be asking why you aren't out there catching the Melbourne mob. They pay money for protection right up to the top, and they don't like being let down."

"But I'm not in that kind of business, Buster. You know me. We worked together in that branch for two years before I enlisted."

Buster coughed again. Harry, followed by Spot, went to the kitchen to get another glass of water. Buster sipped it slowly until his breathing improved. After a while he answered. "Harry, you and I are clean, but where did that get me? Here I am at age fifty-three, poor as a church mouse, and sitting in agony in this bloody chair waiting for God to take me and give me some relief."

"Well, Buster, I'm not going to change. I'm happy doing things my way."

"I'll tell you what I'll do for you, Harry. I'll keep my eye out for when one of these old terrace houses around here comes on the market. They are pretty run down but you could pick up one for your retirement. You and I can sit here together and wallow in our own misery."

Harry sat down and leaned across to Buster. "Well I don't intend to do that for a few years. I have to deal with my present predicament first. So, what would your advice be for me, Buster?"

"Harry, I always admired you for your stubborn, pig-headed attitude, your individuality and the fact that you were never distracted by the shit flying in all directions. You always spoke your mind and wouldn't take a backward step. You were willing to stick it up the nostrils of some of the top brass when they got it wrong. You've got a good brain. You survived in the jungles up north by thinking on your feet and climbing over barriers that most men would walk away from. My advice to you is to use your natural instincts. Don't trust anyone; and I mean anyone. Lie low for a while but don't stop investigating. You can do it, mate. Keep your eyes and ears open and your head down until you get the bastard who did that to you."

Harry walked over to Buster, shook his hand and patted him on the shoulder. "Thanks, digger. I now know what I have to do. If only there were more like you in the police force."

Spot wagged his tail as Harry patted him on the way to the door.

Harry felt sorry for Buster. He was a man who had dedicated his life to the Force; had always done the right thing by his colleagues and the job, but was now spending his last years in agony from arthritis with no sympathy from those with whom he had worked.

On the way to Redfern the car shuddered and stopped three more times. Harry parked it in the lane beside the shed, put the keys in the glove box and walked up to see Aunty Mary and Uncle Joe. He tried unsuccessfully to convince them that what he was doing was the best way to go. He explained that his refusal to tell them his new address was in their interests, in case someone put them under pressure to tell them where he lived.

Aunty Mary put on a wonderful dinner. Harry enjoyed the lamb roast and a large slice of apple and rhubarb pie with custard. After dinner he caught the train back to Stanmore.

Chapter 10
Wednesday

It was eight o'clock before Harry dragged himself out of bed, showered and prepared his breakfast of cereal followed by two eggs on toast. He walked to the radio set in the corner and switched it on to hear the news. The static was bad on most stations so he tuned into the ABC.

The dulcet tones of the newsreader came through.

"You are listening to the ABC. Stand by for this morning's news."

The reader mentioned the continuing celebrations in Burma after the declaration of independence from the United Kingdom. The Australian cricket team was still celebrating their win two days ago in the third test over India, with centuries in both innings to Don Bradman. The meat shortage will continue for some time. A new polar ship will be launched. It has been a disappointing year for British aviation.

"We will interrupt this summary with news that has just come to hand. We have reports of a car parked in a lane in Redfern being destroyed by a bomb blast this morning. One eye witness claims there was a person in the car when it exploded. The identity of the person is unknown. We will keep you up to date as more information comes to hand."

Harry put on his hat, rushed out and ran to the railway station. He jumped in front of a man about to enter the telephone booth. He phoned the Scientific Investigation Bureau, located in Bourke Street, Redfern.

"Tony Jacobs, please? This is urgent. It's Harry Taylor here."

"Hello, Harry, I can't talk. I'm just going out on an urgent job."

"Wait a second, Tony," shouted Harry. "Are you going to that car bomb case at Redfern? If you are, it might be my car. I left it there last night for my mechanic to pick up this morning."

"Holy shit, Harry," gasped Tony. "What are you saying? Do you think that explosion was meant for you?"

"If it's in the lane off Hugo Street, and it's a 1940 Vauxhall Caleche, two-door coupé, it is almost certainly mine. If the shooter saw it there last night, he would assume that I was in the flat and would come out and drive my car this morning to go somewhere."

"Where are you, Harry?" asked Tony, getting more anxious.

"I'm in a phone booth. I can be in Redfern in half an hour."

"Stay away from there. I don't want that area to be a shooting gallery while we're covering that site."

Harry kicked the bottom of the wall in the booth. "If it was a car bomb you'll need expert advice to help you identify what type. A bomb expert will need to check if there are any other explosives there or in the shed. I have a contact in the army. I'll get someone there as soon as possible. Leave that to me, Tony." Harry hung up before Tony could reply.

Harry asked the operator to put him through to the 13th Battalion at the Ingleburn army base.

"Corporal Donaldson speaking. How might I help you?"

"It's Detective Senior Constable Taylor here. Could you put me through to Father Captain Ambrose please. This is an urgent matter."

"Father Ambrose speaking. How may I help?"

"Ambrose. This is Harry Taylor. I want to ask a favour of you. It's urgent, and I need it now."

"Wait until I get my vestments on. Whenever you call I need to bring in the Big Fellow; and he wasn't happy with you the last time. What disaster have you created this time, Harry?"

"I know that I haven't been to church lately, and you can hold that against me, but stop and listen for a moment. This morning my car was blown up in Redfern and there was someone in it when it went up. I think it might have been my mechanic. He was killed. That bomb was meant for me. I need to find out who was in the car and who did it."

"Holy shit, Harry. Why can't you play golf and lead a normal life instead of spending your life looking for and causing trouble. I saw in the paper that you were shot. I would have asked how you are, but you won't tell me the truth; so I won't ask. Now, how can I help?"

"There was some sort of bomb used in that car and I want to know what type and where it came from."

"For God's sake, Harry, I'm a Catholic chaplain, not a bomb expert. I'm not going to ask God to help you because you ignored him the last few times you wanted help."

Harry burst out laughing. "Ambrose, you of so little faith. And here I was going to invite you out to Harry's Café de Wheels for a meat pie."

"Promises, promises. I'm still waiting for the last one you made."

Harry spoke in a more serious tone. "Let's be serious. This is not a social call. I need a bomb expert, and the best ones are in the army. I want one or two of your best men to be in Hugo Street in Redfern within the hour. When they get there they are to report to Senior Sergeant Tony Jacobs."

"Harry, this is the army. Things don't move that quickly here. We are at peace now."

"Ambrose, it's me you're talking to. I saw what you did in New Guinea, and I know you can move mountains when you want to. If you do this for me, I'll never ask for another favour again."

"Harry, I can see storm clouds gathering over the city. You'll be struck by lightning before the day is out. No promises, mind you, but I'll see what I can do. The bomb boys are over at the Holsworthy barracks, but I know the commandant there."

"Thanks, Ambrose. If you can pull this off for me, I'll say a prayer for you."

"Save your breath, Harry. There are others more deserving than me. Just stay out of trouble. Go home and help your father on the farm."

"Thanks, mate."

Harry put down the phone, bought a ticket and took the train to Redfern. He walked along Caroline Street, past Hugo Street and on to the lane that went behind Uncle Joe's place. From there he could see what was happening without being seen. He wanted to observe the scene before moving in to help.

Tony Jacobs and his team had erected a screen on the railway end of the street but Harry could see what was going on from the other end. It was definitely his car. It was a wreck with two doors blown open and twisted and the glass in the doors and windscreen shattered. The front seat was destroyed. The dashboard, seat covers and door linings were severely shredded. The canvas roof had lifted and was badly torn with the frame twisted.

About ten feet away from the car was a tarpaulin that appeared to be covering a body. Harry froze. Could that be Stumpy Baxter, his mechanic? How can Harry explain that to Stumpy's family? That should have been Harry on the road under that canvas. How can you tell someone's family that their husband and father died because you left the car in the lane instead of at Stumpy's garage? He felt so guilty.

"And what might you be doing here, sir?" said a uniformed policeman who was standing behind Harry.

"Constable. That's my car. I'm Detective Taylor."

"Yes, and I'm Miss Muffet eating my curds and whey. But I'm not going to be frightened away by any spider. You're coming with me, sir."

Harry pointed in the direction of the team. "That man there is Senior Sergeant Jacobs. He will be able to confirm who I am," said Harry.

"Well, you come with me and we'll check that out."

"Constable, I'm the officer who was shot last week. That's my car. That explosion was a second attempt to get me. I don't want to expose myself there in case the killer is still around here."

The constable took Harry by the arm. "You're coming with me. You can explain that to Sergeant Jacobs."

Tony looked up from inspecting the car. "Bloody hell, Harry. What are you doing here? Didn't I tell you to stay away? It's okay, Constable. I know this man."

"Tony, it should be me under that tarp. Instead, its my mechanic who is an innocent victim of someone trying to kill me. Can I look and identify him?"

"Okay, but make it quick and then get to hell out of here."

Harry lifted the canvas. It was Stumpy. His upper legs, buttocks, lower back and the clothing covering those areas were shredded. Thankfully it would have been a quick death. It looked as though the impact of the bomb was absorbed mainly by Stumpy's body which explained why there was not greater damage to the car.

At that moment, a khaki-camouflaged Land Rover pulled up. A sergeant and corporal, with the distinctive red-and-gold-spiked patch of the Bomb Disposal Unit on their sleeves, walked briskly to the car.

"Who are you and why are you here?" demanded Tony as he cautioned them to stay where they were.

"Our apologies, sir," replied the sergeant. "We have been sent by senior command to investigate a car bombing here. We are to report to Senior Sergeant Jacobs."

"I'm Jacobs, and I made no such request."

Harry stepped forward. "Tony, these are the experts from the army. They are the best in Australia for dealing with bomb disposal. I asked a friend to send them here to assist with our investigation. We need to know everything about this bomb and how it was set up. These blokes are the best. Give them a go."

Tony paused, staring at Harry as he considered his options. He then turned, put out his hand and greeted the two soldiers. "I'm Tony. Welcome to my team. What would you like us to do?"

"G'day, Tony. I'm Mick and this is Sandy. The first thing to do is to get everyone back at least one hundred yards. Clear this lane and evacuate the houses on both sides. There could still be unexploded ordnance here and we don't want any more casualties. While you are doing that, we will gear-up and start our investigation."

For the next hour Mick and Sandy worked in and around the car. While they did their work, Harry and Tony sat in the police car discussing various aspects of what was before them.

When the army officers finished, they joined Harry and Tony in the car.

"Well, what can you tell us, Mick?" asked Tony.

"The car bomb was a British-made anti-personnel device called an AP Mine Number 3. It was used by the Australian forces in the war and we still have stocks of it here," explained Mick.

Harry looked at Mick. "We used them up north, but you had best tell Tony how they work."

"The bomb has a sheet-metal casing about three inches wide and six inches high. It's loaded with about four to five ounces of TNT. It requires pressure from the top, and when that happens, it ignites the propellant charge that projects the mine upwards. It's not a large bomb but it can be lethal up to thirty yards. They are not like an anti-tank bomb, which carries much more explosive. The explosive material is small in quantity because it's meant only to maim or kill a soldier as he steps on it. Had it been an anti-tank bomb, the car would be scattered across the street."

Tony turned and scratched his nose. "But aren't they normally buried in the ground? How was it used here?"

Mick explained. "The bomber set the bomb on a base of clay to steady it before placing it under the driver's seat. Between the bomb and the seat webbing he placed a bag of nails as shrapnel. When the driver sat on the seat, the pressure set off the explosion. It was severe enough to blow off his arse and cause untold damage to his abdomen, lower back and upper legs. He had no chance."

"Where the hell would a criminal get an army anti-personnel bomb? Or are we looking at someone from the army being the killer?" asked Harry, even more distressed as he thought of himself being the victim.

Mick looked down. "I'll admit to you and I don't want this going anywhere else, but there was a break-in at the Holsworthy military base a month ago. They took rifles, ammunition and a number of these anti-personnel mines."

"How the bloody hell can someone steal from a military base?" asked Tony angrily. "Surely, that type of material in an army camp would be well protected."

"Quite frankly, Tony we don't know, but procedures have become so tight since then that it should never happen again."

"Tell that to the family of that poor bastard lying on the ground over there. I'm sure they'll be comforted by that piece of news. They've just lost a husband and father."

Harry stepped forward. "Thanks, Mick and Sandy. You've done a great job. I wouldn't do your job for quids. At least now we know what we're dealing with, even if we don't know the killer yet. Good work."

As the army officers drove off, Harry thanked Tony and the team and walked up the lane to Uncle Joe's place where he explained all the day's events. By that time they had been allowed to re-enter their home. He used their phone to call the insurance company and requested them to examine his car to assess the cost of the damage. Mary insisted on Harry staying for a meal before he returned to Stanmore.

Chapter 11
Thursday

As Harry walked to the railway station he noticed Eileen Matthews striding briskly in the same direction. She was stylishly dressed in a crisp white cotton dress, broad-brimmed hat and shoes with a low heel; so sensible for a hot summer's day. As she turned he liked the way her dark wavy hair framed her fine facial features. He quickened his pace.

"Hello, Eileen. Where would you be going on this fine day?" he asked.

"Hello, Harry. I'm off to the city. I've just finished my course at Burroughs and I have to collect my results and certificate."

"What did you do at Burroughs?"

"It's a secretarial training college. I learned shorthand, typing and was trained to use comptometers."

Harry scratched his forehead. "What's a comptometer?"

They paused as they bought tickets at the window. "It's an adding machine used in business to do calculations. It's much faster and more accurate than doing it in your head. Now I've finished my training, I'm hoping to get a good job as a secretary. The Burroughs course is well recognised. Now that Robert is no longer with me I need work to survive."

"Are there many jobs in that field?" asked Harry as they stepped on the train.

Being school holidays, the train was not crowded. Three young boys were pretending to play cricket in the aisle. Harry and Eileen found two seats.

"Burroughs is very good. They have recommended me to a company in Parramatta. I go for an interview next week. What are you doing today, Harry?"

Harry shifted uneasily on his seat. "My company has asked me to investigate a car that was bombed yesterday at Redfern. You might have heard about it on the news."

"Yes. That was terrible. Apparently the driver was killed. Who would do such a thing?"

"That's for me to find out." Harry didn't mention that it was his car involved in the bombing.

They filled in the time with small talk before Eileen got off at Central Station. Harry was impressed by Eileen's determination to get on with her life after her husband's death.

He continued on to Wynyard Railway Station where he walked to the insurance company. He met with a claims clerk and filled out the necessary forms for compensation. He was told that an inspector would assess the damage and, if approved, a cheque would be sent to Harry. As it was in the first week of the new year, most of the staff were on holidays, so it could take some time. In the meantime, Harry needed wheels. He thought a motorbike would be the best and cheapest option.

But there were higher priorities. He had to see Stumpy Baxter's family. That would be very difficult. Harry sat on a bench in Martin Place while he thought about it. Should he go? He should have been in that car; not Stumpy. It should be Harry's body in the morgue awaiting the coroner's report and burial. What can Harry say to the grieving wife and children that might lessen their pain? Will they blame him for their loss? What will happen to Stumpy's garage business? Will the family be able to carry on without him? How will the family survive without his regular takings?

Ten minutes later he stood up and strode briskly to Wynyard station. As difficult as it was going to be, Harry was determined to see the family. He took the train to Redfern and walked the short distance to Eveleigh Street. The Baxter's terrace house was constructed from convict-made sandstock bricks. It was a small two-storied dwelling with a door and one window leading onto the street, and an upstairs door opening onto a small balcony with a wrought iron balustrade. It was a simple presentation, but well maintained.

Harry was met at the door by an older man dressed in blue overalls and heavy work boots. His uncombed grey hair fell across his lined, suntanned face. Harry recognised him as Stumpy's father, Chappie.

Chappie snapped through his toothless gums. "Who are you and what do you want? We're busy, so piss off."

Harry reached forward to shake Chappie's hand. "G'day, Chappie. It's Harry Taylor. Remember me? You used to fix my car before the war. I lived down the road behind Uncle Joe's place. Could I come in please?"

Chappie ignored the proffered hand. He squinted to get a better look at Harry. "So, you're the bastard who owned the car that killed my son?"

"Chappie, can we go inside to discuss this? I want to talk to Stumpy's wife, Kitty."

Chappie turned his back and shuffled inside. Harry followed.

"Who is it, Dad?"

Chappie ignored the female voice from the sitting room off to the right and continued on out the back door. Harry turned to see Kitty sitting in a large lounge chair. A boy about eight and a girl about five sat on the floor playing with what looked to be new toys that were probably recent Christmas presents. The atmosphere in the room was sombre. The dark curtains were drawn shut and the central ceiling light was off.

Harry took off his hat. "Hello, Kitty. It's Harry Taylor. May I come in?"

There was an audible gasp from Kitty as she covered her mouth with her hand. Tears streamed from her eyes. "Wait. Stay there."

Kitty turned to the children. "Kids, I want you to take your toys into the kitchen or outside into the backyard. I have to talk to this man."

The children looked at Harry with such disgust as if he had walked in with fresh dog poo on his shoes. They picked up their toys and stomped past. It gave him no comfort to see their deep frowns. Harry walked towards Kitty with hand extended. "Kitty, I'm so sorry. This won't be easy for you, but we need to talk about why this has happened."

Kitty sobbed. "There is nothing you can say, Harry that will bring Stumpy back. It's because of you we've lost a good husband and father. He was such a wonderful person. He wouldn't hurt a fly. He went out there to help you and pick up your car. He's now dead."

Harry sat beside Kitty on the lounge and took hold of her shaking hands. "If only I could swap places with Stumpy now, I would. If I had any inkling that the person trying to kill me would have done this, I would never have had Stumpy pick up my car. He was my friend, such a wonderful bloke. I will never forgive myself for putting him in a position that led to his death. I'm so sorry, Kitty."

Kitty fell against Harry's chest sobbing. "I'm sorry, Harry. I didn't mean to blame you, but it's so hard knowing I'll never see Stumpy again. I can't get my head around it. All I know is that we'll never have our wonderful man with us ever again. It's going to be so hard on the kids. They idolised him and so did I. How can I explain it to them?"

Harry turned to face her. "Kitty, there are some very nasty people in this city and they'll stop at nothing to get rid of anyone who is a threat to their business."

"But why did they kill Stumpy?"

"They weren't trying to get Stumpy. They were trying to kill me. They shot me last Thursday and I was lucky to survive. They put the bomb in my car thinking I would be the one to get into it in the morning. They didn't know I had arranged with Stumpy to pick it up."

Kitty sat forward, blew her nose and wiped her eyes. "Who would do this horrible thing, Harry?"

"I don't know, Kitty but I'll make you a promise. I'll get the bastards who killed Stumpy. I'll swear to that on every Bible in this house. They're not going to get away with this."

Harry spent the next ten minutes explaining to Kitty the main players in the Sydney crime scene. He named the four Mr Bigs and all their henchmen. He told her about the influence of drugs, gambling, prostitution and race fixing in the criminal world, and how dangerous it was to be a part of that mix, or to be investigating crimes in those areas.

"Who do you think did this to Stumpy?"

Harry flattened the hair at the back of his head, searching for answers that might appease Kitty and her family. Of course, that was impossible at this stage. "Kitty, I don't know. It might not even be one of the Sydney mob. There's been a group of Melbourne criminals moving in and trying to take over and that means there will be some fierce battles between them."

"But not my Stumpy."

"I don't have the answers yet, Kitty. I can only assume I have upset some bigwig in the criminal world who thinks I'm getting too close to him. He's obviously decided that I have to be taken out as a warning to others to back off, or else. These people are powerful and they have links to very important people in this state."

Harry heard a shuffle in the hallway. He looked up to see Chappie at the door. His face was red with anger. He held up a tightly-closed fist in front of his face. "Why the fuck are you still here? You're the bastard who killed my son. Get the fuck out of here or I'll throw you out myself."

Kitty got up and rushed to the door. "Dad. Apologise to Harry. He didn't kill Stumpy. They even tried to kill him. Look at him. He's still got all the wounds from last week."

Chappie broke out of Kitty's restraining embrace. "The bastards should have finished the job properly last week and killed him. If they'd done their job then Stumpy would still be alive. I'm not going to say sorry. Why should I feel sorry for him? It's his fault that my son is now dead." Turning to Harry he shouted. "Go on, get out, you bastard. If I see you anywhere near this family again, I'll finish the job they didn't do last week. We don't need your help or sympathy. You're scum."

Harry got up and walked towards the door. "It's okay, Kitty. I understand. I'd feel the same if I was in Chappie's boots. I'll go now. I'm sorry. You've got enough on your hands without me causing you more grief."

Harry eased past Kitty and Chappie and walked out. He was determined to keep that image of Chappie and Kitty in his mind until he put away the perpetrator of that crime.

Chapter 12
Thursday

Harry walked to Redfern station, caught a train to Central and found a vacant telephone booth. After dropping some pennies into the coin-box he was put through to police headquarters.

"Sergeant Tomlinson here. How may I help?"

"G'day, Jack. This is Harry Taylor. Can you put..."

The desk sergeant shouted into the phone, "Holy Jesus, Harry. Where the bloody hell are you? All shit is flying around here since you left the hospital. Everyone is copping it. Nobody knows where you are. For God's sake, get in here and explain yourself."

Harry paused before answering. "No, Jack. I'm not going in there. I've had someone trying to kill me with a shotgun. They blew up my car and killed my mate, Stumpy Baxter, and you want me to just walk in there in full daylight to talk to you and the chief. No way, Jack. I'm not that stupid. Now put me through to Twain."

"Tell me where you are. I'll get someone to pick you up and you can come in the side door. Nobody will see you."

Harry slapped the glass wall of the booth in frustration. After getting through his meeting with the Baxters, the last thing he wanted was to be lectured to by Jack Tomlinson. He liked Jack, but this was going too far. He clenched his teeth and spoke slowly with determination. "Jack, if you don't put me through I'll hang up and make no further contact with headquarters. Now do it."

There was a slight pause before another voice came through. "Where the bloody hell are you, Taylor? I've had the whole damned Force out looking for you. You're causing me no end of trouble. Now get in here right away so we can put you under protection."

Harry waited until the heavy breathing on the end of the phone slowed before answering. "Thank you, Chief Superintendent, for asking about my health and welfare. It never ceases to surprise me how caring we are in this police force."

"I haven't got bloody time for niceties, Taylor. Where are you? Get in here now."

"No way, sir. There's a killer out there and we don't know who it is or where that person will strike next. All your protection didn't stop him blowing up my car and killing my mate. I'll take my chances by myself. It's safer that way."

"I'm ordering you to get in here now. Do you hear me?"

Harry wiped the sweat from his forehead. "You can go and order a meat pie with mushy peas if you like but I'm not going in there."

"We need to meet now," shouted Twain.

"If you want a meeting then listen carefully, because I'll only say it once," Harry said. "Take off your uniform jacket. Put on the civilian coat that you have in your wardrobe. Leave your police hat in the office. Go out and walk along to George Street. Cross over and walk down George towards the Quay. Come alone. If any other police are in sight, this meeting will be off. Do you understand?"

"You can't order me around," shouted Twain. "I'm not going to play your stupid little games of cops and robbers in your backyard. Now get in here."

Harry spelled it out slowly. "If you don't do as I've asked, you'll never see me until I catch that killer. If you want to meet with me, then go to George Street now; and I mean now."

Harry hung up the phone before Twain could answer. He walked to Railway Square and hailed a taxi. He gave instructions to the driver. "I want you to drive slowly down George Street. I have to pick up a mate. He should be down around the Town Hall by now."

It was school holidays, so there was not much traffic. Holiday makers were ambling up and down, going to department stores or to the movies. Harry spotted Twain just past Town Hall, between the Nock and Kirby's hardware store on the next corner and the Marble Bar. He asked the driver to pull over. Harry wound down the window and called out. "Hop in the back seat, Sir. We'll talk when we get there."

Chief Superintendent Twain slipped into the back seat without uttering a word. Harry directed the driver to turn right into Hunter Street, left into Macquarie, right into Sir John Young Cresent, left at the Art Gallery and on to the top entrance to the Botanic Gardens. He got out, paid the driver and led Allan Twain to a small bench seat in a secluded area surrounded by trees and shrubs.

The gardens in summer were a blaze of colour. The last blue flowers from the jacaranda contrasted with the red of the Illawarra flame-tree and yellow of the silky oak. The gardens were alive with colourful petunias, marigolds, dianthus, dahlias, pansies and daisies.

Harry invited the Chief to take a seat on the bench. "Now, sir, we shouldn't be interrupted here. Tell me where you are up to in the chase for my attacker."

Allan Twain looked most uncomfortable. He stood up to take off his jacket. The high summer temperature and humidity with little breeze was in stark contrast to the comfort of his office. They were thankful for the shade of a large Moreton Bay fig-tree. "Harry, we can't have you running around unprotected. We have to concentrate on catching the attacker and, so far, we are using all our resources trying to track you. Come in and we'll protect you in a safe house until we get him."

Harry stood up and surveyed the surrounds before turning to face the superintendent. "With all due respect, sir, your protection hasn't been good enough so far."

"Well, how the bloody hell can we give you protection when we can't find you?"

"That's the point, Sir. If you can't find me, and I'm well known to you and most people in the force, how the hell can you find an attacker who is unknown?"

Twain stabbed his hand towards Harry. "We had you protected in that hospital."

Harry burst into an exaggerated laugh. "Well you stuffed that up, didn't you. I walked out under your noses and you couldn't find me. That says everything about your protection."

Twain twitched. "I have suspended the officer who was supposed to be guarding you."

"If you want my cooperation you'll lift that suspension. It was not Constable Stapleton's fault. He's a good officer and he shouldn't be penalised for having a short break while I went for a wash. There was no relief for him."

"He's got to be taught a lesson."

Harry sat down again. "He's had his lesson and he's paid the penalty. If you want my cooperation, then put him back on duty. We need officers like him."

"Where are you living, Harry?"

"A place where you and others won't find me," was the reply.

"Okay, Harry. Why did you bring me here?"

Three young children ran past the opening between the trees, shouting with excitement at the thrill of open space and grass to run on and play. They were followed by two adults carrying a rug and a picnic basket.

"I want to work undercover to catch the bloke who tried to kill me."

"You can't do that," shouted the chief super. "You're on sick leave."

Harry pumped one fist into his other hand in frustration. "I'm perfectly fit to resume duty and I'll get a doctor's certificate to prove it."

"Look at you," said Twain. "You've still got cuts and stitches all over your face and neck. No way. You'll stay on sick leave until I say so."

"I spent four years in the Islands where wounds like this were just scratches. If we'd stopped to dress them and have a rest, the Japs would have had our guts and I'd still be up there in some muddy burial pit, rotting. I'm fitter than more than half of the people in the Force, so don't try to tell me that I can't do my job."

"I have four detectives working on your case and I don't want you walking in front of them when they are on the track of the killer. I can't have two groups working on the same job, with each not knowing what and where the others are working. That's just plain bloody stupid and I'll have none of it."

"Where are they up to with the investigation? Do they have any positive leads? Has anyone been brought in for questioning?"

"Fred, Joe, Charlie and Bob are the best in the business. You know that. They're the top cops in the Force. Their record speaks for itself. Sit back and let them get on with it."

Harry leaned across so that his face was close to Twain's, his all seeing, unblinking dark-blue eyes focused sharply on the chief. "You didn't answer my question. So, you don't know the answers. That's the problem. Nobody has the answers. And that is why I have to get out there to find it."

"Stay out of it, Harry. I know you're frustrated, but you have to give the CIB boys time to get to the bottom of this mess. I don't want you interfering."

"Frankly, sir, I don't care whether you give me permission or not to go undercover. This is my life. I consider it very precious and I hope to live a few more years yet. I will do whatever is necessary to catch the bastard who killed my mate. I owe that to his wife and kids."

"How are you going to do that?" asked the chief super.

"Are you giving me permission to work undercover?" asked Harry.

Twain stood up and turned away searching for answers. After a pause, he turned to face Harry. "I can't give that permission. That would fly in the face of all protocols and common sense."

Harry stood and pointed down the slope towards the Conservatorium of Music building facing Macquarie Street. "This meeting is over. The Conservatorium is over there. You go that way back to the office. I'll be leaving in the opposite direction. Goodbye, sir."

Twain stood with feet apart, chin jutting towards Harry. "You are suspended until further notice. You'll make no attempt to be involved in this investigation. Do you hear me clearly?"

"Sir, turn around. The Conservatorium is that way. I'm sure you can find the way. Goodbye."

Harry watched as the chief superintendent stormed off across the gardens. He was sure that the man's blood pressure was pumping off the top of the scale. He waited until the chief reached Macquarie Street. He didn't go in the direction he had indicated to Twain. Instead, he turned to follow a path around the eastern side of the gardens towards Government House. He found a quiet nook on the harbour side of the park and sat there to plan his next moves.

Ten minutes later he heard police sirens circling The Domain parklands, the Art Gallery and the roads leading from the gardens towards St Mary's Cathedral and around Hyde Park. Harry wondered how far Twain would go to find him.

Chapter 13
Thursday

For some time, Harry sat and watched the ferries and yachts pass each other on both sides of Fort Denison. The fort was built in the mid-eighteen hundreds to protect the new settlement of Sydney from a possible Russian invasion. But today it was a quiet and peaceful scene that gave Harry time to clear his mind before deciding on his next move. A faint easterly breeze came up from the harbour, providing relief from the humidity. Passers-by ignored the solitary figure sitting on the bench under the tree.

Harry went over his meeting two days ago with Buster Stacey. Buster had never been tempted to take bribes or been the beneficiary of gifts from criminals or police officers. He was clean, and his word could be trusted. Harry respected him as a walking encyclopaedia of policing in New South Wales.

At various stages in his career Buster had arrested and charged most of the Mr Bigs and their henchmen. Their offences included break and enter, theft, bank robbery, drugs, prostitution, assault, manslaughter, murder and SP betting. He was not always successful in his pursuit of those criminals but they had a healthy respect for him.

In the days before the war, Harry, as a new detective in the CIB, had been involved with a number of those same criminals. He had booked Tony Pantano for drug supply, Bomber Earl for receiving stolen goods, Knuckles Elliott for aggravated assault, Bluey Ricketts and Shooter McGill for break, enter and steal, and Curly Peters for running a house of ill repute. These men were hardened criminals who had been in and out of correctional centres since their school days.

It was only natural for those men to hate Harry and, if required by their bosses, they would be happy to cause him harm. But most of them knew that if they killed a policeman, all hell would break loose for the whole criminal community, and the result for some of them could be terminal. Harry put the names through his intellectual meat grinder and concluded that most of them, despite their criminal background, would not take out or take up a contract on him.

Could it be Tom Lebovich? He was a hardened habitual criminal who never took a backward step. It was alleged that he shot and killed another standover man, Tommy Buckett, at a hotel in Woolloomooloo in front of twenty men at the bar. When the police arrived, all of the bystanders had a sudden onset of dementia.

Just before Christmas, Harry and Jock Burns arrested Lebovich for the murder of Knuckles Elliott but he was released by the CIB men. He was a suspect that Harry would have to watch. He was the type who would not hesitate to take revenge for his arrest.

Harry was involved in an investigation into the death of a teenager whose body was found under Lennox Bridge at Parramatta. Harry established that the boy was a minor supplier of drugs and, although he couldn't prove who did the murder, he arrested a well- known Melbourne criminal, Dale 'Flash' Evans, on major drug supply charges. Evans was gaoled for seven years.

Evans was closely associated with 'Splinter' Woods, 'Bruiser' Bignall and, to a lesser extent, their henchman, Tommy 'Scarface' Fisher. They were all well-known criminals from Melbourne who were trying to muscle in on the big crime scene in Sydney. Any one of them could be the person behind Harry's shooting.

Harry watched two couples walk around the garden path below him. The men were dressed in tweed suits with ties, felt hats and brogue shoes. The women wore long woollen dresses, lisle stockings with ankle-high leather shoes. One had a pancake flat, brown felt beret while the other wore a fur pillbox hat. Harry smiled to himself as he questioned how long it would take these new emigrants from England, freshly off the HMS Strathaird moored near the Quay, to acclimatise to the Australian weather.

Harry quickly refocused his mind on the main agenda. How would he find his attacker? He could no longer depend on headquarters for support. For their own safety, most of the officers would want to keep clear of him. He needed a disguise and he needed wheels. As he hadn't shaved since the shooting, he decided to let his beard continue to grow. It would help hide his scars. He would have his thick, wavy auburn hair cut in a crew cut style similar to the American sailors. It was becoming a trend in Sydney.

He stood, stretched and walked around the harbour side of Government House. Slipping out a side gate from the gardens he crossed over to Circular Quay. With all the holiday-makers coming on and off ferries, it was easy for him to merge with the crowd and disappear past the Maritime Services building to The Rocks area.

Harry found an army disposals shop selling excess American Second World War clothing and paraphernalia.

"What can I do for you, digger?" said the shop assistant trying to put on an American accent for effect. "We've got everything a man like you would want."

"I just want some good working gear," said Harry. "I'll look around. Thanks. I'll call you if I need some help."

Harry took his time selecting and trying on some field trousers with webbing belts, a camouflage bomber jacket, shirts, a fatigue jacket with four pockets, a GI cap, a khaki coverall, kit bag and a pair of rough combat boots. When the assistant told him the price, Harry agreed, providing he threw in a tanker hood for good measure. He paid, put the gear into the kitbag, shook hands, and walked out along the street to where he noticed a red, blue and white spiral pattern on the barber pole.

Harry sat and read the popular *Man* magazine as he waited for an empty barber's chair. At two shillings a copy it was too expensive to buy the magazine on his salary, so he caught up with it whenever he went to a barber.

"Next," called the barber as he swept the last man's hair into the corner. "A short back and sides for you, sir?" he asked as Harry sat in the swivel chair.

"No," replied Harry. "I want one of those new crew cuts like the American sailors."

"You're not a bloody Yank are you mate? What's your name? I haven't seen you here before."

Harry laughed. "I'm Fred. Do I look or sound like a Yank to you?"

"I'm Jack. Pleased to meet you. No Fred. But it's hard to tell these days. Why do you want a crew cut?"

Harry pointed to the cuts on his face. "I had a car accident last week and I got cut a bit. I thought it would be better to get more sun on the wounds to heal quicker; and it's going to be easier to keep them clean."

"It's your head mate, so if you want a crew cut I'm the man to do it for you. But I'll have to be careful because you still have stitches in those cuts."

Harry felt for the ones near his left ear. "When I leave you I'm going to find a doctor around here and get them out. They're driving me mad with the itches."

The barber walked around in front of Harry looking at the wounds. "Well, mate, this could be your lucky day. I can take those out for you, if you like. Save a trip to the doctor; and I'll only charge you sixpence more. What do you say to that?"

"But you're a barber not a doctor," replied Harry looking anxious.

"Mate, I spent five years in the sixth divvy fighting in North Africa and Greece. I was the medic. Your wounds are nothing compared to legs and arms blown off. Now, do you want me to do it or not? Make up your mind."

"Yes sure, thanks. My apologies. If you've been through that you can do anything. Go ahead."

Jack picked up his clippers. "I'll do your crew cut first and then do your wounds. Were you in the Forces?"

Harry hesitated. He knew he wasn't allowed to talk about his time in Z Force working behind enemy lines in New Guinea and Borneo.

"Yes, I was in the parachute squadron at various places in the Islands."

"Were you on Kokoda?"

"No. I was at different places."

The two of them talked about the futility of war and the unnecessary losses of their mates but neither spoke in any detail of their own experiences. They understood each other's reluctance.

Jack wiped on some Californian Poppy brilliantine that made Harry's short auburn bristles stand up like a shiny new hairbrush. The splash of Bay Rum aftershave on his neck gave him a fresh, sweet, woody, spicy smell. Harry smiled at his new image in the mirror.

"Now," said Jack, "let me clear around your feet and then I'll remove those stitches. I've still got my very small, fine, sharp scissors and tweezers. The Doc who did this job was good. They will be easy to take out; and your wounds are healing well. With this new haircut you'll have the sheilas falling about you in droves. They won't be able to keep their hands off you."

Jack deftly removed the stitches, dabbed on some iodine to sterilise the wounds and then smeared them with Vaseline. He slapped Harry on the back and laughed as he swept the hair away from his feet.

"Thanks, Jack. Do you know if that motorbike sales place is still in Wentworth Avenue, next to the MG car place?"

"You're not going to go stupid and buy a bike, are you?"

"I need a cheap one to get around," replied Harry.

"Yeah. I think it's still there. Be careful, mate."

"Thanks, Jack. I'll see you next time."

Harry walked around Hyde Park on the eastern side of the ANZAC War Memorial to keep distance between himself and Central Street Police Station until he came to the motorbike sales shop in Wentworth Avenue. The front showroom was filled with brand new bikes. There were Harleys, BSAs, Nortons, Vincent Rapides, Ariels, Matchless and Velocettes. Most manufacturers had by now changed from war production back into civilian models, with more power and speed and flashy colours.

"Hi there. Can I help?" shouted a well-dressed man from the back of the showroom."

Harry adjusted the old kitbag on his shoulder. "I'm just looking, mate."

"I'm John. I noticed you looking at the Vincent. If you're willing to wait a few weeks, we will have the brand new Vincent Black Shadow. I could hold one for you. It will be the fastest bike in Australia. I can see you on one of them."

Harry half-turned away. "I can't afford the prices you have on those new ones. What have you got in second-hand trade-ins?"

The disappointed salesman turned and walked to the back door. "Follow me out here."

Harry looked over the used bikes in the backyard and stopped at a 1939 Triumph Tiger Speed Twin and a 1940 Velocette. "What price have you got on them?"

"They're top-of-the-range bikes and they're the only two I've got. If you don't take them they'll be gone by tomorrow."

"Stop your bullshit, mate. There are hundreds of motorbikes around the city and, if your price is high, I'll go elsewhere. Now what's your best price on those two bikes?"

After some hard bargaining, Harry settled on an ex-wartime model of a Norton 16hp that had been repainted caramelised green. He sat his kitbag across the fuel tank, put the tanker hood over his head and roared off to Stanmore.

Chapter 14
Friday

After a deep sleep Harry staggered out of bed to sit on the toilet. He rubbed his eyes to clear the fog. He ran his fingers through the bristles of his new crew cut. The feeling was different but exhilarating. He had a new lease on life. He was a new man. With a gentle touch he felt each of the wounds on his face, neck and shoulders. He was happy with the way they were healing and estimated that, with the extra growth of facial stubble, in the next few days most of his scars would no longer be visible.

Harry showered but before getting dressed, he took a boot-polish kit from the bottom drawer. He lightly wiped the brush across the black-polish tin and drew it gently through his hair. What a mess, but after wiping it through with his polishing cloth a few times, his rich auburn colour turned dark brown. He smiled as he watched the transition. It wasn't going to fool everyone but it would help him get around looking anything but a detective senior constable. After dressing in his new army outfit he answered a knock on his door.

Eileen stepped back, eyes wide, a startled look on her face. "Harry, what did you do to your hair?"

"Oh that," he replied, trying to appear as nonchalant as possible. "I got a crew cut to help heal my wounds. It lets air and sun get to my skin. And because I don't have to comb it I'm not doing damage to the scars."

"Well that makes sense. For a while, you gave me quite a shock. I came down to give you some fruitcake. My mother gave me a very large one for Christmas, but I don't like it much; and it would be a shame to waste it. I hope you like fruitcake."

Harry took the cake. "Come in, Eileen. Thanks very much. This reminds me of Christmas at home. My mother made cakes like this."

"My pleasure, Harry, but I won't come in. I'm going for an interview today."

"Hey, good luck, Eileen. You'll do just fine. I have every confidence you'll get the job."

As Eileen left, she half-turned, looked quizzically at Harry, smiled and said, "It looks so odd, but you know, I could get used to it. Thanks, Harry."

Harry tried on the tanker hood again. It had been used in the war to keep a soldier's head warm in winter. It was made from a soft lined material that fitted comfortably over the head, covering everything except the face. A flap covered the back of the neck and a chin-strap fixed it in place. In the mirror Harry thought he looked like a bomber pilot, or a tank driver with his head poking through the open turret. As it was too hot for summer, he took his scissors and removed the woollen lining.

After locking up he walked to his bike, kick-started it, and rode off. Harry was surprised how quickly he took to riding the Norton. Having seen too many accidents and deaths of riders in the past, he was not a fan of motorbikes but, being naturally athletic, he quickly felt as one with the machine, weaving in and out of traffic on Parramatta Road on his way to the SIB at Redfern.

Every member of the forensic team stopped what they were doing and watched Harry as he walked in and strode to Tony Jacobs' office. He knocked and walked in.

"What the bloody hell are you doing here?" shouted Tony as he saw who was at the door. "You're supposed to be on sick leave. And what's that stupid thing on your head?"

Harry burst out laughing. "This, my friend, is what the best-dressed men will be wearing this season. You need to catch up with the times, Tony. I'm going to tell Vickie to buy you one for your birthday."

"Take the bloody thing off. It looks disgusting. It looks like a wombat's nappy."

Harry took off the tanker hood and bowed mockingly to Tony. "At your pleasure, sir."

"Oh my God," gasped Tony. "That's worse. Now you look like a dirty toilet brush. Now tell me why you're here."

"I need to know where you put my car. I have to let the insurance company know where it is so they can assess the damage."

"It's in the yard out the back, but we're still investigating," replied Tony.

"What's there to investigate? It's obvious what happened. The army blokes told you that."

Tony walked to the door and called out. "Rita. Could you please come in?"

In through the door walked an attractive tall woman in navy slacks and white shirt, her hair cut in a short bob style.

"Rita, this is Detective Senior Constable Harry Taylor. He's the owner of the car that was blown up on Wednesday. I want you to take his fingerprints."

"Hello Detective. I'm Rita Flynn. I'll get my gear. Won't be a moment."

As Rita left the room Harry exclaimed. "Why the hell would you want my fingerprints? They're on record at headquarters."

Tony replied. "On Wednesday we finished examining your car in the lane and ordered the tow truck to bring it here later in the day. Yesterday, when the team went over it again, they looked in the damaged glove box and found a Cellophane packet containing a creamy-white powder. It has fingerprints on it and we need to check yours against them. You have the right to refuse."

Harry stepped back. "Just hold it a minute. The only things I had in that glove box were my registration papers and my membership of the NRMA. Besides, why is Rita doing this job?"

"As you very well know, Harry, women have been employed in the Force since the twenties."

"But they work in headquarters on matters relating to children or giving school lectures or doing traffic duty."

Tony sat at his desk looking exasperated. "Women are now working with the CIB and are especially good at surveillance of buildings because nobody suspects them."

Harry sat opposite Tony. "Well, what's Rita doing here?"

"Rita showed an interest in fingerprinting. Before she married she had started a degree in science. She's the best operator I've got in that field, and she's going to take your prints to compare them with those in the vehicle and on the Cellophane bag."

Rita came in and opened an ink pad on the table in front of Harry. "Harry, to get good results, I want you to do a print of each finger and thumb separately on each of those slides. Try not to smudge them."

Harry sat back, eyeing Rita up and down as if he was a cattle judge at the Royal Easter Show. Rita remained steadfast, eyes focused on

Harry's face. Harry looked up to meet her stare. There was a pause. "Okay, Rita. For you I'll do it. What do you want me to do first?"

Rita took each finger and thumb, rolled each on an ink pad and then on the glass slide. She labelled each one, picked up her gear and left the room.

Harry sat back. "She seems to know what she's doing."

"We tried a number of recruits and she was thirty per cent more accurate than anyone else. She is even better than any of the other staff. Don't ever underestimate her, Harry."

Harry sat forward somewhat anxiously. "What's this about a Cellophane bag containing a powder?"

"It could be anything, Harry. The boys are analysing it now. Now let's relax and have a cup of tea while they do their job."

Over tea Harry brought Tony up to date about his meeting with the chief super.

Tony looked at the ceiling. "I know it's useless talking to you about this, but I'm going to say it anyhow. Go back to Goonaburra. See your parents, do some work on the farm, catch up with old friends and stay there until the CIB boys catch the bastard who did this to you."

"Thanks, Tony for your fatherly advice but I know you, and if you were in my position, there would be no way you would be off to the country to get away from the action. So don't try to protect me. Let me get on and do what I have to do. Just promise me that you'll be here when I need help."

There was a knock on the door. Tony looked up. "Come in, Jack. You know Harry. What have you got for us?"

Jack Witherspoon, the drug expert on the team, dropped a Cellophane packet on the table. "It's definitely brown heroin."

Harry interrupted. "But that looks creamy, not brown."

"Let me explain," said Jack. "It looks cream but it's known as brown heroin. Pure heroin is white and high quality and is the most expensive on the street. The impure stuff is cream to light brown and the raw material is so impure it is called black heroin. It starts out as brown and becomes whiter as it is refined."

"Thanks, Jack. That explains it better."

Jack sat in the other chair. "Dealers also put in additives such as sugar or flour to make it go further to make more money. They even put in stuff like strychnine and other muck with it and that can result in death to the users."

"Tell me, Jack," asked Harry. "Where does all this supply come from?"

"I'll give you a brief outline of the drug scene here," said Jack. "Let's start with heroin. Australians have been the highest per capita users of heroin in the world since the 1920s. Since the end of the war its use has almost doubled."

Harry stood up and walked around to relieve the stiffness in his neck. "Where does this come from?"

"Most of it comes from Burma and Afghanistan and is processed through laboratories in Marseille in France. But we have recently found some coming through America from Mexico. Some of our big-time criminals now have links with the American Mafia."

Tony broke in. "Tell Harry about the other drugs."

"Cocaine was the big one in the twenties and thirties but authorities took very little notice because it was used mostly by the wives of the rich and famous. The razor gangs controlled the early supply. It was distributed through nightclubs and gambling dens."

"What about the weed, Jack?" asked Harry.

"Cannabis has been grown for years in Queensland. It was not illegal in earlier years but even the *Smith's Weekly* ran an article recently about reefer madness, warning people about the dangers of smoking the substance. It's been in Australia since the First Fleet. In the twenties it was readily available as cigarettes called *Cigares de Joy* until they were banned a few years later."

"Is there a problem now?"

"Yes. In this state it is grown in the Hawkesbury area and the irrigation areas out west."

Tony sat forward. "Jack, tell us about this sample here."

Jack explained. "This type of packet is common with the big dealers. This was no small pusher on a street corner. Drugs like this are supplied by the dealers associated with, and protected by, the big four criminals in the city, as well as in other states such as Victoria and Queensland. Any one of them could have ordered this packet."

"But how did it get into my car?" asked Harry.

"Jack, would you ask Rita to come back in?"

Rita came in and stood at the end of the table. "There are fingerprints on the packet but most of them are smudged. I can tell you with some degree of certainty that none of them belong to Detective Taylor."

Harry breathed a sigh of relief and walked around the room. "Well, Tony, where to now?"

Tony sat back. "I'll pass this information on to the CIB boys and let them go from there. It's out of my hands now."

"But if that packet was in the glove box when the anti-personnel mine blew up, surely it would have burst or been destroyed. This packet is clean and undamaged."

Jack cut in. "Yes, Harry. It appears this was placed in the car after the explosion."

"That means someone was watching my car after the explosion and while the team was examining it," said Harry. "After everyone left, and before it was towed away, someone placed that packet in the car. That also means they saw me at the scene with you."

Tony slapped the desk. "Now, Harry, surely you'll get the message to stay away from here. The killer is watching your every move. Go to the station, get on the next train west and keep going."

Harry stood up, put on his tanker hood and strode to the door. He turned to look at Tony. "No, Tony. This makes me more determined to stay around to catch this bastard. See you all."

He walked out leaving the others shaking their heads with exasperation. However, after he left they expressed their admiration for Harry's guts and determination to catch the killer.

Chapter 15
Friday

Harry rode his bike into the city and parked at Central Railway Station. He bought two meat pies with tomato sauce and walked through to Belmore Park to sit on the bench under a large tree. He needed to think through the implications of the drugs being planted in his car.

The weather was hot but not unbearable. Holiday-makers, going to and from the large department stores such as Anthony Horderns in George Street or to the cinemas, were walking up and down the ramp from the railway. Children were excited going down the ramp or bored and complaining on their return from a morning of being dragged through the shops.

Harry flicked through the files of his mind and focused on cases involving the drug trade. Before the war he and other members of the CIB had been tasked with reducing the impact of drugs in the state, with particular emphasis on cocaine and heroin. They were successful in charging a number of minor criminals, but the drug lords evaded prosecution.

At various times Tom Lebovich, Tony Pantano, Bluey Ricketts, Bomber Earl and Knuckles Elliott had been taken in and charged by Harry and his team. Some were gaoled for short terms while others were cautioned and released. All five were standover men for the big boys but also did jobs on the side for extra cash. Although Harry was investigating them for drugs, those men had their hands in many other criminal activities. Harry didn't trust them but he could not see why any of them would go the extra distance to try to take him out.

Since returning from the war Harry was intermittently involved with investigating the supply of drugs in Sydney but, because murder cases took priority, he never had enough continuity to follow them through to the top of the drug heap.

With the exception of Tom Lebovich, he could not see any of them holding a grudge strong enough to want to kill him. Harry was certain Lebovich had been guilty of murdering other criminals, but that was part of the turf wars that had gone on for some time. However, to kill a policeman was something else. Lebovich, or any other criminal, must have been offered an enormous sum to even think of taking on such a contract. It was not beyond the realms of possibility.

Harry thought again about the influx of the Melbourne mob and their attempts to break into the Sydney scene. He had recently brought in a well-known but low-key Melbourne criminal named Scarface Fisher for questioning. He also led the investigation into Flash Evans' involvement in the Lennox Bridge affair. Evans and Fisher worked for Splinter Woods and Bruiser Bignall, the big operators in Melbourne. Evans, although now in gaol, might have decided to take revenge and let out a contract on Harry.

Harry doubted it was Fisher, but that man could be under instruction from one of the heavies from Melbourne. If Woods and Bignall or the other major criminals in Melbourne such as Jacky Abbott, Billy Stenson, 'Nobby' Clark and 'Darkie' Moffitt were involved, it could only be because they saw Harry as a danger to their efforts to move to Sydney. Harry remembered having run-ins with Moffitt and Clark before the war when they lived in Sydney.

The reality, however, was that if the money was right, someone in the criminal world would be willing to take up the contract. Some two-bit low-life would jump at the opportunity to take a big fat cheque for one night's work and have an opportunity to establish his credentials in the criminal world.

Everyone in the crime business knew that Harry was unconventional and had trodden on many toes, especially since he returned from armed service. They also knew he couldn't be bribed, so a hit might be the only solution to get him out of the way.

As dangerous as it was, Harry needed to get closer to the action. Over the years he had established a relationship with a couple of middle-order and low-order criminals who, on occasions, supplied Harry with vital information. In return, Harry had convinced the magistrate to deliver a suspended sentence with no recorded conviction.

After careful consideration Harry focused on Sandy Blight, a minor miscreant who had convictions for break and enter, receiving stolen goods, drug possession and assault. On one occasion Harry arranged a three-day release from Long Bay Gaol for Sandy to travel to

Dubbo for his mother's funeral. Sandy never forgot and had been a willing but discreet conduit of information ever since.

Sandy ran away from home when he was fourteen to get away from his violent, abusive father. He found it difficult to get work and drifted into petty crime before moving to Sydney where he got a job at the Darling Harbour wharves. It was there he got involved in organised stealing from cargo loaded on and off the ships.

On occasions the wharfies arranged for a load to drop 'accidentally' from the hoist onto the deck. Insurance companies would write off the load and the wharfies shared in the damaged goods. Shipping companies put it down to collateral damage knowing that, if they complained, their ships would be held up in harbour with a strike, costing them more than the damaged cargo.

Sandy always dressed in the same dirty blue overalls, steel-capped boots and greasy hat. A thinly rolled cigarette hung permanently from his lips. The untidy stubble on his sun-tanned wrinkled face gave him the look of a down-and-out, but his country upbringing meant that he was loyal to his mates and he was known as someone who would give up his pay packet for a mate down on his luck. He wasn't the sharpest tack in the tin but he knew who was who in the pecking order at the wharf. He rented a room at a boarding house in the old section of The Rocks.

Harry returned to his bike and rode to Druitt Place, a narrow access joining Sussex and Kent Streets. From there he had a good view over the finger wharves of Darling Harbour. It was a busy day with ships in all but one of the wharves. He watched the hive of activity as hoists took slings of wheat bags from the trucks, lifted them over the sides of the ship and lowered them into its hold. At the adjoining wharf a hoist lifted pallets of 44 gallon drums from the ship's hold onto the waiting trucks.

To get a better view Harry walked down Harbour Street and Wheat Road, stopping briefly in doorways to observe the action below. He pulled his tanker hood forward to cover his forehead. Twice he sat on the step at a door entrance; head down with his back to a group of men walking towards him. They ignored him and moved past. It wasn't until he was near Pyrmont Bridge that Harry spotted Sandy on the wharf. He was leaning against a fully-laden truck lighting another cigarette.

Harry returned to his bike and rode to a warehouse below Market Street where he could sit and wait until knock-off time. When the siren sounded, Sandy walked up the hill to Market Street and turned into York

Street. Harry kept at least fifty yards behind, stopping occasionally to let Sandy to get ahead. Opposite Wynyard Park, Harry accelerated and pulled into the kerb beside Sandy.

"Hey, Sandy," he said. "Hop on the back. We're going for a ride."

"Fuck off. I ain't going nowhere with you. What do you take me for?"

"Sandy, it's me; Harry. Now hop on the back."

"I don't know no Harry, so piss off or I'll call the cops."

"Sandy, it's Harry Taylor. I am the cops. Now get on and I'll give you a ride home."

"Shit, Harry. Is that really you? No bloody way. It's worth more than my life to be seen with you."

"Okay Sandy, I understand, but I need to talk with you. I won't take you home so hop on and we'll go up to Observatory Park where we won't be seen."

Reluctantly Sandy got on, holding his hat in one hand and his lunch box in the other. Harry was happy to take off so that he kept ahead of the full blown body odour. He rode to the park below the observatory, a quiet spot with views across the beautiful Sydney harbour to Luna Park and the Harbour Bridge. They sat on the grass near a Moreton Bay fig-tree.

"Holy shit, Harry, you gave me such a fright. I thought you were dead. I didn't recognise ya."

Harry wiped the sweat from the back of his neck under the hood. "I'm very much alive, Sandy, but if anyone asks, you can tell them I'm dead."

"They told me they had a contract out on you and you'd got the full blast."

Harry turned to face Sandy. "Who put out that contract out on me, Sandy?"

"I'm not certain, Harry, but I heard it was worth a lot of money."

"How much was I worth mate? Why didn't you take it on, Sandy? You could have done it and retired and gone fishing," said Harry with a smile.

"Cripes, Harry. Don't joke like that. This is bloody serious. I wouldn't do that to you, mate. Cross me heart." Sandy got up and nervously rolled another cigarette.

"Alright, Sandy, sit down. Why is there a contract out on me?"

"The trouble with you, Harry, is that you're too clean. You don't take bribes like some of your mates and you were getting too close to some of the top jocks in the business."

Harry stretched his legs. "I'll start naming names, Sandy, and you nod when I'm on the money. Let's start with Whispers Durante. He's into casinos, drugs and prostitutes."

Sandy never moved.

Harry turned and swung his hand in front of Sandy's face. "Well let's try Squeaky Walsh in Palmer Street, or Rosie Travener at The Rocks, or Tony the Greek at Marrickville. What about them?"

Sandy blew smoke away from Harry. "I don't know, Harry."

"You and I know, Sandy, that the Melbourne boys are trying to move in to town and take a slice of the cake. What about Splinter Woods, Bruiser Bignall, Scarface Fisher or Flash Evans. Tell me about them."

"Honestly, Harry, I don't know much about them. I try to stay out of that sort of stuff. I don't get into the big time. That's too dangerous. I leave that to others."

"Then tell me, Sandy; is it drugs, gambling, prostitution or robberies that is the main reason to take me out?"

"It's only a guess, Harry but I'd say that drugs would be the main reason. Since the war they're all going bonkers for drugs. Most people are using them so there's a battle going on between the big uns to get their hands on the extra moolah."

"What drugs are we talking about, Sandy?"

"Heroin and cocaine are the big uns. But lately there's more of that weed they grow in Queensland. You know, that stuff called canna-something."

Harry corrected him. "That's cannabis, Sandy. It's been around for years but it's now illegal. Where else do they get it? Do you get it coming on to the wharves?"

"Very little. Most of the stuff we get off the ships is heroin and cocaine. The weed comes from Queensland but I heard that they're now growing some in the Hawkesbury Valley out past Windsor, and also in the irrigation area down south near some place called Leedon, or some name like that."

"How does it get to the sellers?"

"Don't hold me to it but, I heard that they pack it with the fruit and veggies and it comes into the Haymarket in town and is distributed from there. There's a whisper though that the Melbourne mob are moving into places like Liverpool and Mascot."

"Sandy, who is clearing the heroin and cocaine from the wharves?"

"Harry, that's for you to find out. If I told you that, mate, my body would be put through the mincer and taken out to the middle of the ocean and fed to the fishes. Look, mate I have to get out of here. If I'm seen with you, that's where you'll find me." Sandy stood up to go.

"Thanks, Sandy. You've been a great help. If I want to speak to you again I'll leave a note in your box at the boarding house. It'll give you a day and time, nothing else. You'll know that we'll always meet here. See you, mate. Look after yourself."

Harry waited for Sandy to walk over the rise and back home to The Rocks before he rode back to Stanmore. He stopped at the store to make a telephone call to Keith Tomkin, the Superintendent at Bathurst. He made arrangements to meet him in the morning. After purchasing a steak from the butcher, and some potatoes, pumpkin and beans from the greengrocer, he returned to his flat and prepared a hearty meal to be washed down with a cold bottle of beer.

After cooking the vegetables he heated the pan, wiped lard across the bottom, threw in the steak, waited ten seconds, turned it and waited another ten seconds before placing it on the plate. Harry liked his steak thick and rare.

Chapter 16
Saturday

There was a strong, dry westerly blowing in the window as Harry ate his breakfast of cereal and three pieces of toast. It was going to be a hot day. The early morning ABC radio news talked about the weather, bushfires and the prospects of the visiting Indian cricket team against the lowly-rated Tasmanian side in a warm-up match before the fourth Test. Harry was anxious to get moving. He had a three-hour ride to Bathurst ahead of him.

The early morning trip along the Western Highway was uneventful until he came to a roadblock at Leura in the Blue Mountains. The air was pungent with smoke, ash and dust. Harry asked the constable on duty, "Where's the main fire?"

The constable pointed north. "There's a couple of monster fires coming up from the Grose Valley and they're moving towards us here at Leura and further up the valley. The road is blocked between here and Katoomba."

"Can I ride around the cliff drive and get back on the highway on the other side of Katoomba?" asked Harry.

"If you do it now you'll be okay, but I wouldn't leave it any longer. You never know where the fires will end up around here with a change of wind."

"Thanks, Constable. Hope it gets better for you. See ya."

Harry took the bypass and rode through smoke most of the way to Mount Lambie where he stopped for a meat pie and tomato sauce. He bought a pair of goggles to protect his eyes from the smoke, dust and ash; filled the tank with petrol and took off on the winding road to the west.

Reaching Bathurst, Harry turned off the main street into Keppel Street and stopped in front of the superintendent's house. The red-brick Federation house was a symbol of country solidarity with its impressive leadlight windows. The steps onto the tiled verandah were wide and impressive. It was a fitting dwelling for a respected superintendent of police. The sound from the lion-faced brass knocker on the solid wooden door resonated through the house. As the door opened, a mature lady in a blue linen dress looked quizzically at Harry, her hand firmly on the handle in case she needed to close it quickly.

"Good morning, Mrs Tomkin," said Harry. "I apologise for my looks but I'm Harry Taylor. I've just ridden from Sydney and I'm here to see Keith today. Is he in?"

Norma Tomkin relaxed. "My goodness, Harry. What happened to you? I could have passed you in the street without recognising you. Come in. Keith is out the back. I'll get him for you."

"Sure. That'd be great. Thanks." Harry sat down in the lounge room.

A tall, well-built man in casual long trousers and shirt came into the room. "My God, Harry, you look a mess," said Keith Tomkin as he reached out to shake Harry's hand. "Look at you. You were never one for the rules and regulations, but this is the limit. You've gone feral on me. But then, you didn't look much better the last time I saw you in Goonaburra after that gypsy bloke belted you at the pub."

Harry laughed as he stood up to greet Keith. "Well that's great. If nobody recognises me as a police officer I've got a chance of living a little longer."

"What happened to that gypsy?"

Harry rubbed his nose in memory of that event. "He blindsided and king-hit me good and proper; and the magistrate let him off. That's the way things turned out but that's history. I'm more interested in the present."

Keith called out. "Norma, darling, could we have a cup of tea please?"

They sat in the comfortable large leather lounge chairs. Keith studied the scars on Harry's face. "Tell me about this shooting. Who do you think was responsible?"

Harry placed his tanker hood, goggles and jacket on the floor next to the chair. "I didn't get a look at the shooter but I was lucky that he rushed his shot and hit the frame of the window. Most of my wounds are superficial and are healing rapidly. I came here today to seek your advice because you and I worked in the CIB before the war and you continued with that unit for a few years after that. You know all the players and I trust your advice."

"But why the hair and beard?"

"The shooter knows me but I don't know him, so I want to work undercover and continue investigating where I won't be recognised."

Keith sat forward. "But I heard you were on sick leave."

"Officially I am, but that's not going to stop me from going out there to catch this bastard. If everyone believes I'm on sick leave they won't be out there looking for me on the job. People think that I've gone home to help Dad on the farm."

Norma brought in a silver tray with teapot, cups, saucers, sugar-bowl, milk jug and a plate of freshly-baked scones with jam and cream. "There you go, Harry," she said with a smile. "That'll make the hairs grow back on your head."

"Thanks, dear," said Keith as he poured the tea and handed it to Harry. "Did I hear correctly that your car was bombed? Tell me about that."

Harry explained in detail the bombing of his car, the death of Stumpy Baxter, the forensic analysis by Tony's team and their finding of a Cellophane packet of heroin in the glove box.

Keith sat back and looked up at the ceiling rose in the centre of the room. "Well, you've made one thing clear, Harry. This is no disgruntled small-time crook out for a bit of revenge; this is the big time. But I don't see how I can be of any help to you out here."

Harry licked cream from his fingers. "Keith, you worked in the CIB for many years and knew all of the main players. You put many of them away and you knew the ones who got away from your iron grip. I wasn't there for five years during the war and I lost touch. How do you see the current situation in Sydney?"

Keith topped up the teacups. "In my early days with the CIB we were cleaning up the remnants of the old razor gangs. Immediately before and during the war a new group took over. You know them because they now run the show. There's Whispers, Squeaky, Rosie and Tony. They control seventy per cent of the big crime. Then there is the second layer of standover merchants who do the dirty work for them."

"Do you see any of those four wanting to take me out, Keith?"

"Those people are not minor criminals, Harry. They are very powerful people. We were never able to prove it but they bribed politicians, lawyers, judges and, I suspect, some police officers."

"Yes, we always suspected that, but how far do you think it goes?" asked Harry.

"I couldn't prove anything, but I've had lay-down-misère cases rejected by a judge who I knew was a frequent visitor to illegal gambling casinos run by Whispers Durante. When I raised it with senior officers I was told to shut up and mind my own business."

Harry sipped slowly on his tea. "But why would a judge go against his training, experience and values?"

Keith got up from his chair. "Come on, Harry. Let's go out and get some fresh air."

The two of them walked along Keppel Street to Machattie Park, behind the court house. Harry loved Bathurst. It was a large country city and the focal centre for rail and road transport for western New South Wales. It was rich, having been the financial centre in the early Gold Rush days, and continued later as the market-place for farming produce for one third of the state.

Harry had been a probationary constable there and, on his enlistment in the army, had completed his basic training at the local showground. He loved the friendly people and the fresh clean air. He fully understood why Keith gave up the opportunity to reach the top of his profession, preferring instead to spend the remainder of his career in Bathurst. Like Harry, he was a country boy at heart. Harry had been born and bred at a place called Sandy Creek, near Goonaburra, about two hours west of there.

"To answer your earlier question, Harry," said Keith. "I know that the illegal casinos operate above the nightclubs and several hotels have rooms upstairs for prostitutes. And I suspect that some well-known identities have been offered free visits to those rooms on their gambling nights."

"But Keith," said Harry, "we never really pushed hard against prostitution. It's been around since before Jesus played fullback for Jerusalem. We're never going to stop it so why is this such a big deal?"

"I couldn't care less if a judge has a night with a prostitute, but there is a rumour going around that, in some of those places, the owners set up secret cameras to film their patrons in action."

Harry turned to face Keith. "Wow. That makes a difference."

"Yes," said Keith, "especially when the prostitute is a young boy. How would that look in the Sunday papers? And then there are the politicians who preach morals during the day and go shagging prostitutes at night. Some of them even have prostitutes let in by security through the back door of Parliament House into their private office after a late night session in chambers."

"So the big boys who run these outfits have the men in powerful positions by the short and curlies. If they don't do as they're told, a photograph will appear on someone's table and a promising career goes down the drain."

"Spot on," said Keith. "But we don't have proof because nobody talks. It's a case of you scratch my back and I'll scratch yours. We know it goes on but nobody involved is willing to stand up in court and give evidence because it would be their death warrant if they did."

"Who in the police force is involved in these capers?"

"You and I both suspect some of the officers. We worked with some of them but it is difficult to prove. We know they go into casinos and hotels and mix with well-known criminals, but that is part of gathering intelligence. That intelligence is important to the conviction of major and minor players. Some of the best results have occurred because of that intelligence."

Harry rubbed along a scar across his cheek bone. It was itchy. "I've been offered a free night with a prostitute and some free cases of grog but I've never taken them. Did that happen to you?"

"Yes. In the early years that was quite common. But later on they all knew I was not interested, so they gave up."

"What have you heard about the Melbourne mob, Keith?"

"Nothing much because most of that has happened since I came here. But criminals are criminals; and they guard their turf. I'd watch that area with interest, if I was you."

"What about the drug scene?"

"Australians have always been heavy users, especially with heroin and cocaine. Since the war, with the influence of the American troops here, usage has increased and therefore the big criminals have taken control of the market. I expect a major turf war between the big operators in the near future. Your problem at the moment could very well be related to that area. Being clean, you could be seen as getting too close to the centre of operations. Be careful, Harry."

They walked slowly back to Keith's house, sheltering in the shade of the street trees. As they walked in, Norma called out, "Oh, Keith, while you were out, Sergeant Irwin called to say that the western highway has been closed at Leura, Blackheath and Hartley because of the fires. He's set up warning signs at this end."

"Well, that's put a stop to going back to Sydney this afternoon," said Harry.

"Do you want to stay here, Harry? There's a spare room out the back," asked Norma.

"No thanks, Norma. I'm in no hurry. I'm on sick leave, so I'll go on to Goonaburra and catch up with some of the folks out there. Thank you so much for your hospitality. And thank you, Keith, for your good advice. I promise I'll be careful."

As Harry walked to the door Keith tapped him on the shoulder. "Don't trust anyone, Harry. I mean that. Nobody. Do your homework, trust your instincts and watch your back. Good luck, mate."

Harry rode off to the west.

Chapter 17
Saturday

The mid-afternoon hot, dry air seared Harry's face. His skin felt like parchment. Dust and pieces of wheat straw, whipped up by the strong winds and willy-willies, stung his face as he rode west towards Goonaburra. He was thankful for the protection of the new goggles. Sheep in the paddocks lolled under the shade of the few remaining trees; heads down, tongues panting for any breath of cooler air.

Most of the paddocks were covered in golden stubble from the recent wheat harvest although Harry passed some farmers who were burning off the stubble, believing that the ash was good for the next crop. Harry knew that burning off caused more erosion, but farmers had used that method all their lives. It wasn't against the law, and they weren't going to change because a policeman told them not to do so.

If nothing else, it kept his mind active as he drove into the sun and dust. He avoided a red-bellied black snake slithering across the road. He did not want to run over it because the snake's head would flick back and strike him on the leg. Harry had respect for snakes and he appreciated the good work they did in keeping the mice and other vermin at bay.

Harry drove through flocks of galahs with their distinctive pink and grey plumage. They rose in screeching arcs after feeding on the wheat grain dropped on the side of the road from passing trucks. An occasional locust hit Harry in the chest or splattered on his goggles or face. There was a brief respite as he slowed to drive through the city of Orange with its memories of his court appearances there last year and the reprimands handed out by the magistrate, Mr Hayes.

One hour later as the sun settled lower in the western sky, Harry drove down the main street of Goonaburra. This was the town where he finished his schooling and where he had conducted the investigation into the deaths of two young women last June. Having been born at nearby Sandy Creek, he had fond memories of this place. To him it was sacred territory. He drove past the police station, the CWA, the School of Arts and on to the Railway Hotel where he propped his bike on its stand.

The entrance to the hotel had the same tired look but, then again, so did Harry as he walked through to the public bar, tanker hood on, goggles dangling around his neck and his face covered in dust. He ordered a pint of beer.

"Where did you come from today?" asked Shirley the barmaid as she placed the beer in front of him.

Harry removed the tanker hood, hit it on his leg to remove the dust and placed it and the goggles on the bar. He took a long sip before replying. "I started in Sydney this morning but spent a few hours in Bathurst before coming here. Would you happen to have a bed available for tonight?"

When Shirley heard his voice she jolted back, eyes wide, hands clapped on both cheeks and then screamed. "Oh my God. It's you. It's Harry." She turned. "Ted, come here. Look. It's Harry. Look. It's him. Oh my God. Is this real or am I dreaming?"

Ted Jones, the owner of the Railway Hotel came along the bar. "Well I'll be damned. It is Harry. Where the bloody hell did you come from? For a while we thought you were dead. We heard about the shooting and the bomb and thought you'd copped it good and proper this time."

Shirley rushed around to the front of the bar, stood on tiptoe, and wrapped her arms around Harry's neck and gave him a long hug and kiss. He almost suffocated with her enthusiasm. "Oh, it's so good to see you alive. We've all missed you since you went back to Sydney. Now what can we get you?"

Harry looked up at the drinkers who had turned to see what all the commotion was about. There was 'Nipper' Ricketts, 'Dandy' Lyons, 'Bazza' O'Riordan, 'Rusty' Steele and Charlie McCormack.

Charlie turned and looked at Harry. "Nah. That's not Harry. He was a handsome bloke. This bloke's some blow-in. Wouldn't give him the time of day."

Dandy walked a little closer. "It looks a bit like Harry but the bloody rats have eaten half his head."

Nipper, a long-time friend, walked up and gave Harry a big hug. "Mate. It's so great to see you're still kicking. Come up here and have a drink with us. Shirley, get Harry another drink."

Harry stood and was about to move along the bar but was stopped in his tracks by the booming voice of Maud, Ted's wife, who had come from the kitchen to check on the increased noise. "And where the bloody hell do you think you're going? If you think you can come in here and talk to this riff-raff before you come and see me then you'd better think again. Now get over here and give me a hug, you big mug."

Maud took the tea-towel from over her shoulder, wrapped it around Harry's neck, and pulled him in for a big sloppy kiss and a hug. "Now, before you do anything, get upstairs to the same room you had last year. Go and have a shower before you come back here."

Maud turned to Shirley. "You go up with him and get his bed ready while I get some clean clothes from Ted's wardrobe."

Harry started to complain but Maud thumped him in the chest, turned him around and pushed him towards Shirley and the stairs. "I'll leave the clothes outside the bathroom. Now get going."

When Harry was in Goonaburra last year he and Shirley had a brief but intimate relationship, so it was with some anxiety that Harry followed her up the stairs to the bedroom. She, as a former nurse, had cared for him through his bouts of malaria, and after he was king-hit by the gypsy at the back of the hotel.

Shirley, equally nervous, spoke first. "Harry, darling, when you went back to Sydney, I cried my eyes out for weeks. I have often thought of what would have happened if I had packed up and gone back there with you. Could we have made a go of it?"

Harry walked to the window, staring out at the garage in the backyard. "No, Shirley. Remember, we talked about that. I wouldn't ask you or any other woman to live with me when I'm doing this type of work. It wouldn't be fair."

"That's only your opinion, Harry. You didn't ask me."

"I've seen too many marriages break up in this job. It's not fair on the women."

Shirley straightened the bedclothes and fluffed up the pillows. "Yes. I know you said that before. Anyhow, when I had time to think about it I decided to stay here because a country town like this is the best place to bring up kids. Michael is loving it here and, my mum Noeline, looks after him when I'm at work. She's so involved in the town in her spare time, it's not funny. It wouldn't be fair on them if I went back."

Harry turned back. "Thanks, Shirley. It's best for all of us. You lost your husband, Keith, on the Kokoda Track. That was bad enough. Now look at me. I've just had two attempts on my life in the last two weeks. I should be dead. Someone's still out looking for me. I don't know who the shooter is. I won't have anyone else involved."

"Is there another woman in your life, Harry. You can be honest with me."

"No, there's no one, cross my heart and spit." Harry walked across to give her a hug. "If I wanted someone I would have asked you."

"Come on, you two," shouted Maud coming up the stairs. "I haven't got time to dilly-dally around here. I've got work to do. Go on Harry, get in the shower and toss out your clothes so I can wash them."

Harry diligently walked the corridor to the bathroom. After showering he dressed in Ted's clothes and walked downstairs to the bar. Shirley poured him another beer.

Maud poked her head in. "Harry, you haven't got any luggage so how long are you staying?"

"Just tonight, Maud. The bushfires stopped me from going back to Sydney from Bathurst so I thought I'd come out here to see you. If it's clear in the morning I'll head back."

"Okay. I'll make a dinner for us. I've got roast lamb followed by lemon-cheese tart. It'll be on at seven."

Harry joined the group. They wanted to know about the shooting and the bomb. It was the most exciting thing to happen in Goonaburra since Harry was there last year investigating the murders. Harry gave them a blow-by-blow description of the events since New Year's Eve. After persistent questioning he explained the criminal scene in Sydney and how it was tied up with drugs, prostitution, gambling and theft.

"Why don't you give it all up and come back home?" asked Charlie. "Your old man is not coping and he's gone downhill since you went back to Sydney last year."

"No, Charlie. Farming's not the life for me. My brothers are quite capable of looking after the farm. Dad needs to have confidence in them. They'll do a damn sight better job of it than me."

Nipper ran his finger down the side of his glass, leaving a trail in the froth. "But surely it would be better than getting shot or being killed with an army bomb? You can't go anywhere because the next bloke around the corner could be the killer."

"I know, Nipper, but I like the work I do. I know it can be dangerous but someone has to do it; and I'm happy to be that someone."

Bazza coughed. "Well, better you than me. But I'm sort of glad it's you because we know that you are fair dinkum and you're not going to give up until you get him. Good luck, mate."

Harry stood up to stretch his back after the long ride. "Enough of me. Tell me what's happened since I left. Is Sergeant Walsh still around? What about the others?"

Ted lifted his glass and yelled. "Here's to Walshie. May he rot in hell; because he gave us hell when he was here. He was determined to close us down, but he got shifted to some place near Wollongong on the south coast. He'll be making life hell for the poor buggers down there."

Rusty chipped in. "Yeah, the new sergeant is great. He's easy going and, if you don't do anything stupid, he leaves you alone. And he's good with the young kids who get into trouble. He gets them to chop wood for the pensioners and clean up the garden at the hospital."

What about Mark and Phil?"

Shirley wiped the bar in front of Harry. "Mark Johnstone was transferred to Newcastle, but Phil is still here. You should catch up with him while you're here."

"What else has happened?"

Bazza laughed. "That gypsy bloke you had trouble with, came back once and threatened young Tommy Williams. Tommy hit him a corker of a punch and sat him on his arse good and proper. It took him a minute to get up. He got on his bike and hasn't been seen since."

Dandy tapped Harry on the shoulder. "Young Fritz Henning, the German bloke you had strife with, left here as well and moved to Melbourne. Good riddance, I say."

After a few more rounds of drinks they all helped clean up the bar and moved to the dining room where Maud put on her usual wonderful spread. Shirley left to attend to her son Michael. There was much reminiscing, laughter and good cheer. Harry was relaxed for the first time since the shooting. He was with good friends. At nine-thirty he made his excuses and went to his room and collapsed with contentment.

***

At eleven o'clock there was a light tap-tap at the door. It opened and Shirley walked to the bed, touching Harry on the shoulder. "Harry, dear, I've just come to check your wounds. I'm worried that they might become infected."

She undid the front of her dress, slipped it from her shoulders, dropped it to the floor, kicked off her shoes, lifted the sheet and slipped into bed beside Harry.

Chapter 18
Sunday

The screeching of corellas, cockatoos and galahs in flight and the warbling of a lone magpie on the window sill woke Harry. He ran his hand across the mattress searching for Shirley but it met no resistance. He sat up to find he was alone. It was not a dream; he could smell her perfume on the pillow. He lay back with the memory of last night, contentment overriding the throb behind his ears caused by too much drinking.

The sound of saucepans and crockery from downstairs signalled that Maud was up early preparing breakfast. Harry rolled out of bed and walked slowly to the window where he tapped the glass. Jacko, the magpie, looked up, turned his head from side to side and up and down, then flew to the garage roof across the yard, convinced that Harry had no food for him,.

Harry found his clean ironed clothes outside the door. He showered, dressed and went downstairs.

"Well, look what the cat dragged in," chuffed Maud. "I hope that wasn't you walking around in the middle of the night. I was so disturbed I couldn't sleep. Some people have no respect for the other guests." Maud turned to the stove where she cracked some eggs into the pan. She couldn't hide her grin.

Harry smiled at her cheekiness. "I can assure you, Maud, that it wasn't me walking around. It was probably Ted. He drank so much he was probably up to the toilet a few times."

Ted walked into the kitchen, sat down and started into a big plate of bacon, sausages and eggs followed by toast and honey. "Thank goodness it's Sunday. Maud and I can get a bit of rest today. What are you doing, Harry?"

"I'll check the radio reports and I'll go down to the police station to check on any warnings about the bush fires. If the road is clear I'll go back to Sydney today."

Maud came to the table and slapped the egg slide on the breadboard. "You men have got all your brains in your underpants. There's none up top here for thinking. You're on sick leave, Harry. Stay here for a few days and relax. Catch up with your old friends and family. Spend some time with Shirley. What's wrong with that, eh?"

"Oh, Maud, you are a gem. I'm going to take you back with me to Sydney and put you in charge of the police force. You'll have it cleaned up in no time."

"Don't try that soft-soap dribble on me, young Harry. I didn't come down in the last shower. Ted's not resting today. He's going to tidy the backyard and the cellar. I've been on his back about that for weeks. And you are going to help him."

"I'm sorry, but I've got a killer on the loose, and the sooner I lock him up the sooner I'll be safe again. Being on sick leave gives me the chance to work undercover. I'll go and see Mum and Dad after church. After I go to the police station and check on any road blocks I'll be on my way."

Maud stomped back to the stove. "You men make me sick; excuses, excuses, excuses. You're all full of it. No wonder nothing gets done around here."

"My darling," said Ted. "That's why I give you that enormous allowance every year to pay for all the work you do."

"That'll be the day. When was the last time I got any money to spend on myself?"

Ted got up and walked to the stove to give Maud a pat on the bottom. "My precious princess, I pay you with all the love I give you."

Maud turned sharply and whacked him on the arm with the wooden spoon. "Get out of here and let me get on with my work. Don't think you can smooch up to me and get away with it like that. You men are all the same."

Harry got up and walked across to Maud. He gave her a big hug. "Yes, Maud, we men are like that, but you love every minute of it. Now I'm going to leave you two love birds to yourselves and get on my way. The church service is finishing soon and I want to catch up with Mum and Dad. Thanks so much for everything. You lot are the best thing that has happened to me since I was here last year. Thanks, Maud. Thanks, Ted."

Harry rode back along Main Street, up Myrtle Street and into the car park at the rear of the Catholic church. He entered the church and sat in the back pew as the last hymn was sung. He stood as Father Francis O'Grady led the recessional. As the priest walked past, he looked askance at Harry, but without recognition. Harry had vivid memories of his confrontations with the priest last year.

As his parents came down the aisle he stepped in front of them and ushered them into his pew so that they could talk without the other parishioners present. He gave his mother a kiss and hug but his father refused his outstretched hand.

"How dare you come into this sacred place looking like a drowned rat. You are a disgrace to this family," said his father who started to stand to leave.

Harry gently put his hand on his father's shoulder and guided him back onto the seat. "Dad, I'm not here to have an argument. I'm only here this morning and wanted to catch up with you both."

Harry's mother sat back, hand over her mouth in shock. "What in the name of goodness has happened to you? You look terrible."

"On New Year's Eve someone tried to shoot me. I believe it was one of the big criminals in Sydney. A few days later they blew up my car. I was lucky and was not injured seriously. I'm sure Aunty Mary has told you about that by now. I'm looking like this because I'm working undercover. It's a disguise."

His father waved his fist at Harry. "But why do you offend the church by coming in here looking like this?"

"Dad, everything I have read in the Bible, and everything I've been taught, tells me that Jesus and God accept all men, both rich and poor, clean and dirty, black and white. They welcome everyone, including me."

"How the hell would you know? You haven't been to church for ages."

His mother added to the insult. "And how could you have been friends with that horrible cripple, Hoppy, last year? He committed suicide and he murdered those beautiful young women. Those are mortal sins. He will go to hell for his sins and may he rot there forever. What a terrible man."

Harry changed the subject. "How are the boys going? Did you get a good crop this harvest?"

His mother answered. "The harvest went well and we should get a good price this year. Your brothers were marvellous, thankfully, because you weren't there to assist."

"That's great, because Dad doesn't have to do the heavy work any more. He can sit back and enjoy the fact that he has worked hard all his life to leave a good legacy to the boys. He should be proud of that."

"No thanks to you," shouted his father.

"You're right, Dad. So I want you to give everything to my brothers. They have earned it. I haven't."

At that moment Father O'Grady came in after farewelling the parishioners. Turning towards Harry he asked, "And who have we here, may I ask?"

"I'm Harry Taylor, Father. We met last year when I was investigating the murders of those two girls."

"Oh yes," he replied. "I thought I'd seen the last of you. With all the trouble you caused I'm surprised you would have the audacity to show your face again in this sacred place."

Harry stood up. "Well, I will offend you no longer, Father. I came in here to greet my parents but if your church does not accept sinners like me, then I'll leave. Goodbye, Mother. Goodbye, Dad."

Harry strode out without a backward glance, hopped on his bike and rode down the hill to the police station.

As Harry walked in, young Constable Phillip Simpson looked up from the desk. "How might I help you, sir?"

"You can help me," said Harry, "by not being so bloody formal. Are you trying to get promoted?"

Phil stood up and came to the counter. "Bloody hell. Is that you, Harry? What in the name of goodness are you doing here?"

"Aren't you going to invite me in for a cup of tea? The hospitality has gone downhill since I was last here."

"Come in to the back room and we'll have a cup," said Phil. "Wait a minute and I'll ring the sergeant. He'd like to meet you. You probably know that Mark went to Newcastle and Joe Walsh went to Wollongong. Jack Franks replaced Mark but he's off duty today, and Tom Billington replaced Joe."

As they settled back to have tea, a big bear of a man with a friendly face came into the room. "G'day. I'm Tom Billington. I see that young Phil is looking after you. I've heard a lot about you, Harry, and the investigation you did here last year. Welcome back. Is there anything we can do for you?"

"G'day, Tom, pleased to meet you. I've heard about the good work you are doing here. Yes, you can tell me if the highway back to Sydney is open. It was blocked with the fires after I came through yesterday."

"Phil, give a call through to Bathurst to check it out. I think it's okay but they will know. What brings you back here?"

Without giving any detail, Harry explained his trip to Bathurst as a fact-finding mission.

"I heard about the attempt on your life, Harry. Would you care to tell us about it?"

Phil came back in. "Bathurst said all roads are open at the moment, but there's no guarantee that won't change because the winds are constantly changing direction. You'll have to take your chances Harry."

Harry took his time filling in Tom and Phil about the last two weeks and the problems he was facing in trying to get to the shooter.

Tom interrupted. "I know a few of those characters. I did some time at Darlinghurst and Newtown stations and I worked for six months supervising the cells under the Central Court. I used to see those characters before I escorted them upstairs to the witness box to hear the charges against them. How they reacted down there before their appearance told me a lot about them."

"If you were in my position, Tom where would you look?"

Tom took off his cap. "That's difficult, Harry. It has to be mixed up with the big boys or the Melbourne mob, but if the shooter made a mistake they'll make him disappear until things cool down. Those blokes have some properties up in the hinterland behind the Central Coast and out at Londonderry, near Richmond. They can hide there for weeks without anyone knowing."

"Well, enough of this chatter," said Harry, "I need to get going before the highway is closed again. Otherwise, I'll have to spend another night drinking at the Railway pub."

"Good luck, Harry. Keep in touch," said Phil.

"Watch this young bloke, Tom. He wants your job," said Harry with a smile. "Keep up the good work."

Harry rode off. With only a stop at Mount Lambie and a slow down at Leura, where all traffic had to move into one lane, he got through without further incident, arriving back at Stanmore at seven o'clock. He showered and went to bed.

Chapter 19
Monday

Harry slept in until nine o'clock. It had been a tiring, emotional visit out west and he needed a rest. After breakfast he walked to the railway station and bought a newspaper. After scanning the main news headlines and the sports pages he turned to the funeral notices. He didn't know when Stumpy's funeral was to be held; but there it was, listed this morning in the notices.

> **Baxter,** *Maxwell James. (Stumpy)*
> *Aged 32 of Redfern.*
> *Passed away on the 7th January 1948.*
> *Result of accident.*
> *Funeral to be conducted on Monday 12th January*
> *at 11am at Saint Barnabas' Anglican*
> *Church, Broadway. All welcome.*

When Harry visited Stumpy's house after the bombing, he got a bad reception from Stumpy's father. It would be wise not to go to the funeral. He didn't want to cause any further anxiety for the family. He was also concerned that the shooter would expect him to go because Stumpy was his friend, and it was Harry's car that was blown up.

He wanted to see who attended the funeral and he remembered a hotel that was almost opposite the church on Broadway, between City Road and the Kent Brewery. He walked back to his flat, dressed in his army disposal gear with the tanker hood, got on the bike and rode to Broadway.

He arrived twenty minutes before the start of the service. Turning into Ivy Street he parked his bike in the lane next to the Broadway Hotel. From there he could see the church across the road. The hearse was already parked at the entrance. He recognised many of the people standing outside waiting for the family. The family arrived: Kitty, the two children and Stumpy's father, Chappie. They were greeted by other family members and well-wishers before moving into the church. Harry felt uneasy. He wanted to be there with them to share their grief, but common sense prevailed.

As the family disappeared inside the church, Harry noticed a shiny black Ford sedan move slowly along Mountain Street and turn into Owen Lane opposite the side entrance to the church. Harry kick-started his bike, moved out onto Broadway and turned left into Wattle Street. Riding slowly around the back lanes he came behind where the Ford was now parked, facing the church.

He stopped the bike twenty yards behind the car, got off and walked slowly towards it. He saw two men sitting in the front seat. They were wearing hats and jackets. When he was almost at the back bumper bar, the motor started and the car sped off. It accelerated as it turned into Mountain Street.

By the time Harry got back to his bike, the Ford was well away and he had no idea whether it had turned left into the city or right to go west, south or north. It was useless attempting to find them now. They could have hidden in a garage anywhere in a nearby suburb by the time Harry got out on to Broadway. This was probably their territory.

Harry returned to the Broadway Hotel and observed the mourners as they came out after the service. There were no suspicious persons in the crowd. There were lots of hugs and tears before the hearse drove away slowly, followed by the mourners. The funeral procession was on its way to Rookwood cemetery for the burial. Harry tagged along well behind the last car.

Leaving his bike near the entrance, Harry walked to a cream building in the General Cemetery section. He could see the mourners standing beside the open grave without himself being seen. When the graveside service began with prayers and words of wisdom, Harry noticed two men in pork-pie hats and jackets standing behind a tall crypt about fifty yards away. They were watching the mourners. He pulled his tanker hood down over his forehead, put on his goggles and walked towards the men.

Although he risked being recognised with his new appearance he still took the chance. When the men spotted Harry they turned and ran towards the black Ford, started up, and drove away. Harry knew that he could not catch them. It took him five minutes to get to his bike. They were long gone by then. One of the men was tall and well built. The other was shorter, much lighter in weight and wore a cream waistcoat. The smaller man had a slight limp; however it did little to hamper him when he ran.

Harry didn't get a good look at their faces. Neither of them looked familiar. They certainly weren't one of the big four criminals or their dominant standover men. If not them, then who were they? Were they from Melbourne or somewhere else, attracted by the big contract out on him? In his haste to catch up he failed to note the registration plate number on the car. Harry assumed they were stolen from another car and he guessed that they would be changed again within the hour.

He sat on his bike thinking about the advice he got from Sandy Blight and Tom Billington. They'd told Harry that criminals wanting to disappear for a while, or those from out of town who wanted to lie low, went into hiding at some properties out at Londonderry, near Richmond, west of Sydney. Nobody knew who owned those properties or even asked. They were tucked well away from the main road and were surrounded by bush. Hardly anyone went there. Even the locals rarely went off the main north road except when they went to the local trots meeting. He decided to spend the rest of the day looking at that area.

Harry rode along Windsor Road to Richmond and parked his bike outside Hewston's Real Estate office, opposite the large oval park in the middle of the main street.

"Hi. I'm Tim Hewston. How might I help you?" asked a tall man with a pencil thin moustache, slick Brylcreemed hair, dark suit trousers, white shirt and grey tie.

"G'day," replied Harry, firmly shaking the man's hand. "I'm Harry Forsythe. I've always had a desire to own a small property out this way as a hobby farm. You know, with a few cattle or sheep or goats to give me an interest on weekends and holidays. Would you have something like that?"

"I'm sure that we have something to your liking. You couldn't come to a better place than the Hawkesbury Valley. This is the food basket of Sydney. It's the best farming country anywhere around; and it's close to the city."

"I'm not interested in fruit and vegetable farming on the rich lowlands. That's too much like hard work, and I couldn't afford the price of those properties. I heard that you can pick up small holdings at places like Londonderry, Yarramundi or even further up the river at Wisemans Ferry or the Macdonald Valley. What do you think?"

"What do you do for a living, Mr Forsythe?"

"Call me Harry, Tim. I'm an insurance assessor for Prudential."

"With due respects, Harry, you don't fit the traditional image of 'the Man From Prudential'.

Harry laughed. "Take no notice of my appearance. I had a recent car accident and I'm on sick leave. I got cut up by the broken windscreen. I'm hoping to use the insurance payout to help me buy a farm."

"Phew," Tim relaxed. "You had me worried for a while. Now let's see what I can do for you. If you want to get away from the world, the Macdonald Valley is for you. Only a few families live there; although lately some city folk have been looking to buy small hobby farms in that area."

Harry nodded. "Londonderry and Yarramundi are closer to here. What are they like?"

"Yarramundi has better soil but it does flood close to the river. Londonderry is scrubby country with poorer soils. But if you only want to run a few goats that would be ideal."

"Could you show me around a few places, Tim? I don't know the area so I'm in your hands."

"Sure, Harry, come through to the back. I'll take you in my car."

They walked out the back. "Wow, is this your car, Tim?" asked Harry looking at a clean, 1939, white, two-seater, Singer Bantam Roadster. "You've really looked after it. It's in fabulous condition."

The hood was down and the wind in Harry's hair gave him a sense of freedom. They drove along Londonderry Road, past the Hawkesbury Agricultural College and the race track, before turning off onto the dirt roads that led into the scrub country towards Rickaby's Creek.

With the exception of a few fruit trees there was little sign of cropping. A mixture of beef and dairy cattle roamed through the trees, although not in large numbers; and they weren't in good condition. There were few dwellings visible from the road and they were of poor quality. At one property gate there was an old stove with SMITH crudely painted on the door. It was used as a letter box. It was accompanied by a KEEP OUT sign. At the next property another sign read TRESPASSERS WILL BE SHOT ON SIGHT.

Inside the gate to the second property, two Alsatian dogs had their leads attached to a long heavy-duty wire. They barked and snarled as Tim and Harry slowed near the gate.

"Could you stop here a moment please, Tim?"

"It doesn't look inviting to me, Harry. Let's move on."

At that moment a battered utility truck drove towards the gate and stopped. A bearded man in overalls and army boots with a double-barrelled shotgun under his arm got out. "What the fuck are you two starin' at? Can't ya see the sign? Now fuck off or I'll put a charge up your arse."

"I'm sorry, mate," said Harry. "I'm just looking for a place to buy around here. I didn't mean to disturb you. We'll be off now."

"And don't come back. These places ain't for sale, so piss off."

Tim was so relieved to leave. The little car kicked up the dust until they hit the main road. "Sorry about that, Harry. I haven't been far into that area before. I've sold some places on the main road and closer into town, but not in there."

"Think nothing of it, Tim. Thanks for showing me. Could we go out to Yarramundi now?"

Tim turned left at The Driftway, crossed over the main road at Agnes Banks, drove carefully over the low-level crossing of the Nepean River, and ventured in and out of the side roads in that area.

Harry took in the variety of landscapes. "This is good country, Tim, and it's so different from one side to the other. Near the river there are pumpkins, potatoes, corn, watermelons and sorghum but on the higher farms there are mostly citrus trees."

"Yes," said Tim. "The higher soils are different from the clay silt deposits next to the river that have been laid down from the floods that we get here every couple of years."

"Thanks, Tim. I don't want to grow vegetables. Maybe I could do citrus and it could be good for goats. But I've seen enough. I want to think about it before I make a decision. Could we go back now?"

At Richmond, Harry thanked Tim, said goodbye and rode back to Stanmore. After dinner he sat back to think over the day's events. He was certain that the two men in the black Ford at Stumpy's funeral were up to no good. They weren't there to pass on their sympathy to the family. Their presence most likely had something to do with the attack on Harry. They were trying to find him and report back to their boss.

He shook his head as he thought of Londonderry. It would be the perfect place for a criminal to hide out. That man with the Alsatians and the shotgun was not typical of the good, welcoming folks of the

Hawkesbury Valley. If you were not a local you were at risk of being shot or badly injured. If you were shot and killed and buried there, nobody would know, or even go looking for you. He couldn't imagine the local police going in there unless in an emergency. Harry would have to be very careful if he went there again.

Harry thought Yarramundi was a pretty area compared to Londonderry. The farms, although small, were well maintained and appeared more productive because of their proximity to the river and better soils. He had noticed on one farm at the end of a dirt track another shorter crop growing between the rows of corn. The plants resembled cannabis. That would be worth further investigation..

After finishing his bottle of beer he collapsed into a deep slumber.

Chapter 20
Tuesday

As Harry checked the fuel level in the tank of his bike, Eileen walked out to leave some seed in the tray next to the birdbath. "Good morning, Harry. It's a beautiful morning. What have you got on today?"

"Hello, Eileen. Isn't it a great day? It's a bit cooler and not so humid. I'm going to Wisemans Ferry and the Macdonald Valley to assess some properties for valuations. I don't know a lot about that area so I'll spend the day there."

"You'll absolutely love it there, Harry. Before the war, Robert and I used to go to the Ferry to water ski. We'd tow the boat and take a tent up there on Friday afternoons, and spend the weekend on the water, and come back Sunday night."

"I could take you with me today as my guide. You would enjoy a ride on the pillion. I'll get you a pair of goggles. What do you think?"

Eileen stepped back from the birdbath and stammered. "Aah, Harry, that's a kind offer, but I'm going to stay in today because I have an interview tomorrow and I must prepare for that. But I have a suggestion. When you get to Wisemans Ferry, go over the river at the Webbs Creek crossing up into the Macdonald Valley and come back to St Albans, because they have the best home-cooked pies around. Then come back the other side of the river to Wisemans Ferry."

"That sounds fantastic, Eileen. You know your way around there. Maybe another day. What do you think?"

Eileen brushed her hands down the front of her dress. "We'll see, Harry. No promises. Have a good day and let me know how you go."

"Thanks, Eileen. Let me know how you go at the interview."

Harry called into the local garage and filled the fuel tank. He rode his bike to Castle Hill and on to Glenorie, Maroota and Wisemans Ferry. He swung around the sharp bend to wait for the Webbs Creek Ferry to cross the river.

Riding onto the ferry he leaned his bike against the rail and walked across to talk to the ferryman. "G'day, mate. My name's Harry Forsythe. What do you know about this area?"

"Why do you ask?" replied the ferry master defensively, without turning.

"I'm an insurance assessor and we have clients who want to buy property up in the valley and I have to do valuations for them."

"Are they going to live there permanently or are they some of those bloody Pitt Street farmers who only come on the weekend or holidays?"

"What do you mean?" asked Harry.

"Well the families won't be happy if they're only blow-ins. We've had enough of them."

Harry came around to be beside the driver. "Who lives in the valley?"

"There are three main families in the upper valley. Most of them have lived here for many generations and they don't like others movin' in. They rarely leave the valley. I had to take a girl to Windsor the other day to see the doctor. She's twenty, and that was the first time she's been out of the valley. She was as frightened as a kitten; poor kid."

The ferry pulled against the ropes as the tide ran out. The surface of the water was calm, tranquil and green, reflecting the willow trees on the opposite bank.

"Who are the people moving into the valley?"

The driver slowed the ferry as they approached the other side. "Some of them are okay. One bloke is an engineer who is trying to help us build a bridge over the creek to get our produce out in wet weather, but there are some shifty blokes I wouldn't trust."

"What do they grow on their properties?"

The driver walked to the front and lowered the ramp. "They are mostly in Central and Upper Macdonald. They plant some crops and leave. They only come back every now and then. They don't talk to us and they do nothing for the community. Must go now. See ya."

"Thanks, mate. Might see you on the way back." Harry rode off the ferry.

The narrow, winding dirt road followed the river up the Macdonald Valley. The river flats on one side looked fertile while on the other side the land rose steeply into rugged tree-covered hills. There were some open spaces in side valleys with a variety of crops. In the Lower Macdonald valley Harry noticed a farmer with a rotary hoe who had stopped to light a cigarette. Harry walked across to the fence.

"G'day, mate. If I wanted to buy your nice little farm here how much would I have to pay for it?"

The farmer looked sideways at Harry. "Who's asking and why?"

"Sorry, mate. I'm Harry Forsythe. I'm an insurance assessor. I have some clients who want to buy some property and I need to value it for insurance. What's your name?"

"I'm Terry, and that's all you need to know. Well tell your lot to piss off. We've got enough blow-ins already. They're bloody nuisances. Not worth a pinch of shit, any of 'em."

"I notice, Terry, that you've got a telephone line into the valley there," said Harry pointing to the poles on the other side of the road.

The farmer blew a big cloud of smoke. "There's only one line in and that goes to the school house. But I'll tell you one thing, mate. There's no way I'd have a bloody telephone in my house."

"Why's that?" asked Harry.

"Because if they can talk to you through the wires they can do anything to you. Then they've got you by the balls and you can't do anything about it. I wouldn't trust the bloody government in a fit."

Harry leaned on the fence post. "What do these blow-ins grow?"

"Some of them grow crops like pumpkins, corn or spuds, but most of them just have some horses and cattle."

"How do they get their produce to market, Terry?"

Terry took off his hat and scratched his head. "Well, Don's our carrier here. He comes every day if the river's not up and he takes the cans of milk to Windsor and the fruit and veggies to the Haymarket in Sydney. Without Don we'd be up shit street."

"What happens when the river is up, Terry?"

"The blokes tip the milk into the creek and bury the fruit and veggies."

"Thanks, Terry. I'll try to talk my clients out of coming here so that you can live in peace. You've been very helpful. I'll be on my way now."

Harry rode off through St Albans and up to the narrow valley of Central and Higher Macdonald. There were few houses that far into the valley. There was a small one-teacher school at Central, but little else other than the farming properties. He saw a farmer walking behind a Clydesdale horse pulling a plough. A boy was walking behind dropping cut potatoes into the furrow. Harry got off the bike and walked across the paddock to greet them.

The farmer introduced himself as Jack and his son as Billy. Jack took a water bag from the handles and drank heartily before handing it to Billy. Harry explained his visit to the valley and asked similar questions as he had done with Terry. He got the same answers except that Jack told him of some new farms further up the valley that grew a crop that Jack hadn't seen before.

"I've seen it once when I called in to be friendly like," said Jack. "But I didn't get a good look at it because the owner wouldn't let me go over to the paddock. He was a very unfriendly bastard and had a savage dog on a lead so I've never been back."

"Thanks, Jack and Billy. You've been a great help. I won't hold you up any longer. See ya."

Harry rode to Upper Macdonald and saw the property mentioned by Jack. He rode well past the shed to the top end of the property, got off and crawled through the fence to take some leaves from the plants. He was sure it was cannabis but would have it checked by Tony Jacobs' team. As he rode back down the hill the dogs rushed out to attack him, but he was too fast and left them behind in the dust.

Harry parked his bike outside the historic, convict-built, sandstone hotel at St Albans. Being a Tuesday there were only two other customers at the bar. Harry imagined that it would be more lively on the weekends. He ordered a beer and a home made beef pie. Peter, the owner, asked him what he was doing in the valley. Harry reeled off the same story he had given to the others.

"Well, mate," said Peter, "you have two opposite opinions around here. The older families that have lived in the valley for years hate the Pitt Street farmers who only come on weekends and holidays. Many others, however, want new blood because they bring more money to the valley, and that helps development and better roads."

Yvonne, the waitress, brought out the beef pie in its individual oven dish; it smelled delicious. Harry took a taste. "Hell, that's the best pie I've ever had. Tell me, Peter, do you get any problems with visitors?"

"Most of them are pretty good. They don't cause any problems. Some young blokes come up here for a boozy weekend and play up, but they are mostly harmless. Some forget to put out their fires."

Harry brushed the flaky pastry from his shirt. "What about the new farmers?"

"Most of them are okay but there are one or two I have my doubts about. They never mix, they never spend any time here in the pub. They come and go by themselves and they have their own trucks to take their produce to the market."

"What do they grow?"

"Well there are rumours they are growing some of that weed up there, but I've not seen any evidence. But then I don't go looking for trouble. If they don't annoy me, I don't annoy them."

Harry pointed back up the road. "Would they be the ones right up in the Upper Macdonald Valley near the end of the road at Gorrick's Creek?"

Peter poured another beer. "Yes, there are a couple of new farmers up that way. Old Thommo told me they were damn rude to him when he went up there to welcome them to the valley."

"Do they ever get Don, the carrier, to take their produce?"

"No," said Peter. "They bring their own covered truck. When Don offered to deliver it for them they told him to piss off."

Harry stood up. "I must get going, Peter. Many thanks for the lunch and thank the cook for me. I'll certainly be back. I'll go home on the other side of the river to the Ferry. See you, mate."

Harry took his time looking at the properties on the other side. He caught the ferry and rode back to Stanmore. As he parked his bike near the shed he noticed Eileen at the garden hose.

"Hey, Eileen. You were right. Those pies at St Albans were the best ever. We must go up there some day and have lunch. Did you finish preparing for your interview today?"

"Yes, Harry. It was time well spent and I feel more confident now."

"I must go in and do my bookwork. Thanks again for your advice. Good luck tomorrow."

Chapter 21
Wednesday

When Harry walked into the SIB at Redfern, Tony Jacobs mockingly sighed and threw up his hands in horror.

"Will someone get this tramp out of here?"

The others in the room looked to see what had caught Tony's attention. Those who knew Harry burst out laughing. Harry took off his hood.

George Black walked around Harry looking at his crew cut. "Mate, that's what our mother did to us when we got nits. Then she'd wash it with methylated spirits. Stay away from me. I don't want your bloody bugs."

Jack Witherspoon looked up. "Looks like you got your head caught in a cage with a feral cat, mate. Never mind, your mother will still love you."

Rita Flynn came in from next door to check on the commotion. "Back off, you lot. Harry's been through the mill in the last two weeks, so ease off. Besides, I think the crew cut gives him a fresh, rugged look which is more than I can say for some of you."

"Whoa," said Fred with a broad smile. "Madam Flynn has spoken. We'll have to watch our p's and q's."

They all burst out laughing. Tony stepped forward. "Come on, you lot, get the teapot and mugs. Let's welcome this bag of chaff back to the real world. He's only here to get a cup and a biscuit because he can't afford one at home. He might even tell us what he's doing now."

Harry tossed his head back in mock horror. "I was coming in here for some professional advice, but now I realise that'd be a waste of time." He opened the bag of weed. "I was going to ask you about this stuff."

Jack Witherspoon, the drug expert, stepped forward and took the bag. "Don't you know what this is, Harry? As soon as you walked into this room I detected the earthy, floral, pine-needle smell of cannabis. I was going to arrest you, but I didn't say anything because I didn't want to hit you while you're down. Where did you get this?"

Harry gave them a run-down on his last two days at Londonderry, Yarramundi and the Macdonald Valley.

Tony walked over to sniff the contents. "Why are you so interested in this, Harry?"

"Because there is a strong chance that the attempts on my life have something to do with the supply of drugs."

"Why would you say that, Harry?" asked Fred.

Harry added two sugars to his tea. "Well, let us look at the crime scene in the city. There are four main streams of crime: prostitution, robbery, gambling and drugs. The others such as murder, manslaughter, break and enter and assault can mostly be attributed to those four."

"Yes," interrupted Rita, "but why the emphasis on drugs?"

Harry walked over to Rita. "Let's face it. We don't pay a lot of attention to prostitution and gambling. Politicians and most of headquarters turn a blind eye unless the newspapers kick up a stink and we have a short blitz to make it look good. The Armed Hold-Up Squad covers their area and we respond to murders as required. But the one area that is increasing rapidly is drugs."

Fred sat back, hands behind his head. "But drugs have been around for years and, up to now, we've only paid lip-service to it. The cannabis in your little bag there was not even illegal until recently when the United Nations declared a war on drugs. Australia has only recently ratified that agreement. Why the panic?"

Harry turned to Fred. "Australians are the biggest users of heroin and cocaine per capita in the world, and its usage is increasing. Cannabis has been around for ages and, until recently, was seen as a mild cigarette for rich ladies to ease their tensions. I, like you, haven't been too concerned with the occasional use of one of these drugs for pleasure, but it's now obvious that the crime bosses see these drugs as a way to make big money, and they will fight to take control of what is now an illegal market."

"But if it's confined to the criminal world," asked Rita, "what's the problem? They can kill each other and the world will be better off."

Harry put his hand on Rita's shoulder. "No, Rita. They will push these drugs out into the suburbs and eventually into the country because it's now illegal. Everyone will want to try it and the price will go up; and the crims will make a fortune. They will create the market and then control it."

"But will the politicians take any notice?"

"When different criminal groups get involved, there will be fights and murders. I predict there will be a nasty war between them unless they come to some agreement as to who looks after which territory."

"Why should all of this focus on you, Harry?" asked Tony.

"Before I enlisted I did some work that involved drugs, but since I returned I've been more involved in crimes associated with the increased use of heroin and cocaine."

"But that does not seem serious enough to try to kill you," said Tony sipping his tea.

Harry leaned backwards against the bench. "The big difference I see now is the influx of the Melbourne mob wanting a piece of the action. They know that they can't move into the centre of the city around Kings Cross or Woolloomooloo or The Rocks or Darlinghurst. They'd be wiped out if they tried. So, they're working to get into the suburbs through the hotels. There is a big untapped market, and they know it."

"Why can't the local Sydney boys look after the centre and leave the suburbs to the others?" asked Rita.

Tony stepped forward. "I can see what Harry is getting at. This is turf warfare. There is no way that the locals are going to let the southerners move in anywhere in this city. It would be the same if our mob moved south to Melbourne. They wouldn't last five minutes down there."

"But I thought there was cooperation between some of our lot with the big crims in other cities." said Rita.

Harry explained. "There has been in the past, providing they stick to their own areas and the Sydney mob stay here. I know of cases when we have suspected that a hit man from Sydney has flown in and out of Brisbane or Melbourne in one day to carry out an execution, while the usual local suspects are out of town in a public place to establish their alibis."

"That's pretty serious stuff, Harry."

"Yes it is. But it might be more serious. It's been rumoured that a senior detective from Melbourne, who we know is associated with big crime in Victoria, flew to Sydney and gave Spike Fleming a lethal injection of morphine. Spike was about to give evidence in court against Whispers Durante. The detective was on a plane back home within the hour. We had no proof and no one was willing to talk. There was no record of that flight ever happening."

Fred put up his hand. "But, Harry, why you? Why would they want to take you out? Isn't it a big risk for a crim to shoot a policeman?"

Harry walked back and forth. "To me it's about the turf war between Sydney and Melbourne and I believe it has to do with the increase in drug supplies. Because of my investigations that involved drugs, both sides see me as a danger to their operations. My difficulty is that I don't know who wants to get me. Is it Sydney or Melbourne, or have they both agreed that I must go?"

Tony looked at Jack Witherspoon. "Jack, you're the drug expert. You've been very quiet. Tell us what you think."

Jack folded his arms and looked around the room. "Harry's right. Drugs are increasing in all of its forms. Australians are heavy users. Heroin and cocaine are still the big ones but cannabis is the up-and-coming. It's not as harmful, but it has the most potential to make big money in what is now an illegal market. I believe that once they're hooked on cannabis the users will go further with the hard drugs and the sales will increase."

Tony waved his arms in frustration. "But now that Australia has agreed with the United Nations to make all these drugs illegal, won't that cut the rate of use dramatically?"

Jack coughed. "No, Tony. It's exactly the opposite. The more you prohibit drugs the more people will want to try them, the more they get hooked, and the more the criminals will be involved. Look to America when they put a prohibition on alcohol. It had exactly the opposite result to what they wanted. It'll be the same here."

"Well what can we do?"

"We police will be expected to deal with the mess. The politicians will be screaming blue murder. They'll increase penalties and promise to clean up the drugs but, at the same time, many of them will be in the illegal casinos at night snorting cocaine or smoking heroin for thrills."

Tony leaned forward. "Jack, you're a cynic."

Jack stood up and walked to the door on his way back to his office. "No, Tony, I'm a realist. Listen to Harry. He knows what's going on. Be there to help him when he needs it. I'm going back to work."

Tony looked around the room. "Righto, you lot. Get busy. We have work to do." He turned to Harry. "Come into my office."

They sat at Tony's table. Harry put his hood over his knee. "Thanks, Tony. At least here I know I can talk to your team and they will give me honest answers. They're a top group."

"How can we help you from now on, Harry?"

"I want to be able to drop in at any time to check some evidence. I'd also like to know if I can phone you here or at home, if necessary."

"You can count on it, Harry. But why not the team from headquarters?"

"I'm supposed to be on sick leave. Twain has threatened to demote me. He'll send me back on the beat at Tibooburra if I show my face in there."

"What about the CIB squad? You worked with them and they know you well and trust you. They are also the ones out there trying to get the shooter. Surely, they would want to coordinate their investigations with you."

"They have told me to stay out of it. They don't want to be caught in the cross-fire if the shooter sees me with them."

"You don't have a lot of options, do you?"

"No. But in a way I think it is better this way. I can work independently behind the scenes and, with my haircut, stubble and casual gear, not a lot of people will recognise me."

"Well, Harry, you've got the support of my team. Keep it low-key and in-house and we'll do what we can for you."

Harry stood up and shook hands with Tony. "Thanks, mate; and give my thanks to the team. You don't know how much that means to me."

Harry spent the next two hours down at Darling Harbour watching the loading and unloading of cargo from the ships. He saw Sandy Blight in the distance but made no attempt to talk to him or show his presence. He also noticed some other well-known wharfies who had been involved in various crimes. He made a mental note to check their relationship with drugs and the top criminals.

At the nearby telephone booth Harry phoned Jock Burns' number and left a message with his mother for Jock to meet him at Fig Lane Park at Pyrmont tomorrow morning at eight o'clock.

When that shift of wharfies knocked off work he rode back to Stanmore to relax and think about the last two days.

Chapter 22
Thursday

Because of school holidays the traffic was light and it was an easy ride to Pyrmont where Harry found Jock waiting for him at Fig Lane Park.

"Thanks for coming, Jock."

Jock shook Harry's hand and the two walked slowly around the park. "How's it been for you Harry? How are your wounds healing?"

Harry gave Jock a run-down on his health, welfare and activities since they last met.

"Bloody hell, Harry, you're supposed to be on sick leave. But then again, what else would I expect from you? You've never been one to sit on your bum and do nothing, have you? Does anyone in headquarters know what you are doing?"

Harry stopped and leaned against the fence. "No, and I don't want anyone in there to know. What I tell you here is for your ears only. I'm supposed to be on sick leave. If Twain finds out that I'm still investigating, I'm for the axe."

"But haven't you would been in touch with the CIB boys because they're out there chasing the shooter? Surely, they'll want to keep you in the loop and get your advice."

Harry leaned on the top rail and crossed his legs. "No, Jock. They made it clear that they don't want me around. They are the best and most experienced in the field, so I'll leave it to them. What I'm doing is separate to their investigations. I'm trying to find out why I was shot. I'm more interested in the reason than the result. They'll catch him, I'm sure; and he'll get what's coming to him. But I'm not convinced that the shooter is doing this on his own."

"Who do you think is behind it, Harry?"

"That, I don't know. That's what I want to find out."

Jock leaned back on the fence rail. "Shooting a policeman is one of the worst crimes. It has to involve someone at the top of the tree; unless there's some nutter out there who you've upset and wants to get back at you."

"You could be right, Jock. There are crazies out there with mental problems, or off their rocker with drugs, and are so unpredictable they will do something on the spur of the moment without thinking."

Jock wiped his forehead and started to walk towards the shade of a tree in the corner of the park. "The fact that the shooter missed a certain chance to take you out might suggest that he was a lone amateur. A professional would have taken his time and not hit the framework of the window. At that close range he would have got you."

"But Jock, he followed up the next day with the car bomb. That anti-personnel mine was stolen from the army base. I doubt a lone amateur could pull that off. It smacks of a major crime gang, probably with inside help."

Jock hurriedly brushed some ants from his arm. "Bloody hell, Harry. The criminals are bad enough here in Aussie-land but it's the bloody wildlife here I can't stand. I'm going back to Scotland. If it's not the sharks biting off your leg, it's the snakes and spiders sinking their fangs into you, and then the bloody ants come in to clean away the evidence."

Harry laughed out loud. "Did you notice, Jock that they don't attack me or any other natural-born Australians? It's because they prefer the soft, juicy flesh of you Scots. It comes from eating too much haggis and black pudding. They love the blood in that pudding. They can smell a Scot a mile away. Stick to steak and eggs and sausages and you'll be okay."

"Come to Scotland with me, Harry and I'll give you a hurry up with a thistle between your legs." Jock waved his hand towards Harry's crutch.

"I don't have to go to Scotland, Jock. You buggers brought them out here with you. I spent my early years walking around the farm cutting Scotch thistles and Bathurst burrs with a garden hoe in century-degree heat. You can keep your bloody thistles. What nation would be so stupid to have a thistle as their symbol?"

"Okay, Harry, let's get serious. If it's an individual nutter, it's going to be hard to pick him out, because you don't know who he is, where he comes from, or why he did it."

"Jock, the shooter not only followed up with the car bombing but he planted drugs in the glove box the next day. That packet wasn't something a low-life pusher on a street corner would have prepared. It was neatly packaged in a good Cellophane packet, and in a quantity much larger than a street guy would give away."

Jock loosened his tie. "Yes, I see what you mean. It does point to the big-time operators but could it be a middleman trying to impress?"

"I doubt it Jock. When I talked to my informant he said there was a contract out on me. That means this is big time; not the work of an individual."

"Who's your informant, Harry?"

"Jock, I'm going to give you a piece of strong advice, so listen carefully. If you stay in this field you will find it helpful to establish good relations with someone close to the action who can give you information. They will, of course, expect something in return. It's common for good detectives to have informants, but their trust is only built on silence. It's a relationship between you, them and nobody else. If you break that trust you'll get nothing from them. If you say the wrong thing today someone could die tomorrow."

Jock shifted his weight from one leg to the other. "Okay, Harry, I understand. Can you trust your man?"

"As much as I can trust any criminal. And that's something you must also understand. An informant can feed you a load of bullshit if he's getting paid better by someone else. You have to cross check everything."

"If your information is right and there's a contract out on you, it could be anyone. It seems to me that the most likely person would be a hit man associated with one of the top boys. It doesn't eliminate any low life who suddenly sees a golden opportunity to make a name for himself by showing that he can hack it in the big time and earn some real cash."

"Good thinking, Jock. You're right, and that's my dilemma. If I could eliminate one lot it would make my job much easier."

"Harry, you mentioned that you've been out looking at drug crops this week. What did you find?"

"Let's go and sit on that bench over there." Harry led the way to the bench. When settled, he gave Jock a more detailed run-down on his trips to Londonderry, Yarramundi and the Macdonald Valley.

"That's interesting, Harry, because I've been looking into the same areas in the last week because of my investigations into the murder of that second young bloke in Parramatta."

"Before you tell me that, bring me up to date with what happened with the kid who went missing at Luna Park?"

"Oh, that was nothing. He eventually came home. He was a spoilt young brat from a rich family on the north shore who had an argument with his parents and decided to run away while they were at the Park. He slept under the Harbour Bridge and got belted up by the regular homeless blokes for taking their spot. He went across to the Botanic Gardens but soon ran out of money. He had no experience of the real world so he went back home."

Harry anxiously tapped the bench behind Jock. "Okay, now tell me more about the Parramatta case. Did you have another officer with you?"

"No. Because you're on sick leave, Twain said he was short-staffed. He said his major priority was to get the shooter and the car bomber; and he wasn't worried about some drug pusher at Parramatta. He said he couldn't afford anyone to go with me."

"Tell me what you think, Jock."

"The young bloke was called Drazen Baric; although he was known as 'Doug' or 'Dopey'. He was Yugoslavian and came out here with his parents just before the war. His parents settled on a farm in the Hawkesbury and grew fruit and vegetables. He was poorly educated in his own language and was a failure in school here. Because he found it difficult to get jobs he drifted into crime and was well known to the local police."

Harry sat forward on the bench to get more air to the back of his sweat-stained shirt. "I thought a kid like that was more likely to stay on the farm with his father."

"He did for a while but he was lazy, and he had two older brothers who did most of the work. He did, however, agree to drive the produce to the markets each morning and get it there before four o'clock. He preferred to do that than pick up spuds in the paddock in the heat of the day."

"How long did he last doing that?" asked Harry.

"On and off for the last two years," replied Jock. "But what's more interesting is that he seems to have made some significant contacts there. As you know, the markets have been the centre for the distribution of drugs and contraband for many years and I suspect that Dopey started his involvement in crime there."

"In what way, Jock?"

"I think he started out as a seller of drugs. His arrest sheet shows he was caught selling drugs outside Parramatta station on two occasions, and once outside Auburn station. He was fined and given a suspended sentence and a good behaviour bond on each occasion."

"What happened after that?"

"He probably graduated to a runner, distributing drugs to kids to sell on the streets. The big operators know that the kids only get a slap on the wrist if caught, and the top dogs can keep their distance from the police. They also know that if the kids use their money to buy drugs for themselves, they'll get hooked and have to sell more drugs to pay for their habit."

"But why was Dopey shot?"

Jock stood up and turned. "He probably got greedy. I don't have anything definite because none of my contacts will talk. It's as if he's done the wrong thing and nobody wants to be seen to be involved. It's a wall of silence. That's the problem I'm facing now."

Harry stretched his legs and wriggled his toes. "I've heard that the Melbourne mob have moved into Parramatta. Have you had a chance to find out which hotels they've gone into?"

"I've talked to the local police. They seemed reluctant to give me much information. Maybe it's because I'm not well known there. I got the impression that they saw me as someone not in their league, and therefore not to be trusted."

"You could be right, Jock. We don't know if some of the locals are on the take; so, be careful how you play that out."

"The best information I have for you, Harry is that three hotels around there have activities after-hours. There is one on the south side of the station, one in the centre and one along Victoria Road."

"Thanks, Jock. If your boy, 'Dopey', switched sides from the Sydney blokes over to the Melbourne lot operating out of Parramatta, then there is no wonder he got hit."

"I agree, Harry, but proving it is the problem."

"I suggest that headquarters will put it down to a result of the turf war and give it little priority. But leave it with me and I'll try to do some more digging for you. I'll be in touch when I have something for you. Now I must go. Thanks for your help. See ya."

Chapter 23
Thursday

At eleven o'clock it was an easy ride along Wattle Street, City Road and on to King Street, Newtown, where Harry propped his bike in front of the imposing building of the City Hotel. The bottom half of the front wall was covered in brown-glazed tiles. The top panels between the doors and windows displayed mirrored panels of popular sportsmen promoting beer and cigarettes. The long upstairs wrought iron verandah spanned ten glass doors leading from the rooms. The tessellated wall at the top featured the prominent bas relief of the City Hotel title.

Harry noticed a man sitting on the footpath with his feet in a pit surrounded by a red metal frame with a canvas top. "G'day, mate. It's a bit hot out here for you today. What are you doing?"

The man looked up with a smile. "I'm fixing a telephone cable. There's a major fault here and it's gotta be fixed before I can finish."

Harry looked at the cut ends of the lead covered cable in the man's hands, with hundreds of different coloured wires on both sides of the break. "Better you than me, mate. I wouldn't know where to start."

The man laughed. "It's easy-breezy mate. You just take that one there and hook it up with that one there. Do that three hundred times and Bob's your uncle."

Harry laughed, walked inside, ordered a pint of beer and took it out to the PMG man. "Slip that behind the canvas in case your boss comes along. Good luck, mate."

"Thanks, mate. That won't even touch the sides going down."

Harry walked back in and sat on a stool at the end of the bar against the wall and ordered a middy of beer. There were four older men sitting at the other end and two sitting at a table in the corner. Being lunchtime, most men would be at home or at work. Later in the afternoon, this place would be packed as men tried to drink as much as possible before the compulsory six o'clock closing.

The barman came along and placed a middy of beer on the towel stretched along the bar. He took Harry's money and returned with the change. "I'm Tom. You're new around here, mate. Haven't seen you before."

"Yes," said Harry. "Just visiting from the country. My uncle said this was a great pub for a drink and a friendly smile. So I decided to try it out."

"What do you do for a crust, mate?" asked the barman.

"Oh, a little bit of this and a little bit of that. Whatever comes along, mate," replied Harry, wiping the condensation from his glass.

"So what are you going to do while you're here?"

Harry placed his hood on the bar. "Well, I'd like to have a bit of fun, mate. I heard that this is the pub where you can get some action at night after closing."

"What action are you looking for, my friend?"

"Well, mate, I like a game of cards or baccarat or blackjack, and I heard you've got some nice girls I could meet. What do you think, eh?"

"Well," replied the barman moving back along the bar to the other drinkers. "I don't know anything about that. Nothin' like that here. I just serve beers."

"Well, thanks, Tom. You best get me another one. It's thirsty weather we're having here."

Tom refilled Harry's glass and then walked into the saloon bar. A few minutes later a middle-aged, well dressed woman in a blue satin dress with puffed sleeves and high heeled shoes walked the length of the room to sit next to Harry. Her hair was coiffed to perfection, and make-up perfectly applied.

"Hello, I'm Queenie. I own this hotel. Who might we have here?"

"Hello, Queenie," replied Harry. "I'm Fred. Pleased to meet you. I'm just down from the country. I've heard good things about your hotel and I'd like to get to know it better."

"Tom told me you are looking for some action with cards and girls."

"Yes. I heard that this is the place to come to after-hours for some fun and maybe get a little bit of weed or something a little stronger. What do you say, Queenie?"

The lady turned to face Harry, her eyes cold and steely. "I'll have you know, Fred that I run a good hotel. We provide good service to the drinkers and we provide good accommodation for visitors to our city. There is no way that I'd have anything illegal going on while I'm in charge here. You'll have to go somewhere else if that's what you want."

"I notice that you have several rooms upstairs. Would you have some accommodation available for me tonight?"

"No, Fred. I'm fully booked out tonight."

"When would you have a room available? I might like to stay a couple of nights before I go back to the country."

Queenie stood up. "I'm booked out every night of the school holidays. After that I have bookings for university conferences. Sorry, Fred." She walked back to the saloon bar.

Five minutes later, two men came from the back room and approached Harry. The first one was about five foot ten, stocky and super fit in the style of a wrestler. He walked duck-like towards Harry, shirt sleeves taut over his bulging biceps. The second man was smaller and lighter on his feet, but his face showed that he had spent too many rounds in a boxing ring.

The big man spoke first. "Fred, or whatever your name is, we want you to come with us."

"And who might I be talking to here?" asked Harry, turning to face the men square on.

"We're asking you nicely to come with us. We need to discuss something with you, but not here. Now come with us."

"No. If you have something to say to me then say it here in front of the others. I've got nothing to hide. Now, what is it that's so important that you can't talk here?"

"I'll say it once, Fred. Do you want to do this the hard way or the easy way?"

"Well, I'm not moving because I haven't finished my beer yet and, when I finish this one, Tom will pour me another. So excuse me gentlemen but I'm busy now, so you can be on your way." Harry placed his glass on the bar.

The big man moved forward. "No, you're coming with us." He reached out to grab Harry's shirt.

It happened so quickly the man didn't have time to react. Harry took hold of his arm and continued his momentum forward with such force that the man went head first into the wall and crumpled to the floor. Harry turned and rammed the butt of his hand upwards into the base of the other man's nose pushing it back into the nasal socket. When the man came forward again Harry took out his legs with a perfectly executed sideways karate kick. The man hit the floor and Harry placed his size-twelve boot on the back of his neck and held it there. He was thankful for his martial arts training in the commando training unit before his time with the Z Force.

He called to Tom. "Hey, Tom, get someone to clean up this mess on the floor. It doesn't look good for the regular customers."

Tom rushed out from behind the bar and went into the saloon bar. A moment later Queenie reappeared. She stomped across the room with a stern, determined look on her face, stopped a few feet in front of Harry, and stared at him and the men on the floor. She looked at the imposing six-foot-two figure with a crew cut and two weeks of stubble on his face. She was impressed and took a step back.

"I don't know who you are, Fred, or where you come from, and I couldn't care less, but I'm offering you a job here in this hotel."

Harry focused on Queenie's face and waited until he saw the twitch in her eyelid before he answered. "And why would you do that for a perfect stranger?"

"I like your style."

"What about your two goons?"

"They are no longer employed here."

"You couldn't afford me."

"Whatever you're paid now, I'll double it."

"Would I have to protect the gamblers and the girls at night? Is that what you want me to do?"

"Something like that. Yes."

"Well Queenie, I'll have to say no because I only work for people who welcome me with open arms when I come in. That didn't happen here today so I'll be on my way."

Harry downed the remainder of his beer, put on his hood, walked out the door, kick-started his bike and rode off in the direction of Parramatta Road.

He weaved through the traffic on his way to Parramatta. Harry was satisfied that the City Hotel was a centre for gambling and prostitution at night, and therefore almost certainly a place where drugs were freely available. As it hadn't come across his radar before, it was likely that it was newly involved with those activities. It was possibly tied up with the Melbourne gang. He decided to check the hotels in Parramatta.

***

Harry parked his bike outside the King's Arms Hotel on the south side of the railway line, walked in, surveyed the bar and moved to a space at the end where he could observe all without turning back and forth.

"And what can I do for you, young fella?" asked the portly barman as he walked past carrying four glasses.

"I'll have a middy of Reschs beer thanks, mate," replied Harry.

Sitting around the corner at the other end of the bar was a small man in a pork-pie hat scribbling in a notebook. Harry assumed he was the local SP bookmaker taking bets. He looked like a retired jockey earning a living in his field of expertise. Although Harry was not interested in that form of gambling, he took comfort in the fact that the man was serving the local community with no harm done.

He was more interested in a young man who walked back and forth, eyes darting everywhere as if he was worried he was about to be attacked. His hair was unkempt, his face unshaven and his shirt and trousers unironed. As Harry turned away he was conscious of the young man looking at him. Harry glanced in the mirror behind the bottles on the shelf. The man would turn and walk back to the entrance door when Harry looked in his direction. He looked furtively both ways before coming back in. He appeared very nervous and it took some time before he settled.

When the man returned to the bar Harry turned and called to him. "Hey, mate, could I buy you a drink. You look as though you've had a hard day's work. You've earned it. Come and sit down and relax. It's stinking hot outside."

Harry turned and called to the barman. "Hey, chief. Could you get me another beer and one for my mate here? Whatever he wants?"

The man stuttered. "Gee thanks, mate. Where do you come from? I haven't seen you here before."

"I'm Fred. I've just come down from the country to see some of my folks here but I can only stand being with them for a short time before I need to get out and enjoy myself. What about you? Do you come from around here?"

"Yeah. Been around here all my life. They call me 'Flipper'. Good to meet you, Fred."

Harry smiled and shook his hand. "Well, Flipper, you'd be just the bloke to tell me how to get some enjoyment around here. This is all new to me. What's a man got to do to get a bit of the action here?"

"What do you mean, Fred?"

"Come on, Flipper. You're a man of the world. Where can a man get some enjoyment around here? And I don't mean bingo or Monopoly."

"Well, Fred, if you want to put some money on a donkey, 'Shorty' over there in the corner will fix you up. He's honest and straight."

"But, Flipper, if I want to have a good night out, where would I go to get a girl and maybe some of that stuff I've heard about to give you a lift. They tell me you can get some in the city."

"What stuff do you mean, Fred? There's hard or soft stuff. What do you want?"

"I don't know. I'm new to this. I better start with the soft stuff. What do you call it?"

"We call it weed but it's also known as hash or cannabis."

"What do you do with it?"

"You roll it into a cigarette and smoke it. It'll give you a high, mate."

"Where do you get it?"

"Wait here for a while. I'll be back."

Harry waited for fifteen minutes and was about to leave when Flipper returned with a small roll of newspaper in his hand.

"Give me ten shillings, Fred, and you can have a sample. Get some cigarette papers and roll your own. Good luck."

Harry held Flipper's arm. "Is this the genuine stuff, Flipper. I don't want any shit."

Nervously Flipper responded. "It's the real deal, Fred. It's local stuff and it's fresh, mate, guaranteed."

"Now, Flipper where will I find a good girl to enjoy this with?"

"There are some that hang around the railway station after dark."

"No, I want a good girl. I don't want a bang with some slut in the park. Would there be any that work here at night in a good room?"

"Aah, Fred. I can't say. I mean, I just hang around here. I'm not employed by the hotel."

"Many thanks, Flipper. That's great. I must get going because I'm meeting my cousin and we're going out on the town tonight."

Chapter 24
Thursday

Harry rode his bike back along Church Street and turned into George Street where he parked outside the Empire Hotel on the corner. It was an imposing two storey building in Art Deco style. The bottom half of the lower storey was covered in cream tiles, with the higher levels painted white. Four distinct lines in the rendered surface surrounded the upper level parapet and between the two storeys. There was an entrance on the corner and another on each side wall. The building had a fresh, well-maintained look about it.

There were four men sitting on stools at the public bar; three at the far end and one man by himself eating a meat pie from a paper bag. Harry sat next to the pie man.

"G'day, mate, that looks a great-looking pie. Where can I get one?"

The man looked up, wiped tomato sauce from his chin, and pointed backwards over his shoulder. "Go across the road to the bakery; best pies in town. If you're going to get one, could you bring me another one? I'm still bloody hungry."

"Sure, will do"

Harry walked out, crossed the road, ordered three pies with sauce, returned to the bar, gave the man his pie and ordered a beer. "You look as though you've had a hard day, mate. I'm Fred."

The man shook Harry's hand. "I'm Andrew, but they call me 'Curly'. Yeah, mate, I've just come off shift work. I do the two-to-ten shift at the railway workshop, and by the time I get back here, it's time for lunch and a beer before I go home to get some sleep. What about you, Fred?"

"I'm just down from the country for a holiday and a good time. I'm a farmer and we finished the harvest last week, so it's time to kick up my heels a bit."

"Well, there's plenty of places in the big city to have a good time but, be careful mate because, there are plenty around here who'll take you down for a quid or two without you knowing."

Harry took a sip of his beer. "I'm glad I met you, Curly. You seem to know your way around. Can I get a good time in Parramatta or have I got to go to the city? What do you reckon, eh?"

"Mate, if you want a real good time you'll get it in town. You could go to Kings Cross or Woolloomooloo for sly grog and gambling at the casinos, or go to Darlinghurst, around Palmer Street or The Rocks for prostitutes and drugs. But watch it because they'll have your trousers down in a flash and your money out of your pocket before you can say hooley-dooley."

Harry called for another two beers. "That sounds like good advice, Curly. I don't mind a bet or two. In fact I'd like to have a go at poker, two-up, blackjack or baccarat while I'm here; but I don't want to be ripped off. I've worked hard for my money and I don't want to lose it in one go. Is there anywhere around here where I get some action without being taken down?"

Curly licked some meat and sauce from his fingers, taking his time before answering. "Aah, Fred, you hear a lot of rumours but I don't know how much truth there is in them."

"What are they saying, mate?"

"Well, they say that some of the hotels around here have illegal casinos at night upstairs, but you won't be able to get in unless you know someone who's a regular. They have bouncers downstairs."

"But don't the police know about them and raid those places? I don't want to get caught up in a raid."

"They've raided some new places but they don't seem to bother with the older joints. Maybe they're on the take as well. Who knows? I heard that when the police arrived at one place the bouncers rang a bell that warned those upstairs. By the time the cops got up there, people were playing Monopoly and five hundred and eating cheese sandwiches."

Harry drew circles in the moisture on the bar. "Would anyone else know what goes on around here?"

Curly paused and thought as he pulled the top of his ear. "I'll ask Charlie, the barman." He called out, "Hey, Charlie, have you got a second? My mate here wants to know where all the action is around here. What do you think?"

Charlie was well dressed and groomed with slicked back hair smelling of Californian Poppy. He flicked the tea-towel over his shoulder as he approached. "G'day, boys. I heard that you can get some action up at the Gentleman's Club in Castle Hill, just up Windsor Road; not far from here."

Harry turned his head, listening more acutely. "Where in Victoria did you come from, Charlie?"

"How did you know I came from Victoria?"

"It's your accent," replied Harry.

"What rubbish. We Aussies all speak the same."

"No, Charlie. It's the way you say 'castle'. It's different from the way we say it. Is it Melbourne you come from?"

"Yes. I lived at Carlton."

"Were you a barman down there?"

"Yes. I've been a barman for years. I've worked for the same group of hotels in Melbourne. I worked in hotels in Bourke, Lonsdale and Collins Streets."

"Do they own this hotel and others in Sydney?"

"They recently bought this one and they asked me to come up and manage it for them."

"Charlie, do you have any accommodation available? I think I'd like to stay at a good hotel like this while I'm down here."

Charlie started to walk back to serve another customer. "Sorry, mate, we're fully booked out for the holidays."

Harry turned to Curly. "What do you think, Curly? Would there be any action upstairs in this hotel at night?"

Curly picked some wax from his ear. "I don't know, Fred; but then I'm at work at night. But, come to think of it, I do notice a lot of lights on upstairs in the King's Arms when I'm travelling into work. At that time in the early morning I don't think all the guests are sitting up reading the Bible in bed."

"I know what you mean, Curly. Thanks for your help. I might just look in to see if I can get in there tonight. They can only say no."

At that moment two men wearing balaclavas came in; one from the far door and one through the entrance at the corner. They were carrying two buckets. The bigger man shouted, "You fucking shitbags. Go back to where you came from. You're not welcome here. This will give ya a bit of an idea of what we think of ya. Take this and swim through it back to Melbourne."

They threw the contents of the two buckets over the bar and the floor. The first bucket contained what appeared and smelled like sewage, and the second bucket looked like black sump oil. The men sitting at the the other end of the bar were covered in it. They jumped up, shouting and swearing, trying to run for the door. They slipped in the oil, fell and skidded across to the wall, cursing all around. Charlie leapt over the bar to apprehend the attackers but couldn't get a foothold.

Harry and Curly at the other end of the bar were comparatively lucky, getting only splashes on their shoes. Curly went flat on his face as he tried to rush outside. Harry carefully took little steps towards the closest side door. As he reached the footpath he noticed the two balaclava-wearing men get into a black Ford coupé and drive off at speed. He noted the black and white registration plate: RT 426. By the time he got to his bike the Ford was well gone. He drove around the streets of Parramatta but found no trace of them.

If Harry went to the police station he would have to reveal his true identity, and he wasn't willing to do that at this time. He would get Jock later to check on the registration plates and fill him in on his visits to the hotels.

He decided to go to the third hotel on his list, the Centennial on Victoria Road. It was a solid red-brick construction with an upstairs verandah enclosed by a wooden railing. The glass panels in the doors and windows were stained glass set in solid cedar frames.

Harry parked his bike and went inside. He looked for the toilet and was directed by the barman to an outside building in the backyard. He used wet sheets of newspaper to wash away the specks of muck from his trouser bottoms and boots. When he could smell no more foul odours he returned to the bar and ordered a beer.

"You look a bit flustered, mate," said the cheery barman. "Have you had a hot day at work?"

"No, mate. I'm here on holiday. I came down here from the country to have a good time but I just got caught up with some nasty business at the other hotel up the road."

"Which hotel is that, mate?"

"The Empire in George Street."

"What happened?"

Harry described the incident. The barman asked numerous questions.

"Here, mate, have a drink on the house. You deserve it but can you sit up that end of the bar away from the other customers? You still stink like shit. Three drinks then you'll have to go because I'll have a full bar here in the next hour."

"Thanks, mate," said Harry, happy to get some sympathetic attention at last.

He sat quietly by himself as the barman attended to the other customers at the far end. Every now and then they would look quizzically at him, watching his every move. Twenty minutes later the main door opened and two police officers entered. They approached the barman who nodded in the direction of Harry. The sergeant strode confidently towards him.

"And who might we have here?" he asked.

"And who might you be?" replied Harry.

"Aah, we have a smart arse here, Constable. My name is Sergeant Flannery, and this here is Constable Smith. Now tell me who you are and what you're doing in this hotel."

"Relax, Sergeant. I'm Fred Forsythe. I'm on holidays from the country and I've come in here to have a quiet drink. I'm not breaking any laws and I'm not annoying anyone, so you tell me why you are so interested in why I'm here."

"Well, to start with, you stink like a bucket of last week's prawn shells and the other customers don't like that."

Harry stood up and faced the sergeant. "The good barman invited me to have a drink at this end of the bar away from the others, but if it's annoying them I'll leave."

He picked up his hood and started to walk to the door. The sergeant and constable followed. "You're coming with us, Mr Forsythe, down to the station. We have a few questions for you."

"Are you charging me with an offence, Sergeant?"

"No, not yet, but we have information that you were at the Empire Hotel this afternoon and you are under suspicion of being involved in the attack on those premises."

"Okay," said Harry. "Let's get this over with." He went with the officers to the Parramatta Police Station.

He followed them into an interview room where he outlined in detail the attack on the hotel.

The sergeant stood up and walked behind Harry. "I don't believe a word you've said. You are a member of the gang who attacked that hotel and you are going into that cell until we can gather more evidence. Constable, cuff him and place him in cell two."

Harry thought of taking both of them down but saw that it would only worsen the situation so he went quietly to the cell. "Sergeant, I am entitled to a phone call, aren't I?"

"Not until I say so."

"You know the rules, Sergeant, and so do I, so get me a phone now."

Harry was led into a room where he called headquarters. The phone was answered by Jack Tomlinson, the desk sergeant.

"Sergeant Tomlinson here. How might I help you?"

"Jack, this is Harry Taylor. Do me a favour and get Jock Burns to meet me at Parramatta Police Station now. Tell him to ask for Fred Forsythe when he gets here."

"Bloody hell, Harry. What are you up to now? I can't go around as your errand-boy."

"Jack. Shut up and listen. This is crucial to a major investigation involving Burns. Get him here now." Harry hung up and returned to the cell.

Chapter 25
Thursday

Sergeant Flannery and Constable Smith came back into Harry's cell. They took Harry to the interview room. The sergeant led the interrogation.

"Mr Forsythe, or whatever your real name is, who were your two accomplices at the Empire Hotel this afternoon?"

"Have you got a problem with dementia, Sergeant? Not twenty minutes ago I told you what happened at the Empire. I shouldn't have to repeat it again so soon."

The sergeant sat forward and glared at Harry. "Don't try your smart arse tricks with me, sonny boy, or I'll kick your arse till your nose bleeds."

Harry sat back and smiled. "Isn't that what you police call assault occasioning actual bodily harm?"

Flannery slapped his fist on the desk. "What happens in this room stays in this room." He looked up. "Isn't that right, Constable?"

"Dead set right, Serg; nothing goes out of this room."

The sergeant continued. "Why did you go to the Empire Hotel this afternoon?"

Harry paused before answering. "I know you're having difficulty with memory, Serg, so I'll repeat it. I went there for a drink. Is that against the law?"

"Who were the two men who came into the bar with buckets?"

"I don't know. I've never seen them before. I followed them outside and saw them get into a black Ford and drive away. That's all I know." Harry saved the information about the registration later for Jock.

"Why did you go to the Centennial Hotel?"

"Because I wanted a beer and I couldn't stay at the Empire with all that stink."

"Are your mates planning to do over the Centennial?"

Harry sat forward slowly. "Listen carefully, Sergeant. I'm just an innocent bystander. I came here to enjoy the good will. I was in the wrong place at the wrong time. I don't know any of those people. I just want to enjoy my time here in Parramatta. Now, you can ask as many questions as you like but I'm not answering any more until my friend arrives. He shouldn't be too long."

The sergeant stood up and marched around the back of Harry. Harry could sense his closeness and prepared himself for any eventuality.

"I've just been informed that you were at the City Hotel earlier today and you assaulted two of their customers. What have you got to say about that?"

"I'm getting the impression, Sergeant, that this city is not a friendly, welcoming place. I just wanted a beer. In the first hotel I was assaulted by two bouncers, in the other I was sprayed with shit and sump oil, and in the next one I was arrested by two police officers. What type of town do you run here?"

The sergeant tapped Harry on the shoulder. "Parramatta will be the best place on this earth when we get rid of trash like you."

Harry looked back over his shoulder. "Sergeant, take your hand off my shoulder. If you don't, I'll consider it assault and take the necessary action to defend myself."

The sergeant walked back around to the front of the table and laughed nervously. "And what do you think you can do in this room with both of us here. You don't have a chance."

Harry looked up at the constable and stared unblinkingly until the officer turned and stepped away to the side of the desk. He then stared at the sergeant, slowly looking him up and down. "You might have been fit twenty years ago, Sergeant, but by the size of that fat gut of yours, you couldn't run around this table without collapsing in a heap. So don't threaten me unless you can carry it out."

The sergeant sucked in his midriff and sat in the chair opposite Harry. "Now, why don't you tell me the truth about why you're here in Parramatta?"

Harry sat back and took a slow deep breath. "Sergeant, you've got a job to do and I respect that, but I've told you everything I know about the attack on the hotel. You can keep on asking questions until Parramatta wins the first-grade grand final, in the rugby league, and that's unlikely for at least the next ten years. I don't intend to answer any more questions. So I'll just sit here until my friend comes to sort out this matter."

The sergeant continued to ask questions for the next twenty minutes while Harry sat calmly without uttering a word in response. Young Constable Smith kept getting up and down and pacing the room in frustration because he knew that the man in front of him was in total control of the situation and nothing they did was going to alter that.

A secretary came to the door and announced that a Detective Constable Burns was here to see the sergeant. Jock was escorted into the room.

"Good afternoon, gentlemen, I'm Detective Burns and I'm here to escort Mr Forsythe to CIB headquarters. Mr Forsythe is helping us with our enquiries. I want to thank you, Sergeant, for the good work you have done in holding him until I got here."

"You just wait a minute, Detective. I'm in charge here. I arrested this man on suspicion of being an accessory to an assault on persons and property at local hotels and I'll keep him here until I've finished."

"My apologies Sergeant, I appreciate your good work but, I'm involved with matters that have greater importance than an assault here at Parramatta. So I'm taking Forsythe back with me now."

"Let me make something clear to you. I'm a sergeant, you're a constable. This is Parramatta, and this is my territory. I'm in charge here. The offences took place here and I'm the one who will decide what happens here. Is that clear enough to you, Constable or do you want me to put it in writing?"

Jock stiffened in a regimental way, stepped up to the desk, then leaned forward to look the sergeant in the eye. "Parramatta is a district; the CIB works statewide, and will always take priority over a district. I will be taking Mr Forsythe back with me now."

"Over my dead body," shouted the sergeant.

Jock never moved. "Do you have the phone number of the local funeral director? You'll need his services."

"You can't talk to me like that. I'll have you on report to headquarters. You'll be back in uniform on the beat by tomorrow."

Jock reached across the desk, picked up the phone and dropped it in front of the sergeant. He lifted the receiver and rammed it against the sergeant's ear. "Now dial headquarters and demand to speak to Chief Superintendent Twain. You tell him what you just said. You tell him to sack me immediately."

"I'll do just that," shouted the sergeant grabbing the handpiece.

"But before you do," cautioned Jock, "you must understand that I'm here on the direct orders of Chief Superintendent Twain. If you know the chief super well, you'll also know how he's going to react when some piss-ant sergeant from the suburbs tries to tell him how to do his job and refuses to cooperate with his specific instructions. I'll see you in Tibooburra next week, Sergeant."

The sergeant put down the phone. "What's so bloody important that I can't continue to investigate this matter here?"

Jock stood back behind the chair. "Sergeant, you do a good job here but the matter I'm dealing with has a much higher priority. The chief super is oversighting this personally, so don't even question it. Be thankful you're not involved. We are dealing in a life-and-death situation and this could get out of control. This is big time. It's not some minor assault."

"Well, what's Forsythe got to do with it?"

"I can't discuss that with you or anyone outside the immediate team other than to say that he's an important link to our investigations and to any follow-up action. I'm leaving and I'm taking Forsythe with me."

"How long will it take?" asked the sergeant.

"How long is a piece of string? I don't know, but you'll be the first to know when we're finished with him. I'll inform the chief super of your cooperation. Thanks." He turned to Harry. "Come on, Forsythe. And don't give me any grief or I'll have you back here as quick as you like and let the sergeant deal with you."

Jock and Harry got into the police car and drove off.

As they turned the corner, Harry laughed and looked at Jock. "Well, what a clever little dick you are. Keep up performances like that and you could become commissioner."

Jock smiled. "It was nothing, Harry; just part of the day's work."

"But didn't you come across that sergeant and constable when you were investigating the Parramatta murder?"

"No, it was another sergeant and two constables. I'm not certain I could have gotten away with it if the senior sergeant had been there."

"If Twain finds out you took his name in vain, your work day will be very short, mate. But what a performance. You deserve an Oscar for that."

"So, where do you want to go?"

"Drive into Parramatta Park over there. It'll be quiet and we can have a chat."

They got out of the car and found a bench under a tree. Harry filled in Jock on the day's happenings. He asked him to check the registration plates of the black Ford even though he was sure they were stolen.

"Where do we go from here, Harry?"

"We know that the three hotels I visited today are connected. We know that there is gambling, drugs and prostitution at the King's Arms. We know that the management of the Empire comes from Melbourne and we know that someone is trying to put them out of business. The Centennial is most likely the third hotel in the chain and they have close links with the local police."

Jock nodded his approval of Harry's summary. "Yes, I agree with that and it confirms my investigations into the other case. I don't know whether 'Dopey' was connected to the Melbourne mob or the ones from Sydney. He probably didn't know what he was getting himself into. He was an accident looking for some place to happen."

"Jock, I want you to keep going on that case if the boss allows you and see if there are any more connections with the big-time boys from either side. You can drive past the Centennial Hotel so that I can pick up my bike, and then you get off home. It's getting late."

"What are you going to do?"

"I'm going to take a run up to Castle Hill to look over that club they mentioned and then I'll hang around after dark to check out those hotels again."

"Be careful, Harry. Do you want me to stay with you?"

"No, Jock. You'd stick out like a Scotch thistle in a bed of petunias. No, it's best that I go alone in my casual gear. Thanks, mate for your help."

Harry picked up his bike and rode to Old Northern Road, Castle Hill, where he found the Gentleman's Club set back with well-groomed gardens and a gravelled driveway that curved under a large portico at the entrance. Harry parked the bike and walked up the steps to the front entrance.

A man in a top hat, tails and waistcoat greeted Harry. "My dear fellow, the tradesman's entrance is around the back."

Harry removed his hood. "Well, sir, I'm not the plumber. I'm a grazier down from the country and I was told that this club welcomed us country cousins while we're in town. I've decided to join and enjoy some of the action on offer."

The doorman tilted his head backwards to look down his nose at Harry waiting on the step. "I don't know what you mean, my man."

"Oh come on, my good fellow. My friends who come to all the Sydney sheep and Royal Easter shows told me you can have a drink after-hours, some gambling, and maybe meet some nice girls."

"Are you a member, sir?"

"No. But I'd like to join."

"That's impossible sir. You can only join this club on the recommendation of three members and have the approval of the Board."

"Thank you, sir. When I get home I'll have three members do just that. Will you be able to look after me then?"

"I'm sure that we will take good care of you. We pride ourselves on looking after our members."

Harry rode off. He was convinced the club was another outlet for gambling and other enjoyments, but it was unlikely to be involved in the current war between the Sydney and Melbourne mobs.

After dark he rode around the streets of Parramatta observing the various hotels and, in particular, the three he had visited earlier that day. In all three he noticed customers being let through the back doors which were guarded by bouncers. In all three hotels the lights upstairs were on.

He was about to ride away from the Centennial Hotel when he noticed Sergeant Flannery, in civilian clothes, entering a side door. He noted the time and rode off to Stanmore to get some rest.

Chapter 26
Friday

It was ten o'clock before Harry woke. He was not only tired from his adventures yesterday, but he felt a fever coming on. He recognised it as another touch of malaria that he picked up in the Islands during the war. He thought he was over it, as he had not had a return of the disease since the middle of last year when he was working on the murder case in the country. He knew that it took time to get out of his system, so he took a quinine tablet and a Vincent's headache powder washed down with a cup of tea.

During a breakfast of bacon and eggs he went over in his mind the events of the last few days. There was no doubt that gambling, drugs and prostitution were active in Newtown and Parramatta. That, in itself, was not a surprise because almost any suburb in Sydney would have some of those three operating at any time. But, with the hotels he visited yesterday there was evidence they were controlled by big crime figures, not just the low-key local operators. In at least one of them, Melbourne was involved. There was a strong suggestion that all four were connected.

At least one Parramatta policeman was complicit in what was going on, and that meant Harry could not trust the other local officers. All three hotels he visited in Parramatta, as well as two others, were active after-hours. That couldn't happen without the knowledge of the police, officials from the local council and maybe the local politicians. Whether those officials were actively involved in the after-dark activities or merely turned a blind eye, was still in question and would require further investigation.

Harry remembered the advice he received last Friday from his informant Sandy Blight who told him that the Melbourne mob were also moving into Liverpool because of the nearby army camps and into Mascot because of its closeness to the airport. He made a mental note to look them over. Recently, in those areas, there had been shots fired and premises set alight as a result of disputes between the newcomers and the locals who had been running crime there beforehand.

As Harry turned the radio on to the ABC, the announcer read the hourly news headlines.

"In breaking news, the Chief Superintendent of the New South Wales police, Mr Allan Twain, has informed the ABC that the top detective from the Criminal Investigation Branch, Detective Senior Sergeant Sherman, was fired upon late yesterday at Rosebery by a well-known criminal from Melbourne. Detective Sherman returned fire and fatally wounded the man. The chief superintendent said that the criminal was a major suspect in the shooting of Detective Senior Constable Harry Taylor two weeks ago."

Harry dropped everything and ran to the railway station to get a newspaper. The *Daily Mirror* had it as their lead story. The headlines were extra large:

SHERMAN TANK SHOOTS CRIME BOSS.

Top cop, Detective Fred Sherman, has shoot-out with a well-known Melbourne crime boss in a vicious fire fight in a dark alley near Mascot late yesterday afternoon.

Yesterday, Detective Fred Sherman, regarded as the best detective in NSW and as the man who, single handedly, has brought more criminals to justice than anyone else, survived an attack on his life by a well-known Melbourne crime boss. Detective Sherman was extremely lucky to survive the attack.

Detective Sherman and three colleagues were visiting Rosebery, near Mascot, as part of their investigation into the shooting of Detective Senior Constable Taylor two weeks ago at Redfern. The three other detectives were door knocking in the street at the time and were some distance from the main action. By the time they rushed to assist Detective Sherman, the criminal was fatally wounded. Detective Cross tried to revive the man but he died at the scene.

Detectives Rockwell and Crow, who were walking along the street, said they saw the man, now identified as Tommy 'Scarface' Fisher, emerge from a house at the end of the street and fire shots at Detective Sherman before Sherman returned fire and killed him.

Chief Superintendent Twain praised the work of the four detectives, especially that of Fred Sherman, and reminded the public that it was only because of the brave work of men like him that NSW was a safe place. People could be confident walking the streets of Sydney because of the good work of the NSW Police Force and its brave officers.

There will be an official inquiry into the death of Scarface.

Our special crime correspondent, James Bolton, will be following this story for our readers.

Harry walked back to his flat and reread the article. He chuckled when he saw the group photo that accompanied the article showing Chief Superintendent Twain at the centre, controlling the interview with the press. The big joke in the Force was that the most dangerous place on earth was between Twain and a camera. No one else was game to venture into that zone.

But something bothered Harry about the article. Scarface Fisher was not a top crime boss. He mostly worked for the big boys such as Splinter Woods and Bruiser Bignall, and was a known associate of Dale 'Flash' Evans. He was never seen as a killer. Harry dismissed his concern as an attempt by the newspaper to sensationalise the story.

He locked up his flat and rode to Redfern where he entered the laboratories of the Scientific Investigation Bureau. He went straight to Tony Jacobs' office.

"You took your time to get here," said Tony. "We were on this case yesterday. Where have you been?"

Harry threw his hood on the table and sat down. "I only just heard about it. What can you tell me about it?"

"Well, so far we don't have much more than what you've heard or read in the news. There was a shooting at Rosebery, near Mascot; and Scarface was killed in the shoot-out with Fred Sherman."

"How soon after the shooting was your team called in?"

"Joe Cross called headquarters immediately after the shooting, and they called us. We were there in well under an hour."

Harry walked around anxiously trying to visualise the scene. "Was the body still there?"

"Yes. It was covered by a blanket. You can see it here in the photos that George Black took at the scene yesterday afternoon."

Tony placed some photos on the table. The first photo showed a blanket covering what looked like a body on the verandah of a small cream weatherboard house at the end of the street.

Another photo showed the body slumped on its side on the verandah without the blanket covering. Under the victim's right hand was a revolver that Harry recognised as an Enfield No.2 Six-Shot Service revolver, which was in common use during the war.

The next photo showed the body lying on its back after it had been turned over. There were two wounds in the centre of the chest. They were about three inches apart, slightly left of centre. The dark red-black wounds were not large and were clean breaks of the flesh. There was little blood on the surface.

"Were there any exit wounds, Tony?"

Tony pointed to another photo showing the back view of the upper half of the body after the clothes were removed. There were no wounds on the back or side. "The evidence so far would indicate that the shots were fired from a handgun which has a lower velocity than a rifle of the same calibre. One shot hit a rib and fragmented into the heart and other organs, while the other shot penetrated the lung."

"What did Joe Cross say about the body when he got there?"

"He said that Scarface was making a sucking noise which is characteristic of a punctured lung. He said he pressed his hand against the wounds to stop the bleeding but the victim died soon after."

Harry looked through the other photographs. "There are no photos of Fred Sherman or Charlie Rockwell. Were Joe Cross and Bob Crow the only ones present when you got there?"

Tony looked up. "Joe told us that Charlie wanted to take Fred to the hospital to have him checked out for shock or other injuries, but Fred refused. Fred asked Charlie to drive him to headquarters so that he could report the incident to the commissioner and Allan Twain."

"Were there any shell casings at the site?" asked Harry.

"Yes," said Tony. "There were two .38s on the verandah of the house and two .45s on the grass near the steps."

Harry scratched his ear. "That would suggest that Scarface fired his shots from the verandah and Fred responded from the front yard in front of the steps. The .38s would be from the Enfield while the .45s would be from the police issue Webley. Is that what you're seeing, Tony?"

"Yes, the placement of the shells would suggest that."

"Were there any fingerprints on the shells?"

Tony called to Rita Flynn. "Come in here, Rita. Tell Harry about the scene from your perspective."

Rita looked her usual smart self in a short-sleeved emerald green blouse tucked into her neatly-ironed cream slacks, and burgundy mid-heeled brogue shoes.

"G'day, Harry. It looks as though they got your man. There were traces of prints on some of the shells but not clear enough to identify anyone in particular. The two .38s were almost clean as if they had been wiped. Scarface's prints were found inside the house."

"It's odd to me," said Harry, "that a top criminal like Scarface couldn't hit Fred when, according to reports, he fired two shots first and they were standing only a couple of yards apart. And why would the prints on those shells be wiped clean?"

"What makes you say that, Harry?" asked Rita.

"Look at this photo here. The shells from Scarface's Enfield are at the front of the verandah near the steps. The others from Fred's Webley are next to the base of the steps, only three feet away. Even if Scarface fired from the doorway the shells might have rolled to the front of the verandah, but that would be only nine feet away."

"Scarface could have been running at Fred," suggested Tony.

"Yes, that might explain it. And that could be why the wounds shown in that close-up photo suggest that they were fired from close range. Fred was close to him when he fired."

Tony put his hand on Harry's arm. "What are you going to do now, mate?"

"It depends on the autopsy. When will you have the full report?"

Rita patted his shoulder. "Relax, Harry. They got your killer. He's out of your way. He can't hurt you any more. You need to take some time off and go away and forget any of this ever happened."

Harry nodded and smiled. "Thank you, Rita. That's good advice but I haven't got anyone to go with. Besides, I'm not going to take your suggestion just yet. There are a few unanswered questions I have to look into and I need more time to do that. Thanks, Tony. I'll be in touch when the autopsy is complete. Must go now."

Chapter 27
Friday

It took little time to ride into the city and park beside headquarters in Central Street. Inside, Harry spoke to Jack Tomlinson, the desk sergeant.

"Bejesus, Harry. Where have you been? We don't have your address or phone number. We've had everyone out looking to give you the good news. Where are you living?"

"Thanks for your concern, Jack. It's touching. I'm in a flat and it has no phone. That's all you need to know at this stage."

"The chief super is going off his brain because we couldn't find you. I'll let him know you're here."

Harry reached for Jack's phone. "Put that phone down, Jack. I want to talk to the boys in the CIB first. They were the ones who did the job yesterday. Are they in?"

"Fred and Charlie are on leave until further notice. They have to have medical checks. Joe and Bob were in this morning but I'm not certain if they are now. I'll check."

Jack dialled through to the CIB. After a short conversation he put down the phone and turned to Harry. "Joe and Bob are in but they said that they are busy at the moment."

"Thanks, Jack. I'll just wander around to see how busy they are. I might be able to help."

As Harry walked into the CIB wing, Joe Cross and Bob Crow were in an interview room having a smoke and a cup of tea. "G'day, my friends. I came around to thank you blokes for getting rid of Scarface. They tell me that he was the one who shot at me two weeks ago."

Joe turned around with a scowl. "Didn't Jack tell you we were busy?"

"Yes. He said you were busy having a smoke and a cup of tea, so I thought I'd come around to have one with you. Remember it was me Scarface was trying to kill. I thought I'd like to be here in the follow-up and help you blokes finish your reports."

Bob sat forward and scowled. "You weren't there, Harry so you know fuck-all about nothing. So how could you help with the reports?"

"You're right, Bob. I'm sorry for intruding, but could you tell me about what happened yesterday?"

"Haven't you heard about it on the radio and read it in the newspapers? It's all there."

"How's Fred and Charlie? Are they okay?"

Joe turned around. "Fred was close to getting it yesterday but he handled it very well; as he always does. He's as tough as nails. You've got a lot to thank him for. He saved your arse by taking out that monster, and he did it by taking an enormous risk to his own life."

Harry walked over to the bench, found a clean mug and poured some tea. "Yes, I fully understand. I had that same feeling two weeks ago when Scarface shot at me and then blew up my car. I owe Fred a bucketful of thanks. You blokes did a marvellous job yesterday. What put you onto him as the main suspect?"

Joe stood up and filled his cup again. He added three sugars and stirred. "We've been investigating the Melbourne mob for some time and we have reliable informants who have been keeping us up to date with what's going on."

"Did your info come from Melbourne or was it local?"

Joe smiled and sat down. "Now, Harry, what a stupid question. You know a good cop never reveals his sources. I'd never ask for yours. Just put it this way: they're damn reliable."

Harry sipped his tea. "Why would Scarface want to take me out?"

"If it wasn't Scarface, Harry," said Joe, "it would've been someone else. There was a contract out on you."

"But why me? I've had nothing to do with Scarface. I knew about him but never met him, and wasn't involved in investigating him."

Bob turned. "Remember, Harry, before you went out to the country last year for that murder investigation, you were involved in a number of cases involving drugs in southern and western Sydney. The blokes involved were mostly the Melbourne boys trying to break into the Sydney scene. When you came back to the city you were involved again in those same type of investigations."

"But what has that got to do with the attack on me?"

Joe cut in. "Rightly or wrongly, the Melbourne mob saw you as being on to them and about to put them out of business. They were copping enough aggro from the top dogs in Sydney who were protecting their territory. They must have thought you were working for them.”

“You must be joking, Joe. I’ve got nothing to do with Whispers, Squeaky, Rosie or Tony the Greek. I’m not in their pockets, and never will be.”

“But the Melbourne mob think you are. They believed you were getting too close. Most of those cases you worked on were in southern and western Sydney, and that’s where they are setting up their businesses in the hotels. Your mate, Burns, has been investigating drugs in Parramatta with that Lennox Bridge case. They see the two of you as a danger to their welfare.”

Harry sat back absorbing the impact of what Joe just said. “Then I best warn Jock that he’s also a target.”

“That would be good advice, Harry.”

Harry stood, picked up their mugs, walked to the bench and switched on the jug. “Let me get you two some fresh tea. Now, tell me a bit more about what happened yesterday.”

“It’s much as you read in the newspapers, Harry,” said Joe impatiently.

“Why did you go to Lever Street at Rosebery?”

“We had a reliable tip off that Scarface was living in a house at the end of the street. We didn’t know which one, so we had to do a house-by-house search. Fred and Charlie went to the end while Bob took one side and I took the other.”

“What happened then?”

“Bob and I came out of houses about three from the end when we heard four shots; two followed almost immediately by two more. We rushed to the end of the street to see Fred standing over a body on the verandah. Charlie ran up the steps. When I got there I could see it was Scarface. He was in a bad way. I ripped open his shirt to see two wounds. I applied compression but he died soon after. I went into the house and phoned headquarters to let them know.”

Harry turned to Bob. “What did you see, Bob?”

“Just as Joe told you. He went to Scarface. I went to Fred to check him out. When I saw he had no injuries I took him aside and asked him what happened.”

“What did he say?”

"He told me he was walking up the path towards the steps when Scarface rushed out of the front door firing a revolver at him. Fred said that he quickly stepped to the side, took aim and shot him in the chest with two shots."

"How could Scarface miss at that distance? What handguns were involved?"

Joe cut in again. "When I got there Scarface was crumpled on the verandah. He had what looked like an Enfield revolver under his hand. He was half on his side so I pulled back his shirt and held my hand over the wounds. He didn't last long."

"Scarface must have been a crook shot," said Harry. "He had first shots, and he must have been only three to four yards from Fred when he pulled the trigger."

"Probably what saved Fred," said Joe, "was that Scarface had to come around the gauze door to get a shot at him. He would have been swinging his arms in an arc to get a bead on him."

"Did you turn him over to check for other wounds?"

"No. There was no need. He was dead. I left him on his side."

Harry noted that Joe's explanation was consistent with the photos he saw at the SIB.

Bob walked around the table. "Charlie took Fred by car to a hospital to check him out although he said that he wasn't wounded. Scarface missed with both shots. Joe and I waited until SIB came to carry out their work. We answered questions and went back to headquarters to report in."

"Yes, Bob, I saw your photo in the newspaper with the chief super," said Harry.

"Well, you know the super, Harry. He always wants to make the most of it when there's a big story like this. He wanted Fred there but he refused. He said he didn't want to be the next target, so he went home."

"What weapon did Fred use?"

Joe turned to answer. "He used his service Webley. He's one of the few blokes who is consistently accurate with it. I don't like them. I've been pleading with the commissioner to supply us with something more modern and accurate. But I'm talking to deaf ears."

"I agree with you Joe," said Harry. "The Webley's a heap of rubbish. It's been around since well before the war. There are much better handguns out there. I've had the same response from the top brass.

Fred's probably a great shot because he has those big strong arms that are rock solid when he's firing; and his concentration is just as good."

"Yes, but the trouble is that the bloody crims are better armed than us."

"Now that Scarface is out of the way how do you think the Melbourne mob will react?"

"Well," said Joe, "they won't be happy. They are determined to move into Sydney and the locals are determined not to let them in. They are looking to move into hotels in the suburbs because they see that as the future market. They're not out to compete in the inner city, but the Sydney lot don't see it that way."

"Yes. I agree," replied Harry. "The locals will see any move by the southerners as a way of getting into the big stakes in town and it'll be a fight to the finish."

"As you know, Harry, they are working into Liverpool, Mascot, Newtown and Parramatta, and our intelligence says that they are about to move into Lewisham and Marrickville to tap into the Greek and Italian population."

"That means that Tony the Greek will be in the thick of it."

Bob coughed on his cigarette. "Most people think that Tony is at war with the others in town like Whispers, Rosie and Squeaky. I can tell you, when it comes to an outsider moving in, those four are as thick as thieves. For some time now there has been an uneasy truce between them. Against the southerners, their hit men will work together."

Harry leaned against the back wall. "That means that I'm almost certainly still a target and my partner, Jock, will also be in the line of fire. It's possible that getting rid of Scarface has upped the ante more so. I'll need time to think this through."

"I don't agree. It's time to get back to work, Harry." said Bob. "I think you should be safer now that Scarface is out of the way."

Harry took another sip as he pondered his answer. "I'm not sure, Bob. The chief super has put me on sick leave until further notice. I'll have to talk with him."

"He was screaming his head off the other day because he couldn't find you. He wants you back on the job now. He's short-staffed and he thinks you've had enough time to recover from your wounds and, now that Fred and Charlie are off, he wants you back on duty today."

Harry turned as he walked to the door. "We'll have to see about that. Thanks for your help and thanks for taking out Scarface."

Chapter 28
Friday

Jack Tomlinson shouted to Harry as he came along the corridor from the CIB. "Harry, come here. It's urgent."

"Calm down, Jack. I can't see anyone shooting up the place, so what's your problem?" asked Harry as he ambled towards the main desk.

"The chief super has heard you're in the building and is going berserk because you didn't see him before going anywhere else."

"What is it about this building Jack that makes everyone in it go troppo with a little heat and humidity? Open the windows, Jack. Let in some fresh air. It'll do all of you the world of good."

Jack sneered. "Thanks for your smart advice, Harry. I'll phone the chief super to let him know you're here. I'm sure he'll enjoy your jokes."

Harry walked along the corridor and knocked on the door. He waited and knocked again. A booming voice shouted. "Wait." He walked slowly back to the main desk.

"Hey, Jack. I thought he was in a hurry to see me. I'll come back later when he's in a better mood."

At that moment the door along the corridor swung open and shuddered into the stone wall. Chief Superintendent Twain grasped the door jamb. The scowl on his face would have frightened a mallee bull.

"Taylor, get in here now."

"Good morning, sir. It's so good of you to make time in your busy day to see me."

The chief slammed the door shut. "Don't try your smart arse comments on me. Now sit down there and tell me where you've been. We've been looking all over for you. Even your partner, Constable Burns, didn't know where you were."

"I've been on sick leave, sir. Remember, you were the one who told me to go home and stay away from any investigations. I've been following your orders, sir."

"And why do you have the audacity to come in here looking like a bag of rubbish. This is the New South Wales Police Service and we do have standards."

"I'm sure that you're not suffering dementia, sir, but you'll remember that you..."

There was a knock on the door and Jack Tomlinson entered with a file.

"Get out of here, Sergeant. I don't want to be disturbed."

"But this is the file you requested sir," replied Jack.

"Get out. I'll call you when I'm ready and not before."

"Yes sir." Jack closed the door.

Twain got up, paced the floor, then turned to face Harry. "We have no address or phone number or any way to contact you."

"That's correct, sir because I'm not going back to my flat at Redfern. I'm not going to give the shooter another go at me. I'm not that mad."

"He's dead. Get over it. Why haven't you told us where you're living?"

"With due respect, sir, I've been shot at, had my car blown up and drugs planted in it, I don't trust anyone any more, so I'll keep my residence secret until this matter is all over."

Twain sat back at his desk, fingers tapping angrily on the writing pad. "But you are no longer in danger because Fred Sherman got your man yesterday."

"Yes Sir, Fred and the boys did a great job at Rosebery in getting rid of Scarface, but I disagree with you on the matter of danger. Because of that killing yesterday I'm now more at risk. The Melbourne mob will be determined to get me in retaliation for that."

"Absolute rubbish," shouted the chief super, banging his fist on the table. "They wouldn't dare do anything now that they know we have our top cops from the CIB on the job. They'll lay low or go back to Melbourne."

"I disagree, sir. I believe they're deeply entrenched in the suburbs. They've had time to rope in some of our police, together with local councillors and maybe politicians." Harry sat back to watch the reaction.

"Hogwash," screamed Twain. "You be careful, Detective. You're accusing police and politicians of being corrupt. You're treading on very thin ice."

"That might be so, but that is my opinion now and I'm not putting myself in the firing line until I'm certain."

Allan Twain jabbed both hands onto the writing pad. "Name the police officer involved in corruption now or retract that allegation."

Harry opened wide his hands wide. "I'll name those officers when I get more corroborating evidence; and not before."

"But you can't go around making such allegations against other officers without proof. They'll have your balls for breakfast."

"Sir, the Melbourne group have already moved into Newtown, Parramatta, Liverpool and Mascot, and are about to move into Marrickville and Lewisham. Blind Freddy can see what is going on and they can't do that unless they have some of the local coppers and local government officials on side."

"You can't say that without proof. And if you go around making false allegations about my officers, I'll see you in gaol where I'm sure some of the inmates will be pleased to share a cell or yard with you."

"With all due respect, sir, you've worked in some of the toughest areas of policing and come across the biggest criminals, and you are well aware of the current state of affairs in the big crime scene in this city. You either know of, or are very suspicious of, some of our members who are linked with major crime figures and are probably corrupt."

"I know that good detectives, including you, have links with criminals as informants. It is a valuable means by which we gather intelligence that leads to arrests and convictions. But that doesn't mean that those officers are corrupt."

Harry twisted in his seat. "I apologise, sir, if my comments have offended you or implied that good officers are corrupt. That certainly was not my intention. I'm merely pointing out that there have been very few arrests for gambling, prostitution, drugs or assaults in regards to the well-known criminals from here or from Melbourne."

"Look, Detective, gambling, drugs and prostitution have been around since Adam chased Eve under the fruit tree. The public demand it and, if it's doing nobody any harm, I'm not going to get too excited about it. I'm short of staff and I'll put those resources where they are most needed."

With increasing frustration Harry tapped the desk and leaned forward. "But we are now looking at a major turf war between the Sydney and Melbourne mobs, and people are dying as a result of it."

"And that, Detective, is where I'm putting my resources. You don't see everything that goes on in here, so don't jump to conclusions when you're not involved."

"Thank you for that advice, sir."

The chief super stood up. "I want you back on duty on Monday. That's an order. And give the desk sergeant your address and phone contacts on the way out."

"Before I go, sir, would you reconsider letting me work undercover on this battle between the drug lords?"

"No. Now get out here. I've got important business to attend to."

Harry left the office and walked to the main desk.

Jack looked up. "Well, Harry, how did that go?"

Harry chortled. "He was so pleased to see me he gave me a big hug and a kiss and promoted me to Superintendent. So, smarten up young Jack or I'll have you back on the beat."

"Oh, Harry," laughed Jack. "You've made my day. You're like a breath of fresh air even if you're just a big bag of wind. Now, let's get serious. Give me your address and phone contact."

Harry leaned on the counter taking his time to respond. "Jack, I'm going to give you what you need to fill in your register. It'll keep the boss happy, but it won't be accurate."

"You can't do that, Harry. What if we need to get in touch?"

"Jack, I'll tell you how to find me on the condition that you tell nobody else; and I mean nobody. If anyone questions it you can plead ignorance. You can blame me for giving you the wrong information. Now, is that a deal?"

"I don't like it, Harry but I know that you're not going to tell me the truth so let's get on with it."

"For the record, Jack, my address is 5A Eveleigh Street, Redfern, and my phone is MJ-6210. But if you have to find me in an emergency, contact Constable Burns. He's the only one who knows where I am."

Jack coughed to clear his smoker's throat. "But why all the secrecy, Harry? They got Scarface Fisher yesterday and he was the one who took the shot at you. He's out of the way, so there's no more danger to you."

"No, Jack. Yes, he's out of the way, but there'll be ten others wanting to pick up the contract on me. Take it or leave it, mate but that's the way it's going to be. Now I'll be off. I'm still on sick leave until Monday."

As Harry left the building he saw Jock Burns walking towards him along Central Street. "Come on, Jock, turn around. I'm taking you back into George Street for a drink at the Great Southern Hotel. We need to talk."

"But I'm supposed to see the chief super this afternoon before I knock off."

"Mate, I just saw him and he's in such a stinking mood, he'll throw the desk at you if you go anywhere near him. Leave it until Monday. Tell him you had a blow-out and you didn't have a spare tyre."

"I don't like it, Harry. You know what he's like. He'll be furious if I don't turn up."

"Jock, if you and I are going to work together you'll have to trust me. He just told me ten minutes ago that I'm back on duty on Monday, but he didn't tell me what case I'm on. So we'll have to go in first thing Monday to see what he wants us to do. You can tell him then what happened."

"Okay, Harry, but it's on your head if this blows up."

"It's okay, Jock. With my crew cut it'll just blow off. Relax, mate."

They found two stools in the back corner of the bar and ordered beers. Harry outlined his visit to the CIB and his meeting with Joe and Bob.

Jock wiped the froth from his mouth. "That's great, Harry. Now they've done their job you can relax."

"No, Jock, I can't relax. As I explained to Jack Tomlinson, there will be others wanting to pick up the contract on me. My difficulty is that Twain wants me back on normal duty on Monday. I wanted to go undercover, but he said no."

"Is there anything I can do to help?"

Harry explained his meeting with Jack. He told Jock the address of his flat at Stanmore.

"Jock, you mustn't tell anyone; even on threat of death. If you have to contact me slip a note under the door. I'll still contact you at your mother's place."

The two of them settled back over another four beers before leaving to go their separate ways home.

"See you on Monday, Jock, at the super's office."

Chapter 29
Saturday

After an overnight sub-tropical storm with strong winds and lightning, the morning air was as thick as grandma's pea soup. As Harry rode his bike to Rosebery, moisture was rising from the road. His shirt and trousers below the knee were damp from the spray thrown up by the cars and trucks in front. He wiped the droplets from his goggles. He hadn't bothered with his oil skin coat because it was too hot.

On entering Lever Street he slowed to a walking pace while he surveyed the houses. Most of them were small, probably with only one or two bedrooms. They were likely occupied by workers and their families from the nearby industrial areas. An elderly man in singlet and shorts, a cigarette dangling from his mouth, a newspaper tucked under his arm, was walking his dog. Harry suspected that the man was about to study the form guide for the day's races. An elderly woman with rollers in her hair was sweeping the footpath in front of her neat cottage.

At the end of the street Harry recognised the small weatherboard house with a gauze door and verandah where the shooting took place. He'd seen it in the photos at the SIB. He parked his bike nearby, walked back to Middlemiss Street on one side and returned on the other. There were ten houses on each side. The cottage occupied by the woman sweeping the path was neat and freshly painted white. It had a well-maintained garden full of colourful summer flowers. Other houses were in need of a good coat of paint with gardens overgrown with weeds. Two had rusted-out cars parked in front.

From where he stood Harry focused on the positions where Fred, Charlie, Joe and Bob were when the shots were fired. He decided to door knock the nearby houses to find anyone who might have seen the action. He approached the woman sweeping the footpath.

"Good morning, Madam. I was just admiring your garden. You must be very proud of it. My mother, who lives out in the country, keeps her garden like that and it's refreshing to see it in the city."

The woman wiped her hands on her apron before resting on her broom. "Well thank you, Sir. That's so nice of you to notice. And what brings you to this part of town?"

"Please excuse my casual gear but it's Saturday. I'm a reporter with the *Daily Mirror* and I came out here today to look at the place where that nasty criminal was shot on Thursday."

"Oh, that was terrible. I was so shocked. I didn't know what to do. And this has been such a good street for all the time I've lived here; until that horrible man moved in at the end of last year."

"My name is Fred. What might I call you?"

"My name is Nellie, but you mustn't put my name in the paper. I don't want to get into any trouble."

Harry touched her on the shoulder in reassurance. "I promise you, Nellie, that I won't mention you at all, but I'd like to ask you some questions. Could we sit on your verandah out of the heat?"

From his vantage point Harry had a direct view of Scarface's house at the end. "Where were you, Nellie, when the shooting took place?"

"One of the detectives came to my door to check if this was the house where that man lived. We were standing right here when the shots were fired. I thought it was New Year's crackers going off with some of the kids in the street. The detective left me and ran to the end of the street."

"How many shots were fired?"

"I'm not sure. Me ears aren't as good as they used to be. I think two shots, but it could have been more."

"What happened next, Nellie?"

"The man in the front yard went up the steps to check on the man who was shot. He put something down on the verandah and then it looked as though he took the man's pulse."

Harry sat back. "Did you see what he put on the verandah?"

"No. Me eyes are not that good. And the policeman moved, so I couldn't see any more. The detective who was here ran up to check the man lying on the verandah and I saw him put his hand on the man's chest."

"What can you tell me, Nellie about the man who lived in that house?"

"I hate speaking bad about anyone, especially about the dead, but he was a nasty piece of rubbish. I was out there sweeping my gutter one day and he shouted at me to get off the road. He said, 'Get off the road you old bitch or I'll run you over'. I was so upset and frightened. I'm alone now since my husband, Andy, died last year."

"Did anyone else live in that house?"

"I don't think so, but there seemed to be people coming and going at all times of the day and night. It was annoying when you're trying to get to sleep with car lights coming through the window."

"Did those people go inside the house when they went there?"

"Some did, but a lot of them just went to the door and walked away with what looked like a letter in their hand. I didn't want to be a stickybeak and I didn't want him to see me staring at him; because I was scared of him."

Harry stood up. "Thank you so much, Nellie. You've been very helpful, and I promise I won't mention your name. Your secret is safe with me. Did anyone else see what happened on Thursday?"

"Talk to Clarrie. He's two doors down. He was sitting on the verandah when it all happened."

Harry knocked on Clarrie's door and introduced himself as a reporter from the *Daily Mirror*. Clarrie was a retired fitter and turner who had worked all his life at the Eveleigh Railway Workshop. He still had a bounce in his step and invited Harry in to have a cup of tea. He said he felt privileged to have been chosen for an interview for the paper.

"Did you bring your camera with you? Will my photo be in the paper? Wait until I tell me mates about this. They might shout me a free beer at the pub."

Harry smiled. "No, Clarrie, I forgot the camera today, but I'll get a photographer to come on Monday. Now tell me about that bloke in the end house. Did you have anything to do with him?"

"Horrible piece of shit. Good riddance, I say. The police deserve all the praise for getting rid of him but it was a close thing for that big copper."

"What do you mean, Clarrie?"

"One of the coppers told me that the bastard took two shots at their mate first before the copper shot him dead."

"Did you see the man shoot at the detective?"

"No, I was just standing up to walk inside when the shots were fired. When I turned around I saw the other fella falling on the verandah."

Harry sat back to try to get away from the cloud of smoke from Clarrie's cigarette.

"How many shots were fired, Clarrie?"

Clarrie scratched his nose and puffed again on his cigarette. "Aah, jeez mate, I'm not sure. It could have been two, three or four. It was over before I turned around."

"What happened next?"

"It looked to me as though the big copper put his gun on the verandah near the body and checked the bloke's pulse. Then the other copper ran up and pushed his hand on the man's chest. After a few minutes they went inside, got a blanket and placed it over the body."

"Did the big copper pick up his gun again from beside the body?"

"I didn't see him do that; but then I could have been mistaken. It all happened so quickly."

"Nellie told me that there were lots of people coming there at all times in the day and night. Did you notice anything?"

"Yeah, the bastards kept me awake at all hours. They didn't stay long. I reckon they were up to no good. Maybe they were doing drugs or something like that. But hey, I didn't say that. Don't print that or the bastards will come around here and knock me off."

"Don't worry, Clarrie. I'll be very careful in what I write. I won't say anything that will cause you any concern. I'm very grateful for your help. You're a real champion. If we had more people like you the world would be a far better place. Thanks for everything. I must get going."

Harry walked to the house where the shooting took place. He slipped under the police tape and went to the back door. He picked the lock and entered the kitchen. There were dirty plates and cutlery in the sink. The rotting scraps of food on the table made the atmosphere putrid.

The occupant of the house was certainly not house-proud. The furniture was covered in dust and there were muddy footprints on the lino floor. The washbasin and bath had scum rings. The beds were unmade. Curtains and blinds were drawn shut. Harry noted that all the drawers and cupboard doors were open but he assumed that was a result of the investigation by the SIB team.

When he re-entered the kitchen he noticed two faint dusty boot prints on the hard shiny surface of the Formica table. Looking up, he saw the manhole. Climbing onto the table he removed the cover and hoisted himself into the roof space. He waited until his eyes adjusted to the dark. He crawled over the roof trusses, wiping away spider webs, and saw a small sheet of Masonite that had been nailed across the beams. He reached under that sheet and found a paper bag and an old biscuit tin.

He placed them on the kitchen table, opened them and smelled the contents. The paper bag contained what he believed to be cannabis, and the tin contained small packets of cream powder.

Harry walked to the backyard where he noticed an outside toilet and a garden shed. On the wall of the outside dunny was an old telephone book hanging from a nail. Beside it was another sheet of Masonite tacked across the studs. Harry squeezed his hand behind the sheet, pulled it away from the wall and found four smaller tins. He found more in the garden shed. He returned to the kitchen, found a calico bag, placed the tins and bags in it, walked out and rode his bike to Tony Jacobs' place at Coogee.

Tony greeted Harry at the door. "What the hell are you doing here? I've got guests, mate, and I really am not in the mood to be doing police work or having a booze up with you. Go away, Harry."

"Thanks for the welcome, Tony. I won't come in. I've just been to Lever Street, Rosebery, to see the place where Scarface was shot on Thursday and decided to look into the house where he lived."

Tony put up his hand. "Stop there, Harry. You've just told me that you broke a police line and went into that house without permission. We've already been through that house. What the hell were you doing there anyway?"

"I wanted to see for myself what I'm up against."

"Harry, go home and leave that to us."

"I will Tony but I thought you might like to have these. I found them in the roof, in the outside dunny and in the garden shed hidden behind sheets of Masonite. Your team missed them. I wanted to give them to you and nobody else. You can thank me some other time. I'll go now to let you get on with your barbecue. See you, mate."

Harry walked out and rode back to Stanmore.

Chapter 30
Sunday

As Harry stepped outside the flat he noticed Eileen leaving her back door, dressed in her Sunday best, ready for church. She moved with style. There was a certain grace about the way she walked down the path.

"Good morning, Eileen," said Harry with a broad grin. "You look stunning this morning. You must be going to church. I can give you a ride on the back of my bike, if you wish."

"No thank you, Harry, not in my good dress and hat. What happened to your lovely car? I liked that one."

"Oh, someone ran into it while it was parked at Redfern and the insurance company wrote it off. So I'm getting around on a bike until I get another car. You could ride side-saddle if you like. I'm sure that'll get the congregation talking this morning."

Eileen burst out laughing. "You are a cheeky one, aren't you? It must be because your wounds are healing. Go on, be off with you. Thanks, but I'll walk."

"How did your interview go?"

"Very good. I got the job. I start tomorrow."

"Congratulations. I'll have to get a bottle of champagne to celebrate. Will you say a prayer for me today because I can't be there?"

Eileen laughed. "Will it do any good?"

"Probably not." He waved and walked to the gate.

Harry rode his bike into the city and parked outside Sandy Blight's boarding house in The Rocks. He knocked on the door three times before it opened. A scruffy unshaven old man stood there looking at Harry.

"We don't want any, so piss off." The man spat on the floor, snarled at Harry and grabbed the door handle. Harry's boot moved just in time to block the door being slammed in his face.

"I'm not selling anything, and I don't belong to any church or religious society, so listen up," said Harry in his commanding voice. "Go and get Sandy Blight. I want to talk to him."

"He ain't done nothin' wrong. Why do you want him?"

"You're right. He hasn't done anything wrong. He's a friend."

"Pull the other leg, mate. It plays Dixie."

Harry grabbed the man's shirt-front. "Now, either you go and get my friend, Sandy, or I'm going to walk right over you and get him myself. What's it to be?"

"Okay, okay, keep your shirt on. At least you could show some manners when you come here." The man shuffled off down the corridor mumbling under his breath. A few minutes later Sandy came to the door.

"Holy bejesus,, Harry. What the bloody hell are you doing here?"

"Sandy, I want you to be up on Observatory Park in half an hour; usual spot."

"Bloody hell, Harry, it's me day orf and I ain't had breakfast yet."

"Sandy, I'm not asking a question. This is an order. Be there. I'll pick up a meat pie or a dim sim on the way and have it ready for your breakfast."

On the hill a family with three children were about to set up for a picnic under the tree, but Harry convinced them that the area was reserved for a wild, boozy celebration and they should move to a different location. They were not happy but were not willing to argue with the big untidy-looking man.

Half an hour later Sandy ambled over the rise and down to the bench under the tree. He plonked himself on the bench. "What the bloody hell is so important that a man can't have a sleep in on a Sunday morning?"

"I need information, Sandy, and I need it now."

"You should be so happy, Harry. They shot Fisher the other day."

Harry handed Sandy a meat pie. "Who did Scarface work for?"

"I think he worked for the Melbourne mob."

"But who in that group? There are a number of top criminals in Melbourne and they all hate each other's guts. Now tell me who he worked for."

Sandy brushed the pastry flakes from his shirt. "I really don't know, Harry. The message is that Splinter Woods and Bruiser Bignall are the main two trying to set up here. But then there are rumours that Jacky Abbott and Billy Stenson are also butting in."

"If all four of them are coming here, there could be more strife between them than there will be with the Sydney boys. Are any of them here in Sydney now?"

A child ran past with a kite. Harry turned back to Sandy who scratched his neck before replying. "I've been told that both Splinter and Billy Stenson have been here for short trips to suss out the area and buy up some hotels. They tell me that they fly in and out on a private plane."

Harry stretched his legs and rubbed his knees. "Who did Scarface work for in Melbourne?"

Sandy licked his fingers and lit a cigarette. "They tell me that he always wanted to work for himself but he did a lot of work for Splinter and Darkie Moffitt."

"Does that mean the contract on me came from one or both of those men or Billy?"

Sandy sat back and scratched the stubble on his chin. "Well that depends."

Harry stood up and faced Sandy. "For God's sake, Sandy, stop frigging around. I want answers and I want them now. It's my life that's on the line, not yours."

"Calm down, mate. It's not that I don't want to tell ya but it's not very clear. You see, Scarface Fisher was born here in Sydney and was a young criminal when he met up with a lot of the others in juvenile detention, and later in Long Bay Gaol. He knows all of the hit men here."

"Who did he work for in Sydney?"

"You probably didn't come across Scarface in Sydney because he only came out of juvenile when you went away to the war, and he left for Melbourne in forty-five before you returned."

"Did he work alone?"

"On small jobs he worked alone, but he linked up with any of the others when a big job was on. He often did break and enters and he used standover tactics while collecting debts for any of the big boys. He worked a lot with Bomber Earl here when there was a major bank heist or an armoured van job."

Harry sat down again. "So, he's well known to both sides, and that means he could have been working for either a Sydney or Melbourne syndicate."

"That's right, Harry, and that's why it's not clear who's paying the contract now."

"What would be your honest opinion, Sandy?"

"Aah jeez, Harry, that's a tough one. It could be any one of them, or both. But if I had to put money on it, I'd say Melbourne."

"Which of them would be most likely, do you think?"

Sandy blew some smoke rings before answering. "I'd say it would be between Splinter or Jacky Abbott."

"Why Jacky Abbott?"

"Jacky is the most cunning bastard of them all. I hear that in Melbourne he's the one taking over most of the big drug deals, and he supplies to the others. He's made a fortune and now wants to use that to set up in Sydney."

Harry shifted uncomfortably on the bench. "But from what you've said it might not be the Melbourne mob. It could be here in Sydney. What else are you hearing around the traps, Sandy?"

"Well it's a bit of an each-way bet, Harry. Scarface was so well known here that they could have contracted him to take you out, and if the Melbourne mob heard about it they might have set up Scarface to have him taken out by the CIB as revenge."

"Sandy, do you think someone is feeding the CIB boys with information?"

"Most of the money would be on the Melbourne boys doing this to you but, some close to the action say it's Sydney."

"That doesn't help me much, Sandy."

"Well, the main message is that the contract is still out there on you. Getting rid of Scarface didn't stop that. So be careful, Harry. Don't trust anyone."

Harry lifted his shoulders and tightened his gut muscles. This was not good news. "Now Sandy, tell me how the drugs get in from overseas."

Sandy outlined how the drugs from overseas came in by cargo ship, sailing boat or plane. He could only talk with confidence about the shipping cargo on the wharves. He explained that the drugs were hidden in furniture, or cans of fruit and vegetables, packets of lollies, and things like pipes or water hoses. Some customs agents were on the take and let them through without examination.

Harry was anxious to find out the whole story. "But how does it get to the customer?"

"Be patient,, Harry. Some of it goes to the Haymarket. It's a main centre for distribution. There are a couple of big codgers who control it from there. The rest of it is picked up from the wharf by the runners who work for the big boys. They have sheds around Mascot and Botany."

"Who controls it at the wharves?"

"That's Boris Weller. Be on your guard with him, Harry."

"Who are the key operators in the Haymarket?"

"Harry, I wouldn't go anywhere near them. They are very nasty bastards. If you cross them forget about breakfast tomorrow. You'll go through the mincer and come out as cat food or you'll be fed to the fish out at sea."

"Sandy, I have to know who is controlling the action. If they're out to get me I want to know where the bullets are coming from. I need to be ahead of the game. Remember, mate that I can't be of any use to you when you get into trouble if I'm shark bait. Now tell me who they are."

"Okay, but you didn't hear it from me. There are two blokes. They supervise the arrival of goods into the markets. If you don't look after them then you don't get in. There's an Italian bloke called Angelo Romano and a nasty Hungarian bastard called Bozsi Gabor. Everyone calls him 'Boss'."

"How do they operate?"

"They have control of who gets into the market. They take a cut from the stallholders. If they don't pay up they get kicked out. If they argue they get done over. Those two also have their own coolrooms to store vegetables, and they also have secret compartments there to store the drugs."

"What about the weed? Do they control that as well?"

"Yeah. That's becoming more popular now, so they have farmers out in the Hawkesbury and down south near Leeton and Yanco who supply the stuff. The farmers put the stuff in special bags and hide it in with the fruit and vegetables. The truck is locked so that the driver does not see what's in the back. When he gets to the markets the driver goes off to have breakfast and Boss' boys move in, unlock the truck and take the stuff into the secret room."

"How is it moved from there?" asked Harry as the picture became clearer.

"Angelo and Boss have a team of runners who distribute the goods to the main buyers. Those blokes then deliver to the next mob who break it down, mix it with additives and then they use young blokes who have been hooked to sell it on the street."

"So if a kid gets caught he gets a slap on the wrist and he doesn't know who was the main supplier."

Sandy rolled another cigarette. "That's right, Harry. The big boys don't get caught."

"Okay, Sandy. Thanks a lot, mate. You've been a great help. Here, take this and shout yourself a big steak."

Harry handed Sandy a ten pound note and waited until he was well over the hill before walking back to his bike.

Chapter 31
Monday

It's Monday morning and Harry had to report for duty. He'd been ordered back on duty by the chief super. No more Fred Forsythe. No more army disposal gear. No more masquerading as an insurance inspector. The main problem was that he would now be exposed as a walking target in full view of all those willing to take up the contract. Harry felt uneasy, but he had a job to do, and it wouldn't be the first time he'd been in a dangerous situation. At least in the war he knew the enemy and the direction from which they came. This would be different.

While having breakfast, Harry went over the feedback he got yesterday from Sandy. Scarface Fisher's death did not put a stop to the contract on him; others would pick that up. What was unclear was who wanted him out of the way. He couldn't see Rosie Travener or Squeaky Walsh being involved. They had their patch and stuck to it.

That left Whispers Durante who controlled the Woolloomooloo area, and Tony 'the Greek' Stavros in Marrickville. Both of them wanted to expand their empires. There was strong evidence that Tony had been involved in a murder and a manslaughter, but all those present at the time weren't willing to speak up and the cases never went to court. Harry doubted that Tony would pull the trigger. These days he had enough henchmen to do his dirty work. But who could that be? For Harry, there lay the problem.

Tom Lebovich wouldn't hesitate to do it. It was only his association with the older CIB men as an informant that saved him from being charged with the murder of Knuckles Elliott. But surely those same officers from the CIB wouldn't let Lebovich get involved in an attack on one of their colleagues. Tony Pantano, Bluey Ricketts and Shooter McGill were all standover men and wouldn't hesitate to take out a contract on anyone.

If the money was right they weren't fussy who they got rid of. It was rumoured that McGill had already been involved in at least three

murders. In only one of those cases was the body found, and that was so
mutilated it was difficult to identify the victim.

Bomber Earl liked to work by himself but would team up with
others on big jobs like bank robberies or armoured van hold-ups. Bomber
fired off shotguns in banks to scare the staff and customers but Harry
didn't think he would go as far as murder, so he put him in the not-likely
list.

Then there was the Melbourne mob. If Sandy was right, all four of
the big boys were involved in the recent move to Sydney. From
intelligence reports, Harry knew that Splinter Woods and Jackie Abbott
got on reasonably well but, the other two, Bruiser Bignall and Billy
Stenson, were having their own private war in Melbourne.

Now that Scarface was out of the way, there were three main hit
men who worked for the top dogs. They were Dale 'Flash' Evans, Nobby
Clark and Darkie Moffitt. If the rumours were right, all three of them
were in and out of Sydney in the last twelve months. They were all
ruthless, nasty, habitual criminals. Evans was out of the picture because
he was in gaol; unless, of course, he organised the hit from inside.

Darkie Moffitt was believed to be responsible for knifing another
prisoner to death in Pentridge Prison but there were no witnesses.
Another story was that he strangled his girlfriend to death. He put her in
the boot of his car and went to the club with his mates to celebrate his
winnings at the races, before taking her out to sea to feed her to the
sharks the next morning.

By the time Harry finished breakfast he had more questions than
answers. He'd have to be more careful than normal. He needed 360-
degree vision at all times. Jock Burns was a good partner but he was still a
bit raw and Harry didn't want to put Jock in the line of fire.

Harry was never one for self-pity, so he quickly washed his dishes,
put on his hat, walked to the railway station and took the train into the
city. He was early for his meeting with Twain, so he and Jock went to the
interview room where Harry told him about his meeting with Sandy.

Harry looked Jock in the eye. "Mate, I'm the target; you're not.
So, if you want to be assigned to another officer, I'll understand. I don't
want to put you in a situation where you might be hit instead of, or
because of, me. In fact, it might be better if I work alone. That way I'll be
less conspicuous. I can talk to the chief, if you like. What do you think?"

"Mate, you can't look in all directions at the same time, so you'll need someone to ride shotgun for you, and I'm your man. Don't think you can get rid of me that easy." Jock laughed and tapped Harry on the shoulder. "And by the way, Twain has appointed me as your babysitter because he doesn't trust you to follow orders."

Harry sat back, laughed and slapped his thighs. "Bloody hell, Jock, it'd be okay if I could only translate what you're saying. Speak the bloody King's English, mate so I can understand what you're going to do." He sat forward, smiled and took Jock's arm. "Mate, thanks. You and I'll make a good team. Let's go and see the chief."

At that moment Jack Tomlinson came into the room to announce that the chief super was ready for them.

"Well, at least you look a bit more respectable than you did on Friday," said Twain as he pointed to the chairs to indicate his order to sit. "From today you'll be back on full-time duties."

Harry sat forward. "On Friday I asked you if I could work undercover to get to the bottom of this case, but you refused. Since then, Constable Burns and I have discussed this and we would like to work again as a team, if that has your approval."

Twain jutted his chin forward. "There's no problem any more, Harry. Scarface has been put out of business, thanks to Fred Sherman and his team, and that case is closed. It's time to move on and I'm happy for you two to work together. For God's sake, you need someone to look after you."

Harry did not look at Jock who was grinning. "Thank you, Sir. Now where do you want us to start?"

"There was a fire at a hotel in Marrickville in the early hours of this morning. It could be a put-up job for insurance, or it might have been a fire-bomb from some angry customer or some rival group. Get out there and wrap it up. It's good to have you back on duty, Harry."

***

Harry and Jock took the train from Town Hall to Marrickville and walked to the Fitzroy Hotel on Illawarra Road. It was an imposing three-storey brick building with a cantilevered awning, curved around the corner. Two porthole windows indicated the stairwells at both ends. The upper two floors appeared to be for accommodation. The three doors entering the bars and main entrance were blocked with tape. A lone policeman stood at the main entrance.

Harry and Jock approached the young constable. "G'day. I'm Detective Senior Constable Harry Taylor and this is Detective Jock Burns. What have we got here?"

"I'm Constable John Collins. I'm from the local Marrickville station. We got a report about three o'clock this morning of a fire here at the hotel. By the time we got here the lower floor was ablaze. The firemen got it under control quickly. The owner is in there with the fire inspector now. The owner told us that there were seven guests staying here, but they were leaving when we got here."

"Where are they now?" asked Jock.

"I don't know. We were more interested in checking if there were any others in the hotel who needed help."

"Were they in pyjamas or carrying luggage?" asked Harry.

"Neither. They were dressed in normal clothes."

"Did you interview them?"

"No, because by the time we came out they were gone."

"Thanks, John. Where's the owner and the fire chief?"

"In the saloon bar."

Harry found them coming into the office area and introduced himself and Jock. He pointed to the man in civilian clothes. "Are you the owner?"

"Yes. I'm Angus McLean. How might I help?"

"Did all the occupants get out safely?"

"Yes. There were no injuries and we can thank the wonderful fire brigade for their swift action."

"Jock, will you stay here with Mr McLean while I go with the Fire Chief?"

Harry turned to Chief, Fred Blake. "Fred, let's go for a walk and you can give me your assessment of this situation."

"Okay," said Fred. "Let's start in the bar. You'll see that this fire was no accident. Two of the bar windows have been smashed inwards. There was an accelerant and it appears to be kerosene and methylated spirits. The most intense heat was over there, directly opposite the smashed windows. You can see the V-shaped burns up the walls. In the foyer area the top of a lounge chair burned but the floor underneath was okay. The ash smothered that lower area together with some kerosene splashes that didn't burn."

"Did the fire reach upstairs?" asked Harry.

"No. We are just around the corner and arrived here in a few minutes after it started. We managed to confine it to the lower floor and the bottom of one staircase. We got the visitors out the other end."

"From all your experience, Fred, does this look like an insurance scam?"

"No. This hotel has recently been refurbished. All the electrics are brand new and we got the call early. By the time we got here it hadn't travelled far. There was no indication of fire in the kitchen with hot fat or rubbish. Everything was very clean. There was no obvious fuel added except for the kerosene and spirits. It looks more like an act of hooliganism or a deliberate act by someone who was unhappy with this hotel or its owners."

"Thanks, Fred. Is it safe to look upstairs?"

"Yes. Go ahead. There's no structural damage, but go up the other stairs."

Harry called out to Jock. The owner came out of the office and called out. "There's no need to go upstairs. The firemen confined the fire to downstairs."

"Well, that's for me to say, Angus. Come on, Jock. Let's take a look upstairs."

After looking at the two top floors they returned to the office. "Sit down, Angus. We have a few questions," said Harry. "To start with, how many guests were staying here last night?"

"Seven."

"And where is your accommodation register?"

"That got burned in the fire."

"That was very convenient. Was it totally destroyed or just singed?"

"It was sprayed with the kerosene and totally destroyed in the intense heat."

"But seven adult guests slept in two beds. Is that right? The other beds were not touched."

"Some of the guests were playing cards with my wife and me."

"Where's your wife now?"

"She went with friends to their house."

Harry stood up and paced the room. "At three in the morning? Who were those guests? Why are two of the top rooms set up for playing cards and baccarat?"

Angus ran his fingers through his hair. "I don't remember their names; and the register's destroyed. So, I have no record. My family and friends like playing games for fun. There's nothing illegal in doing that."

"First you tell me that you had seven guests staying here and now you tell me that they are family and friends playing cards; and you don't know their names. Don't answer because you and I both know why they were here."

"Honest. They were..."

"Stop, Angus. I've heard enough of that. I'm curious now about another thing. Why would you have a camera fitted to the wall between the curtains opposite the bed in the end room?"

"Oh that," replied Angus nervously. "That would be my son. He likes to take photos of himself in various poses to show off his muscles. I'll go and get it down."

Harry walked towards the door and turned. "There will be no need, Angus. I've already taken it down. I'll take it with me and bring it back later. Come on, Jock. Let's get out of here. I've seen enough for now."

At the main entrance he asked the young constable to follow the owner wherever he went until they returned later. "Don't let him out of your sight. We shouldn't be too long."

Chapter 32
Monday

It was hot and sweaty in the Red Rattler railway carriage. A distressed mother was trying to control her three screaming children. The looks on the other passengers' faces said it all. Why didn't she stay at home or give them a good belting? Two older women shook their heads knowingly. It wouldn't have happened in their day. Harry and Jock removed their coats and sat at the end of the carriage.

"Should we have spent more time there, Harry?" asked Jock. "It didn't look or smell right to me."

"Not now, Jock. Let's go straight to Redfern to the SIB. I want this film developed. We'll ask Tony and his team to get out to Marrickville and go through that place thoroughly. Let the experts do it."

"What will we do?"

"I'll wait for George to develop this film. When I know who's in the photos we'll return to the hotel with Tony's team. I'm not expecting to find the muscle-bound son on this film."

"No," said Jock. "Nobody mentioned a boy in the group that left the hotel and nobody else was in there except the owner and the fire chief when we got there."

The pair walked from Redfern station to the SIB building where they met Tony. Harry explained the situation and asked George to do a rush job on the film. He asked Tony if he could have his team do an inspection of the hotel. Tony looked at Jock and laughed.

"Jock, I want you to ask for a transfer. This bag of rubbish with you thinks he runs the police force. Forget the other ten thousand who urgently want jobs done by us. He creates the problems and then expects us to clean them up."

"I agree with you, Tony but the chief super has assigned me to look after him. I know it's an impossible job but someone's got to do it."

"You deserve a medal. Now, what do you want us to do, Jock?" said Tony without looking at Harry.

"I'd suggest we take Rita for fingerprints, George for photographs and Jack for drugs. Could you spare them for a couple of hours?"

"Certainly, Jock. It's so good to deal with people who know what they're doing and are not too demanding; not like some people I know." Tony looked at Harry with a broad smirk.

Harry got up, walked towards Tony and put his hands around his neck. "Jock, what I'm about to do is justifiable homicide. The state needs to be rid of pests like this one. I'll be doing the community a service." They all had a good laugh.

"Okay, I'll get the team together. Let's go," said Tony.

Harry raised his hand. "Could we wait until George has developed that film? He should be finished by now."

George walked in and laid the still-wet photos on the table. Tony, Jock and Harry looked them over.

Harry snorted. "Well, if that's Angus McLean's son then he certainly knows how to flex his muscles. Look at this."

"It couldn't be his son. That bloke looks as old as Angus," said Jock.

"Let me have a better look at him," said Tony. "I think I know him. It's a bit hard from this angle in this first photo. In that one I'm only looking at his big bum. But the other one where he is lying exhausted on the bed with his big fat belly is a better shot and I can see his face. He surfs at Coogee beach. Always big-notes himself. Tells everyone he can get things done for the surf club but nothing ever happens. I think he's a politician or a local councillor. He's in government somewhere."

Harry patted Tony on the shoulder. "And I suppose you know the girl as well? You being the forensic man, you'd easily recognise that beautiful body."

"I couldn't afford what she would be charging. That jacket and dress on the chair are quality material."

Jock interrupted. "Would that bloke be paying or would this be on the house?"

Harry stepped forward. "That's what we'll ask Mr McLean. Come on, let's go."

Tony, Harry and Jock got in one car while George, Rita and Jack took another one. They arrived at the Fitzroy Hotel to find Angus McLean and Constable John Collins in the office having a cup of tea.

Harry introduced the team and took them for a walk around the inside of the hotel while Jock stayed with the owner.

He left the other team members to get on with their examinations while he went back to the end bedroom where he had found the camera. He pulled back the red lace curtains to reveal two small holes in the wall; one for the cable connecting to the camera and the other as a peep hole, like those in the front door.

In the adjoining room he saw a bookcase covering the holes. On removing some books he saw the other end of the camera cable next to the peep hole. He looked through directly at the bed in the end room. Obviously the cable was used to activate the camera at the right moment.

Harry walked along the corridor to find Rita. He asked her to take prints of the books, cable and the bracket used to fix the camera to the end room wall. After that he wanted her to dust the bedhead and the side tables as well.

Rita looked at Harry with mock horror. "And how was it Harry that you knew about this room? And I thought that you were a good clean-living young man."

Harry laughed. "Okay, Rita, now you know the truth about me. I've got no secrets any more. You forensic people always find the truth. What can I do to redeem myself?"

"I'll have to think about it, Harry. Now, out of my way so I can get on with my work."

Harry went downstairs. He told the constable to have a break for a couple of hours.

"Now, Angus, we need to have a talk; and this time I want the truth."

Jock sat to the side with his eyes fixed on the owner's face but said nothing.

Angus sat back smugly. "How can I be of assistance? I answered your questions this morning."

Harry leaned forward but took his time before speaking. "This time, Angus you'll give me the right answers. To start with, name the guests who were here last night."

Angus fidgeted before answering. "I can't remember and, as I told you earlier, the guest register was destroyed."

Harry said nothing but stared unblinkingly at the owner. After a minute of silence Angus spoke. "Well, there was my wife and son."

Harry remained quiet. Angus looked nervously around the room looking hopefully for someone to rescue him. "The others were casual guests."

Harry stood up and walked behind Angus but said nothing. Angus half-turned. "I think one of the guests was called Adrian, and I think his wife was Mary."

Harry walked to the front and held the back of his chair. Angus looked up at his unflinching stare. "Adrian and Mary have been here before. They come to Sydney from the country. They are nice people."

"What's their surname?" asked Jock.

"I can't remember. It would have been in the register."

"Which bedroom did they sleep in?"

"I don't know. My wife organises that."

"Where is your wife and son?"

"With friends."

Jock stood up. "Are they the same friends who were here last night?"

"Yes. They live in Campsie."

"If they are friends, and they live so close, how come you don't know their full names and why were they booked in for accommodation? Pick up that phone and tell them to get back here now."

Angus stuttered. "They will probably be asleep. We were up late last night and early this morning."

Jock, in his broadest Scottish accent, shouted. "Are you bloody deaf, man? Get on that bloody phone now or I'll send Constable Collins around to their place with the police siren blaring to wake them up and drag them back here. Do you understand?"

Angus lifted the phone and dialled. After some time there was an answer and he passed on the message.

Harry sat back down at the desk. "Now, Angus, I'm going to show you some photos. Look at the first one. Is that your son in that photo? Is that the way he flexes his muscles?"

"That is not my son."

"Then who is it?"

"A guest."

"Does that guest have a name?"

"I can't remember."

Harry laid out all the photos. "Who took those photos?"

Angus shifted forward and then back; perspiration appeared on his brow. "I don't know. The guests probably took them for their own amusement."

"How do they take photos from the camera on the wall, operated from next door, while they are bonking here on the bed?"

"The camera probably had a time-lapse trigger."

"What? In the next room? You must be joking. That fat bloke couldn't trigger the camera in the next room and get to that position in the other room in under ten seconds without dying of a heart attack."

Harry picked up the photos and placed them back in the envelope. "I'll take them down to the local council chambers. The people there know all the local identities. They'll be able to tell me who these people are. I'm sure those on the bed will want a copy of them and want to know where I got them."

Angus got out his handkerchief and wiped his brow. "That won't be necessary. That man is a local council representative. He was a guest here."

"Is the woman a prostitute or a call girl?" asked Harry.

"She's a nice call girl; nothing sleazy."

Harry banged the desk. "Supplied by you free of charge and the stupid local government official didn't know he was being photographed secretly by a hidden camera from the next room."

"Well, I have to have some insurance, don't I?"

"Taking those photos without their permission is a criminal offence. Blackmail is even more serious. I'm sure that when it goes to court the local official will be very angry; especially when the photos appear in *The Sunday Mirror* where they will be seen by his wife and kids."

Angus stiffened but then sat forward with more confidence. "Look, what's wrong with someone having some fun if his wife doesn't know? I provide a service; everyone is happy. This doesn't have to go any further. I can look after you two blokes. I have very powerful rich friends. I know you police never make much money and you take all the risks for everyone else. Be like some of your friends and let me look after you."

Harry stood up and towered over the owner. He spoke firmly and slowly. "Are you telling me that you are offering me and Detective Burns a bribe?"

Chapter 33
Monday

Angus McLean's head moved back and forth searching for something on the desk to hold his attention while his thoughts fought to form a reasonable answer. "No, no. Aah..., no, I wouldn't call it a bribe," he stuttered. "Let's say that it could be like a loan, you know? Aah..., not like a gift, but more like a helping hand. Do you see what I mean?"

Harry and Jock said nothing and waited. Angus looked from one to the other searching for a response but got cold stares in return. "Well aah, let's call it an interest-free loan with no timeline for repayment. How about that? Would that be okay with you fellows?"

Harry turned to Jock and winked. "Detective Burns, does that sound like a reasonable deal to you?"

Jock caught the meaning of Harry's wink and went along. "It sounds very tempting. We poor coppers get paid so little that I can't afford to buy a bottle of Scotch except at Christmas; and I have to share that with my family."

Harry turned to the owner. "And how far would this loan go?"

Angus, now more confident that he had them on the hook, sat forward. "Well, the sky's the limit. Do you want to buy a new car or boat or put a down payment on a new house for you and the missus?"

"And how would this loan be paid to us?" asked Harry.

"I would suggest that we give it to you in cash so that there are no bank records. It's safer all round that way."

"And how long would I have to pay it back?"

Angus spread his open hands. "Take your time. There's no time limit. And maybe you could pay it back in kind, if you know what I mean."

Jock walked around behind Angus. "I'm sorry, but I'm having trouble translating what you're saying into English. Could you explain that a little clearer?"

Angus sat forward. "Look, you two are men of the world. You know what goes on in our business. You scratch my back and I'll scratch yours. Let's look after each other and we'll all be happy."

At that moment Rita walked in with her ink pad and other gear. "I'm going to take Mr McLean's prints, and I want you lot out of here so that I can dust this office."

"Go ahead, Rita," said Harry getting up to stretch his legs. He and Jock walked outside.

Out of earshot of Angus and Rita, Jock turned to Harry. "What an arsehole. He's trying to bribe us by putting us on his payroll."

Harry grinned. "Come on, Jock. You could get yourself a fast red Alpha Romeo sports car and hoon around the streets. All the lassies will be lining up to jump in with you."

"No way. Not on your Scottish heather. But don't tell me you're thinking of taking it?"

Harry turned. "No, but he hasn't told us what he wants in return. Let's play on that a bit further. Let's take our time. We want to know who's behind this. I think he's only the front man for this hotel. He's not the one paying the money."

Ten minutes later Harry and Jock found Angus at the bar cleaning the beer taps. Harry pulled up a stool. "Angus, if I looked up the licence details of this hotel, who would I find to be the owner?"

"I manage it for a company."

"And who might own that company?"

Angus turned to wipe the bottles on a shelf. "I really don't know and don't care. The company is called Big Timber Pty Ltd. They pay me a good salary; it's always paid on time and I do my best to run a good hotel for them."

Jock interrupted. "Didn't you meet these people when you applied for the job?"

"I was approached by two businessmen who offered me the opportunity to run this hotel, and they agreed to pay for my removal from Melbourne plus an extra allowance for other expenses."

"Did those two have names?"

"They introduced themselves as Mr Smith and Mr Jones."

"Had you ever met them before?"

"No."

Harry brushed some ash from the bar. "Angus, you're not paying us this loan, as you call it; the owners are, and we want to know who they are. Otherwise this is no deal. Stop feeding us crap and tell us what we need to know now."

"Honestly, I only know them as Smith and Jones."

Harry stood and leaned on the table. "Angus, you are a Scotsman. So you would appreciate it when I tell you that Detective Burns, here, is an accomplished Gaelic martial arts expert who is a whiz with the dirk and the shillelagh. I'd hate to let him loose on you when he gets angry. What makes him very angry is when someone is not telling him the truth."

Angus looked at Jock who stood with feet apart and arms folded and a cold stare that could pierce metal. Angus tried to explain. "I didn't think it was their real names but, it was such a good offer, I didn't question them."

Harry paced slowly around the room as he thought. "Let you and me work this out, Angus. The company is called Big Timber. Do you think that name might have some reference to Mr Bignall and Mr Woods, two well known identities in Melbourne?"

"That could very well be the case. I've heard they are big in the business world."

At that moment Jack Witherspoon walked in and placed two small sachets on the bar. "Mr McLean, could you explain how those packets got into your hotel?"

"I don't know. What are they? I've never seen them before; must have been brought in by the guests."

Harry stood up, reached into his pocket and pulled out a large pocketknife. He opened the long blade and placed it on the desk, pointing at the owner. "Angus, you don't look like a man who's ever lived in the country on a farm, and therefore you wouldn't understand what we do in the lamb-marking season."

Angus took out his handkerchief to wipe his face. "No. I've always lived in the city."

"Let me explain," said Harry. "When the lambs are born we select the best males and keep them for breeding. They are the good honest-to-God quality beasts. With all the others, we clip their ears with our mark of recognition and, then we castrate them. Do you get my message?"

Harry moved his forearm holding the knife, slowly in arcs across the desk with the sharp end always pointing at Angus. He waited for a response.

"Well, what can I say?"

"You can start by telling us the truth. Those drugs on the desk didn't fall out of the sky; they're not a gift from heaven; they didn't grow on the mushrooms you serve for breakfast; and they didn't hop into those neat, little parcels by themselves. You have them and you supply them to your customers."

George walked in and laid the photos on the desk. "We found some of those drugs in the bedroom where those photos were taken. They contain cocaine. I suggest that we go around and charge the man in this photo with illegal possession and use of drugs. Angus; we can inform him that you said that he brought them into the hotel to sell."

Jock cut in. "Why don't I go and get him and bring him back here for questioning, and then we can compare his and your answers, Angus?"

"I don't think that will be necessary," said Angus.

"Before you go on," said George, dropping more loose packages on the desk; "I found these taped to the back of the bedside tables in your bedroom. You might like to explain why you have cannabis in this establishment."

Angus gulped, took a deep breath and sighed. "They must have been there from the previous owner."

"No," said George. "Rita has just confirmed that the fingerprints on the packages belong to you. I'm going back up to check the other rooms."

Harry looked up at Jock. "Constable, would you have your dirk in its sheath on your belt?"

"Aye, and I'm fecking ready to use it."

Harry looked again at Angus. "Now keep your eyes, ears and brain open and say nothing until I have finished. Do you understand?"

Angus nodded.

Harry closed his pocketknife and put it back in his pocket. "We are about fifteen minutes from Long Bay Gaol down the road at Malabar. You can get three good meals there every day, and free accommodation. I'd say that the judge would be looking at giving you fifteen years, with maybe a couple of years off for good behaviour."

"But I haven't done anything wrong," shouted Angus.

Harry thrust out a cautionary hand. "Don't you dare say another word until I'm finished. The charges against you at this point are: running a house of ill fame, prostitution, illegal gambling, use of drugs, dealing in drugs, pornography, taking explicit photographs without permission, attempting to bribe a police officer and serving alcohol out of hours. And that's only for starters. How do you plead?"

"I only manage this hotel. I don't own it," gasped Angus; head down, exhausted.

"Are you saying that the owners of this establishment direct you to carry out these crimes?"

"The owners are very happy with the management of this hotel."

Harry raised his arms in a mock show of surprise. "I'm sure they are. They are making a fortune out of crime and you are helping them to do that, but as you will not tell us who they are, then you'll have to do the time for them."

"I told you. They are Mr Smith and Mr Jones."

"Yes," said Harry. "And Detective Burns here is Santa Claus and he has some presents for you unless you tell us who they really are."

"Well, I did hear them on one occasion refer to each other as Bruiser and Splinter."

"Now, Angus, that wasn't difficult, was it? I can assure you that was easier than being in a cell with Spud Murphy. He's in for life, so anything he does to you doesn't extend his sentence one day. So, we now know that the owners are Woods and Bignall who have set up a dummy company called Big Timber."

Jock turned to Harry. "Can I put my dirk away now?"

"I'd keep your hand on it. We haven't finished here yet." Harry turned back to Angus. "Now tell me why you have put out a contract on my life."

Angus jumped up and slammed his hands on the desk. "Look, everything in here might not all be above board but there is no way I'd get myself into anything violent like trying to kill you. I didn't even know you until you came here today."

"But you knew that there was a contract out on me. I saw it in your expression when I introduced myself this morning."

Angus fidgeted. "I'd heard there was a contract, but it has nothing to do with here."

"And what about your good friends, Woods and Bignall?"

"You'd have to ask them. I don't know."

"You don't get it, Angus, do you? I don't have to ask them; you do. I'm going to give you a couple of days to think about this. You go and talk to all your mates, here and in Melbourne. If you want to keep running this hotel you'll give me straight answers. You can stick your bribes where they belong, but from now on you're going to give me information. If you tell me one lie I'll arrange a bed for you in the cell at Long Bay with Spud Murphy. Detective Burns and I can be very discreet. We can keep this within these four walls."

Jock walked towards the door. "Harry, can we go? I'm not feeling well in this company."

"Sure, Detective. I think we're done here for today. But we'll be back. We need to go now or you'll be late for your martial arts practice."

Chapter 34
Monday

On the train back to Sydney, Harry and Jock talked about the events at Marrickville. Jock was so angry about the owner with his offer of a bribe. Harry took time to explain the realities of the criminal world and how some police gave in to such temptation. He also explained how some high profile police used those contacts to gather intelligence. Sometimes it was difficult to tell the difference between the bad blokes and the good ones.

"Have you ever accepted a bribe, Harry?" asked Jock.

"No, never. It's not that I haven't been offered one because I have, but on each occasion, I told them where to shove it. I believe now that the big crime bosses know that I won't take a bribe, so they don't bother asking any more."

"But they get away with involving others; and that's not right. Which of our blokes are involved?"

"Jock. Don't go there. If you can't prove it leave it alone. It's very dangerous territory. I look at it this way: I've got a job to do, and at least they see me as straight and honest, and they stay away. It means that I can move in hard if I want without favour to anyone; but I still have to watch my back."

***

When they reached headquarters they were shown immediately into Twain's office.

"Well, what did you two find out about the fire at Marrickville?" asked the chief super.

Harry outlined the day's events and the involvement of Tony Jacobs' team in the investigation.

"Why do you think the hotel was fire-bombed?"

Jock broke in. "It appears to me, sir that it's the result of a battle between the Melbourne criminals and the established ones here in Sydney."

Twain turned. "Is that your opinion, Harry?"

Harry sat back and folded his arms. "I agree with Jock. There is strong evidence that the Melbourne mob are moving in to the suburbs by buying hotels and setting them up as brothels, and drug and gambling centres."

"What evidence have you got to prove that?"

"Well, it was obvious there today, and in the last few weeks I have witnessed the growing influence of the Melbourne mob in suburbs like Newtown, Parramatta and now Marrickville. Intelligence suggests that the next move will be into Lewisham to involve the Italian community."

"Where did you get that information?"

"I've been moving around keeping my eyes and ears open, sir."

"I haven't heard about this. Where's your report?"

Harry opened his hands in mock defence. "There is no report, sir. I was on sick leave."

Twain thumped the desk. "Were you investigating while on leave? How dare you disobey my direct orders."

"Sir, I visited some hotels to enjoy a beer but when I was there I observed certain activities that were suspicious and asked some questions."

"Like what?" Twain demanded.

Harry described his visits to the City Hotel in Newtown and the King's Arms, Empire and Centennial hotels in Parramatta.

"They are very serious allegations. What proof do you have?"

"Not enough to lay charges yet, sir. At this stage it's just strong suspicions. But I'll keep an eye on developments there from now on."

"What else have you got?" Twain snapped.

Jock leaned forward. "We found cocaine and cannabis on site today. Jack, from Tony's team, has the proof and will take the necessary action. The set-up in the bedrooms is obviously designed to accommodate prostitutes or call girls, and the use of the cameras ensures that people of influence are trapped, guaranteeing that they will allow those activities to continue without government restriction."

Allan Twain got up and paced the room. "Is there any evidence that the person caught with the call girl in the photo is receiving a bribe?"

With a tilt of his head Harry answered. "No, but the fact that McLean was willing to offer us a bribe was evidence enough that he would do it with others in exchange for protection."

"But you have no concrete evidence."

"No, but we know it goes on in all areas of the criminal world. I'm sure that some of our own colleagues are on the payroll of the crime bosses."

Twain thumped the desk. "Name them."

Harry put up his hands. "I have nothing at this stage that would stand up in court; but give me time. Something will drop on the table in the future."

"That's not good enough, Harry. If you have no evidence then drop it. I'm not paying you to try to convict our own officers. For God's sake man, the place is full of criminals. Go and find them and lock them up or get out of the service and let someone else do the job. Now leave and let me get on with real work. Be back here in the morning."

Harry and Jock walked around the corridor past the CIB room where they noticed Charlie Rockwell with his feet up on the table having a smoke and a mug of tea.

"Have you got BO, Charlie?" said Harry cheekily. "Did all the others leave to get some fresh air?"

Charlie coughed and blew smoke into the air. "I'll give you bloody BO, mate. And I'll give you a kick up the arse as well for being such a dickhead."

Harry laughed and walked around to give Charlie a pat on the back. "Just stirring you up, mate. I thought you were having a sleep. How's things going, my friend?"

"Not too bad, Harry. I'm just relaxing for a bit before I have to write up my report. Twain's still screaming that I haven't finished mine from the Fisher case."

Harry and Jock sat down at the desk. "Charlie, could you tell us what happened on that day when Fred shot Scarface?"

"Come on, Harry. Let it go. It's over. Bob and Joe have already told you what happened. You don't need me to tell you all over again."

"I'd just like to hear your side. You were closer to the action than Joe when the shots were fired."

Charlie slowly sipped his tea. "Fred and I were walking up to the gate. I was a bit further back behind Fred. I had been checking out the house next door. When Fred got inside the gate, Scarface ran out of the door onto the verandah and fired at Fred."

"What happened next?"

"Fred ducked to the side, steadied and took two shots, hitting him with both. Joe's much younger than me and he reached the verandah first and checked out Scarface but he died soon after."

"What did you see when you got there?"

"Scarface was lying on the verandah with a revolver in his hand. Joe was pressing his hand on his chest."

"What did you do then?"

"I rushed over to Fred to check that he was okay and then I checked the victim to make certain he was dead. Joe told me that he and Bob would stay and call the SIB team in to secure the site. He suggested that Fred and me should go to headquarters to report to the boss."

"Is that what you did?"

"Yes. I didn't want to, but Twain insisted that Fred and me had to be with him when he talked to the media. You know I hate that crap. Anyway, Fred refused to go there and we went to the Marble Bar to relax and unwind. Joe and Bob did the photo stuff later on."

Jock put his mug on the desk. "Charlie, how did you know it was Scarface that took a shot at Harry?"

"We had reliable intelligence that the Melbourne mob were getting worried that Harry was getting too close to their involvement in Sydney."

Jock scratched his head. "But why Harry? Why not me or you or Fred or Joe or Bob?"

"It's well known that Harry has been sniffing around the drug scene over the last few years. It's to do with the cases he's been on. The Sydney boys have been concerned, but the Melbourne lot are more concerned because they think Harry's work might make the suppliers here cut off supply to them."

"But couldn't they get it from their known supplies down south?"

Charlie coughed and farted at the same time. "Sorry about that boys, but it's better out than in. Yeah, about the drugs. They get supplies of heroin and cocaine from overseas through the wharves in Melbourne, but they want to get more of that weed. They want to control the supply from the Riverina."

Harry sat up. "Is that because Leeton is closer to Melbourne than Sydney?"

"It could be, Harry, but the market here is bigger and our Sydney boys have a strangle hold on the supplies so far; and they want to protect it."

"But why would they worry about me, because I'm not in the market and I have no connection with the suppliers or any of the four big blokes involved here?"

Charlie scratched his ear. "Harry, everyone in the business knows that when you get your teeth into something you're not going to give up until you get to the bottom of it. The Melbourne mob think you're on to them and so they want to take you out of the picture. It's as simple as that. You've got to go."

"Charlie, I've worked with you blokes before and after the war. You've been around longer than any of us and have more knowledge in that head of yours than anyone else. How do you see all of this working out?"

"You're right Harry. I've been around a long time, but I won't be around much longer. I'll be looking for retirement in the near future. I'm getting too long in the tooth for this. This is a mug's game and it's time to pass it on to you young blokes. To tell you the truth, it's not going to get any easier. I see this war between Sydney and Melbourne getting worse, not better."

"Why doesn't it happen with other states?"

"Aah, that's easy, Harry. We have better relations with places like Brisbane. The commissioners here and in Brisbane are great mates and they get together to organise meetings with us senior blokes with their top detectives. We had a great time up there on the Gold Coast just before Christmas; and they'll come down here next month. We share intelligence."

"Why don't you do the same with Melbourne?"

"Down there they think that their shit doesn't stink. They say they don't trust us and so we told them to go fuck themselves. There's no way now that we'd work with them unless it's a formal court case."

"Charlie, I've been told that the contract on me is still out there. What chance is there that it will be picked up by one of the Sydney hit men?"

"That's a good question. There are lots of blokes here who'd kill their mothers if the price was right. My advice, Harry is to not trust anyone." Charlie pointed to Jock. "And you, young bugger, have to cover his back. You're a sharp young tack but you need to be more than that. You've got to cover all four corners of the room. Harry's life could depend on that. Do you understand?"

"Hell yes," said Jock with determination. "Harry and I work together as a team. If they take him on they'll also have to deal with me."

"Thanks, Jock," said Charlie. "That gives me more confidence. Harry upsets a lot of people but I've always looked upon him as someone who'll get the job done. I think you two will be a good team, but you'll have to jump some pretty high walls to get through. When I retire I hope you two will fill the gap."

Harry stepped up and shook Charlie's hand. "Thanks, mate for those thoughts. Knowing we have your backing gives us a lot of confidence. We'll be off now."

As they walked to Town Hall station Jock broke the silence. "Harry, I'm confused. The rumours are that Charlie is on the take from some of the big boys in Sydney but in there, he was so helpful and supportive to us. It doesn't make sense."

Harry changed stride. "Nothing much makes sense in this game, Jock. I think Charlie is hoping to get out of this crazy world with his reputation intact. He's probably reflecting on some past indiscretions. He hopes that being helpful to us will result in some redemption. It's like asking for forgiveness without doing so. I might be wrong, but it's worth considering. There's my train. I'll see you in the morning."

Jock waved. "See you, mate."

Chapter 35
Tuesday

When Harry arrived at headquarters Jock was already there writing up his report of the events at Marrickville. "Well, look at goody-two- shoes," he said. "Are you looking for a commendation from the chief?"

Jock smiled. "I decided to get it out of the way while it was fresh in my mind. How about you?"

Harry patted him on the back. "I did mine last night. I'm not a slacker like you."

For the next half-hour Harry and Jock talked with other detectives about their cases and shared their experiences. There was general discussion about the Sydney-Melbourne clashes and the shooting of Scarface. Nothing was said that was new or enlightening. Most of them wanted to know more about the attempt on Harry's life and the bombing of his car.

Jack Tomlinson burst into the room. "Harry, Jock, come quick now."

The two jumped up and followed Jack to the main desk. "There's a bank hold-up in Kogarah. You two are to go there immediately. The criminals are holding the manager and staff hostage in the Commonwealth Bank on the corner of Belgrave Street and Railway Parade. They broke in when the manager opened the back door at nine. There's a squad car waiting at the door with a driver. Get going."

Harry stepped up to the desk. "Jack, call in all the cars from Cronulla, Strathfield, Mascot, Heathcote, Liverpool, Parramatta and Newtown. Tell them to block all roads from the bank. I want that place surrounded. We'll be there as soon as we can."

Constable Dave Smith, the driver, put on his siren and drove at speed down George Street to City Road and on to the Princes Highway. Although most workers were off the road the traffic was still heavy and a lot of the journey was spent on the wrong side of the road. As they approached Kogarah the highway was blocked with a police wagon, side on to the traffic. The constable on duty waved Harry's car through.

They turned off the highway and drove towards the railway line. As they turned into Railway Parade they could see that other police wagons were blocking both exits. Another car blocked Belgrave Street at the other end from the bank.

Harry surveyed the area. "It looks as though the local boys got here quickly. The road exits are blocked and the other side of this road is the railway line. If these blokes are still in the bank we've got them cornered."

Jock pointed out the four uniformed officers. One was standing next to the high arched front door. The second stood at the corner of the building. The third was in a police wagon blocking Railway Parade and the fourth blocked the railway crossing.

Harry asked Dave to stop in Belgrave Street. He and Jock walked to the door of the bank and spoke to the officer.

"G'day. I'm Harry Taylor. What can you tell us?"

"G'day. I'm Doug Edwards. We got the call and have surrounded the area and blocked the roads. We were told to wait for you. We haven't seen any activity in the bank yet, and nobody has come out."

Jock looked around. "I'm going to let down the tyres on those two cars parked over there. They might be the getaway ones."

Harry checked the arched windows and the doors in front and on the side. "Doug, I want two of your men to guard those two doors. In a minute Jock and I will try to get attention through the back door. If nobody responds we might have to break it down."

"I've got a sledgehammer in the wagon. I'll go get it."

When everyone was in place, Harry, Jock and Doug walked to the back door. It was still twenty minutes before the ten o'clock opening time for the bank.

Harry knocked and stood to one side with Jock and Doug on the other side. He noticed a peep hole in the centre of the door. "Open up. This is the police. Put down your weapons and come out. You're surrounded."

He banged on the door again and shouted. "Drop your weapons and come out now."

The door handle turned slowly. Harry and Jock had their Webleys out and armed. They spread their legs, raised their arms and pointed the handguns at the opening. The door opened about three inches. Harry could see a safety chain across the opening and the figure of a mature man in a suit. The man froze. Harry broke the tension. "I'm Detective Harry Taylor. Are you safe? Who's in the bank with you? How many are there?"

The man stuttered nervously. "We're not open for business yet. It's not ten o'clock."

Harry stepped closer to the door. "I couldn't give a stuff about your opening hours. We've been told there's been a robbery at this bank. What the hell is going on?"

The man looked at the handguns and stuttered again. "I think you must be mistaken. It's not this bank. The only people in here are the staff."

Harry lowered his voice. "If there is anyone else in the bank, blink your right eye."

"I'm sorry but you must have been given the wrong message. There is no one else here but me and the staff. We are getting ready to open up."

"Remove the chain and open the door slowly."

"I'm Anthony Egan. I'm the manager. Please come in so I can shut the door again for security."

Harry, Jock and Doug walked in and quickly surveyed the scene, each covering a different sector. There were three tellers in the cages counting out the money. In one office they found the accountant and in another, a man identifying himself as the loans officer. There was nobody else in the building, there or upstairs.

"Anthony, did anyone in this building call the police to say there was a robbery taking place?"

The manager sat down. "No. When one of the staff got off the train, they noticed the police at the end of the street but there certainly hasn't been any robbery here. Wait a minute and I'll ring the other banks in Kogarah."

Five minutes later he came from his office. "No. All the banks are secure. There's been no incident here this morning."

Harry walked into the office. "I'm going to use your phone."

He dialled through to headquarters and spoke to Jack Tomlinson. "Bloody hell, Jack, you've sent us on a goose chase. There hasn't been a robbery in this bank or any other bank in Kogarah. Who told you there was a robbery?"

"We got three separate phone calls to tell us that armed men in balaclavas had smashed the back door of that bank and stormed in. We sent you straight away and organised the road blockages."

"Well call them off. This was a hoax. But if this is a genuine hoax then it was on purpose and probably done to divert us from another job."

"What do you mean, Harry?"

"Tell me, Jack, have there been any other calls come in this morning?"

Jack paused. "Oh hell. A call came in just a while ago about a hold-up of an armoured van."

"Where the bloody hell was it, Jack?" shouted Harry.

"At North Rocks shops. I've just sent Bob Crow out there to investigate."

Harry banged the desk. "Can't you see what's happened, Jack? This was all organised as one operation. The armoured van robbers got three of their mates or wives or girlfriends to call in to tell you that there was a bank robbery in Kogarah. They knew that we would throw everyone into that area. Even the Parramatta police were on their way to cut off Parramatta and Woodville Roads so that they were nowhere near North Rocks. That gave the robbers plenty of time to get the job done before we got the message to go there."

"You might be right, Harry."

"I know I'm right, Jack. Jock and I are going to North Rocks now. You can call off all the boys from Kogarah."

"But I've already sent Bob out there."

Harry had already put down the phone.

Dave put on his siren and arrived in North Rocks in twenty minutes. Harry and Jock walked to the armoured van where they met Bob Crow who had arrived a few minutes earlier. The van was parked outside the Post Office that also served as a branch of the Commonwealth Bank.

"G'day Bob," said Harry. "How do you see this mess? Do you think it's linked to the hoax at Kogarah this morning?"

Bob drew at length on his cigarette, smoke curling past his eyes. "Nah. I don't think so. I just heard about that. Most crims couldn't think that far ahead. I think it was pure coincidence. I just talked to the security guards from the van. They're pretty shook up, so I've left them for a while. I'll talk to the woman in the Post Office."

Harry and Jock introduced themselves to the driver and his mate, took them into a milk bar and got them a chocolate-malted milkshake. When they had almost finished Harry tapped the table with his finger.

"Take your time and tell us what happened."

Both men were still shaken. They fidgeted and looked nervously at every movement and sound. Sweat poured from their foreheads.

"Thanks for that, Harry. I'm Beefy Watkins and this is Freddy Allcott. When we pulled up we did our normal checks and it looked okay. There was only one customer in the Post Office. Freddy waited at the door while I went inside to pick up the boxes. Freddy kept watch while I loaded them. We were about to close the door when two blokes in balaclavas came from around the front of our van."

Freddy broke in. "They took us by surprise. Both of them had sawn-off shotguns. One of them whacked me on the head and took my gun. The other bloke took Beefy's gun and made him carry the boxes to their car. They shoved us in the back of our van, closed the doors and took off."

"How's your head, Freddy?" asked Jock, standing up to look at the damage.

Freddy shook his head. "Not too bad. It could have been much worse but I'm thinking of getting out of this business. My wife can't stand it any more."

"Describe those two blokes," said Harry.

"We couldn't see their faces. One was short and stocky and the other bloke was tall and well built with big hands. On the big bloke's right hand, just above his glove, was a bit of tattoo. I couldn't make out what it was. It all happened so quickly. They weren't mugs; they were experienced. They knew what they were doing."

"Did they speak?"

"Only the big bloke," replied Beefy. "He was the one controlling the action. He seemed to have a slight limp but he was very fit."

Jock interrupted. "How much did they get?"

"We don't know. We've done three pick-ups already this morning, and we had some supplies for the hotels in Parramatta after we finished here."

"That means that it was a big haul. Did they get it all?"

"No, but they would have got a motser. We won't know until the security firm gets here to check it out."

"Could you see from in the van which direction they took?" asked Harry.

"No. From here they could go anywhere. They could have gone to Windsor Road and into Parramatta, or west towards Windsor, or south. Or they could have gone back the other way to Pennant Hills Road and gone in any direction."

"Did you see the car?"

"When we arrived we saw a dark blue V8 Ford Pilot sedan in front of us, but we couldn't see any passengers. It was similar to some of your police cars. They made me load the boxes in that car."

Harry thanked them and walked out to talk to Bob Crow.

"How did you go, Bob? Did you get any information from the woman in the Post Office?"

"No. She didn't see anything. They didn't go in there and she was busy with a customer."

"What about the other shops?" asked Harry.

"One bloke said he saw a blue Ford drive off in a hurry headed for Windsor Road, but he couldn't see their faces; they had balaclavas on."

Jock spoke up. "Bob, you're experienced in this field. What do you make of it?"

Bob wiped his nose along his forearm. "It was a professional job. I'd say it was the Melbourne mob trying to get some ready cash to help set up themselves in their new premises."

"Is there anything more we can do here, Bob?"

"No. I don't think so. I've called in the SIB to work it over but those blokes had gloves on and they're too smart to leave evidence. You lot might as well go back."

Harry shook his hand. "Thanks, Bob. We'll take your advice and move on. See ya."

Chapter 36
Tuesday

As they drove away from North Rocks, Jock wanted answers. "What's this all about, Harry?"

Harry paused before answering. "We've just been played for suckers by two professionals. They got their mates to phone headquarters this morning, all at the same time, to say that two men in balaclavas broke into the Commonwealth Bank in Kogarah. They knew that we would get all of the police cars for miles around to converge on that bank. By doing so it took those police away from the North Rocks and Parramatta area near where they planned to do the armoured van robbery."

"Why North Rocks? It's only a small Post Office with a Commonwealth Bank branch attached. It isn't big enough if they wanted to get a huge haul."

Harry wound down the window. "It wasn't what was in the Post Office. It was the amount they were carrying in the van. The drivers did some pick-ups this morning but they also had lots of cash to deliver to other places. That van was full. The criminals probably had inside information, and there were few people around here to get in the way."

"Where do you reckon they went?"

"A shopkeeper said they headed for Windsor Road. From there they could go anywhere; but we won't find them. They would have ditched the car by now."

Dave turned. "While you've been talking, a report just came through the radio that a car is on fire in Parramatta Park."

Harry tapped the dashboard. "Dave, turn at the next corner. Go past the gaol and then up to the park."

They drove into the park, crossed the bridge to the far end towards Westmead where they saw the fire. The car was well alight. The fire brigade had just arrived. They waited until the brigade got the fire under control.

Jock walked around the vehicle. "It certainly is a dark blue Ford V8 Pilot and therefore it's probably the North Rocks getaway car."

Harry nodded. "You're right, Jock. Look at the pattern of streaks down the bonnet. This car was doused with a flammable liquid. They knew what they were doing. There will be no evidence left in that mess, and the culprits will be long gone by now."

The brigade captain who was standing nearby agreed with Harry.

Jock looked around the park. "I'll go and talk to those people on the verandah across the road. They might have seen something."

Harry pointed to another house. "You do that one and I'll do the other one further down. Dave, you can report in what we've found here."

When they returned, they compared notes. Jock went first. "The old couple saw it all. They couldn't see their faces but one bloke was tall with a slight limp, and the second was shorter and stocky. They said a third man was in another car that looked like a Hillman Minx. It was cream in colour. He looked younger."

"Thanks, Jock," said Harry. "That's the same story as the other couple. They saw them load the boxes into the cream car and take off in a hurry. The couple were too far away to see their faces."

Dave came around to look into the burnt-out vehicle. "Well, Harry, there's not much use hanging around here. You'll get nothing from those ashes there. Do you want me to take you two back to headquarters?"

"No," said Harry. "Get in the car. We're going to Tempe."

"Why Tempe?" asked Dave.

"Because that's where Ben Bomber Earl lives. The descriptions of the two robbers match that of Bomber Earl and Tom Lebovich. Bomber is the expert with bank robberies and armoured van heists. The description of the short bloke fits him. He's done time twice already and it's suspected that he's been involved in a number of others."

Dave drove out of the park and on to Parramatta Road towards the city.

"What about Lebovich?" asked Jock.

"He normally doesn't do bank robberies but, if he or his boss wanted some ready cash to do a drug deal, they'd get someone experienced in van robberies like Bomber to do the dirty work for them. This was well planned and has the stamp of Durante or Tony the Greek. The hoax at Kogarah was a master stroke."

"Could it be the Melbourne mob?"

Harry scratched his nose. "I don't think so because the second bloke sounds like Lebovich, and there's no way that he would work for the southerners. Whatever you think of him he is loyal; and always has been. Bomber Earl and others, like Shooter McGill, will do jobs for anyone who pays the right price."

"What about McGill?" asked Jock. "Would he be the second man this morning?"

"I don't think so. He's about the same size as Tom Lebovich, but the man this morning had a slight limp and that points to Lebovich, not Shooter."

Dave took the shortcut from Strathfield to Tempe. Crossing the railway line at Sydenham he turned towards Edgar Street where he stopped outside a small brick house in need of repair. The brick fence was broken. The iron gate was off one hinge. The gutter on the small verandah was sagging at the end. The blue paint on the door sadly needed a new coat. The sagging sheer curtains inside the three front windows were discoloured a light nicotine colour. The laneway to the right was overgrown with weeds except for two distinct tracks indicating parking for a car or trailer.

The three officers walked up the front steps. Harry knocked on the door. A curtain on the front windows parted slightly and a small face looked through the gap. Harry knocked again. The door opened. A small middle-aged woman in a loose unironed brunch coat, with her hair in rollers and a cigarette hanging from her mouth, peered out. "What do you want? Because I don't want none. So piss orf."

"Hello, Betty," said Harry. "Long time no see. You're still living in the same place, I see."

"Who the fuck are you? I ain't seen you before, so piss orf."

"Betty, I'm Detective Senior Constable Harry Taylor. This here is Detective Jock Burns and the other gentleman is Constable Dave Smith. Is your husband Ben in?"

"Now I know who you are, you fuckin' bastard. You're the one who put my good husband Ben away on a trumped-up charge of bank robbery. It was a put-up job and he did time for nothin' he did wrong. You owe him, ya bastard."

"Betty, Ben was caught red-handed in the bank with a sawn off shotgun and the cash in bags. He was guilty. He did the crime and did the time. Now tell me where he is."

"He ain't 'ere."

"Where is he?"

"He's gone fishin'"

"Where?"

"In the river."

"Which river?"

"Cook's river"

"When did he go?"

"Early this morning. If you look in the lane you'll see that his trailer and boat is gone."

Harry walked to the end of the verandah and saw a cream Hillman sedan. He walked around and looked inside the car and in the boot. There were a few scraps of paper and some greasy rags but nothing to help Harry link it to the robbery. He was about to walk back but turned and put his hand on the bonnet. It was still warm. He stepped back onto the verandah.

"Do you drive, Betty?"

"No way. I couldn't trust you other bastards on the road. I leave the drivin' to me good husband. He's the best."

"Where does he put the boat in the water?"

"In at the recreation reserve; and he goes out on the river into the bay. He'd better bring back a fish or he'll be starvin' tonight."

"Thanks, Betty. We won't disturb you any more. We'll be on our way. Tell Ben we'd like to have a talk with him when it's convenient. Will you do that for me?"

"Tell 'im yourself." Betty slammed the door shut.

Harry told Dave to cross over the Princes Highway and go to the Recreation Park. They parked and walked to the launch ramp. He took down the number plates of all the utilities, trucks and cars with tow bars. The three of them walked to the kiosk, bought pies with tomato sauce and sat on a bench under the big fig tree.

"Why are we down here, Harry?" asked Jock.

Harry wiped the sauce from his chin. "There's no doubt that Bomber was involved in the robbery this morning. The description fits him. The car in the lane next to his house fits the description given by the people at the park in Parramatta. The bonnet of that car was still warm and his wife doesn't drive. He and his mates will be out there on the river or in the bay fishing; the perfect alibi."

"Have we got enough to book him?"

"No, and he knows that. When he comes in he'll be as cocky as a bantam rooster."

"If we can't charge him why are we hanging around here?"

"I want to see if Lebovich is with him. I don't think so because they would have split up soon after they burned the car. They wouldn't want to be seen together after that. This was a very professional job."

Dave pointed out to the water. "There's a small tinnie with an outboard motor and three blokes in it coming across the river towards us now. I wonder if it might be Bomber's boat."

They waited until the boat was driven onto the ramp. One of the men walked to an old utility and backed it and the trailer towards the boat where it was loaded. They pulled the plug at the back to drain the water. As the water poured out, Harry, Jock and Dave walked to the water's edge.

"G'day, Bomber. How was the fishing today? Did you catch any?"

Bomber looked up. "What the fuck are you doin' here? Can't a man have some peace from you bastards? It ain't against the law to catch a few fish, is it?"

"No, Ben. It's okay to fish here. Tom mentioned to me this morning that you might be down here fishing."

"Tom who?"

"You know. Your mate, Tom."

"I don't have a mate called Tom."

"Who are your other mates here?"

"This is my son, Garry, and me mate, George. We go fishin' together."

"When did you go out?"

"We started early this mornin' and we just got back in."

"Did you have any luck?"

"Yeah, look in the boat there. We got two flathead, three mullet and five whiting."

"How do I know that you didn't buy them at the fish shop down the road this morning?"

"Ask the boys."

Garry stepped forward, flexed his muscles, spread his elbows ready for a fight. "Are you callin' my father a liar?"

"Do you think he's telling the truth?"

"I'll fuckin' show you the truth."

He threw a wide-arced left hook. Harry blocked it, brought his left elbow up under Garry's jaw and followed it with a karate kick to Garry's right knee. He went down in a heap, cursing Harry with a string of expletives. Harry stepped on his hand to keep him on the ground. George came forward with guard up but had second thoughts and stepped back.

"Ben, haven't you taught young Garry the moves yet? If he's going to follow in your footsteps he'll want to do better than that; otherwise, the big boys in Long Bay Gaol will have him on toast for breakfast. Now, get going out of here. Betty's waiting to cook those lovely fresh fish you have there. But I might want to talk to you and Tom again about the hold-up this morning."

Bomber Earl, his son Garry and their mate George got into their utility and drove off.

Jock looked at Harry. "What the bloody hell was all that about?"

"We know we don't have enough to book them but I wanted to alert him that we know he and Tom did the job this morning. That means they have to be very careful how they spread the loot. I want them to be worried because that's when they will make mistakes."

"What now?" asked Dave.

"Get in the car and let's go back to the office."

Chapter 37
Tuesday

Dave let them off at the main door and went off to park the car. Harry and Jock asked if they could see the chief super.

Jack Tomlinson dialled through and gave them the all-clear.

"Well," said Allan Twain as he put some papers into a filing cabinet, "what did you find out?"

Harry outlined the day's events at Kogarah, North Rocks and Tempe.

"Did you arrest Bomber Earl?"

Harry stood behind the guest chair. "No. There was not enough evidence that would stand up in court. He had a good alibi."

"What rubbish," shouted the chief. "Bring him in here and work on him. He'll break. He's a miserable skunk. You're too soft on them, Harry. Use all your army skills I've been hearing about. He'll be screaming for mercy in no time. Get young Burns, here to hold him while you work him over. I expect a result before the day is out."

Jock remained at attention, not wanting to get involved when the chief was in such a mood. Harry pulled out the chair. He paused as he looked at the chief, watching for a change in expression. Only when Twain sat down and leaned back did Harry speak.

"No, sir, I'm not going to work him over because I'm not going into a court to be ridiculed by the defence lawyer and the judge for a badly presented case. Bomber will have witnesses who'll say he was nowhere near North Rocks, and he'll tell the court that we were there watching them come back to the park in their boat. I'll wait. He'll make a mistake and then I'll have him."

"What nonsense." Twain turned to Jock. "What have you got to say for yourself, young man? You were there. What do you think we should do?"

Jock stiffened. "With all due respect sir, I think Detective Taylor is correct. I think we should bide our time."

Harry interrupted. "I'm more interested whether Tom Lebovich was there this morning. If we can prove that, then we will have a direct connection to the person who organised this stunt."

Allan Twain looked to the ceiling. "I don't think Lebovich would have been involved. It's not his style. He's a standover man, not a bank robber."

"It's for that reason he would have linked up with Bomber to do the job and split the spoils. I believe he was working for one of the big boys here in Sydney."

"What utter nonsense. I heard that Bomber Earl is working for a new Melbourne lot. Rumours say that he's changed sides. Now bring him in and belt the hell out of him until he confesses."

"No, sir. I'll get him but it'll be my way." Harry sat down.

"Bloody hell, are we breeding a bunch of wimps here? Maybe a stint back in uniform on night shift down at the Cross will do both of you the world of good. Get out of here before I change my mind. What's the world coming to?"

Harry remained seated. "Before we go, sir, could you tell us your views on the changing nature of drug supplies in the city and whether that might be the main reason for the current battle between the Sydney and Melbourne mobs?"

Allan Twain snorted. "We've always had drugs here but we have kept it under control. You should know because you've locked up a few of them. Why all the attention now?"

"Well, sir, I believe that there's a bigger influx of drugs from overseas and locally than ever before, and Melbourne are trying to move in to get a bigger slice of the action."

"What evidence have you got?"

"My informants tells me that there's a lot more activity on the wharves involving the importation of cocaine and heroin by ship. Up till now that supply has been controlled by the four big bosses here. Rumour has it that there is now more supply coming in from America because at least two of the big operators here have links with the Mafia in the States. That is in addition to the usual supply from France."

"Who's your informants?"

"With due respect, sir, I will keep that information to myself at the moment. They are reliable but very nervous, and I don't want anything to upset our arrangement."

"What poppycock. Don't you trust me?"

"That's not the point. I'll protect his identity until I have more information."

Twain thumped the desk. "Unless you can put evidence on the table I'm not interested. Get out of here and put boots on the ground. Do some real police work and stop wasting my time."

"If I could waste your time a little longer, sir, I want to bring to your notice the sudden increase in the use of cannabis. What was once a recreational drug for rich ladies is now becoming a major problem and there is an increased supply from local sources."

"What are you talking about? Cannabis is nothing. It was only recently made illegal. It's fairly harmless, and if a few ladies get a bit high, and have some fun why should we be worried. There are more serious crimes to deal with. Stop wasting my time."

Harry stood up and pointed to the map of New South Wales on the wall. "I believe, in addition to Queensland, the major suppliers are here in the Hawkesbury Valley, on the Central Coast and down here in the Murrumbidgee Irrigation Area around Leeton."

"What evidence is there?" shouted the chief.

"When I was on sick leave I went to Londonderry, Yarramundi, Wiseman's Ferry and the Macdonald Valley. I saw it for myself. I believe we should nip it in the bud before it gets a bigger hold."

Twain brushed a stray hair from his uniform. "Look, I know that some people have been smoking these things for ages. What do you call them? Cigares de joy? But they're not causing any real harm. Let them have a little fun and you two get on to the real crimes in this city."

"The difference now, Sir is that the major crime bosses are moving in on this trade. Most of those supplies are being funnelled through the markets and I believe that both Angelo Romano and Boss Gabor at the Haymarket are heavily involved."

"So? What's new?"

Harry sat down again. "Rumour has it the Melbourne mob are wanting more of the action. Up till now I believed that Romano and Gabor have been fairly loyal to Whispers, Tony the Greek and, to a lesser extent, to Rosie and Squeaky, but they are brutal, hard men. When the southerners offer them a better deal, loyalty goes out the window. This could lead to a major battle."

"What do you suggest?"

Harry raised his head in hope. "I suggest, sir that you give Jock and me permission to travel to Leeton to investigate the growth of this weed and trace the supply and money trail back here, and then do the same with the growers in the Hawkesbury and Central Coast."

The chief stood up. "Not on my time you won't. We have murders, bank robberies, rapes, armoured van heists and other big crimes happening on our door step, and you two want to junket off to the country to see some of your mates and have a holiday. Nice try, Harry, but I didn't come down in the last shower. Now, get out of here."

As Harry and Jock walked out, Joe Cross caught up to them in the corridor. He laughed and slapped them on the shoulders. "And how was the ring-a-ring-a-roses this morning, eh? Or was it hide and seek you two were playing?"

"Okay, Joe, have your fun," said Harry. "We might have missed them this morning but we'll get them. Have you got a minute? Tell us how you see the current situation."

The three of them went into the tea-room, got a cup and sat down. Joe put his feet up on the table. "There's a bit of argy-bargy going on but it's not as serious as everyone is making out."

Jock took a sip. "I reckon the Melbourne mob are moving in big-time and the locals are not going to let it happen. I can see that it will end up in a major dust-up before long."

Joe leaned back. "You're right, Jock, but so long as the southerners keep to the hotels in the suburbs and leave the Sydney boys to control the city and the race game, then things might be okay. There'll be some minor scuffles, and some might die, but so long as they don't hurt the public, who cares?"

"But, as you say, they will kill each other."

"Better them doing it than us. We're safer watching it happen and then move in to lock up the culprit after the event."

Harry looked exasperated. "Joe, you've got better contacts in this field than us. What are you hearing on the grapevine?"

Joe lit a cigarette and blew clouds of smoke into the air. "Look, there have always been drugs ever since Pontius Pilate was banging nails into the cross, but mostly they have done very little harm. What's wrong with a few people having a bit of fun?"

"But the way I see it, Joe," said Harry, "is that it's beyond just having a little snort or a puff of some weed on occasions. This is now big-time with the top criminals about to have a war over who will control the supply and distribution in this city."

Jock added his comment. "Australia has been the biggest user of heroin in the world for years so it has always been a problem. Now we have this extra concern with the weed. Throw in the entrance of the Mafia from America and I think we have a real problem."

Joe looked at Jock with a half-sneer. "That's schoolboy stuff, Jock. Look, you've got more people killing themselves on grog and cigarettes, and they're legal, so why are you hell-bent on stopping a few people having a bit of fun with this other stuff?"

"Because they are not having turf wars over grog and cigarettes, that's why."

Joe sat up. "Okay, a few of the bad boys will do some damage to some other bad boys and one or two might disappear as a result. The good thing is that they are not hurting the public, and if they get rid of someone from the other side, it'll save us from doing it. And if they die, it'll save the government a stack of money looking after them in gaol."

Harry interrupted. "Who do you think was involved in the Marrickville fire-bombing yesterday and the hold-up this morning?"

Joe thought for a minute. "Bomber Earl was the man today."

"What about the second man? It looked like Tom Lebovich."

Joe paused. "Nah. I don't think so. It's not his style. I've never known him to get involved in that stuff. I reckon it'd be more like someone like Billy Knobbs. He's been a bit down on his luck lately with his gambling debts to Tony the Greek, so he'd do anything to keep on Tony's good side."

"What about the fire at Marrickville, Joe?"

"Ah, forget about it. It's probably some local who's angry about the extra noise at night, or another pub getting jealous about the extra competition. They'll sort it out."

"Thanks, Joe. You've been really helpful."

"I'll give you two a bit of advice. I used to do some refereeing of rugby league and an old fellow ref gave me some good advice. He said 'don't stick your head too far into the scrum looking for trouble or you'll be the one who gets punched. Stand back and you can see all the action.' I found that was good advice also for this job. Now, I'm off. I've got some serious drinking to do. See ya."

Chapter 38
Wednesday

Harry arrived at work early. He wanted to write up his report of yesterday's events before starting the new day. He had hardly started when Jimmy Wilkins, who was filling in for Jack on the main desk, came bursting in to tell him he was needed immediately at Woolloomooloo. There had been a drive-by shooting at the Elegant Lady nightclub.

"You're needed there now, Harry," said Jimmy. "The local police have secured the site but the boss wants you to take over the investigation."

"Okay, Jimmy, I'm on my way. When Jock Burns gets in, tell him to follow me. Call Tony Jacobs and tell him to send his team there as soon as possible."

Harry took the keys to a car and drove to Bourke Street and parked beside the club on the corner. It was an imposing red-brick building with three storeys and a closed-in balcony upstairs on both sides. On a corner of the first floor there was a large arched window. There were eight windows along each side of the first and second floors. The main entrance was on the corner with service doors along the side street. A hinged lift -up door on the footpath was the entrance to the cellar.

Harry noticed four of the glass panels in the doors downstairs and two of the upstairs windows facing Bourke Street were shattered. There were two bullet holes in the front door. He approached the constable on duty. "G'day, I'm Harry Taylor. What can you tell me?"

Constable Gerry Sampson shook Harry's hand. "G'day, Harry. We got a call this morning that there had been a shooting at the nightclub so we got here as quick as we could. The manager, Arthur Birch, and his wife, met us here. They said that someone drove along Bourke Street and sprayed the side of the building with what sounded like machine-gun fire. No one was hurt."

Harry went inside where he found the manager and his wife. The man was nervously pacing the floor while the woman, sitting at the dining table, puffed anxiously on a cigarette. The room was set up as a top-class restaurant. The tables were covered with starched white linen tablecloths, silver cutlery and fine crystal glasses. The chairs were upholstered in burgundy velvet. A piano and microphone were on a small stage in one corner. Swinging doors led to the kitchen in the far corner.

Harry asked them to describe the shooting.

Arthur wiped his brow with a napkin. "We were sound asleep. We had been up until three this morning. After our last customers left we cleaned up and set up the restaurant. You can see it's ready for tonight."

"I'm Kathleen," said his wife, stubbing out her cigarette into a crystal bowl. "I thought at first it was a motorbike backfiring, but then I heard glass breaking so I jumped out to see what the commotion was. By the time I got to the window it had stopped. Whoever did it must have been in a car or on a bike."

At that moment Jock Burns came in, introduced himself and sat down. Soon after, Tony Jacobs, together with Rita Flynn, who did fingerprints, George Black, the photographer, Jack Witherspoon, the drug expert, and Archie Ingram, the ballistics specialist, came in.

Tony introduced his team. "Where do you want us to start, Harry?"

Harry pointed to the entrance door. "Archie, I want you to start outside because some of the shells would have hit the walls, and then you can do the top two floors as some of the windows up there were shattered."

The manager stood up. "You won't have to go upstairs. There's nothing there. The damage was all at this level."

Harry turned to face Arthur. "Arthur, I noticed some windows upstairs were broken. The team will cover all levels. Are there any guests upstairs?"

"No."

"Then there's no problem. Go to it, Tony. Jock, you go upstairs and help the team. I'll be up shortly."

Harry turned back to the managers. "Now, Arthur and Kathleen, who have you upset enough that they want to shoot up this joint?"

Arthur half-covered his mouth with his hand. "I can't think of anyone. I think it must have been some hoon showing off. He was probably drunk and letting off a bit of steam after a night on the grog."

"Do you think it might have been someone who lost money on your gambling tables and wants revenge?"

"We don't do gambling."

"Or could it be someone who didn't get satisfied by one of the call girls who visit here?"

Arthur wiped his brow again. "We don't do call girls here. If a lady comes here and meets a man and they go off together, that's none of our business, is it?"

"Could it have been someone who got high on drugs from one of the suppliers who work in this area?"

Kathleen interrupted. "Well it certainly wouldn't have happened here. I won't tolerate drugs on these premises."

Harry looked around the room. "You have a nice set up here. I suppose you have to book well in advance."

Arthur stood up and waved his arm around the room. "We are very popular and we serve only top-class food and drinks. We are booked out well in advance, but we can find a table for you and your lady."

"No thanks, Arthur. It'd be way out of my salary range."

"It'll be on the house, Harry. It'll be our pleasure. Just let me know what night you want to come."

Harry gave him his steely cold stare and waited until Arthur wiped his forehead again. "I'll leave you two here and go upstairs."

On the next level he found Tony, Archie and George doing their thing. "Well, what have we got here? I bet Arthur downstairs will tell us that these baccarat and card tables and roulette wheel are for family entertainment."

Tony pointed to the corner. "I'd almost believe that if it wasn't for the well-equipped bar. They've got everything."

Archie came over with a shell in his hand. "This one is squashed, but it's a .45. And if their description of a machine-gun attack is right it would appear to me that an Owen gun was used."

Harry reminisced. "My favourite weapon. We used them in the Islands. It was the ugliest thing around but, you could throw it in the mud and dirt and, it would still fire. It was the best weapon for close-quarters fighting in the jungle. But it's only available to the army."

Archie turned back. "My information, Harry, is that some Owen guns were stolen from the army camp with the land mines and other weapons."

"That means it's big-time crims involved, not some wild hoon on a drunken spree. I'll go up to the top level."

Tony laughed. "I wouldn't if I was you, Harry. You are so young and innocent. I don't want your mind polluted like that."

Harry climbed the stairs where he found Rita and Jack walking along the corridor from room to room.

Rita smiled and took him by the arm. "Now I want you to close your eyes, Harry and dream of your wildest fantasy. I'll let you open them at each room and at the end of the corridor you'll have to pick which one you like best."

Harry reluctantly let her guide him to the first bedroom. The walls were black with photos of nudes in various seductive poses. The ceiling was bright blue with stars. The four-poster bed was draped in sheer lilac and purple material. A whip and leather straps were lying on the silken gold bedspread which was adorned with an image of a tall attractive nude with knee-high leather boots and fish-net stockings.

Harry turned. "Rita. I thought you were all pure and innocent and here you are leading me astray. Are the other rooms better or worse than this one?"

"That's for you to find out. Close your eyes. Come on."

The next room was themed with serving maids in white caps, four-inch-deep aprons and knee-high white stockings. The third room had an Egyptian theme with a nude Cleopatra being attended to by well-built eunuchs. The fourth had images of young girls in scanty school uniforms. The fifth showed a nude Johnny Weissmuller-like Tarzan swinging from the jungle over a skinny-dipping Esther Williams.

"Rita, how could you? My mother warned me about girls like you. She told me to be careful of girls who led me into the bedroom. She said they're all brazen hussies wanting only one thing."

The two of them burst out laughing. "Have you had enough, Harry or do you want to look at the other corridor?"

"No, Rita, it might be too tempting for a young innocent boy like me. Have you got any prints?"

"Yes, plenty, but they might be useless unless we can match them with a suspect we bring in for questioning."

"Good work, Rita. Thanks for that." Harry turned to Jack. "And what have you got, mate?"

Jack handed a packet to Harry. "These sealed packets of condoms appear to have white powder in them."

"Wow," said Harry. "Does that mean he gets a hit at both ends?"

"Seems so. And I found some hash in one of the bedrooms in the other wing."

"Does this look like stuff a man would buy off the street or is it a professional preparation?"

Jack laid out the drugs on the table. "All these samples have been prepared in neat Cellophane packets. This is not the work of a street seller."

"Could it be that this joint is supplying drugs to their customers as part of a deal to get them here for the gambling?"

"Not conclusive but it looks that way."

"Alright you two, take Tony, Archie and George downstairs and I'll meet you on the ground floor with the managers."

When they had gathered in the dining room Harry started the questions. "How long have you been running a gambling den?"

Arthur Birch snapped back. "We don't run a gambling den. All of that equipment is used by the family. We get enjoyment playing for fun and there's nothing illegal about that. When our kids and some relatives come to stay, we play. That's all."

"Do the kids stay in the bedrooms upstairs?"

"Yes. They enjoy the atmosphere of the rooms. It's a fun thing."

"Do your kids do drugs?"

Kathleen slapped the table. "No way. Not in our place. We have brought up our kids properly. There's no way I'd let that thing happen in my house."

Harry stood up and walked behind them. He paused, waiting for them to turn and face him. They didn't. "Then tell me why there are drugs in some of the bedrooms."

Kathleen snapped her head around. "You must have planted them there. I've heard you coppers do that to get a conviction. Well, you're not going to do that to us. I'll fight you in court if you try that on me."

Harry looked up. "Jack, put the evidence on the table."

Jack spread the condoms and other packets on the table. "You might like to explain these." he said.

At that moment Joe Cross came in the front door.

Chapter 39
Wednesday

Joe walked to the bar, poured himself a glass of squash and sat back at the table. "Hi everyone. Now, where are we up to?"

Harry watched Joe's entry with his obvious attempt to show that he owned the joint and that he was in charge of the situation. "G'day, Joe. It looks like you need a bit of the hair of the dog. Did you have a late night? But don't worry; we've got everything under control here."

Kathleen stood up, walked to the bar and poured a glass of water. "Thank goodness you're here, Joe. You know that we run a good nightclub here and we wouldn't do anything illegal. These mongrels here are trying to plant drugs on the premises and stitch us up for something we didn't do. And I'm not going to put up with that nonsense. Why don't you take over this investigation? We trust you."

Joe took another sip of his squash. "Well, Kathleen, Detective Taylor is a fine investigator and he's in charge. I'm sure that he's just trying to find the truth, so I want you to answer his questions and cooperate." He sat back, lit a cigarette and put his feet up on the next chair.

Tony Jacobs pointed to the condoms and other packages. "There's nothing illegal in using condoms. In fact, men should use them more often to save unnecessary back door abortions. The illegal back room operators around here are causing untold damage to young women because the doctors won't do it for them. However, we will be analysing the powders in those packets and the other samples when we get back to the laboratory."

Arthur wiped his brow again. "We didn't put them there. If a customer stays here and brings in drugs you can't blame us. Tell them, Joe. You know we're clean."

Joe puffed his cigarette and took another sip but said nothing.

"Let me clear something up here, Arthur," said Harry. "You two are only the managers. Who owns this establishment?"

"It's owned by a company."

"What's the name of the company and who owns it?"

"I don't know. Kathleen and I and the staff get paid by the company. An accountant arrives here each fortnight and hands out the monies. I give him the details of the staff wages and the accounts for all the supplies. It's as simple as that."

"Would the owner be a gentleman known locally as Whispers Durante?"

"I don't know. It's got nothing to do with us. We just mind our own business and run a good nightclub."

"Do you have your wages book?"

"We don't keep a wages book because most of the staff are casual. I give the accountant a list of the work done and he gives me the money to pay the workers in cash. It's all above board and nobody complains."

Harry looked at Kathleen. "Tell me about the bedrooms upstairs. Are you running a brothel or do call girls rent those rooms from you by the hour?"

"How dare you suggest that. We run a respectable place. We have accommodation rooms upstairs. Many people from the country and interstate like to stay here; especially in the school holidays and when the Royal Easter Show and the Sheep Show are on. After a tough year on the farm they love to come here for a bit of excitement. You can't blame them for that. There's nothing wrong with a bit of fantasy. The wives love it."

George cut in. "Can they have their photograph taken in the rooms?

"I suppose they can if they bring their own camera."

"And are they allowed to use the gambling tables?"

"Sure, if they like, but they only play amongst themselves as a family. A bit of fun."

Arthur spoke up. "Why the hell are you asking all these questions about the accommodation? There's been a bloody shooting. We could have been killed and you're worried about beds and sheets. I think you've got a real problem."

Harry paused while he slowly looked the manager up and down. When Arthur pulled out his hanky again Harry spoke. "That's the point, Arthur. The person who riddled the side of this building with .45 calibre bullets is no amateur, and obviously has a score to settle."

"I don't believe that. Nobody has ever complained about our service."

"Let's speculate," said Harry as he stood and paced around the room. "Would he have got food poisoning in the club? I doubt it because as I can see here, this is a very clean setting. Would he have lost his life savings gambling? But you've told me that doesn't happen here. Would he have been ripped off by some prostitute or their pimp? Again you have told me that there are no prostitutes or call girls here."

"Well," said Arthur, "that settles it doesn't it? There is no sound reason, so it must have been just a wild hoon showing off and it just happened to occur outside here."

"That's good thinking, Arthur but let's take it one step further. I've heard that there are nasty people from down Melbourne way who want to move in to Sydney, and they want to do away with good places like yours because you're too big a competition to them. What do you say to that?"

"I think that's utter nonsense. We've been well established here for years. We have very important clientele. I doubt that anyone would be stupid enough to try to wipe us out. Even some of your top policemen come to our nightclub to celebrate a special event with their wives. I'm sure they wouldn't tolerate someone else shooting up this place while they are sitting here drinking a celebratory champagne and listening to fine entertainment."

"Is there any reason that the shooter is targeting you or Kathleen? Have you got outstanding debts or upset anyone lately?"

Arthur was indignant. "Definitely not. I always pay my debts on time. If we have customers who drink too much and upset our other patrons we have security staff to deal with them. I don't get involved."

"And who are they?"

"We have a number of security staff. We rotate them."

"Thanks very much, Arthur and Kathleen. We're finished here now. Senior Sergeant Jacobs and his team will work on the material collected. Myself and Constable Burns will look into other related matters." He turned to Joe. "Are you coming with us, Joe or have you got another case?"

Joe dropped his boots off the chair. "I'll see you later, Harry. I've got a few things to do down this end of town first."

As Harry and the team stepped out onto the footpath a tall, well-built man with a slight limp approached. He tugged the brow of his hat forward over his eyes as he attempted to move past the team into the building. Harry recognised him as Tom Lebovich.

"Hello, Tom. How are you today? You're a bit late, mate."

Lebovich looked up, sneering. "What do you mean?"

"Arthur and Kathleen have been waiting in there for you. There's been a drive-by shooting."

"I don't know what you're talkin' about. Now, can ya get out of my way? I've got more important things to do than stand around talkin' to you."

Harry held up his hand. "By the way, Tom, why didn't you go fishing with Bomber Earl the other day? He and Garry got a good catch. We had a good yarn on Tuesday. You could have taken some home to the missus."

"Get out of my way or I'll call the police."

"Nice try, Tom. You have a good day."

Tom pushed past into the club, almost knocking over Rita Flynn and causing her to drop her gear on the footpath.

After Tom had disappeared inside she asked. "What was all that about, Harry? What a rude bastard."

Harry explained to the group the events on Tuesday at Kogarah, North Rocks and Tempe. "I'm sure that the two who pulled off that heist were Bomber Earl and Tom Lebovich. It was a very professional job and I suspect that Lebovich was there on the orders of Whispers Durante, the owner of this fine nightclub here."

"Why didn't you arrest them?"

"Because they had a good alibi. The hoax at Kogarah gave them time to pull off the robbery and get back in a fishing boat at Tempe by the time we caught up with them."

"Why the little tête-à-tête with him there?"

"I wanted to let him know that I'm on to him and it won't be long before I get him. I just made it clear to him that I know he was there."

"What does he do in the club?"

"He's the hit man, bouncer and standover merchant. He does the dirty work for Whispers and Rosie and a few other nasty men."

"Aren't you playing with fire, Harry considering what has already happened to you?"

"Yes, Rita but I've got a good extinguisher on my belt."

"Be careful."

"I will, and I've got Jock here as backup. They're not going to take him on. He sprinkles dry Scotch thistles on his cereal every morning for breakfast."

Rita laughed and walked off to catch up with Tony's team.

Harry and Jock drove back to headquarters and spent the remainder of the day analysing the evidence and preparing their reports. At the end of the day Harry took the train back to Stanmore. As he walked out of the station he saw Eileen crossing the street. He quickened his pace and caught up.

"Hi, Eileen. Have you had a busy day?"

"Oh, hello, Harry. Yes I have. I'm still getting used to the new work. It's very demanding but I'm getting there. How about you?"

"Yes. We had a major investigation today so it'll be good to get home to relax."

"I've got a good idea, Harry," said Eileen, looking up into Harry's face. "I cooked up some corned silverside last night and have enough left over for both of us tonight. Would you like to come over? I can do some salad to go with it and a rich customer at work left a bottle of a new wine from Portugal called Mateus and the boss gave it to me. I don't know what it's like."

"That sounds better than a cold sausage and tomato sauce and a bottle of beer. I'll be over shortly."

Harry had a shower, got changed into casual gear and walked to the house.

Eileen was fussing around the kitchen sink. "Harry, would you do the honours and open that bottle? I wouldn't know how to do it. I don't know what it's like but the man said it was very nice. I only have an occasional sherry. Tell me how your day went."

Harry uncorked the bottle and poured two glasses. "We had a major investigation today. There was a drive-by shooting down at Woolloomooloo last night and we had to assess the damage."

"If you can carve the silverside, Harry I'll finish the salad. Gee, that's dangerous work. It doesn't sound too safe to me."

Harry sharpened the knife on the steel and cut the meat finely. They sat at the small round table covered with a starched linen tablecloth and a small vase of petunias in the centre. Harry raised his glass of Mateus in a toast. "Thank you, Eileen for inviting me here. This is such a welcome relief after a difficult day."

"Tell me about it, Harry. I'm interested to know."

"Well, to start with, I have a confession to make. I'm not an insurance agent. I'm a detective and my name is not Forsythe, it's Taylor."

Eileen sat back startled. "But why the cover up?"

"I'm genuinely sorry that I had to tell you a myth but I was working undercover. I was the detective who was shot on New Year's Day. My injuries were from the shattered glass and pellets from the shot. I'm now okay and back on normal duties."

Eileen took a gulp of her wine. "But are we safe here from whoever was trying to kill you?"

"Relax, Eileen. Nobody knows where I live; not even the commissioner. And, if anyone asks, I'm still Mr Forsythe, the insurance agent."

Eileen settled back enjoying the taste of the wine. The two of them had a relaxed time talking about their life experiences while they enjoyed the meal and followed it with an ample helping of apple pie with cream. After dinner they moved to the large two-seater lounge where they spent the remainder of the evening.

Chapter 40
Thursday

"You look very relaxed, happy and pleased with yourself this morning, Harry," said Jock with a smile as he poured two mugs of tea. "You must have gone to bed early last night."

"Yes, something like that," replied Harry. "Now, let's get on with this report."

"Harry, can you tell me what the hell Joe was doing there yesterday? He didn't look at anything. He didn't ask questions. He made no comment and he didn't want to come with us to follow up. He seemed bored by the whole exercise."

"You have to realise, Jock that some of the top dogs in the CIB have close connections with the people who operate illegal casinos, brothels and drug outlets. They use those people as informants."

"But isn't that illegal?"

"Jock, men like Joe Cross, Fred Sherman, and to a lesser extent, Charlie Rockwell and Bob Crow, bring more top criminals to justice than anyone else. They can do that because they get the best information."

"But that means they're mixing freely with the top criminals in places like where we were yesterday."

"Don't worry, Jock. They're in good company. Some of our most prominent politicians, police, lawyers, judges and business leaders are in there with them."

"But those politicians are always on about cleaning up crime. They publicly preach about morals and family values and the teachings of Christ and they condemn gambling, prostitution, drugs and the evils of the demon drink."

"Jock, we're going to make a good detective out of you yet. You're right, they're all hypocrites. But that's the reality of life in this big city. Welcome to the real world."

"How do you feel about it, Harry?"

"Well, there's no denying that the CIB boys get results. They have a record equal to no others and the politicians, media and public love them for putting away some of the nastiest criminals in this country. They are the champions of the police force. If that means mixing with the meanest bastards in illegal casinos, then that is the price we pay for results."

"Would you do that, Harry?"

"I have informants, but not in those places."

"Have you ever visited those casinos?"

"On occasions, but I've never accepted offers of a night with the girls or free holidays or any other gift. I use my visits to get information; to check on who's with who."

"We should have locked those two up yesterday. It was obvious that they run an illegal casino with prostitutes and drugs."

"Relax Jock. No one was gambling when we were present. There's no law against having that equipment for your own personal use. No prostitutes were present on the premises nor any customers, and it would be difficult to refute their statement that the drugs were left by people having a holiday in those rooms. The judge would laugh us out of court."

"Well, what are we going to do?"

"We will keep our eyes and ears open and do our job. They'll make a mistake and that's when we move in. Be patient."

"But what about the drive-by shooting?"

Harry pointed his finger at Jock. "Now you're getting to the main point. Nobody goes around firing off an Owen gun or similar weapon at a building, well known as an illegal casino, drug outlet and call girl centre, just for kicks. This is serious."

"Is it the Melbourne mob?"

"Well I don't think it's one of the other Sydney bosses. They seem to have a mutual agreement about who controls what. I can't see Rosie Travener, Squeaky Walsh or Tony the Greek trying to take on Whispers Durante. He's got more fire-power and influence than the other three put together. I've seen them together at the races at Randwick and Canterbury, and they all seem happy with each other."

"Which of the Melbourne mob would have done this job?"

Harry thought for a moment before replying. "I don't know. If I had to guess I would say it is most likely the person who owns the Fitzroy Hotel at Marrickville. I suspect this is a revenge attack for the fire-bombing of that hotel."

"And who might that be?"

"We still need to check out the business register for that hotel and the others at Newtown and Parramatta. I'll get you to do that, Jock. You could find it difficult because you might find a couple of dummy companies before you get back to the original owners. Accountants these days are getting clever at running paper trails here and overseas to hide the real identity of the owners. They set up dummy companies at places like Norfolk Island and transfer monies from one to the other under false names."

Jock stood up to stretch his legs. "And what then, if we find out who they are?"

"I doubt they would have pulled the trigger. They all have their bodyguards and they can hire hit men to do any job they want. They are the people we'll start tracking."

At that moment, Jimmy Wilkins came to the door. "Harry, I've got some woman on the phone who's screaming her guts out and wanting to cut your balls off. Can you speak to her and get her out of my hair? I don't know what she's on about."

"Sure, Jimmy. What's her name?"

"I think she said Beth or Betty, but I'm not sure."

"Put her through."

Harry picked up the phone. "Hello."

"You stinking rotten fucking bastard. What have you done with my Benny? Shits like you should be shot on sight."

"Is that Betty Earl speaking?" asked Harry.

"Of course it is, you dickhead. Who else would it be? You know what I'm on about. Now what have you done to him?"

"Just hold your horses, Betty. I don't know where Ben is. Tell me what's happened."

"My Ben went down to the pub yesterday at lunchtime for a drink and he ain't come back. Garry went lookin' for him this morning and found his car at Marrickville. His keys were in the car but he's not there."

"Are you at home now?"

"Yes. Where else would I be?" she shouted.

"Stay there. I'm coming out. I'll be there in half an hour."

Joe Cross walked into the room, went to the bench, got a mug and poured some tea.

"G'day, Joe," said Harry. "I've got to go out on an emergency. Could you talk to Jock and give him your thoughts from yesterday about the shooting at the Elegant Lady, and he'll write up the report for the chief. Thanks, mate."

Joe nodded and sat down. "How long will you be?"

Harry stood up to leave. "Don't know. It could be all day."

He picked up the keys from the desk and drove to Tempe. He was met at the door by Ben's son, Garry, and was escorted into the kitchen.

"About bloody time," shouted Betty. "I'm goin' out of my mind with worry. What have you done to my Ben?"

"Honestly, Betty I've done nothing to Ben. If he's missing let's get the ball rolling and try to find him."

"Why would you want to help? You hate him."

"I don't hate Ben. I don't like what he does but that's no reason to dislike him as a person. Now, Garry, tell me what happened last night."

Garry sat at the table. "Dad and I went for a drink at Marrickville yesterday. I only had a couple with him because I was going on to me mate's place to play cards last night. I didn't get home until after midnight."

"So you took two cars? Is that right?"

"Yes. Dad parked outside the pub there. I didn't know Dad was missing until Mum woke me this morning at ten o'clock."

Harry turned to Betty. "Why did it take you until ten to realise he wasn't here this morning?"

"I didn't wake until nine and when I saw he wasn't here, I thought he'd got up early and gone fishin'; but he's always back by ten. When he wasn't here I woke Garry."

Garry put down his cup, brushed the unruly hair from his eyes and coughed. "Yeah, I saw that the boat was still in the lane. I went to the recreation park but his car wasn't there. So I went to the pub and it was still there with the keys in the ignition."

Harry looked at Garry. "Did you ask at the hotel?"

"Yeah, but they said they knew nothin'. They said that Dad left the pub at about two o'clock yesterday arvo. They ain't seen him since."

"Which hotel in Marrickville?"

"We went to the Capitol."

"Isn't that the one owned by Tony the Greek?"

Garry stepped away and put his cup on the sink. "I don't know who you're talkin' about. We just drink there sometimes."

Harry got up and stood beside him. "Now Garry, let's put all of our cards on the table. You two were drinking at Tony's pub yesterday. Down the road is the Fitzroy hotel that was fire-bombed the other morning. It's owned by the big criminals from Melbourne. That's not just a coincidence."

Garry stammered for an answer. "I don't know what you're talking about."

"Well let me make it a little clearer. You and Ben and Tom Lebovich did the armoured van job at North Rocks the other morning. On occasions Lebovich works for Tony the Greek, Whispers and Rosie. The Melbourne mob are moving in to Marrickville. The Fitzroy gets fire-bombed. Do I need to say any more?"

Betty leapt out of her chair and banged Harry on the arm. "You rotten bastard. You're trying to stitch up my Ben and Garry for a job they didn't do. They were out fishin'. Is that the way you get your kicks?"

Harry gently edged her back to the chair. "Now, Betty, calm down. I'm not here to arrest anyone. I'm here to find Ben, but if Ben and Garry are mixed up with that lot, anything might have happened. Until Garry tells me the truth I can't help you."

"I don't know nothin'" said Garry as he sat down again.

"Garry, tell me where the money is that came from the van the other day."

"We ain't got any money. If we had money do you think we'd be livin' in a dump like this?"

"Garry and Betty, you and I know that Ben is a compulsive gambler and is in serious debt to Tony the Greek, and maybe other bookmakers. If they organised that heist at North Rocks they certainly would have taken their cut first. Is that what happened?"

"All I know," said Garry with head in his hands "is that we never got no money."

"Thanks, Garry. Now we are getting somewhere. That means that Lebovich took the loot and gave it to whoever was behind this robbery. Of course, we won't know because the money would be well hidden by now."

"Well what are you gunna do about it?" shouted Betty.

"If Garry is willing to stand up in court and tell us who was on the heist and who got the money, we might have a chance."

Garry thumped the table. "There's no way I'm goin' to court to say nothin'. I'm not mad. I wouldn't last five minutes when I got out."

"If you're not going to cooperate with me I can't do much. I'll put out an all-points bulletin for Ben, but it doesn't look good. The big operators don't take kindly to blokes who squelch on their debts; and Lebovich is not a nice man. I'll go now, but if you want to talk again leave a message for me at headquarters."

Harry drove home where he worked on his plans for tomorrow.

Chapter 41
Friday

It was three-thirty in the morning when the alarm rang. Harry dressed in his army disposal gear, ate a banana, put on his tanker hood and goggles, walked outside, kick-started his bike and rode to Parramatta Road. There was little traffic. The light mist was cool and refreshing. He continued through to Broadway and turned into the Haymarket.

The place was a hive of activity. Trucks, vans and utilities were lined up on both sides of the laneways. Trolleys of boxes and bags were being wheeled in and out of the sheds. Men in leather aprons were rushing back and forth shouting at each other in a variety of languages as they moved the produce. This was the beating heart of food in this big city. Produce from the farms had been brought in overnight.

Greengrocers, restaurateurs and big food store buyers were bargaining with the stallholders for the best deals. What looked like utter chaos was in fact a well-oiled machine. Each buyer would trolley the boxes or bags out to their van and drive off. Big burly men controlled the flow of traffic. It was best to keep on their good side, and it was not uncommon for a driver to slip them a ten shilling note to get a favourable position.

Harry walked along the lanes and into the sheds to watch the action. He looked into the big Number Six building where Paddy's Market was located, but was more interested in the fruit and vegetable markets where he believed the movement of drugs took place. He knew much of this market was controlled by the two big crime bosses, Angelo Romano and Boss Gabor.

Inside the door of one of the sheds Harry spotted a leather apron on a hook and a nearby trolley. He slipped on the apron, put two empty boxes on the trolley, and walked off. With his tanker hood on, he looked like any of the other workers in the market. He wheeled the trolley from shed to shed, watching the activity. He was surrounded by boxes of fruit; oranges, peaches, apricots, nectarines, bananas and pineapples. Stacked on other pallets were bags or crates of potatoes, pumpkins, carrots, cabbages, cauliflowers, lettuce and other vegetables.

Moving in and out of each shed, Harry looked like any other grocer buying daily supplies for their shop back in the suburbs. He moved quickly to give the impression of urgency to match that of the other buyers. He tried not to get involved in conversations.

For over two hours he walked in and out of all the sheds, watching the cunning bargaining between the farmers and dealers on one side, and the dealers and shop owners on the other. He could see that the dealers had the upper hand. Watching the Italian stallholders gesticulate and remonstrate, as if their mother's life depended on the deal, brought a smile to Harry's face. The farmers who had worked their heart out to bring their produce to the markets walked out with disgusted looks on their faces.

When Harry had done the rounds of all the stalls he returned to one of the biggest sheds where he had noticed a large cool room at the back. He bought a hot dog with sauce from a nearby stall, stood just inside the door and watched. A big-framed Goliath of a man, black beanie on his head, two weeks stubble, tattoos on both arms and neck, an oversized gut and a dirty leather apron, sat at a table outside the room.

Harry noticed two other workers go in and out of the room with a nod to Goliath each time. They carried out trays of strawberries or cherries. During the next hour, three other men walked up separately and talked to the big man who stood up and escorted them into the cool room. Each time he shut the door behind them. After each man walked out, Goliath counted cash in his hand and put it into a big pocket in his apron.

Harry followed the third man to his motorbike. The man was about to kick-start it when Harry stepped in front of him. "Hey, mate," he said. "Could ya sell me a bit of weed?"

"Git out of me way or I'll run ya down," was the snarling reply.

Harry took hold of the handle bars and turned them sideways. "Come on, mate. I've got money to pay for it."

"Who the fuck are you?"

"I'm a mate of Bomber Earl. He said you could get me a hit."

The man grabbed the handlebars again, straightened them, kick-started the bike and glared at Harry. "Fuck off. I ain't got none."

Harry stepped back and let him ride off with a deep-throated roar of the bike. He walked back inside, picked up his trolley and moved towards the cool room. When he saw one of the two regulars walking towards the room, he quickly moved in to follow him. The man turned. "What the hell are you doing in here?"

"I want to look at your strawberries and cherries. I want to get a couple of cases," replied Harry.

At that moment a booming voice behind him announced. "Get the fuck out of here. Who the bloody hell are you?"

Harry turned to see 'Goliath'. "I'm Tommy Forsythe. I've just bought a fruit and veg shop at Parramatta and I want some stock. Those strawbs and cherries look great. Can I get a couple of boxes?"

Goliath took Harry's arm and led him out. "Let me make it clear to you fuckwit; nobody goes in there unless I say so. Have you been cleared with Angelo?"

"I'm new around here. I've just come up here from Melbourne. Who's Angelo?"

"Angelo runs these markets. If he says no, you're not even allowed to breathe the bloody air in here. Do you get what I mean?"

"Where do I find this Mr Angelo?"

"See that man upstairs in that room up there? That's Angelo. He's looking at you now. So piss off out of here. I won't tell you twice."

Harry decided to back out. He had seen what he wanted. He walked back to the first shed, hung the apron on the hook and returned the trolley to its position. As he walked towards his bike he noticed two men come from what looked like an office at the entrance, and drop in behind him. They quickened their pace until they reached him and took him firmly by both arms. "You're coming with us," said the man on his right.

Harry jolted suddenly to a stop and then jagged slightly forward. As he did so he swung his fists back, hard into their testicles. As their grips on his arms relaxed he kicked backwards at the first man catching him up under the rib cage. Continuing his movement he spun around, swung his other leg in a high arch, catching the other man square on the jaw with the side of his boot. Both men went down in a heap. Harry walked to his bike, kick-started it and drove to Broadway and on to headquarters.

It was only seven-thirty, so Harry walked to his favourite café in George Street and ordered bacon, eggs and mushrooms on toast. He went over in his mind the events at the markets. He now knew where Romano operated and the tight organisation and security around that cool room. He assumed the large cool room in the other shed was owned by Boss Gabor. Cool rooms in other units were much smaller.

Harry knew that he had no evidence to charge anyone but he had seen small and large loosely-packed bags stored at the very back of the cool room behind the boxes of strawberries and cherries. He didn't have time to check the contents but he had seen a few green leaves at the top of one bag, and suspected that it was cannabis. He needed more information before he moved in; and a search warrant.

He remembered seeing a large truck from Leeton. It had the owner's name on the door; Arthur Frankston, Carriers, Palm Av, Leeton, Phone 659. He wrote down the details.

After breakfast he walked to headquarters where he almost collided with Chief Superintendent Twain at the entrance.

"What the hell are you doing coming to work like that," said the chief super. "Haven't you got any decent clothes?"

"My apologies, sir, but I've been doing some surveillance down at the markets early this morning."

"Why the hell are you wasting your time doing that? Didn't we talk about this the other day? Have you got any concrete evidence that anyone has committed a major crime there?"

"Not yet, sir, but I expect to have some in the near future."

Twain threw his bag on the chair in his office and pointed to the door. "What rubbish. Get on and do some real policing. Get out of here and let me do my work."

As Harry walked past the CIB room he saw Bob Crow having a mug of tea. "G'day, Bob. Mind if I join you?"

"Come on in, Harry. How are things going?"

Harry filled him in on his morning visit to the markets. "How do you see all this playing out, Bob?"

Bob drew deeply on his cigarette. "Well, Harry, you're on the right track. The markets are the centre of activity for drug distribution, and Angelo and Boss control most of the action."

"Why haven't we knocked them off before this?"

"Because we've never had enough evidence. And the powers that be don't want us to waste time on a few smokes when there are real crimes like murder out there that take priority."

"Yes," said Harry. "I know what you mean. Tell me, Bob, what do you think about Bomber Earl disappearing?"

Bob took a slow sip. "That's interesting. I've heard that he's been getting mixed up with the Melbourne mob; so maybe he's playing with fire. There's no doubt that he was on the North Rocks job, but he was cunning enough to set up the Kogarah hoax and the fishing trip. I didn't think he was that smart."

"He might not have been the one who set it up. I think it was more likely to be Tom Lebovich," said Harry.

"I don't think it was Lebovich," said Bob. "I heard he's had nothing to do with Bomber these days. They had a falling out a year ago over some gambling debts."

"Then who do you think was the second bloke on the job the other day?"

Bob blew smoke towards the ceiling. "I heard via the grapevine that it was Darkie Moffitt. He used to do jobs for Woods and Bignall in Melbourne, but he seems to be more in Sydney these days. Coming back to his old stamping-grounds."

"Could he still be working for them up here?"

"I'd put money on it," said Bob.

Harry stood up. "Thanks, Bob. I've got to go now. See you later."

He left the building and rode his bike to Tempe where he visited the Earl family. Neither Betty or Garry could give him any more information about Ben. Harry assured them that he had Ben's disappearance still high on his agenda, but had no more leads.

As he was walking out he took Garry aside. "You and I both know that you were driving the getaway car at North Rocks. Who was the other bloke in the car?"

Garry pushed open the door. "I don't know what you're talkin' about."

Harry poked his finger firmly into Garry's chest. "If you want my help, Garry, I need yours. Do you get what I mean?"

"I know nothin'," said Garry as he closed the door.

Harry rode back to Stanmore.

Chapter 42
Saturday

Harry turned on the radio while he ate breakfast. The only news worth listening to was the results from the fourth cricket Test between Australia and India in Adelaide. Neil Harvey made his debut but didn't score many runs, but Don Bradman made 201, Barnes scored 112, Hassett got 198 and Miller put on a handy 67. There was no way India could win after those scores.

The night before, Harry had decided he would go to Leeton to see for himself what others had been talking about. It was 350 miles each way, but he had the whole weekend to get there and back. He packed a change of clothes into his kitbag, strapped it to the seat behind him and, after breakfast, took off.

The trip on the Hume Highway to Goulburn and Yass was uneventful so Harry decided to take the short cut through Harden and Temora. The winding narrow road cut through miles of freshly-harvested paddocks. The stiff yellow wheat stalks stood bleached in the over century temperature. Harry dodged the occasional rabbit, kangaroo, snake and wheat truck. The horizon shimmered in the heat. Wheat straw and galahs flew up in his face. Willy-willies danced in the paddocks. The road from Temora to Leeton through Narrandera, was mostly hard corrugated gravel. Maybe this was not the best way to come.

After stopping at Temora for lunch he arrived in Leeton at two o'clock; tired, dirty and sweaty. He looked for a hotel where he could stay the night. He thought the Hydro was too expensive so he settled on the Wade Hotel in the main street. He showered and changed before phoning the police station.

He asked to be put through to Sergeant Mansfield.

"I'm sorry, sir but Sergeant Mansfield is not on duty this afternoon. Could I be of assistance?"

"No thanks. I'll catch up with the sergeant at home."

Harry called 512. "I wish to talk to Senior Sergeant Chicka Mansfield. I have been sent here by the commissioner and the chief superintendent to pass on to the sergeant their personal congratulations on the outstanding work he and his team have done in the Leeton area. The chief is putting forward his name for a special commendation. I would like to meet the sergeant while in town."

For a moment there was a slight pause on the other end of the line, then a loud guffaw. "I know that bloody voice. When did they let you out of Long Bay, you bastard? Please don't tell me you're in Leeton. I'll have to call out the whole squad. Harry, please piss off. This was going to be a quiet weekend for me and Norma."

"Chicka, you old bastard. What other welcome would I expect from you? I'm down here on a job and I need to talk to you this afternoon. Where can we meet?"

"The last time I saw you was when you got us to help you raid the gypsy camp at Euroley Bridge, and you stuffed that up and got us all abused by the magistrate in Orange."

"That was Sergeant Walsh's sloppy work. I didn't know who slugged me at the pub in Goonaburra. But enough of that. That was last year. I'm more interested in what's going on now. Can I come to your place to have a talk?"

"Just give me enough time to hide the bottles."

Harry rode along Yanco Road until he came to a neat weatherboard house set back from the street. He was greeted by Chicka's wife, Norma.

"Hello, Harry. So pleased to see you again. Chicka and I often talk about you, especially after that terrible shooting recently. How's things now?"

"Great, Norma; and even better for seeing you."

Chicka shook hands with a grip that could crush bricks. "Come out on the verandah and have a beer."

Harry filled them in on all the action of the last three weeks since his shooting at New Year. Norma was shocked; Chicka was not surprised. "Even when you were a probationary constable in Bathurst I told you not to keep putting your fingers in the snake's mouth; you'll get bitten. But you never took any notice, did you?"

Harry laughed. "That, folks, is the third reading from the gospel according to Saint Chicka."

"Okay, Harry, what the hell are you doing in Leeton, because I'm damn sure you're not here to bring me and Norma a present?"

"All my information points to the fact that this area is becoming a main supply of cannabis. I know that it has never been a high priority. In fact, it was only recently made illegal."

Chicka waved his hand. "We've known that some farmers grow a bit of that stuff and that it's been used by rich ladies in the cities, but the powers that be have not been interested in it. Why the big interest now?"

Norma brought out a plate of Christmas cake and rum balls. "I'll get another bottle of beer."

Harry refocused on Chicka's question. "There's about to be a major turf war in Sydney between the locals and the big crime bosses in Melbourne who are trying to move into the city and take over. A major part of that scene is the control of the drug market. The Sydney mob has a stranglehold on the heroin and cocaine market, but the Melbourne mob want to take control of the cannabis which they see as the up-and-coming drug for everyone; not just the rich."

"But is cannabis any more dangerous than tobacco? Most of the men in this country smoke and the tobacco companies sponsor our big sporting events. Don't trust a man who doesn't smoke, they say."

"I know what you mean, Chicka. And a lot of the top brass think the same way and don't want to waste time chasing up this matter; but it's bigger than that. The big crime boys can see an opportunity well ahead of us and it's developing into a major dust-up."

"But what can we do to help you here?"

"I've heard on the grapevine that there's a group of Italian farmers involved and they live in the Corbie Hill and Merungle Hill area. What can you tell me about them?"

Chicka stood up and scratched his upper thigh. "A lot of Italians came out here earlier this century. They left tough times in Italy and found the soils and climate here similar to back home. They worked their guts out and earned enough money to buy their own properties."

"How do you find them?"

"A lot of the people around here call them wogs and spags, but I find them good citizens. And they don't give me many problems; which is more than I can say about some others."

Harry took another sip of beer. "I'm not worried about someone producing a bit of weed for themselves or their neighbours, but I've heard that some farmers are now moving into it big-time and sending loads of it to the markets in Sydney."

"What happens to it there?" asked Norma.

"It goes to the Haymarket where it's distributed by the two big criminals who control the market: Angelo Romano and Boss Gabor. A lot goes to the big crime bosses but the rest goes to smaller dealers who take it to other dealers who take it to young boys, who sell it on the street and use it themselves to get a high."

"So how can we help you?"

"I understand that there are carriers here who take local produce to the markets in Sydney, and they also carry bags of the weed."

"Do you know who?"

"I saw one carrier there: Arthur Frankston. I don't think he's personally involved because when he arrived at the markets, he went off and the market workers unlocked his truck and unloaded the goods."

"I know Arthur; great bloke. I'd trust him with my life. I'll give him a call."

Twenty minutes later Arthur arrived and was introduced to Harry who cautiously explained his problem.

Arthur wiped the condensation from his glass. "As far as I'm concerned, all the farmers here are great blokes. I do a lot of business with them. They always pay on time and I get free fruit and veggies as well. I've often had them to my place, and their kids and mine are great mates."

"What do you carry for them?"

"We do a lot of carrying for them and other farmers around here to Sydney and Melbourne. It's mostly fruit at the moment; especially oranges."

"Describe the trip for me."

"The good thing about the Italians is that they do the loading and unloading. We take a truck to their farm in the morning and they load it. We go back in the afternoon and me or my sons drive it overnight to Sydney. When we get to the markets we go off for breakfast while they unload. With my crook back, that's like heaven."

Harry scratched his ear. "Why would they load and unload?"

"They produce the best oranges in the country; especially the ones for export. And they're fearful of others hijacking their load or ruining the fruit by poor handling. They've got family in the markets in Sydney who do the unloading."

"When's your next trip?"

"Tomorrow. We drive on Sunday to get there before the early Monday morning market. It's always big when the retailers stock up again after the weekend. Tomorrow we'll load two trucks, drive overnight and be in the markets before four in the morning."

"Where do you pick up?"

"Tomorrow we have four farms: Frank Marino, Alex Foti, Giuseppe Lagano and Mario Morabito. They are four great blokes. They give back a lot to the community. They've done a lot to help the local Catholic school."

"Thanks, Arthur. You've been a great help. But can you promise to keep Sergeant Chicka, here under control? I've tried and failed, but I think you can do it."

"No, Harry. I'm not into miracles yet, but I'll share a beer with him any time because I don't want to end up in the clink."

Arthur said his farewells, thanked and hugged Norma, and drove off.

Chicka poured another glass. "Well, did that help, Harry?"

"Yes. That gives me a clearer picture. What I need to do now is to drive around the area to get a better feeling for the country and the farmers here."

Chicka looked at Norma with a grin. "Well love, that says goodbye to our afternoon nap. When this bag of rubbish comes to town he wants our full attention."

Norma laughed. "Well, darling, let's be kind to our city friend. We'll just have to wait until next weekend."

Chicka took Harry in the car, crossed over the main canal and up into the Corbie Hill area and then to Merungle Hill. He pointed out the properties of the four farmers where Arthur would do his pick-ups tomorrow.

Back at the house Norma insisted that Harry stay for a roast lamb dinner with steamed pudding and custard for dessert.

"When are you going back, Harry?" asked Chicka.

Harry licked some custard from his finger. "I'll go around on my bike tomorrow to have a closer look at those farms and then head back to the city in the afternoon. I want to be at the markets when they open on Monday morning."

Harry went back to the hotel and slept soundly.

Chapter 43
Sunday

Harry slept in and, after a long shower, went to the dining room where he ate a hearty breakfast. The big oval plate, overhanging with bacon, sausages, toast and eggs told Harry that he was back in a country town; big breakfasts for big, hard working men.

At ten o'clock he paid the hotel, got on his bike and rode to Corbie Hill. He spent the next hour riding past the nearby farms, then on to Merungle Hill. He wanted to get a feel for the area. This was prime farming country; good rich soils with plenty of water from the irrigation canals nearby. The Murrumbidgee Irrigation Area was one of the major suppliers of fruit and vegetables for the Sydney and Melbourne markets, as well as for overseas.

Oranges and other citrus trees were dominant; although, Harry saw many farms producing stone fruit such as peaches, apricots and nectarines which he knew were canned at the local factory. On the flatter paddocks he saw crops of tomatoes, peas, pumpkins, beans and cucumbers. The farm houses ranged from tin sheds on the smaller properties to modern mansions on the better farms.

Harry went back to Corbie Hill where he rode to the big shed on Frank Marino's farm. Four dogs bounded out, barking. One tried to bite the rear tyre of the bike. Harry patted the lead dog and they settled. A short man in overalls and a shapeless hat walked out. "Whosa you, and whatta you want?"

Harry walked towards him with hand outstretched in greeting. "G'day. I'm Freddie Forsythe. I was just wondering if you had any jobs for a fruit picker. I've been workin' on a sheep station out the back of Booligal. It's so bloody hot and dry out there that the water boils in the billycan in the sun, and the bloody flies suck the water out of ya spit before it hits the ground. Decided to have a change of scenery and cool down a bit."

Frank Marino looked him up and down and shook his head. "No, mate. We've gotta our own workers here. Ride back through da town to the north side. You getta plenty of jobs over there."

Harry thanked Frank and rode on to Giuseppe Lagano's farm. Parked next to the packing shed was one of Arthur Frankston's large vans. The reception was not so friendly.

"Watta the fuck are you doin' here? This issa private property. Piss orf. We don't want whatever ya sellin'. Now git goin' or I'll sool the dogs onta ya."

Harry put up his hands in defence. "Sorry, mate. I'll go now. I was just looking for a fruit-picking job. But I see that you're busy so I'll be off."

He rode on to the other properties of Alex Foti and Mario Morabito. Another of Arthur's trucks was at Mario's farm. His reception was not as cold as Giuseppe's, but it was distinctly cool and protective. On three of the properties he saw plants that looked like cannabis growing. On Alex's farm it was growing between the peach trees. On Mario's it was in the corn paddock, and on Giuseppe's it was growing wild in the timber paddock on the hill behind the shed.

As he rode back into Leeton he thought of his long-term future and wondered whether he would like to finish his career in the country like Keith Tomkin, the superintendent at Bathurst. Coming from the country he understood the people and the way of life. In many ways it was a hard life, but the people were more open and honest than in the city and more likely to help each other. However, he had a job to do and now was not the time to get sentimental. He parked the bike in front of Chicka's house.

"I'm not stopping, Chicka but I wanted to let you know of my plans for the next twenty-four hours. It's important for you to know in case there is some blowback from headquarters. They might try to get up your nostril."

"What are you on about, Harry?"

"I've just been to the four farms Arthur is picking up from today. I'm certain that there are bags of cannabis in those loads. Arthur's not involved because the stuff is loaded here by the farmers and unloaded in the markets by their mates. I hope to catch them in the act at the markets in the morning."

"But how's that going to affect us here, Harry?" asked Chicka.

Harry banged the dust from his tanker hood. "You and I know that the big brass haven't given a stuff about the weed up till now. It's only just become illegal and they see other things as being more important. But this drug scene looks like becoming bigger than the film production of *Gone with the Wind*. It's going to be the major part of the Sydney and Melbourne turf wars."

"But that's in Sydney, not here."

"If everything goes to plan in the morning, I'll be locking up some of the big boys involved in the drug trade. When that happens the shit'll hit the fan and head office will want to know about it, including why they didn't know about the Leeton connection. I've told them before, but you know what they're like. When the pressure is on the chiefs suddenly get dementia and blame everyone else. This time they'll be looking for scapegoats."

"What do you want me to do?" asked Chicka.

"I'll be telling them that you alerted me to the problem here and that you assisted my investigation. You have to understand that some of your mates here are going to be caught in the middle; so be prepared."

"Thanks, Harry. Be careful, mate. I know what they're like in the city. I worked there for five years. That's why I'm happy to be back here in the country."

Harry got on his bike and kick-started the motor. "Sometime tomorrow I'll call you to let you know what's happened and who's involved." He rode off.

Arthur had mentioned yesterday that his drivers stopped at the trucker's stop at Jugiong, between Gundagai and Yass, to fill their tanks and have a meal. They stop there again on the way back. Harry remembered his travels in the country. The best meals were always at the trucker's stops. He rode to Wagga Wagga where he had a break, before going on to Jugiong where he waited for Arthur's trucks to arrive.

The first driver stopped and went inside to order a meal. When the driver started eating, Harry walked behind the van, out of sight, and picked the lock. He climbed past the boxes of oranges and found small sugar bags of green leaf. It smelt like cannabis. He took a small sample, closed and locked the door and rode on to Sydney.

***

On arriving at the Haymarket early Monday morning, Harry approached a young constable on duty at the gate. He showed him his badge. "G'day, Constable, I'm Detective Harry Taylor. I'm here on a job at the markets. What station are you from?"

"G'day, Harry. Yes, I know who you are. I'm Gavin McDougall from Redfern station. How can I help you?"

"Phone through to the station and get a wagon here as soon as possible. And I want at least one other officer to stay here as well. Tell them to wait with you at the gate until I give you the signal."

Harry walked along the lane towards Angelo Romano's big shed. He found a tea and breakfast room opposite and settled in to watch the movement of goods in and out. He had a narrow line-of-sight through to the cool room where Goliath was guarding the door.

Thirty minutes later Harry noticed a scruffy young man in dirty sandshoes and an army slouch hat, walk into the shed. He approached Goliath who entered the cool room and came out with a half-filled sugar bag which he exchanged for some cash. Harry waited until the man headed for the gate.

"Constable," Harry shouted. "Stop that man. Hold him there."

The big constable grabbed the man's shirt-front and held him firm. "What do you want me to do with him?"

Harry walked up and took the sugar bag from the man, opened it and smelled the contents. To Harry's nose it was distinctly cannabis. "Take down his details, read him his rights, charge him with possession and dealing in an illegal substance, and throw him in the wagon."

Harry walked back to the breakfast room. Two more men approached Goliath and came out with large paper bags. He followed quickly and walked past them before they reached the gate. "You take the one on the left, Constable; I'll take the big one on the right."

As the men approached, Harry challenged them. "Stop there. I'm Detective Taylor. Hand those bags over to the Constable there." The man on the right made a sudden dash for the gate but Harry's foot was quicker. His boot flicked the man's ankle and he went sprawling across the bitumen. Harry held him down and cuffed him before leading him to the wagon. The other man went quietly. The second constable helped lock them in.

As Harry walked back he noticed one of Arthur Frankston's trucks reversing towards the big shed. The driver got out, talked to one of the men inside and walked away to the breakfast room. Harry followed but sat on the opposite side.

The man in the leather apron went to the back of the van, opened the doors and called two others workers. They carried the sugar bags over to Goliath who, after checking them, pointed to the back of the cool room. When that was finished the boxes of oranges were unloaded onto the open warehouse floor for all the buyers to see. Boxes of other fruit and vegetables not available in the Leeton area were loaded onto the van for the return journey. When the driver finished his breakfast he returned to the van and drove off back to Leeton.

Harry walked to the gate and asked the constables to drive the police wagon to the big shed. "We are going to arrest that man at the entrance of the cool room. He's a big man, and he won't come easily, but you two and I can handle him. We will then take the sugar bags at the back of the cool room with us as evidence."

Harry approached Goliath. "I'm Detective Taylor and I'm arresting you on charges of possession and dealing in illegal substances. You don't have to say anything but you will now accompany me to the wagon."

Goliath stood up, picking up a large bag hook from the table. "You and fucking who else do you think is gunna put me in that wagon? You've got another think comin', shithead. I ain't goin' nowhere."

He swung the bag hook in a wide arc. Harry blocked that arm and jammed the knuckles of his other fist deeply up under the man's rib cage causing him to bend over and vomit. Harry kept the man's momentum going forward until he hit the ground. Harry applied an arm lock. The constable came across and cuffed the giant.

"Good work, Constable. Now you two get those sugar bags at the back of the cool room and load them into the wagon. Drop them off at the SIB and tell Tony Jacobs that I'll see him later. Then take those blokes to the cells and charge them. I'll be there soon."

Another of the workers in the shed came up to Harry. "What the fuck do you think you're doin'? You can't just come in here and take our men away like that. This is private property. Where's your warrant?"

"For this I don't need a warrant. Now get back to your work or you'll join your mates in the wagon."

Harry stepped onto the running board of the wagon until it got to the gate where he jumped off and rode his bike to the Redfern police station. He asked the officer-in-charge to arrange with the prosecutor to have an early hearing. After formally charging the men he rode to the SIB where he met Jack Witherspoon, the drug expert, who had already identified the contents of the bags as cannabis.

He rode back to Stanmore, showered, dressed and took the train back to the city.

Chapter 44
Monday

Getting off the train at Redfern, Harry went to the police station where he asked to interview the first man arrested that morning. Constable Gavin McDougall and Senior Sergeant Scotty Duff were there to meet Harry.

"Hell, Harry," said Scotty. "You've really stirred up the rats nest. Have you got a death wish?"

"Good to see you again, Scotty. No, mate. Just doing my job. How have the prisoners reacted since you brought them in?"

Gavin cut in. "The big bloke you called Goliath has tried to wreck the cell. His real name is Aubrey Simpson, although he's better known in the crime world as 'The Brute', or Simmo. He has a record as long as your arm. He's done stints for manslaughter, numerous break and enters and assault, and other minor offences. The other three blokes are fairly quiet. The first bloke we took is very worried about what will happen to him."

"What's his name?"

"Tom Walsh. He has no previous record other than traffic offences."

Harry rubbed his chin. "Bring him into the interview room. Gavin, I want you in there with me to take notes."

Gavin escorted Walsh into the room. "Sit there and take off that hat."

Harry looked him up and down. The man seemed very nervous, fidgeting with the brim of his hat and pushing the hair out of his eyes. He looked at Harry with fleeting upward glances. Gavin settled in the other chair and took out his notebook.

"Where did you serve?" asked Harry.

"Huh? What?"

"Where did you serve in the army?"

Walsh seemed surprised. "In New Guinea."

"Where in New Guinea?"

"On the track. Kokoda."

"Then you were unlucky to be there but lucky to survive it. I know what you went through. You lost a lot of good mates up there."

"Yeah. Sure did. It was a shithole."

"I agree, but enough of that for now. Tell me why you were at the markets today."

"I just wanted some weed to have a smoke. It's me nerves. Since I was demobbed from the army I can't get work. Me missus left me, the kids won't talk to me and I've been sleepin' rough."

Harry paused and walked out of the room for a minute. When he returned he sat and watched Walsh without talking. Tom got edgy.

"When we were up north in the army they gave us free tobacco to keep us going," he said. "But now I need something stronger. The doctor's useless. He told me to just suck it up and get on with my life."

"Joey, let's cut the bullshit," said Harry. "Half a sugar bag of hash is not what I'd call for personal use. Now tell me the truth."

"Honest-to-goodness. Dinky-di. I wouldn't tell you a lie."

Harry turned to Gavin. "Have you got all that written down, Constable?"

"Just give me a minute sir," replied Gavin.

Harry paused then said. "Tom, right now you're pooing your pants. You're scared shitless. But it's not me or Constable McDougall that's making your bowels work overtime, is it?"

Walsh asked to go to the toilet. Gavin took him. When he returned he seemed more composed.

"Okay, Joey," said Harry, "start talking. Tell me who you're working for."

"I don't know what you're talkin' about."

"Put it this way, Tom. You've come back from the war and your life's turned upside down. You don't have a job and someone comes along to offer you a golden opportunity to get some easy money for very little work. It's too good an offer to give up."

"Honest, I just use it for meself."

"Where did you get the money to buy half a bag of it, Tom?"

"Me brother gave me a loan. He felt sorry for me."

Harry paused again. Tom looked down at his feet and scratched his arm and around his rib cage.

"You didn't get into that cool room this morning unless you knew Simmo at the door. And with that quantity you must be working for someone big. You've got a choice, Tom. Tell me who you're working for and I'll only charge you with possession; and you'll probably get a slap on the wrist. If you don't, you'll go down for dealing and that means a long stint in Long Bay. Now, what's it going to be?"

"I don't know what you're talkin' about."

Harry looked up. "Take him away, Constable. We'll hit him for big-time dealing. It's a pity the silly fool doesn't know what they're going to do with him when he goes to Long Bay. They'll have him naked on the bunk in no time."

Gavin took Tom by the arm and led him out of the room. Five minutes later they returned. Gavin explained. "Tom's had second thoughts. He would like to talk with you again."

Harry paused while he watched Tom fidget in the chair. "Well, what have you got to say?"

"What's in it for me?"

Harry sat back. "Tom, you've been through hell up north against the Japanese. You're doing it tough. You need a break. If you tell me what I want to know, I'll get you a job on a farm with a mate of mine out in the country at a place called Goonaburra. But if you touch the weed again you go straight into Long Bay."

"What do you want to know?"

"Who supplies it to you and who do you sell it to?"

"I get my supplies from The Brute at the cool room."

"And who does The Brute get it from?"

"I only work with The Brute but when I started, a big bloke called Angelo took me into a room and threatened me with death if I did the wrong thing. He was scary."

"And where do you sell it?"

"I get a bag or half a bag each week. I break it up into smaller parcels and sell it to blokes out at Liverpool, Marrickville, Newtown and Parramatta."

"How did you know who to sell it to?"

"The Brute told me."

"And where do they sell it?"

"I think they sell it in pubs out that way; but I'm not sure."

"So you must be making a fortune, Tom."

"No, because I still owe The Brute money for the weed I've used; and he also covered my gambling debt with Tony the Greek."

"Okay, Tom, I can't make you promises because the decision is up to the magistrate, but I'll put in a good word if you promise to go to the country. Don't forget your slouch hat, digger; you earned that. Wear it with pride." Harry shook his hand. "Take him back to the cell, Constable, and bring in Simpson."

Harry could hear Simpson complaining along the corridor. Gavin had difficulty forcing him into the chair. He stood behind him in case the prisoner tried something stupid.

Simpson snarled. "What are you lookin' at, shithead?"

Harry paused before he read him his rights and listed the charges against him.

"You ain't got nothin'. My lawyer will throw this out in five minutes."

"Who do you work for Simmo?"

"Meself."

"Do you own the shed and the cool room?"

"No."

"Who owns them?"

"Dunno."

"Who do you pay the rent to?"

"A man picks it up each week."

"Who is that man?"

"Dunno."

Harry looked up. "Constable, take him back to the cell. We'll see him later in court."

"My man'll make mincemeat outta you in there."

"Does he swing a bag hook as badly as you, Simmo?"

Gavin took him away and brought in the other two men.

Young Toby Lyons was meek and mild when he sat down.

"Now, young fellow," said Harry, "you had best tell me the truth about this morning; and I mean the whole truth."

Lyons opened up and told them of his own experimentation with cannabis and how he was offered a chance to pay for his own weed by selling it to others. He would have liked to give it up, but he was now making money and felt that it was an opportunity to set himself up later in a business of his own. He implicated Simpson, Angelo Romano and a third person who had a slight limp whose name he didn't know.

"Take him back to the cell, Constable."

Harry turned to the other man. His name was Cecil Phillips. He had a similar story to Lyons so Harry went through the same routine.

Senior Sergeant Scotty Duff came into the room to inform Harry that the prosecutor had phoned and wanted to talk to him before the prisoners went before a magistrate at three that afternoon.

Harry took the train to the city and walked to the Central Court complex, next to headquarters, where he met with Lincoln Harris, the prosecutor. They had an hour to prepare the case.

"Tell me about these four men, Harry."

Harry described Simpson first and his association with Angelo Romano.

"But are you bringing Romano into court as well, Harry?"

"No. He wasn't directly involved this morning, so we can't do that. I'll save him for another day. I'm sure we will find another link."

"What about the other three?"

Harry described the situation with Walsh and his army background. He also mentioned that he had been in touch with his friend Nipper Ricketts, at Goonaburra, who promised Harry that he was willing to give Walsh a job working in his garage providing he stayed clean of the drugs. Harry wanted the court to go easy on him and only charge him with minor possession. A suspended sentence would be fair enough.

"What about the other young blokes?"

Harry again wanted a suspended sentence with the threat that another charge would lead to a custodial sentence. He wanted them to promise to go into rehabilitation. It was a chance to get them out of the trade in drugs.

"From what you've told me, Harry I have two concerns. You broke into that truck without a warrant, and you entered that cool room without one as well. Felix Prima will be defending Simpson, and he is one of the top lawyers in this state. Someone like Romano will be paying for him, I bet."

"Is he the one they call Prima Donna?"

"Yes, and for good reason. When he takes the floor it is always a grand display. Be careful with him, Harry. He'll try to crucify you."

"Thanks, Lincoln. I'll go and freshen up before we get called in."

Chapter 45
Monday

At three o'clock Harry was called into the courtroom. The magistrate, Campbell Anderson, called the room to order. Harry had never met him before but was impressed by the way he took command.

Tom Walsh was called to the witness box. He was extremely nervous. Being unrepresented he was at a distinct disadvantage in a situation with which he was not familiar. Lincoln Harris, the prosecutor, could have made mincemeat of him, but thankfully he took note of Harry's advice and treated him gently. After some preliminary questions to Walsh, Lincoln called Harry to the stand.

"Detective Taylor, could you outline to the court the circumstances that led to the arrest of Mr Walsh."

Harry confined his comments to his observation of Tom at the markets and his subsequent questioning.

"How serious do you see the actions of this man?"

Harry looked at Tom who sat with head down. "The quantity was well beyond what one would expect for personal use, but I believe there are circumstances that I wish to put to the court for consideration."

"Go on," said Lincoln.

Harry outlined his interview with Walsh and the fact that he had cooperated with his inquiry. He told the court of his conversation with Nipper at Goonaburra and his offer to take Walsh on trial as a worker in his garage. He turned to the Magistrate.

"Your Worship, this man has been to hell and back in New Guinea. He has served his country well and he has hit hard times readjusting to civilian life. I ask that he be given a chance to redeem himself in a place where he is less likely to re-offend."

The magistrate looked over his glasses at Harry. "How well do you know this man whom you call Nipper?"

"I've known him and his family for most of my life. I guarantee that he will give Walsh every chance to get back on his feet in a town where he'll be surrounded by a caring community."

"You seem to know these people," said the magistrate.

"Yes, Your Worship. I was born in the district and still have family there. I know most of the people there and I know they'll give him a fair go."

The magistrate turned to Walsh. "Mr Walsh, are you willing to take up Detective Taylor's offer of a job at Goonaburra?"

Tom looked around, first at Harry, then the prosecutor and back to the magistrate. "Yes, sir but I don't have any money for the train fare."

Harry broke in. "Your Worship, I'll arrange for a train ticket and a spending allowance to tide him over until he gets his first pay. Nipper has agreed to put him up in the shearers' quarters on his family's property. If you agree, I'll have him on the Western Mail train tonight."

Mr Anderson called for Walsh to stand. "Mr Walsh, I find you guilty of possessing illegal substances with the intention of selling them to persons unknown. I sentence you to twelve months in gaol but I will suspend that sentence if you agree to take up the offer from Detective Taylor to work with his friend at Goonaburra. Are you willing to do that?"

A wave of relief washed over Walsh's face. "Yes, Your Worship. Thank you and thanks to Detective Taylor. I won't let you down."

"You best not let us down because if I see you in this court again, you'll be going to gaol for a long time. You are dismissed."

Toby Lyons and Cecil Phillips were brought to the stand, one after the other. In their cases, Harry convinced the court that they were minor users rather than big dealers, and that they should be given second chances on the proviso that they undergo rehabilitation. The magistrate agreed and handed down a suspended sentence of three months, not to be registered on their records.

The magistrate called for a break of thirty minutes. When they returned, Aubrey 'The Brute' Simpson was in the box. Lincoln Harris read out the charges and commenced the questioning but despite his repeated cautions, he was having difficulty getting Simpson to give direct answers.

"I don't have to answer your stupid questions. You're a bunch of drop shits, the whole fucking lot of ya."

Magistrate Anderson called for order. "Mr Simpson, you'll behave in my court and if you don't, I'll hold you in contempt. You are obliged to answer Mr Harris' questions. Now let's proceed in a more orderly manner. Proceed Mr Harris."

Simpson shouted at the top of his voice. "I don't have to answer any of your fucking questions. Ya can't make me; so there. Stick that up ya arsehole."

The magistrate looked down at Felix Prima, the defence lawyer who, up until now, had spent his time cleaning his fingernails without a word spoken. "Mr Prima. I'm going to call a halt for ten minutes. That will be sufficient time for you to advise your client on matters relating to court proceedings and the penalties that will apply if he continues to abuse this court."

Upon resumption Harris continued his questioning. "Mr Simpson, please tell the court how you came to be in possession of a large quantity of the illegal substance cannabis?"

"I know nuffin'."

"A large quantity of that substance was in your cool room and you were seen selling some of that to Walsh, Phillips and Lyons."

"I know nuffin'."

"Do you agree that you control the flow of goods in and out of that cool room?"

"I know nuffin'."

"Who owns that cool room at the Haymarket?"

"Me lawyer said I don't have to answer no questions. So stick that up ya nostril."

Mr Anderson sat forward. "Mr Simpson. I'll remind you of my earlier caution."

"Sorry, sir but I'm just tellin' ya what me lawyer said."

"Mr Simpson, you don't have to answer the questions, but you might do your case harm if you don't. Do you wish to answer the question?"

"Na."

Harris continued. "Did you attack Detective Taylor with a bag hook?"

"My fucking oath. Pity I didn't kill the bastard. Those coppers are always trying to plant somethin' on us. I saw him in the markets three days ago in plain clothes and he put that stuff in the cool room. The bastard's trying to set me up. I ain't done nuffin'."

"Do you agree that you sold cannabis to Walsh, Phillips and Lyons this morning?"

"I know nuffin'."

"I have no further questions, Your Worship."

Felix Prima rose slowly to his feet. "I have no questions Your Worship."

Lincoln called Harry to the stand. "Detective Taylor, will you tell the court why you visited Leeton over the weekend."

"I have been investigating a number of leads that involve the increase in drugs in this state. Recent intelligence indicates a dramatic increase in the use and supply of cannabis."

"But why Leeton?"

"It's not only Leeton. I have investigated a number of properties also in the Hawkesbury Valley where it is also grown."

"What did you find in Leeton?"

Harry described his visits to the farms at Corbie Hill and Merungle Hill and the plants he observed growing there.

"Tell us about how the drugs are transported to the Haymarket in Sydney."

Harry described his trip via Jugiong.

"Were the drivers of the trucks involved?"

Harry sat back. "No. The trucks were loaded and unloaded by the farmers and their friends in the market. The van was locked and the drivers had nothing to do with the contents."

"And what are the local police in Leeton doing about this matter?"

"I was alerted to this problem by Sergeant Mansfield in charge of the Leeton station. He has had this matter under observation for some time. It's been his good work that led to the arrests made here today."

"Why didn't he make the arrests in Leeton?"

"Because we wanted to track the supply to the outlets here in Sydney."

"Thank you, Detective. I have no further questions."

"Over to you Mr Prima," said the magistrate.

Felix Prima spent the next couple of minutes shuffling papers on the bench. He rose and looked at Harry without speaking. Harry stared back, unblinking.

"Detective Taylor, did the commissioner or your chief superintendent know that you were in Leeton on the weekend?"

"Probably not."

"Were you on official duty or on a folly of your own?"

"I consider that when I'm on a case I'm always on duty. Unlike you, sir, days of the week don't matter to us. Criminals don't confine their nefarious activities to the daytime from Monday to Friday."

"Why did you enter the properties at Corbie Hill and Merungle Hill?"

"Intelligence indicated that those farms were growing and supplying cannabis; and I found that to be correct."

"Did you identify yourself as a police officer?"

"No, because I wanted to continue to track the material to the market."

"Did you read those farmers their rights before you interviewed them?"

"No. I wasn't charging them, so it was not necessary at that point."

"Don't you agree that what you did was entrapment?"

"No. I was investigating, not charging. I didn't encourage them to commit a crime."

Felix paused for a minute. "You stated that you inspected the produce in the truck at Jugiong. Is that correct?"

"Yes."

"Did you ask the driver's permission?"

"No."

"Did you pick a lock to enter the vehicle?"

"Yes."

"Did you have a warrant to enter that vehicle?"

"No."

"When you and the other officers entered the cool room at the market did you have a warrant to search?"

"No. I didn't need one because I knew that the bags of cannabis had been delivered to that room that morning. I saw them taken in. I wasn't searching for something I didn't know was there on the off-chance that something might be there. We went in to retrieve the bags as evidence. We knew they were there"

"Did you have authority from your superior officer to carry out that search and seizure?"

"No, that wasn't necessary."

Felix Prima stomped his foot and banged his fist on the bench. "Your Worship, I ask that you throw out this case against my client immediately. Here you have a bunch of bushrangers holding up a legitimate wagon on its way to market. They burst in to arrest my client and others for doing nothing more than their hard day's work. This detective is the one you should lock up. He is a disgrace to the police force."

"Thank you Mr Prima but I'll decide what happens in my court; not you."

"But, Your Worship, this officer searched farms without identifying himself and without a warrant. He illegally broke into a private vehicle and searched it without a warrant and he searched the cool room of my client without a warrant. How much more evidence do you need to put him away?"

"Have you finished your cross-examination, Mr Prima?'

"Yes, Your Worship. I want nothing more to do with this scum. I'll be putting a report through to his superior officers."

In his right of reply Lincoln Harris kept his questions brief. He didn't want to give the court any more ammunition to fire at Harry. Following that, the magistrate delivered his verdict.

"Mr Simpson, I find you guilty of assaulting Detective Taylor, with a bag hook and sentence you to sixty days detention. Because of the nature of the search conducted by Detective Taylor and the lack of warrants to do so, I am dismissing the charges of possession and dealing in illegal substances. Take the prisoner away. Detective Taylor, I want you to remain after the court is cleared."

Harry and Lincoln remained seated after the others left. The magistrate called them to the bench. "Detective Taylor, I gave you a lot of leeway today. I appreciate what you have been through in the last three weeks with two attempts on your life, but that is no excuse to insult this court with amateur stunts like you pulled today. I'll not have it my court again. I'll be talking to your superior about this. Do you understand?"

"Yes, Your Worship. I appreciate your concern, but I felt it necessary to strike while the iron was hot to prevent this trade from developing into a major concern in this community. There is a threat of a turf war between major criminals from Sydney and Melbourne."

"I think you're exaggerating, Detective. Cannabis has been around for centuries without any major outbreak of crime, and I can't see that changing in a hurry. You're dismissed."

Harry thanked Lincoln and went to Central Railway Station where he waited for Tom Walsh. He bought a ticket to Goonaburra and handed it to Tom with a ten pound note.

Tom looked a little brighter than in the court. "Thanks, Detective. I won't let you down."

Chapter 46
Tuesday

In the morning on the way to the station Harry bought a copy of the *Daily Mirror*. He stopped in his tracks as he read the headline on the front page:

Detective Slammed by Court

He read on:

Detective Harry Taylor, a highly-decorated officer who recently survived two attempts on his life, was castigated yesterday by the magistrate in the Central Court.

The magistrate, Mr Campbell Anderson, admonished Detective Taylor for arresting four men on drug charges without a search warrant. In court, Detective Taylor outlined the nature of his trip to Leeton in the Murrumbidgee area over the weekend where he observed cannabis being grown on farms. This is an illegal substance on the increase in this city.

He followed the trucks containing the harvested crops to the Haymarket where he saw four men dealing in this illegal substance. One of those men, Mr Aubrey Simpson, is well known to police. He attacked Detective Taylor with a lethal weapon and was sentenced to sixty days in gaol.

Detective Taylor has been working closely with the local sergeant of police at Leeton who has been monitoring that activity for some time.

Our special crime reporter, James Bolton, has for some time been following the increase in the supply, dealing and use of this terrible drug. He can now report that yesterday morning, the local Leeton police destroyed three acres of cannabis plants. Sergeant Mansfield and his team are to be congratulated on saving the public from this horrible curse.

Reliable sources have informed James Bolton that the sudden increase in sales of this substance is connected to the recent influx of Melbourne big-time criminals into the Sydney area. It is alleged that they are moving into hotels in the suburbs, and setting up gambling rooms with prostitutes and drugs, in competition with the well known criminals already operating in the city area.

It appears that the politicians, judges and police are not interested in taking action about this new threat to society. The public needs answers.

It is anticipated that there could be a tribal war between the big crime bosses. One informant told James that the attempts on Detective Taylor's life were connected to his investigations into these matters.

Why would the court and the hierarchy of the police treat Detective Taylor so shabbily when he is doing what others before him should have been doing?

Neither the Commissioner nor the Chief Superintendent of Police have responded to James' many requests for an interview.

The public need to know, and James will continue to follow up on his investigations.

Harry was stunned. He was unaware that James Bolton was in the courtroom yesterday. He was even more surprised that Bolton was saying something positive about him after the way he was treated by the same man last year when Bolton was a reporter for *The Central West Daily.*

As Harry entered the corridor of headquarters he saw Fred Sherman who beckoned him into the CIB room. Joe Cross, Charlie Rockwell and Bob Crow were having cigarettes and mugs of tea.

Fred turned and with a savage snarl on his face shoved a copy of the *Daily Mirror* onto Harry's chest. "What the fuck do you think you're doing? You'd better start explaining yourself. What do you want? Another fucking medal? We're supposed to be a team and you piss off trying to make a big star of yourself and making us look like fools. Now start talking."

Harry pushed Fred's hand away, put the paper on the table, walked to the sink and took his time pouring himself a mug of tea. He turned and faced the group.

"Let me start by saying that I didn't know Bolton was in the court yesterday; and I haven't talked to him about this case."

Joe shouted. "Then how did he get that information? And why is he your friend?"

Harry took a slow sip of tea. "I can assure you that he's no friend of mine. He tore the guts out of me twice last year when I was involved in that case out at Goonaburra."

Fred coughed and blew out a belch of smoke. "I don't believe you."

"Well that's your problem, Fred, not mine. Let me make it clear to all of you. I'm the one they've tried to kill twice; and I'm still the target."

"That's over," shouted Fred. "Get over it. We got Scarface. He's out of the way."

"Fred, you know the contract is big enough for someone else to pick it up, and at this stage we don't know who that is. I'm trying to get to him before he gets me. It's my life, not yours."

Joe broke in. "But what's all this bullshit about cannabis? A few rich old ladies smoke it to give themselves a bit of a thrill or get over their depression. Why should we bust our guts about that? Come on, get real."

"My information is that it's much bigger than that. You blokes know what's going on with the Melbourne mob. Surely people like Lebovich, Durante and Tony Stavros have let you know about the southerners."

"Why would you say that?"

"Because you're in regular contact with them."

Fred snorted. "Have you been fucking spying on us? There's nothing lower than a scumbag rat in the ranks. We get rid of snitches."

Harry paused and stared at Fred. "No. I've got better things to do. But it's well known in here that you meet with them to gather information. That's why you blokes are the best in the business; because you get the best intelligence right from the source."

"You better believe it, and we don't like doing business with anyone who doesn't cooperate with the team. From now on you'll let us know what you're doing before you go off to be a media slut in the newspapers. Do you get my message?"

Harry slowly rinsed his mug in the sink. "I take my orders from the chief."

Fred snorted and chuffed with what looked like a half-smile. "Well, you get in there now because he's about to kick your arse inside out. Don't complain that we didn't warn you."

Harry walked out and along to the main desk.

Jack Tomlinson held up his hand. "Harry, for God's sake, don't go anywhere before you see the chief. He's about to explode about that newspaper article this morning. Stay there and I'll call him."

As Harry entered Twain's office the chief paced the room slapping everything in range, shouting abuse at Harry who waited patiently until the explosion subsided.

"Why did you deliberately disobey my orders?"

"I didn't disobey any orders."

"I told you to concentrate on your inquiries here, not in Leeton."

"Well, sir, I went to Leeton on the weekend in my own time at my own expense. I wasn't on duty. I'm entitled to do that as a normal citizen."

"Don't try your fancy words on me, Detective. I didn't come down in the last shower. You went there to chase some fancy idea that this was the next big thing since the razor gangs. You deliberately disobeyed my orders."

"I went there to catch up with some old friends and get away from the intensity of the last few weeks; and that's what I did."

"Sit down. Who were your friends?"

Harry shifted the chair to the side and spread his legs. "Sergeant Chicka Mansfield. I worked with him as a probationary constable at

Bathurst, and we caught up again last year when we worked together on the gypsy case."

"So, you two have conspired to pull off this stunt without consulting us. That's insubordination."

"No, sir. That's good policing. It was Sunday. You weren't in the office and neither was the commissioner or any other senior officer. When we saw the extent of the growth of cannabis we talked to the man who owned the transport company that took the produce to the markets. It was obvious he wasn't involved with the drugs, so I followed the goods to the markets where I made the arrests."

"I should have been told."

"I guessed that you would not have been pleased if I had rung you at midnight from Jugiong when I saw the evidence in the trucks."

"But you didn't have a warrant to search the cool room at the markets, or the truck at Jugiong."

"If I had waited to get a magistrate to give me a warrant to search the truck at Jugiong it would have already been unloaded at the market and been on its way back to Leeton."

"What about the cool room?"

"I wasn't searching for the goods. I already knew they were in there. I was merely recovering those goods. I didn't need a warrant."

"That's a matter of opinion."

"Yes, Sir. That is what the magistrate told me."

"Yes, I have his report on my table. But it was the report in the papers this morning that was the straw that broke the camel's back. The commissioner wants me to sack you, immediately."

Harry shifted in the chair. "And are you going to do that, sir?"

"I have a good mind to do it. You disobeyed a lawful instruction."

"No, sir, I didn't. I went on a private trip to Leeton. While I was there I became aware of a major crime taking place. Like any good police officer I took the necessary action to bring the criminals to justice. Had I not done so you would have a good reason to sack me."

"But you picked up a couple of small-time users."

"Yes, sir I did, but we treated them with the respect they deserved and they have been given another chance. It was the fourth man who was the problem. Brute Simpson tried to kill me."

"Come on, he took a swing at you. Are you getting soft, Harry?"

"A large bag hook is a solid weapon capable of causing serious injury or death."

"But you handled it with ease. Why the fuss?"

"He's a key henchman for Angelo Romano who, with Boss Gabor, controls what goes in and out of those markets. Both of them are connected to the big crime bosses in this city. I suspect that Romano is changing sides to join the influx of Melbourne boys, and that means trouble between the two sides."

"But now you've opened a can of worms with the press. How are we going to deal with them?"

Harry sat back. "Sir, there is no one on this planet who can handle the press better than you. Tell them that you and your officers have been working undercover on this case for some time as it was necessary to gather the evidence before moving to convictions. Congratulate your officers and assure the public that you have everything under control."

"Get out of here and don't try to pull a stunt like that again. Do you hear me?"

"Loud and clear, sir. Thank you."

Harry walked back to the tea-room.

Chapter 47
Tuesday

Jock looked up as Harry entered. "Well, who's the big media tart today? How much did you have to pay that reporter, Harry? Cover your eyes boys. The flashbulbs will be going off soon."

"Okay, Jock, okay. Have your fun. I've had enough flak from everyone else here, I don't need any from you. Let's get out of here. We'll go around to the café in George Street."

Harry ordered two mugs of tea and two helpings of grilled cheese on toast. They sat back in the corner. Harry filled in Jock on the events of the last three days.

"Why didn't you tell me?" said Jock. "I would have gone with you."

"I didn't want to get you in the poo, Jock. I knew what I was doing and I knew that I was going to cop a bucketful this morning. But now that it's hit the fan we might get some support."

Jock shook his head. "I don't think so, Harry. Everyone I talked to this morning wants to keep their distance from you. They think you're sucking up to the reporter to big-note yourself and make everyone else look like fools; and they don't like that. They're not happy, mate."

"Yes, I can see that. I got a rough reception from the CIB boys this morning, but I bet we get some results from now on."

"Well, what are you going to do now?"

"We still have an unsolved missing person who was deeply involved with this mess. We need to get out there and find some answers. That is, of course, if you still want to work with me. Are you in or out?"

"Sure and begorrah mate. We're like black pudding and haggis; we go together. So what do you want to do?"

"We'll pay another visit to Garry and Betty Earl. Let's see if they want to tell us more about Bomber."

As they walked into the house at Tempe, Betty was sitting at the kitchen table sipping her tea and blowing clouds of smoke over the dirty dishes. Garry walked in from the back door with another young man who was introduced as 'Buster' Floyd, his mate with whom he had been playing cards last Wednesday.

"Well, what have your bastards got for us? Where's my Benny?" shouted Betty.

"Hello, Betty," said Harry sitting at the table and shifting the dirty cup and plate to the side. "We've had no response from our all-points bulletin. He's disappeared. Are you sure he didn't have another woman?"

Betty screeched. "He wouldn't dare. He knew that I'd cut his balls out if he did."

Garry stepped to the table. "I can tell you for sure that Dad wasn't like that. No way."

"Have you been back to the hotel where Ben was drinking?"

"Yeah, they told me that dad left the pub with another man. They had never seen that bloke before. He was a pretty tough looking bloke but was well-dressed. Someone said they saw Dad get into a car with him."

Harry told him to sit at the table. "Now, Garry, we need to clear up the details of the robbery at North Rocks the other day. Your Dad and Tom Lebovich organised it and you were the getaway driver."

Betty screeched again and banged the table. "Get out of here you mongrels. You're not gunna stitch up my Benny and Garry for that job. You bloody cops'll do anything to get us poor people into trouble."

Harry reached out and placed his hand gently on her arm. "Just calm down, Betty. Whatever has happened to Ben is connected to that robbery, and we have to know what went on so we can get to the bottom of Ben's disappearance."

Garry spoke up. "Honest-to-goodness, Harry, I wasn't there. Buster here can tell you that. Can't you, Buster?"

Buster was standing at the door fidgeting with the buttons on his fly. "Yeah. Garry was with me."

"Where?"

"We were handline fishing down at the Recreation Park and then Garry went out on the boat with his Dad."

"Did your dad use the money to pay off Tony Stavros?"

Garry twitched. "I know nuffin' about that."

Buster shifted his position and spread his legs apart across the doorway. "Now don't you two go pickin' on me mate, Garry. He had nothin' to do with that job."

Jock walked across, took his arm and guided him to the table. "Now, Buster, you just tell us who really was on that job."

"I don't know, but someone at the pub said it was Billy Knobbs, who was the driver; but it wasn't Garry."

"Is he that tough little bloke who does the debt-collecting for Tony Stavros?" asked Jock.

"Yeah. He's a little mongrel of a bastard. I wouldn't trust him, but he's a great driver."

Harry looked at him. "And where will I find Billy Knobbs?"

"You'll usually find him at the Capitol Hotel in Marrickville."

Harry stood up. "Thanks. Come on, Jock."

"What about my Benny? What ya gunna do about him eh?" Betty sniffled.

"Calm down, Betty; we're still investigating. We'll let you know when we have more information."

***

Harry and Jock drove to Marrickville where they found Billy Knobbs on the verandah at the back of the hotel. They introduced themselves. Billy was a short, stocky man with a round face and receding hair. He had the look of a man who could handle himself in a tight situation.

"Now, Billy, we have it on good advice that you were the driver of the getaway car at North Rocks the other day. What do you say to that?"

Billy jerked around to face Harry. "No bloody way. You can't pin that on me. The bastard's lying. You ask the blokes here. They'll tell you I was here on that day."

Harry chuckled. "Yes, Billy, I'm sure that you could get five blokes here to swear on the Bible that, on that day, you were in heaven washing the feet of Jesus and then went off playing the harp with the Vestal Virgins. Now tell us the truth."

"Honest to God I wasn't there."

"Don't bring Him into it unless you really believe it; and I haven't seen you in church lately. So cut the crap and tell us what really happened."

"I heard that Bomber Earl's son, Garry was the driver that day."

"That's interesting, Billy, because he and his mate reckon you did it."

"That scumbag. They should have done him in with his old man."

Harry and Jock said nothing. Billy looked from one to the other waiting for a response, his eyes flicking back and forth. "Go and pick him up. He's the one who was there."

Jock decided to sit down next to Billy making his physical presence felt. "What happened to his old man, Billy?"

"I don't know."

Harry reached forward and lightly held Billy's arm. "You just said that Garry's dad was done in. We know he's disappeared. What happened to him?"

"I don't know."

"Let me jog your memory, Billy. You just admitted that Bomber Earl has been killed. It's not looking good for you because I'm holding you on charges of murder, assault and robbery; and that's just for starters."

"You can't do that. I wasn't there."

"Yes I can. I have witnesses. It's my guess that you'll get at least twenty years. But you'll have company. Bomber has some very good friends in Long Bay and Goulburn maximum security. He's been good to them over the years and they are not going to take too kindly to you when you go in."

"Come on, you can't do that. My lawyer will wipe the floor with you."

"Do you mean Tony Stavros' lawyer? Well, that'll be okay because we might call Tony to the witness stand as well. Bomber owed him a lot of money. Tony won't like having to sit in the witness box again. He won't want to be connected to Bomber's disappearance, with a possible murder charge against him."

Billy started to get up but Jock put his hand on his shoulder and eased him back into the chair. "You can't put that on me. I ain't gunna cop it like that."

"Well, Billy, you had best start talking. Who was driving that car?"

"Bomber's son, Garry, was the driver; and if he tells you otherwise, he's lying."

"But Bomber didn't get his cut of the takings on the day, did he?"

"I don't know, but I heard that he owed a lot of money for gambling debts."

Harry let go of his arm. "Now, Billy, everyone knows that you are the debt-collector for Tony. How much did he owe and how many times have you given him a visit?"

"I saw him a few times. He'd do a job and pay back some of it, but he never caught up with the lot."

"So the North Rocks job was a way of him paying off the big debt, and he got nothing for himself. Is that correct?"

Billy shuffled back and forth in the confined space of the chair. "You could say that."

"Well, why did he disappear?"

"I don't know, but someone said he threatened to go to work for the Melbourne mob. He's been seen talking and drinking with Nobby Clark and Darkie Moffitt; and they were mates of Scarface Fisher who was shot by your mob."

"Were Clark and Moffitt involved in his disappearance?"

"Oh, God no. He wanted to join up with them, but we think those two were involved in the drive-by shooting at the Elegant Lady."

"But surely, that's no reason to kill him."

"Maybe not, but the word goin' around is that he was willing to go to court and give evidence that Lebovich, Stavros and Durante had organised that North Rocks robbery, and that you were protecting him."

Harry and Jock looked at each other. Slowly Harry turned back to Billy. "Bomber disappeared last Wednesday afternoon at two o'clock. Where were you at that time?"

"I was at the Canterbury races."

"And who else was there?"

"Most of me mates was there. It was a big mid-week meeting. You should have been there. All the blokes from the CIB were there having a celebration. They can vouch for us. They could see us from their table up in the stands."

"Let's get back to Bomber's disappearance. What happened to him, Billy?"

"I told you. I don't know."

"It's your choice, Billy. Do you want Long Bay, or would you prefer Goulburn maximum or Grafton high security?"

"Come on, you bastards. You're trying to stitch me up for something I didn't do."

"You tell us what we need to know and I'll see what I can do for you; but I'm getting impatient."

Billy got up to go to the toilet. Jock followed. When he returned, Billy remained standing. Jock stood beside him. "Promise me that you didn't hear this from me."

Harry looked up. "I can't make any promises until you tell me the truth."

"Honest-to-goodness, it's the gospel truth. I swear."

"Go on."

"I've been told that the bloke who picked up Bomber at the Capitol Hotel was a big-time detective from Queensland."

"Yes, Billy, and I'm the Easter Bunny, but you're not getting an Easter egg until you tell us the truth."

"Honestly, Harry, ridgy-didge."

"Why would a detective from Brisbane want to meet with Bomber?"

"The rumour has it that he's very closely linked to some of the big crime boys here and in Brisbane."

"Did this detective have a name?"

"I don't know his name but I think it was like a German name."

"But why Ben the Bomber? He doesn't have any record with Queensland."

"The message was that Bomber was wanting to switch sides to the Melbourne mob and take all the loot from the North Rocks job to them, and then go to court to blame Tony Stavros and the others. He had to be got rid of to teach everyone a lesson, but the locals couldn't be seen to be involved."

"What happened?"

"They tell me that the big detective flew in from Brisbane at lunchtime, picked up Bomber at the hotel, and drove to Bankstown Airport and took off back home. It was all over in about an hour."

"Does that mean that Bomber's in Brisbane now?"

"No. The rumour has it that he took a dive out of the plane about twenty miles off the Coffs Harbour coast and is swimming back."

"Wow. That story better be true, Billy or you're in strife. Get going before I change my mind."

Billy jumped up and walked away quickly without turning back.

Harry turned to Jock. "Come on, mate. Let's go back to the office. We'll go to Bankstown first thing tomorrow morning."

Chapter 48
Wednesday

Jock drove to Bankstown while Harry thought about what Billy had told them yesterday. It seemed too weird to be true. Why would a senior detective from Queensland get involved with an armoured van robbery in Sydney? Harry knew that there had been exchanges of detectives between the two states since 1940 and he had met some of the Queensland men. On occasions a small group of the top New South Wales detectives would travel to Brisbane for a combined conference with their colleagues up north, and they visited down south at a later date.

Of all the Queenslanders that Harry had met, one man stood out; and he had a German name. He was Max Kruger. He was known up north by his nickname 'Killer'. He was renowned for his ability to bring in the big criminals and for his bravery at facing the toughest of them. He was often accompanied by his partner Albert Muller. Both of those men had German names but that was not uncommon. There had been a large influx of German migrants into southern Queensland late last century and early this century, and many people in Queensland had German heritage.

On reaching the Bankstown Airport, Harry and Jock went to the office and asked to see the register of flights in and out on the Wednesday when Bomber disappeared. The officer-in-charge showed them the register but there were no entries for any flights from Queensland.

Harry queried the entries. "Would it be possible that a flight from Queensland might have stopped at Newcastle or Armidale or Coffs Harbour and not be registered as coming from interstate?"

"That is possible, but the only one on that day was out of Newcastle, and he is a regular traveller. He's a top lawyer who sometimes has to appear here in Sydney. He had his regular hire car pick him up. There were no other flights from up north."

Harry thanked him and walked to the toilets. He was followed in by a young man from the office.

"Excuse me. Are you the detective asking about flights last Wednesday?"

"Yes," said Harry. "I'm Detective Harry Taylor. How can I help you?"

"I was on duty on Wednesday and I can tell you that another plane did arrive on that day that wasn't registered."

Harry did up the buttons on his fly. "Why wasn't it registered?"

"I don't know, but when I queried it with the boss he told me to shut up about it and it was none of my business."

"What type of plane?"

"It was a Piper with a pilot and one passenger. But when it took off about three o'clock it had two passengers."

"Did you recognise anyone on the plane?"

"No. Never seen them before. They're not regulars."

"Describe the three men."

"The pilot wore a cap, white shirt and navy trousers. He stayed in the canteen while the big man drove off in a car that was parked here. He returned with the other bloke, who was smaller, and they flew out of here."

"Was there any problem with them?"

"No. They seemed to get on okay. The two blokes squeezed into the back seat."

"And who might you be?"

"I'd prefer not to say. I don't want to lose my job."

Harry shook his hand. "Thanks very much. If you need to talk more, leave a message at police headquarters. Now get back inside before they want to know what you're up to."

Harry asked Jock to pull in to the shopping centre at Bankstown. They found a café and ordered lunch.

"Do you believe the rubbish that bloke told you in the toilet?" asked Jock.

"Well, I don't disbelieve it because we have nothing more to go on. Let's look at what we've got."

"What we've got, Harry is a bunch of scumbags who couldn't lie straight in bed."

"You're right, Jock, but, in all their talk, there is a grain of truth and we need to sift that from the rubbish. Let's put down what we already know."

Harry took out his notebook. In turn they suggested points to include in the list:

- Attempt on Harry's life at the flat.
- Car bombing. Murder of Stumpy Baxter.
- Murder of Knuckles Elliott.
- Possible involvement of Tom Lebovich.
- Shooting of Scarface Fisher. Fred Sherman. CIB.
- Criminals at Londonderry.
- Cannabis at Yarramundi and Macdonald Valley.
- Fire-bombing of the Marrickville hotel.
- Drive-by shooting at Elegant Lady.
- Turf wars between Sydney and Melbourne.
- Hoax at Kogarah.
- North Rocks armoured van robbery.
- Lebovich and Earl involvement?
- Cannabis at Leeton.
- Market arrests. Simpson, Walsh, Phillips and Lyons.
- Court case.
- Disappearance of Bomber Earl.
- Possible involvement of Billy Knobbs.
- Possible involvement of Queensland detective.

"Okay, Jock," said Harry. "You're the smart new bloke on the team. What's the answer?"

"Well, all of those things tie together. They're interrelated. The problem is to sort out who's on whose side. It comes down to a turf war between Sydney and Melbourne over gambling, prostitutes and drugs."

Harry sat back with hands behind his head. "I agree, Jock but it still doesn't tell us who did each of those crimes."

"To start with, I think Lebovich murdered Knuckles Elliott."

"But we've been ordered off that case. What does that say to you?"

"It could be, as they say, that Lebovich is involved in something more important and we have to back off so as not to ruin another investigation."

Harry sat back. "Yes, that could be right, but something stinks there. I can't put my finger on it and nobody's talking about it."

274

"Everything points to Lebovich being involved in the North Rocks job, but we can't prove it. What do you think, Harry?'

"I still think that Bomber Earl, his son, Garry, and Lebovich did that job. But Bomber tried to do the wrong thing with Lebovich or Tony Stavros and it all went wrong for him."

"But what about Billy Knobbs?"

"I don't think he was on that job but he's very much involved elsewhere. He and Tony Pantano are the bouncers for Squeaky Walsh and they do jobs for the other big boys."

"I agree. I'm putting him in the spotlight for the fire-bombing of the Fitzroy Hotel."

Harry coughed. "I agree. And he suggested that Nobby Clark and Darkie Moffitt did the drive-by shooting."

"The best information could come from them."

"Yes," said Harry. "When they knew who did the fire-bombing they probably took the necessary action to even the score."

Jock nodded. "But what about Billy Knobbs? I don't trust him."

"I did some checking on him. He was in an artillery battalion in New Guinea, and he was an expert with explosives. I wouldn't be surprised if he was the one who did the break-in at the army camp and set up the anti-personnel mine in my car. If so, then it's the Sydney mob who want me out of the way."

"Will we go back and pick him up now?"

"No. I want to do some more checking first. I think we've done enough here today. Let's drive home. I want to go over all aspects of this case this afternoon before we start again in the morning. You can drop me off at Stanmore on the way back."

***

As Harry walked in the back gate he saw Eileen pushing a lawn mower over the small patch of grass in the backyard. He walked across and took hold of the mower. "It's too hot for you to do that, Eileen. Leave it to me. I need the exercise."

"It's okay, Harry. I can do it. I've been doing it by myself for the last few years since Robert left for overseas."

"Then you need a rest. If you get me a cold drink I'll do the lawn."

"If you do that I'll go and prepare some dinner for the two of us."

"That's a deal, Eileen."

Harry stripped off his shirt and finished the lawn. After showering and getting dressed in clean shorts and shirt he walked to the hotel to buy some beer and a bottle of sherry. He picked a rose from the neighbour's garden. He gave the rose and sherry to Eileen and poured a beer for himself and a sherry for her.

"Harry," said Eileen anxiously. "Was that you the papers were talking about this morning?"

"Yes, Eileen, but don't take much notice of it. It's all paper talk."

"It sounds much more than that to me, Harry."

"It's just a case I've been working on."

"But couldn't the magistrate see that you're trying to clean up this city from those terrible drugs?"

"Don't blame him. He's just doing his job. He has to stick to the law; and so do I. Sometimes I tend to cut corners with those rules in order to bring a criminal to justice. It works sometimes and on occasions it doesn't."

"But it doesn't seem right," said Eileen sternly.

Harry reached across the table and gently took her hand. "Eileen, I don't want you worrying about me. You've got enough on your mind with your new job. Tell me about it."

Over a good meal, a few beers and a couple of glasses of sherry, the two of them chatted about her job and her life before she lost her husband. As the night progressed the tensions of the day fell away. The atmosphere mellowed.

They finished the evening with another sherry and some apple pie. The extra helping of double-thick cream did the trick.

Chapter 49
Thursday

Jock watched Harry as he came into the room. "Well you look as happy as a kookaburra in a snake pit, this morning. Did you have a good sleep last night?"

"You could say that," replied Harry with a smile.

"You know, Harry, if we knew who was involved in stealing that gear from the army camp we might get a link to who bombed your car."

Harry smiled. "Because I had a good night's sleep last night I woke with a fresh mind this morning and I had the same idea. I'll give my friend, Father Ambrose, a call."

"Are you going to get him to call the Big Fellow upstairs?"

"No, Jock. I don't have any credits up there any more and I believe we have to keep our feet firmly on the ground with this case."

Harry called the army camp at Ingleburn and was put through to Ambrose.

"I don't talk," said Ambrose, "until I get my two meat pies with mushy peas from Harry's Café de Wheels that you promised me last year."

"Sorry about that, Ambrose. It must have slipped my mind."

"Now, if I was a reporter from the *Daily Mirror* I would be taken to Andre's Nightclub in the city for a big nosh up and entertainment but, because I'm just a lowly army chaplain, I get nothing."

"Don't worry, Ambrose I'll say a prayer for you when I go to bed tonight."

"Please don't. I don't want the start of World War Three. Now, how can I help?"

Harry laughed but then became serious. "I heard that the army carried out an investigation into that break-in at Holsworthy with the theft of those guns and mines. You know everyone, Ambrose. Could you get us a meeting with the chief over there? We need information quickly."

"He's Colonel Taffy Hayes; a great bloke. When do you want to see him?"

"Now."

"I have to go there this morning. Add a good bottle of wine at Andre's nightclub and I'll see what I can do."

Half an hour later Ambrose phoned back. "Taffy will see you at ten-thirty. I'll see you there when you arrive. I've asked the guard not to shoot you on sight."

"Thanks, mate."

Harry and Jock drove to Holsworthy camp where they met Father Ambrose and Colonel Taffy Hayes.

After introductions Ambrose stood up. "I'm going off to save some souls. There's no use wasting my time on you lot unless, of course, young Jock, here, hasn't been contaminated too much from working with Harry."

"He's as pure as the driven snow," said Harry. "But I'm working on him."

"See what I mean, Taffy? Tell them nothing and piss them off. Harry's nothing but trouble unless you want to get your face on the front page of the paper. He's got contacts there."

They all burst out laughing. Ambrose left the room.

"Taffy, thanks for seeing us. We believe that you carried out an investigation into the break-in here and you have locked up one of your men for being an accessory. We'd like to interview him to see if we can find a link to the outsiders involved. Will that be possible?"

"Sure, Harry. Ambrose told me of your time together in New Guinea. You certainly made an impression on him, and I respect his work here. The soldier responsible for letting in those blokes is Sergeant 'Bluey' Shrimpton. I'll get the guard to take him to the interview room in the guard house. The Stick Orderly will take you over there."

"Thanks, Taffy."

As Harry and Jock entered the room the guard and Shrimpton snapped to attention. "Stand easy, men," said Harry. "Sergeant Shrimpton, you sit there. Guard, you can wait outside. Relax, this man is going nowhere."

Jock placed his chair behind Shrimpton, between him and the door. Harry faced the prisoner across the table. "Sergeant Shrimpton, tell me about your time in the army."

Bluey explained that he joined the army in 1941 and, after a short training, was sent to New Guinea. Not long after he arrived he was part of an early advance group on the Kokoda Track, but he slipped into a ravine, badly tearing tendons in his knee. He was declared unfit to continue. He was sent back to Port Moresby to work in the stores and he continued in that role until after the war.

"Sergeant, I understand you were behind the recent robbery of arms and ammunition from this army base. Tell us what happened."

"I'm not guilty. I wasn't at the store when the robbery took place."

"But you are in charge of that store. Is that correct?"

"No. The Regimental Sergeant Major is in charge."

Harry waited before continuing. "But the RSM is not in the store each day. In fact, I put it to you that he left the running of the store to you."

"Well, I did most of the work, but I have other soldiers helping me."

"Where were you on the evening of the robbery?"

"I was in the sergeants' mess having dinner."

Jock cut in. "That's a handy alibi, isn't it?"

Harry stood, walked to the window and turned slowly. "Is it true that you took out an army vehicle that afternoon?"

"Yes. I had to pick up some gear from Liverpool Railway Station."

"But the records from the gate state that you returned on foot."

"I don't know what you're talking about. I brought that truck back."

Harry paused. Bluey became more agitated. He asked permission to smoke. It was denied. Harry walked back to the desk, leaned across and looked Bluey in the eye. "No you didn't. That truck returned at dinner time with two soldiers in the cabin. You were already in the mess hall."

"That's a lie. I brought that truck back in the afternoon."

Harry looked up. "Jock, would you go out and get a jug of water and three mugs? This conversation is getting very dry."

When Jock left, Harry leaned across the table and spoke quietly. "Bluey, let's stop mucking around. The army has found you guilty of negligence in your duty to keep proper security of the store. I'm going to add to that and have you charged for aiding and abetting a robbery from that store, and an accessory to murder. Those robbers did not break and enter. They didn't have to. You left the store unlocked."

"That's not true. I always lock up before I leave."

"You also provided the army truck and two uniforms to your friends so that they could drive in and take the goods. You went out after dark and drove the empty truck back to the camp. The record at the gate shows that."

"You can't put that on me. I wasn't there."

Jock returned with the water. He took time to fill the mugs. Bluey took two nervous sips. Harry took his time drinking his. He sat back, his pyramid of fingers locked under his chin, eyes fixed on Bluey who turned side on to avoid the stare.

"Bluey, is it true that you and your brother joined up with a bloke called Billy Knobbs?"

"I don't know anyone by that name."

"Have you got dementia, Bluey?"

"No. What do you mean?"

"Well, Private William Knobbs joined up on the same day as you and slept in the same tent. At the end of hostilities he worked in the store with you at Port Moresby for a year to decommission all the equipment."

"I can't remember him."

"That's funny because he remembers you well. He said you and him were great drinking mates."

Harry turned. "Detective Burns, what do you think?"

Jock walked slowly around the table, stopped behind Harry and stared at Bluey. "He's lying like a pig in mud. Do you want me to have a private conversation with him? He might be more forthcoming in a quiet one-on-one situation."

Harry paused. "Not just yet. We'll save that for later, if necessary. I think Bluey is ready to talk."

Bluey blinked nervously. "I've told you everything I know."

"No, Bluey. You haven't even started yet. Now let's get to the serious stuff. I'm not here to talk about negligence in leaving the store open. The army can deal with that. I'm talking about murder; and you're up to your neck in it."

"What do you mean? I ain't done anything."

"I'm going to charge you with conspiracy to commit a murder, robbery, assault and being an accomplice to property damage. It looks like you will be going down for twenty-five to thirty years. Say goodbye to your wife and kids."

Bluey leapt out of the seat screaming. "You can't do that. I have my rights."

Jock shoved him back into the chair. "If you do that again I'll tie you to the chair."

Harry resumed. "I put it to you, Sergeant Shrimpton, that on the day of the robbery you drove an army truck out of this base. Two other men dressed in army uniforms dropped you back at the gate late in the afternoon. Those two men returned at dinner time, drove to the store where they loaded guns, ammunition and anti-personnel mines and left the camp with papers, signed by you, stating that they were carrying garbage to the dump. They returned later that night where you met them at the back gate. You drove the empty truck back into camp."

"That's a lie."

"One of those men was Billy Knobbs, your friend from New Guinea. The other man was probably Barry McGill, also known as Shooter McGill. He's a hit man for the big crime bosses in this state. They, or someone close to them, took out a contract on me. One of them took a shot at me. When that failed they used one of the anti-personnel mines stolen from this camp to blow up my car, hoping I was in it. I wasn't, but it killed my mate."

"What's that got to do with me? I wasn't there."

Harry walked around the table and tapped Bluey lightly on the shoulders. "But you organised the robbery from your storeroom. You are an accomplice. An accomplice is just as guilty as the man who pulled the trigger; or the one who set and exploded the mine in my car. You are guilty of murder. You are going down for the rest of your life unless you cooperate with us."

"What do you mean?"

"Confess to your part in this and give us details of the operation."

"No way. I ain't confessing to anything"

"Put it this way, Bluey. If you tell us, it could be the difference between staying in gaol for the rest of your life, or doing ten years with good behaviour. It's your choice."

"Can I think about it?"

"Sure. Jock, call in the guard. We'll leave you alone in here for half an hour."

One hour later Harry and Jock left with a written confession.

They called in to thank the colonel for his cooperation.

"What do you want me to do with him?" asked Taffy.

"Just keep him here for a while until we do some more investigating. When we tie all the pieces together he'll have to face extra charges in court."

Harry and Jock went back to headquarters where they wrote their reports before going to the chief superintendent to get warrants to search the properties of Billy Knobbs and Barry McGill.

At first, Twain was in doubt about this operation but, because it involved the attempt on Harry's life, he finally agreed.

Harry and Jock visited the court complex nearby and convinced the chamber magistrate that there was good reason to issue the search warrants.

As they walked out Harry said, "Let's call it a day. Be here at eight in the morning and we'll go to Billy Knobbs' place to do a search. He lives in Malcolm Lane, Erskineville. Ask Redfern station to give us two backup men. See you in the morning."

Chapter 50
Friday

Harry and Jock drove to Redfern police station, picked up two constables, Phil Westacott and Angus Bishop, and continued to Malcolm Street, Erskineville, where they found the terrace house where Billy Knobbs lived. The two-storey facade looked tired but clean. A good coat of paint would have improved the presentation. A 1940 Humber Super Snipe in good condition was parked at the kerb. Harry asked Phil to go to the back lane and cover that exit. Harry banged the brass door knocker in the shape of an ancient sailing ship. A young boy answered the door.

"Who are you?" he asked.

"Is your dad at home?" asked Harry.

"Yes. I'll go get him."

Billy came to the door, his thinning hair ruffled. He was dressed in a blue singlet, dirty shorts and slippers. When he saw Harry he slammed the door shut and ran through the house; but he hadn't turned the lock. Harry opened the door and he, Jock and Angus entered. A woman and three children were sitting at the kitchen table having breakfast. The children were dressed for school. Phil Westacott came in the back door with a firm grip on Billy's arm.

Harry explained their visit. "Billy, we have good reason to believe that you are in possession of stolen goods on these premises and we have a warrant to search this house."

He turned to Billy's wife. "I suggest, Mrs Knobbs, that you send the children off to school before we start. We don't want them missing out on their education."

Billy's wife, Jean, who seemed a meek and mild person, ushered the children out. She seemed embarrassed by the events unfolding in her house. When the children had gone, Harry ordered the search.

"Phil, you stay with Billy and his wife in the lounge room. Angus, you get that stool next to the bench and climb up through that manhole in the hallway into the roof and check it out. Jock, you go out to the shed and toilet in the backyard and I'll look through the bedrooms and bathroom."

Before long, Jock came in from the backyard carrying a large metal ammunition box. He opened it to reveal clips of .303 bullets and magazines full of .45 shells. Harry recognised the magazines as those used in the Owen guns. He had used them in the Islands and was very familiar with them. His trusty Owen gun had been his lifesaver on a number of occasions.

Angus called out from inside the roof cavity. "Can someone take these for me?"

Harry stood in the hall and took two Owen guns, a box of grenades, three Enfield .303 rifles and four anti-personnel mines. After helping Angus he went to the bedroom where, in a cupboard, he found two Enfield revolvers and one Webley.

Harry got Phil to put the cuffs on Billy. He read Billy his rights. "Put him in the car, Phil. We'll take him back to Redfern. Angus and Jock, load that gear in the boot."

"What about Mrs Knobbs?" asked Phil.

"Leave her here. I doubt that she had anything to do with this, even if she did know the weapons were here. It's more important for her to be here for the children when they come home from school. I'll arrange for Welfare to look in on them later."

They loaded the car and drove to Redfern where they took Billy to an interview room. Harry reminded Billy of his rights to have a lawyer in attendance.

"I can't afford no lawyer, and I don't need one, 'cause I didn't do nothin' wrong."

"You can make a call, Billy. Surely, Tony Stavros will get a good lawyer to represent you. He always looks after the men he trusts."

"I don't need no help."

"Billy," Harry cautioned, "we have a car load of stolen military equipment found in your house, and you're going to try to tell us that you had nothing to do with that. Then you'll tell us that someone broke into your house while you, the wife and kids were down at the beach getting a suntan and you weren't aware that it was there."

"Yeah, that's right. That's what really happened. How did you know?"

"By the way, Billy, your mate Bluey Shrimpton, asked us to pass on his regards to you."

Billy wriggled on the chair and leaned forward to look down at his singlet where he found a crumb of toast. He flicked it off. "I don't know who ya talkin' about."

"That's odd, Billy because you were in the same artillery unit in New Guinea, and you were an expert with explosives. At the end of the fighting in Port Moresby, you worked with Shrimpton decommissioning that artillery. You were great mates then, and still are."

"I don't know him."

Harry put in front of Billy a sheet of paper containing the list of goods taken from his house this morning. "We know that you were in the army truck that entered the camp. You drove it to the stores and loaded these goods. Who was the other man in that truck?"

"I don't know what you're talkin' about."

"You and your mate drove to your place and hid the goods. You returned to the camp where you handed back the truck to Shrimpton at the back gate of the camp."

"That's a bloody lie. That bastard is trying to set me up. You wait till I catch up with him."

"Thank you, Billy, for admitting that you know Shrimpton. He's not happy with you either because he thinks you led us to him. It should be a great party you have when you meet up in gaol."

"I ain't going to gaol because I ain't done nothin'"

"Detective Burns, would you like to discuss the car bombing with our friend, Billy?"

Harry got up and Jock came around to take his seat. "Sure and begorra I would. Now, Billy, I'm not going to muck around like Detective Taylor. He's too kind, but I haven't got the time to waste on scum like you. I'm going to charge you with murder."

Billy spun around to face Harry who was casually taking notes in his book. "He can't do that. I have rights. Get this bastard out of here or I'll put in a complaint to the commissioner."

Harry continued taking notes. Jock slammed his fist on the table and shouted. "Pay attention to me, Billy. I'm the one asking the questions. You weren't honest with Detective Taylor but begorrah you're going to start talking to me now."

"I ain't done nothin'"

"You stole anti-personnel mines from the army camp. You are an expert in explosives. You spent most of your time in New Guinea working with mines. You set one of those mines under the seat in Detective Taylor's car and had it set to go off when he sat in the driver's seat. That explosion killed a man. I'm charging you with murder."

"I didn't do it. Honest-to-God."

"If you didn't, who did?"

"I don't know but it wasn't me. Honest."

"Now let's go to the next crime. You were driving the getaway car in the North Rocks hold-up and, at the time, you were carrying an Enfield army revolver stolen from the camp."

"That's a lie. I wasn't there. My wife will be able to tell you I was at home."

Jock paused then sternly spelled out his message. "If you do anything to hurt your wife or make her lie to protect your hide, I'm going to come after you. You won't know what hit you. I can't stand scumbags who treat their women like dirt to be trodden on. Do you get my message loud and clear, Billy?"

"I wasn't there and you can't prove otherwise."

"You were there because Bomber Earl told us."

"Well that's a lie, because Bomber's not here to tell you."

Jock sat back with a smile and waited for Billy to think about what he had just said. "Well now, Billy, if you know that Bomber's no longer with us then you had a part in his disappearance."

"I don't know what you're talkin' about."

"Billy, we all know that you're the hit man for Tony Stavros and Whispers Durante and anyone else who is willing to pay the money. You arranged Bomber's disappearance, so we'll add conspiracy to murder to the list."

"You can't pin that on me. I wasn't nowhere near him."

"Where were you when it happened, Billy?"

"I was home with me missus."

Jock slammed the desk again. "I've just told you what I'll do if you hurt that woman. I'll hang your balls on the front verandah of your house to show everyone what a bastard you are. Your wife doesn't deserve scum like you."

Harry coughed and stood up. Jock looked up and moved out of the seat, walked around and stood directly behind Billy. Harry settled back into the chair opposite Billy. He put his notebook on the table and started writing. Billy fidgeted as he waited and waited.

"Now, Billy, let's have a look at the drive-by shooting at the Elegant Lady nightclub. The shooter was using an Owen machine gun. He sprayed the walls and windows with bullets. As you were the only one in town who had possession of such weapons and the right ammunition, you were the one who did that job. So I'm now charging you with that offence. We'll add it to the murder charges mentioned by Detective Burns."

"You bastards. You're trying to pin all these things on me. I didn't do it."

"What interests me, Billy is that the Elegant Lady is owned by Whispers Durante, your boss. Why would you want to shoot up the joint of your boss. Have you got a death-wish?"

"I didn't do it."

"It looks to me Billy that you and Bomber were doing deals on both sides of the table. I think you are now working for the Melbourne boys."

"That's a lie. I heard that it was Nobby Clark and Darkie Moffitt who did that job."

"But you supplied them with the Owen guns and you can't deny doing that fire-bombing at the Fitzroy Hotel at Marrickville."

"I didn't give them anything, and I wasn't there."

"You're not going to tell me that you were with your wife, are you?"

Jock rested his hands on Billy's shoulders.

"No. I was playing cards with me mates."

"Well, Billy, let's summarise where we are up to. We have you for murder, conspiracy to murder, arson, break, enter and steal, discharging firearms in a public place, property damage, robbery and having unlicensed weapons. How will your poor wife and kids survive while you spend the rest of your life inside?"

"You rotten bastards. This is a set-up. You won't get away with this."

Harry looked at Jock. "Take him out to the car. We'll take him to the magistrate for a preliminary hearing."

They drove to the court complex in the city where Harry arranged for a hearing. After listening to Harry and Jock's presentation, and Billy's complaints, the magistrate determined that Billy would appear again in February on the charges relating to the army camp robberies, but was not convinced there was sufficient evidence to support the other charges. He released Billy on bail with the proviso that he report daily to the Redfern police.

Harry and Jock walked to headquarters where they met Charlie Rockwell. He invited them to a special party at Randwick Race Club the next day to celebrate Bob Crow's birthday. He handed them tickets to the Members' dining room.

Chapter 51
Saturday

There was very little food in Harry's flat so he spent the early hours shopping for supplies. When he returned he saw Eileen taking out parcels to put in the garbage bin. Harry dashed out to help her.

"Thanks, Harry. I miss having Robert here to do these jobs. If you're not doing anything I'll make a cup of tea."

"That would be great, Eileen. I'll be there in a minute."

Harry took out the garbage, washed his hands and walked up to Eileen's kitchen. Eileen had a fresh sponge cake and scones on the table. She poured two cups and sat down.

"You know, Harry, it was good being with you the other night. It's great to have company. Since Robert died, it's been so lonely. It's okay in the day because I'm at work but at home I miss him very much."

"Yes," said Harry. "That's the problem with war. It's not just the men who die but it's the women and kids left behind. That's the real tragedy."

Eileen sat up and shook her head. "But enough of that. I have to get over it. Now, how's your investigation going?"

Harry licked the icing from his fingers as he ate the last slice of the sponge. "Fairly hectic. We've been working on a couple of nasty cases."

"What are they?"

"Just a missing person case, a drive-by shooting and some robberies."

"You seem so casual and easy going about it, as if it is a stroll in the park."

Harry reached for another scone. "It's much more serious than that, but I don't like others worrying about it. It's best handled by us as quietly as possible."

"What have you got on for the weekend?"

"I have to go to the races at Randwick this afternoon because we are celebrating the birthday of one of the CIB detectives."

Eileen poured another cup. "I can't see any sense in putting money on donkeys running around a track."

"Neither can I. But it's for Bob, not the races."

"If you're doing nothing tomorrow would you like to have a roast for lunch? I don't bother cooking a leg of lamb just for one person."

"Thanks, Eileen, that'd be great. It'll be like Sunday lunch at home in the country. Now I must be going."

Harry caught the train to Central and a tram to Randwick. He was shown to the Members' dining room overlooking the finishing post. It was crowded. Sitting at a large table near the window were all of the CIB detectives together with the chief superintendent, Tony Jacobs and a couple of area superintendents. On the next table were the Minister of Police and a few well-known judges, magistrates and lawyers.

Harry walked around to Bob Crow and handed him a birthday present; a fine bottle of aged Scotch whisky.

"Thanks, Harry. By the feel of the parcel it's not a pair of socks or a hanky. I think I'll enjoy this."

As Charlie walked past, he slapped Harry on the arm. "Come over here with us, Harry. Jock is already here."

Sitting at the end of the table were Fred Sherman, Joe Cross and Jock. Fred handed Harry a beer. "How are you going Harry? I hear that you're stirring up a few possums."

"G'day, Fred. No, mate, only a few bull ant's nests. Nothing to worry about."

"That's not what I've been hearing, Harry. Are you okay now that we've got rid of Scarface for you?"

"Yes, that was great of you and the boys to get him out of the way. He was a nasty bit of work but there are still three others linked to the Melbourne mob who regularly come to Sydney."

"Who are they?"

"Nobby Clark and Darkie Moffitt are regulars here now, and I'm half-expecting Billy Stenson to get involved soon. What do you think?"

"You're right, Harry. The big danger here now is the influx of the Melbourne mob. We've been doing a lot of intelligence on them lately. The attempt on your life, the fire-bombing of the Fitzroy and the shooting of the Elegant Lady were all done by them."

"But why would they fire-bomb the Fitzroy? I thought that hotel was owned by the Melbourne mob."

Fred snorted. "I think it's owned by Jackie Abbott, but he's at war with Billy Stenson and Splinter Woods down in Melbourne. They're all crazy down there. I wouldn't trust any of them. They've been at each other's throats down there for years and there's nobody in their police force who can keep them apart. That's why we have to get rid of them from here."

Harry sipped his beer. "What's the intelligence coming out of Melbourne?"

"We used to have good relations with the blokes down there and then they got a new commissioner, and he said he didn't trust us. So, stuff the lot of them. We don't need them. We've got our own contacts down there."

"Have you got any information on the North Rocks armoured van robbery?"

Fred scratched the side of his nose and laughed. "That was that stupid Bomber Earl. He had a good thing going until he decided the grass was greener on the Melbourne side, and he and Billy Knobbs thought they could do that job for them and get away with it."

Harry took another sip. "We pulled in Billy yesterday, and have him on toast for the army camp job and hope to get him for the van robbery as well. Bomber's disappeared. Have you got any leads on where he might be?"

"My guess, Harry is that he grabbed the loot and took off for Melbourne. I'd say that one or a few of the big four down there will be looking after him. Check out Splinter Woods, Bruiser Bignall, Jacky Abbott or Billy Stenson. They'll be up to their necks in it."

"There was a weird story going around the other day that a senior Queensland detective flew here, kidnapped Bomber and dumped him somewhere off the coast on the way back to Brisbane. Have you heard that?"

"Yes. I've never heard so much bullshit in all my life. I was talking to Tony Stavros the other day. He said the Melbourne boys are spreading that rumour to distract us away from them. There's absolutely no reason why Brisbane would want to be involved in anything down here. They've got enough problems up there."

"I know some of them up there, but not everyone," said Harry.

"I know all of them," said Fred. "We have combined meetings to share intelligence. Ask Joe."

Joe turned around, beer in one hand and cigarette in the other. He shifted the chair so that he could get a good look at the finishing post.

"G'day, Joe," said Harry. "We've just been talking about the wild rumour that a detective from Brisbane came here to take out Bomber Earl."

Joe drew on his cigarette and coughed out the smoke. "If you believe that rubbish, Harry, you'll believe in pixies at the bottom of the garden. That's just a smoke screen put out there by those bastards from Melbourne to take the attention away from them. Don't fall for that one, Harry."

Allan Twain and the Minister of Police walked past on their way to the bookmakers, nodded in recognition and continued without a word.

Charlie Rockwell looked at Harry. "G'day, mate. Didn't see your photo in the paper this morning. Must be a bad news day."

"No, Charlie. I asked them to keep the space for the race details today. What are your big tips for today?"

"I like the favourite in the third race but I'll wait until Tony Stavros comes and gives me some tips. He'll be here shortly."

Three waitresses came from the kitchen and placed a large birthday cake with sparklers on top in front of Bob. Two waiters walked around the table pouring champagne into tall glasses for all the guests. When everyone had a drink Fred Sherman called the gathering to order.

"Good afternoon, Ladies and Gentlemen. Thank you for coming today. I'm surprised that we're here today celebrating the fifty-fifth birthday of this old bear. Many people over the years have tried to stop this event from taking place but the old bastard has beaten them every time. He's as tough as a mallee bull, with a hide as thick as a Territory crocodile and a gut as big as a bull elephant. He's taken on the toughest crims in this country and come out on top every time. He's not the prettiest animal on earth, but all the sheilas want to hug and kiss him, and he won't tell me what gives him that magic charm. So let's raise our glasses to the old bull and wish him a happy birthday."

They all drank and sang *Happy Birthday.*

Harry noticed that Tony Stavros, Whispers Durante and Rosie Travener all came around to Bob to give him a present and wish him good luck. The three of them mixed freely with the other guests around the table. Whispers approached Harry and Jock who, by then, were standing in the background, and spoke in his raspy voice.

"G'day, Harry and Jock. I heard you two have been busy lately. Keep up the good work. People like Billy Knobbs and Bomber Earl are the scum of the earth and should be put away for life."

Harry smiled and shook his hand. "Thanks, Whispers. It's good to see you supporting us crime-fighters. We need more like you."

"Any time, Harry. By the way, if you two want a night out, give me a call. I'd like you to enjoy our hospitality at my nightclub, the Elegant Lady, as a thank you for catching up with those two mongrels who shot up my joint. It's the least I can do as a thank you."

"Thanks, Whispers. I'll give a call if I have a free night."

As Whispers walked away Jock turned to Harry. "Do you mean that you're going to that joint to get free grog, a night at the gambling tables and maybe a girl in the bedroom?"

Harry laughed. "Come on, Jock. Don't tell me you're not interested to see what goes on there."

"No thanks, Harry. Not for me."

"I don't have any free nights either. I'm fully booked for the next few months."

Jock gave a sigh of relief. "But it's obvious that some of our blokes go there."

"Yes. The CIB boys do. That's where they get vital information. The top brass and the politicians love it so they will always support them."

After the horses passed the winning post in the third race, Joe Cross walked across and whispered to the group. "Tony Stavros mentioned number six in the fourth race but don't put on any bets until two minutes before the race starts; and not with the same bookmaker. Spread yourselves around. Good luck."

As Joe walked away Jock asked. "What the hell was all that about, Harry?"

"Tony Stavros controls most of the SP betting in this city. He owns racehorses and he pays jockeys to run dead when he decides it's necessary. He's only got to control one race each day and he makes a fortune."

"But why wait until the last two minutes?"

"He lets his mates know but, if they put it on too early, the price will drop quickly. That horse is listed now at 10-1 or 12-1. If some of us rushed in now, the price would drop to 3-1. If we all go at the last minute the price will stay high."

"But race fixing is against the law."

"Welcome to the real world of racing, Jock. This is why they say that betting is a mug's game."

"Are you going to put on a bet, Harry?"

"Yes, because I had already decided that I liked the look of that beast. I worked with horses in the country and I can pick a good horse when I see their deep chest, alert eyes, a good coat and strong hindquarters."

The afternoon continued with much drinking, cheer, laughter and good will for Bob on his birthday. Harry and Jock left after the last race and went home. Harry used some of his winnings on the last race to buy a bottle of Mateus, and a bunch of red roses.

<h1 style="text-align:center">Chapter 52
Sunday</h1>

The kookaburras laughed at Harry as he dragged himself from his bed and staggered to the shower. The cool water cleared his head. He shaved and dressed ready for a casual day of rest. He was half-way through his toast and eggs when there was a knock on the door. Harry sensed it wasn't Eileen as the knock was too strong. He opened the door cautiously to see Jock standing there.

"Sorry to disturb you, Harry but we've a job to do. I got a call from headquarters this morning. A fisherman has picked up a body out at sea. He brought it in and we have to go and investigate."

"Did you tell them it's our day off?"

"Sure did, but they said that there was nobody else available. So we drew the short straw."

"But you could have gone, Jock and left me to go to church."

Jock laughed, reached across and took half of Harry's toast. "Thanks, mate. I didn't have time for breakfast."

"Where's this body?"

"The fishermen work out of Gunnamatta Bay and are now tied up at Cronulla at the ferry wharf."

"Has anyone contacted SIB?"

"Yes, I did that; and they'll have their team there when we arrive."

"Okay, Jock, let's get going and get it over and done with."

Being Sunday morning there was little traffic and they made the journey to Cronulla quickly. They found the fishermen and their boat at the wharf. The owner's name was Spiro Raptis, and his son was Pedro. They were very anxious to get rid of their unwanted cargo.

Harry and Jock walked to the boat. On the forward deck was what looked to be a large roll of canvas caught up in some fishing net.

Harry turned to the owner of the boat. "Spiro, tell us about your trip this morning."

Spiro scratched his bearded chin. "Pedro and I went out last night and set the nets. We went out from Port Hacking and motored north and out from Kurnell. We have a good spot straight out from the point. When we pulled in the nets early this morning we found this heavy bag. We pulled it in and got it up on the deck. It was pretty heavy. It took both of us to get it on board."

"You did well. It wouldn't have been easy with only two of you."

Jock and Harry climbed onto the deck. With help from Spiro and Pedro they untangled the net and separated it from the canvas bag. Harry looked up and saw the SIB wagon pull up with Rita Flynn, Jack Witherspoon and Archie Ingram on board. He called for them to come on deck.

"At least, Harry," said Rita, "if you're going to invite me out on a Sunday you could take me to lunch at a good restaurant. A plate of oysters followed by some grilled snapper and chips and then an ice cream sundae would go down well, followed by a walk on the beach. What about it, eh?"

"Are you leading me to temptation on the sabbath, Rita?"

"No, I'll let you take the lead, Harry."

They all burst out laughing and then Archie stepped forward. "Come on, you lot, let's get this over and done with. I've got a golf match this afternoon."

They undid the ropes around the canvas and spread it out.

"Well, look who we have here," said Harry. "It's our good friend, Billy Knobbs. Come and have a look, Jock."

Jock stepped towards the front of the boat. "Yes. There's no mistaking Billy. He's still wearing his blue singlet, dirty shorts and slippers he had on when we saw him on Friday."

"What were you doing with him on Friday?" asked Jack.

"Young Billy's been a naughty boy. We had him on a break, enter and steal from the army camp. We believe it was those explosives that were used in my car bombing. The drive-by shooting of the Elegant Lady was done by an Owen gun taken from the camp. We think we could also have got him for the North Rocks armoured van robbery with Bomber Earl, and possibly for the fire bombing of the Fitzroy."

"But hasn't Bomber gone missing?" asked Archie.

"Yes," said Harry. "It's all too complicated at the moment. One rumour had it that a Queensland detective flew to Sydney to grab him and dump the body at sea, but the CIB boys yesterday said that was nonsense. They think that he and Billy have jumped ship from the Sydney blokes and joined the Melbourne mob."

"If they had," explained Rita, "that would be a good enough reason for the Sydney boys to do both of them in. It's no surprise to see this happen to Billy."

Archie looked at the wound in the centre of the forehead. "This looks like a professional job. I'd say it was a .38 shell at close range, but I'll do more testing later."

Jock cut in. "That could be from an Enfield revolver. We found a couple of them in Billy's house on Friday. He could have sold off some from the Holsworthy robbery and then got shot from one of them. That's justice for you."

Harry bent over. "Give me a hand to take off all of this canvas and examine the rest of him."

The group slowly unwrapped the canvas covering. They noticed that the left kneecap was shattered. Archie reasoned that it was done by another bullet. There was deep bruising on both legs, the abdomen and back. It was consistent with being beaten by a solid piece of timber or water pipe. The tibia and fibula on the left leg were broken in at least two places.

Rita took out her kit and took prints. Archie took photos. Jack did a thorough search of Billy's pockets and the canvas wrapping. He also took notes for the other two. Harry walked over to Spiro and Pedro.

"We won't be long. You blokes will want to get on with your work. Thanks for bringing this in. It's important to a major investigation we are carrying out and you've been very helpful. If someone dumped this at sea, why didn't it just sink and disappear? Why did it float and get caught in your net?"

Spiro scratched his beard again. "I can't be certain but I think it's because the canvas they used is polished and water resistant. It was wrapped fairly tight and therefore would have trapped air inside. Had we not picked it up in the nets it would have eventually got water logged and sank."

"That makes sense. The killers are probably sitting back at a barbecue today thinking they have committed the perfect crime. Let's hope that they left some evidence in the bag to tell us who they were."

"Can we go now?" said Spiro.

Harry looked to the others. "Give the team a few minutes and they'll load the body in the wagon and be on their way. Then it's all yours. Thanks again."

Harry and Jock helped wrap the body again and carry it to the wagon. The others packed up their gear and drove back to town. Harry and Jock drove to Billy's house in Erskineville. The door was answered by the same boy who greeted them on Friday.

"Is your mum in?" asked Harry.

"Hey, Mum, those bastards who were here the other day are back again."

Harry and Jock walked into the hall and waited until Jean came through. "Mrs Knobbs, I want you to sit down here in the lounge room. We have some bad news for you."

Jean stopped, put her hands to her mouth and gasped. "What have you bastards done to Billy? He didn't come home last night or the night before."

Harry took her arm gently and led her to a chair. "We haven't done anything to Billy. He left the court on Friday and we haven't seen him since. He was supposed to come home. But we have to tell you that he has been found today. He was murdered and his body was dropped out at sea."

Jean screamed in agony. The children rushed in to see what happened to their Mum. Harry asked Jock to take the children to the kitchen and explain why Billy was not coming home. Harry spent time trying to console Jean before asking questions about Billy's movements.

"Did Billy come home on Friday, Jean?"

"No. We didn't know where he was. He didn't phone."

"Do you know any reason why anyone would do this to Billy?"

"Billy never talked about what he did, but he had an argument with Bomber Earl last week. I don't know what it was about. I stay out of it and look after the kids."

"Would it have been about money or was it about the guns and ammunition we found here on Friday?"

"Honestly, I don't know."

"Other than Bomber, has anyone else been here to the house to see Billy in the last week?"

"Only his usual friends he goes fishin' with; except one bloke who came last Thursday. He was different to all of Billy's mates. He was young and well-dressed in a spivvy sort of way. You know, shiny new black shoes, tie, hair slicked back. Looked like he had money.”

“What did he talk about?”

“I dunno. I went out the back. I stay out of it.”

“Thank you, Jean. I have no more questions. I’ll phone Welfare to see if they can be of help. Someone will be in touch for you to identify Billy. They’ll pick you up here and bring you back home. That will be tomorrow. We’ll leave now.”

Jock dropped Harry off at Stanmore. He had just enough time to shower, get dressed and, with his bottle of Mateus and his bunch of roses, he walked to the back door of Eileen’s house.

“Just in time, Harry. I’ll have the meal on the table in twenty minutes. Thanks for these gifts. That’s lovely. Would you do the honours and open the bottle?”

“Did you get to church today?”

Eileen took a sip of wine. “Yes, and the sermon was on the evils of drink, and here we are drinking this beautiful wine. You are quite naughty to lead me astray like this.”

“Eileen, you will always have a special place in heaven. I’m sure that He will forgive you for a minor misdemeanour. So, let’s enjoy it before the sky falls in on us.”

“How was your morning, Harry? I saw you going out early with another man.”

“That was my partner, Jock. We had to go and investigate the finding of a body found floating off Kurnell by a fisherman.”

“Oh, what a horrible thing. I don’t know how you do those things.”

“I don’t know how you can sit in an office all day at your typewriter and calculator. I enjoy doing what we do. Someone has to do it.”

Eileen served the meal. They took their time and talked about their early life; Harry on the farm, Eileen in the western suburbs. Eileen tried to get Harry to talk about the war. He was reluctant. He knew that he was not allowed to discuss what he did in the Z Force.

The more they talked the more relaxed they became. It was a relief for Harry to take his mind off the events of the last four weeks; and Eileen was great company. For Eileen, it was wonderful to be with someone in a normal setting again instead of thinking about herself all the time and worrying whether she was doing the right thing. They felt comfortable in each other's company.

The roast lamb dinner reminded Harry of the traditional Sunday lunch at home in Sandy Creek. He was more at ease with Eileen than with his mother and father who were so angry that he had joined the police force and gone to war when he didn't have to.

Eileen served a wonderful lemon curd tart with three dollops of thick cream for dessert. They took their time finishing the last drops of Mateus.

"Come in here with me, Harry," Eileen said as she stood up and walked to the bedroom.

As she stood beside the bed she undid her dress and let it slide to the floor. She pulled back the sheet and slid underneath with her hand outstretched towards Harry. He took the hint, got undressed and slid under the sheet beside her. A summer storm was brewing. The street lights came on. Lightning struck.

Chapter 53
Monday

Rita looked up as Harry entered the SIB office. "Well, don't we look all bright and breezy? What's your secret, Harry? A good night's sleep maybe? Not like some of us who had to stay up all night working."

Harry laughed. "When you have a clear conscience, Rita, you always sleep well."

"Ha," snorted Rita. "When was the last time you had a clear conscience?"

Tony Jacobs walked in. "Okay you two, are you ready for a meeting?"

"Sure," said Harry. "Let's get the team together."

Tony, Harry, Rita, Jack, Jock and Archie went to the meeting room.

Archie opened the discussion. "Although Billy was beaten badly, the cause of death was a single shot to the head by a thirty-eight calibre bullet, probably fired from a revolver at close range."

Rita continued. "Fingerprints identify this person as William Knobbs, a person well-known to police. He has a long record of offences reaching back to his early teens."

Jack Witherspoon added his comments. "The autopsy showed that he had consumed a large amount of alcohol in the previous twenty-four hours which was not unusual, going on his earlier records. There was no trace of other drugs."

"What about other evidence?" asked Jock.

Jack replied. "What is more interesting was the vegetative matter trapped in the canvas and on his clothes."

"What do you mean, Jack?" asked Harry.

Jack placed a number of Cellophane bags on the table. "The team took samples of greenery, particles of soil and grease from the canvas for examination. Some of the greenery was dried, other bits were fresh."

Harry flicked his fingers over the bags. "What's your analysis, Jack?"

"These bags here contain vegetation from such things as fruit trees, celery, lettuce, cabbages and members of the cucurbit family such as pumpkin, watermelon or cucumber."

"Are we looking at a farmer?" asked Jock.

"Could be," said Jack. "Or it could be from somewhere like the markets. But to follow up with Jock's suggestion, we tested the soil particles and found a high proportion of particles consistent with soils found more in the western part of the state."

"What's in this other bag?" asked Tony.

"It's cannabis."

"Are you suggesting, Jack, that this piece of canvas has been used on a fruit and vegetable farm, probably out west, and maybe in the Murrumbidgee area?"

"Not necessarily, because we have to do some further analysis of the soil. But it points in that direction."

Harry looked again at the soil samples. "Could it be that this canvas came from the markets and was used to cover supplies from different areas like the Hawkesbury or Central Coast or even interstate?"

"Yes, that's definitely possible. We can't say that the vegetative material all came from the same area but our botany expert recognised seeds and leaves from the Weeping Myall and Yellow Box trees that are prevalent in the Riverina including the Murrumbidgee area."

Tony looked at Harry. "What do you think, mate?"

"Well, if it comes from the Murrumbidgee, it would most likely be our friends in Leeton or their associates. This canvas could have been used in the trucks that brought the produce to the markets. It could have been left at the markets to cover produce in the warehouses."

"Does that tie in with your other evidence?" asked Tony.

Harry picked up a packet. "It could. We know the Leeton men deal with Angelo Romano at the Haymarket, but I suspect that some of them also deal with Boss Gabor. The trouble is that we blew our case with Romano in the court because we didn't have a search warrant."

Tony stood up and walked to the blackboard. He wrote the names on the board. "Who else do we need to tie to these characters?"

Harry pointed to the board. "Romano is tightly tied to Whispers Durante, while Boss deals with whoever has the most money; and I think he might also be dealing with the Melbourne mob."

Rita raised her hand. "But surely those men wouldn't be out there shooting Billy Knobbs or getting rid of Bomber Earl."

"No," said Harry. "The Sydney blokes would use their standover men to do the job, and that brings in people like Tom Lebovich, Tony Pantano, Bluey Ricketts or Shooter McGill."

"What if the Melbourne mob did the job?" asked Jock.

"Well, we can eliminate Scarface Fisher and Knuckles Elliott because they're both dead. So that leaves people like Flash Evans, Darkie Moffitt and Nobby Clark."

"What's your best guess, Harry?" asked Tony.

"I'd say either Lebovich or McGill from Sydney, or Clark or Moffitt from Melbourne. Evans is in gaol, and I don't see the others as shooters. The others will break your leg, pull out your toenails with pliers or fire bomb your house but not use a gun."

Rita looked at Harry. "So what's your plan from here?"

"When we saw Jean Knobbs to tell her about Billy, she mentioned that she had been visited by a spivvy bloke who was asking about Billy. If he was the person who organised his disappearance, that would more likely fit the image of McGill. I'm going to visit Jean today with some mug shots and see what we come up with."

Tony got up. "Okay, team, get on with your reports and we'll get them to Harry by tomorrow morning."

"Thanks, team. Thanks, Tony. I think we're getting closer to sorting out this mess."

Harry and Jock drove to Erskineville. Billy's wife Jean led them to the lounge room.

"I'm sorry to disturb you again like this, Jean," said Harry, "but this is urgent. We need to get the man who did this to Billy, and we need your help."

"I don't see how I could be of help. I had nothin' to do with Billy's friends, and he didn't tell me what he was doin'. He just gave me the money to pay for everything."

Jock laid out the photos on the table. "I want you to take your time and tell us if you recognise any of these men."

Jean blew her nose loudly and tucked her hanky up her sleeve. Her hand was trembling as she fidgeted with the photos. Jock and Harry waited patiently. After five minutes she sat back and sobbed. "I don't think I know any of these men. They all look so rough."

Harry took her hand and gently squeezed it. "Take your time, Jean. Remember that these photos were taken at a police station when these men were arrested. They are not dressed up and many of them are unshaven with their hair out of place. Have another look."

After a while Jean pointed at one photo. "I think I've seen Billy with this man."

Harry recognised a photo of Bomber Earl. "Yes, Jean, that was a friend of Billy. Now look at the others."

After some time Jean pointed at two other photos. "That man looks as if he could be a brother of the smart bloke who came here the other day. And I've seen that other bloke but don't know his name."

Harry turned to Jock. "The first photo is Barry Shooter McGill and the second is Don Flash Evans from Melbourne."

He turned back to Jean. "How often have you seen the second man?"

"He was here about three times in the last couple of months. I dunno what they talked about. I just leave 'em alone. It's none of my business."

"Thanks, Jean. You've been very helpful. If you have any problem with Welfare give me a call at headquarters."

When they got back in the car Jock spoke first. "Evans from Melbourne had been a regular visitor earlier on but it was McGill who came the other day before Billy disappeared. What do you make of that?"

"It seems to fit in with what others are saying. It seems that Billy and Bomber, who were always closely associated with the Sydney bosses, have recently changed camps to the Melbourne mob."

"But surely they must have known that was dangerous?"

"Bomber was deeply in debt to Whispers and Tony Stavros, and the southerners must have made him a great offer to pay off his debt if he worked for them. He convinced Billy to go with him. Follow the money trail, Jock. It usually gets you to the target."

Harry asked Jock to drive to Darling Harbour. They parked near the wharves. He explained that he wanted to talk with Sandy Blight when he knocked off work. They waited in Wheat Road. At three o'clock they heard the knock-off siren and saw the wharfies coming up on their way to the trains or trams. As Sandy came by, Jock got out and asked him to get in the car.

"Hello Sandy," said Harry. "Meet my partner, Jock Burns. You can trust him. We'll drive you home but let's go to Observatory Park first."

"I don't like this, Harry. If my mates see me with you, I'm dead."

"That's why I asked Jock to meet you on the path. They don't know him."

They walked to the tree on the hill. Harry explained the disappearance of Bomber Earl and the death of Billy Knobbs. "What's the word going around, Sandy?"

Sandy rolled a cigarette and lit up in a cloud of smoke. He drew deep and long on that cigarette before answering. "Well, they had it coming to them."

"What do you mean, Sandy?" asked Jock.

"Whispers and Tony have been good to those bastards. They've protected them and made sure that, when they got into trouble with the police, they got an easy hearing."

Jock tapped him on the arm. "What the hell are you saying?"

"Come on, Jock. Don't tell me you don't know. Go and talk to your mates in the CIB. Your blokes get good information from the big boys and, in return, they want favours."

"What went wrong?"

"Billy and Bomber got greedy. When the Melbourne blokes came here they had a couple of suckers ready for the pickin'. It was like takin' lollies from a kid."

Harry looked at Sandy. "What's this about the copper from Queensland and Bomber? Is there any truth in that?"

"The word is that it's true."

"Why would a copper from up north be involved?"

"They tell me he's corrupt as hell and in thick with Mr Big in Brisbane who happens to be a great mate of Whispers and Tony. They often meet together up there at the races. The locals here wanted someone from outside to do the job so that there was no suspicion on any of them. All the Sydney blokes were at the races down here at the time and had an alibi."

"Is there any word on who took out Billy?"

"Not sure, but it was probably one of the Sydney boys. Billy, the stupid bastard, got caught in a five-way crossroads. He worked for Whispers and Tony but then got caught up with Splinter Woods and Bruiser Bignall from Melbourne."

"Was that enough to get him killed?" asked Jock.

Sandy continued. "Then he decided to tag along with Bomber Earl and got mixed up in the drugs cross-fire between Angelo Romano and Boss Gabor at the markets. He had to go. If there was an open competition between Billy's brain and a pea, the pea would win hands down every time."

Harry stood up and walked around the seat. "Tell me a bit more about Scarface Fisher who they reckoned took that shot at me."

"Believe about half of what you hear, Harry. I think Scarface was set up."

"Why would you say that?"

"From what I hear he wasn't a shooter. He was a small-time rogue always in trouble. I can't see him taking up a contract on you."

"But he shot at the CIB blokes when he was cornered."

"It's my opinion that he didn't have a gun when he came out of that house; and I know that he was a left-hander."

"Are you trying to tell me that the gun was planted on him after the shooting?"

"That's for you to work out, Harry. You're the detective. I don't know nothin', and I must get going."

Harry shook his hand. "Thanks, Sandy. You've been very helpful. I'll let you walk home. The exercise will do you good."

As Sandy walked away he turned. "Take my advice, Harry. Clean the shit out of your own nest first."

Jock dropped Harry at the station for the train home.

Chapter 54
Tuesday

Jock poured a mug of strong tea for Harry as he sat in the interview room. "Tell me, Harry, what did we get out of all that yesterday? Do you honestly believe Sandy, or is he having you on and leading you up the garden path?"

"How far can you trust any criminal? How loyal are they really?" replied Harry. "I always check everything he says but, of all the criminals I've known, he's the most reliable."

"But would he stand up in court and swear on the Bible?"

"No; and I wouldn't ask him to do so. He gives me information and I've helped him on occasions. That's our relationship."

"Are you telling me that you take bribes from him in return for favours?"

"Goodness no. You saw my car before it was blown up. Was that the sort of car a man on the take would be driving? Come on, Jock, give me more credit than that. It's because he's not paying me a bribe that Sandy's information is more reliable."

"Okay, boss, what are we going to do today?"

"Yesterday we found out that Flash Evans from Melbourne had visited Billy a few times, and Shooter McGill saw him the other day. To me that looks like Evans was the go-between for Splinter Woods and Bruiser Bignall; and they are the two biggest operators from down south. McGill is a hit man for anyone willing to pay the price but, he does a lot of dirty work for Whispers and Tony Stavros. If Billy and Bomber shifted camps to Woods and Bignall, then McGill would be the logical man to be hired to take them out."

"But they're not going to come in voluntarily and give themselves up."

"No, Jock. So let's be like good sheepdogs and circle around and lead the flock to this door here where we can sort the rams from the wethers. Let's go to see Tony Pantano who works for Squeaky Walsh, and who was a friend of Billy Knobbs."

Harry and Jock drove to Palmer Street, Darlinghurst, and stopped outside a two-storey Victorian terrace building, with a lane to the back. It was from this building that Tony operated as a pimp and bouncer in the brothels owned by Squeaky Walsh. They knocked and were met by a tired looking Tony Pantano. "Fuck off, you lot. Can't a man have a decent sleep around here?"

Harry put his size-twelve boot in the doorway to stop it closing suddenly. "Good morning, Tony. My friend here is Detective Burns. Let's go in and have a cup of tea. If you've got some bread I'll put on some toast for your breakfast."

"What do you bastards want?"

Harry found a jug, filled it with water and switched it on. The sink was covered with dirty plates, cups and saucers but he found three mugs in a cupboard above the cooktop. He scooped four spoonfuls from the tea caddy into a stained teapot. He gave up looking for bread to make toast.

Jock removed some dirty clothes from the kitchen chairs and threw them into the laundry before sitting down. Harry brushed crumbs off the table and sat down. Tony lit up a cigarette.

"Tony, we would like to have a talk about your good mates Billy Knobbs and Bomber Earl."

"They're not my mates," snorted Tony as he drew on his cigarette and followed with a deep racking cough.

"That's not what Billy told us. He said you and some others were playing cards the day Bomber disappeared. Is that true?"

"Well yeah, but that doesn't make us mates."

"Calm down, Tony, we're not here to arrest you or accuse you of any crime. We just want information. So stop stalling and talk to us. We all know that you and Billy were great mates and did a lot of jobs together, and you and Bomber did that bank job in Campsie a few years back."

"You can't pin that on me. This is a set-up."

"We know you did it but we don't have the proof to stand up in court. So forget about that for now. We're only interested in what happened to Billy and Bomber."

"Those bastards got what they deserved."

"Why would you say that about your mates?"

"They're not my mates any longer. They ratted on us and wouldn't pay their debts; and they jumped ship to those mongrel Melbourne bastards."

"So who did them in?"

Tony picked the wax from his right ear and wiped his fingers on his left breast pocket. "I don't know nuffin'."

Harry took a long slow sip on his tea. "Tony, we're not blaming you. We just want information. Is there anything in the story that Bomber was knocked off by a Queensland detective?"

"Why are you asking me? You should know."

"What do you mean?"

Tony got up and walked to the sink to get a mug of water. He scratched his bottom and tightened his belt. "The rumour has it that you're the bloke who got him here to do that job."

Harry got up, walked to the sink, took Tony by the shoulders and turned him around. "Now, tell me straight to my face. What did you say?"

"Around here they're saying that you got cranky because Bomber made a fool of all of you when he pulled off that North Rocks job and this was your way to get back at him."

"Tony, you know me and you know that's rubbish. So, whoever did the job is the person spreading that rumour. Who do you think that might be?"

"I dunno, but I'd say it would be someone closer to you than to me or my mates."

Jock turned in his chair. "What about Billy?"

Tony lit another cigarette. "Billy was his own worst enemy. He could have stayed doing what he did for Tony and the others and he would have been well treated, but he thought that he could do better with the Melbourne boys."

"Who did it, Tony?"

"I dunno, but I think it's more important to know who ordered it rather than who pulled the trigger."

"And who was that, Tony?"

"Well, I can tell you it wasn't Squeaky. I suggest that you should look closer to home."

Harry sat up. "What do you mean by that, Tony?"

"I ain't sayin' nothin'. I know where my bread comes from and I want to keep on livin'. You two go and look somewhere else. Now get out. I'm gettin' allergic to you two and I'm gettin' the itches."

"Okay, Tony, we'll let you go back to sleep but we'll be keeping in touch so don't go on any long trips."

Harry and Jock sat in the car and talked about Tony. "You know him better than me, Harry. What do you think?"

"Tony can get very nasty with people who abuse his girls or try to take down his boss, Squeaky. But he's loyal to him and rarely strays away from his own patch."

"But what was he saying about the killer being closer to us than him?"

"I don't know but it seems he's suggesting the police could be involved."

Jock started the car. "I can't believe that. Where do we go from here?"

"Let's go visit Nobby Clark. He works with the Melbourne mob but he's come back to live in Sydney. In fact he once did work with Whispers Durante and Rosie Travener. He now lives back in Marrickville."

They drove to a small house in Gorman Street. It was a semi-detached with a narrow verandah leading to a small arched-doorway. The three-panelled window to the right covered faded curtains. Harry knocked. The door opened slowly. A man in his late thirties or early forties with thick, black wavy hair and a three-day stubble appeared in the narrow opening. He was dressed in a blue singlet and khaki shorts with no shoes.

"Hello, Nobby. Long time no see," said Harry. "Meet my partner, Detective Burns. May we come in for a minute? We have a few questions. You might be able to help us."

"Hello, Harry. I haven't seen you since before the war. Come in."

"This is where you lived when I last saw you before I joined up. How are your parents?"

"They both passed away, Harry. I've got the house to myself now."

"Is that why you came back to Sydney?"

"Partly the reason, but there's more work up here."

"What are you doing these days?"

"I do security work for some of the hotels. I still keep fit; and it pays well."

"I hear that you work for Splinter and Bruiser. Is that right?"

"I work for a company that owns the hotels. I don't ask questions and they don't give answers; and that suits me."

"Have you kept in touch with Bomber Earl and Billy Knobbs since you came back? I heard that you worked with them before the war."

Nobby picked up a piece of Christmas cake from the table and took a bite. "Yes, I got Bomber to come and work for us. He was happy because he got more money here than he did with the other mob."

"But what happened to him?"

"I don't know but you can be certain that it wasn't our mob who did it. We had no reason to do it. He was working for us."

Harry looked at the cake and picked up a crumb to taste. "Did you cook this Nobby? It's good. I'm going to have some more. Here, Jock, you try some too."

"No. My girlfriend made it for me."

"What's the word around town about Billy?"

"They tell me that he got too greedy and tried to play off Angelo Romano against Boss Gabor to get more involved with the drugs. How stupid can you get? That's like sticking your head up between the machine-gun posts on one side and twelve pounder artillery from the other side."

"Who did the job on him?"

"I don't know, Harry. It was all to do with something he was involved in before he came to work for us."

Harry tapped the table. "But, Nobby, you keep your ear to the ground. You know what's happening. It's what keeps you alive."

"I'd say you should be looking more at the centre of the city and Woolloomooloo. I can't help you any more."

"What about your mate Scarface?"

"That was a set-up and he was stupid to let himself get caught in the middle of it. Talk to your mates. They'll tell you."

Harry stood up. "Thanks Nobby. Keep your nose clean. And if you have any more information, give me a call."

Harry and Jock drove back to Central Street station. As they walked past the main desk Jack Tomlinson called out. "Hey, Harry, the chief super wants you immediately. Go straight to his office now. It's bloody urgent. I'll tell him you're here."

Harry knocked on the door and entered. The chief scowled at him, picked up a file and banged it on the desk. "Come to attention, Detective. I'm suspending you as of this minute. You will hand in your badge and weapon to the desk sergeant and take no more part in any work until this matter is fully investigated."

"Excuse me, sir, but I don't know what you're talking about. Please explain."

Twain slammed his hand on the file. "I have here clear evidence that you have been taking bribes from criminals and hiding them in secret bank accounts. See Sergeant Tomlinson on the way out and report here tomorrow morning, and every morning, until this investigation is complete. Now get out of here."

Chapter 55
Wednesday

It had not been a good night's sleep for Harry. At first he put that down to the cold Spam and tomato sauce sandwiches he had last night for dinner, washed down with a couple of bottles of beer. In the cold light of dawn, however, he realised that he was facing a major investigation into charges of corruption for which he had no answer. How can you prove your innocence when you don't know who is behind it, or the circumstances behind the charges? Too many questions and no answers.

The hot, humid day and Harry's woollen suit made it an uncomfortable trip on the overcrowded, standing room only, train from Stanmore to Central. The walk to head office was no relief with everyone in a rush to get to work and out of the heat. On entering the building he headed for the tea-room where he took off his hat and coat, got a mug of tea and settled into a corner to think through what might happen next.

He had little time to think as Jack Tomlinson came in, demanding his presence in the chief superintendent's office. On entering the office Harry recognised Inspector Kevin Thornett, a highly respected officer with whom Harry had worked briefly in Redfern just before he enlisted into the army. Harry was not invited to sit.

The chief stood behind his desk and, in his most formal voice announced: "Detective Senior Constable Taylor, complaints have come to our attention that you have received payments that can only be described as bribes, and you have taken action to hide those payments in secret accounts at the bank. As a consequence of those complaints I have asked Inspector Thornett to carry out an investigation into these matters and report back to me. I am ordering you to cooperate with his investigation. In the meantime, and until this matter is concluded, you are suspended from duty."

"I have no knowledge of these matters," said Harry. "I will fully cooperate with the inspector's investigation."

Kevin Thornett stood up. "We have cleared an interview room here so let's go and get this matter under way. Come with me."

When they entered the room Kevin closed the door. "Before we start, take off your coat. There is no reason why we can't do this in more comfort."

"Thank you, sir. That's a relief in this hot weather."

"Harry, this is not a pleasant duty for me. Nobody wants to be involved in internal investigations involving complaints against fellow officers; but it must be done. So, let's get on with it. These complaints involve allegations that you received bribes from persons unknown, but certainly from those believed to be involved in criminal activities in this city, and that you created a secret account for depositing those monies. What have you to say about that?"

Harry stretched his neck and shoulders to relieve his tension. "I haven't taken bribes and have not opened secret bank accounts. I have no knowledge of anything relating to these matters."

"Do you have any bank accounts?"

"Yes, one. It is with the Bank of New South Wales at Redfern. When I receive my pay packet each fortnight I try to get to the bank to deposit what I don't need in the coming days. I had a Commonwealth Bank savings account when I was at school, but I let that lapse when I joined the army."

Kevin reached into his briefcase. "I have here bank slips signed by you that show you opened a second account at that same bank and, on occasions, the amounts deposited far exceeded your fortnightly pay. I want you to explain how that came about."

Harry took his time to study the deposit slips. "I have never seen these before, and I did not fill them in."

"Do you agree that those slips came from the Redfern branch of your bank?"

"Yes, the stamp says it is from that bank; but I haven't seen them before."

"Do you agree that the signatures on those slips are yours?"

"They look like mine, but they can't be, because I never filled in those deposit slips."

"Pick one up and look closer at it."

Harry sat back and pulled his hands back from the table. "No. I won't touch any of them because that would put my fingerprints all over it. Are you trying to stitch me up?"

Keith coughed and sat forward. "No, certainly not."

Harry stood up. "I will not proceed with this investigation until these documents have been examined by experts that I can trust. I demand that Tony Jacobs from the Scientific Investigation Bureau together with his team members, Rita Flynn, the fingerprint expert, and Michael Sturgess, the forgery and handwriting expert come here to do a thorough examination."

"That won't be necessary, Harry. It's just a simple case of you telling me if you had anything to do with these bank slips."

"Kevin, I worked for you before the war and had a lot of respect for the way you went about policing, but in this case I'm being set up and I want to get to the bottom of it. I'm sure you don't want to go to court and tell the judge you refused my request to have these exhibits examined by professional experts."

"Okay, okay, I'll call Tony. I'll pack these up and I'll call you back in when the team has finished their examination."

"No, Kevin. I'm staying here and so are those papers and passbook. There is no way they are going out of my sight until the team gets here to examine them. I'm prepared for you to have someone else in the room to ensure that I make no attempt to destroy or alter them."

"How can I trust you?"

"I guarantee you, Kevin that I won't touch them. They are too valuable. Those pieces of paper contain the evidence to show who is trying to set me up. It's up to me and Tony's team to find it, not destroy it."

Forty minutes later Tony Jacobs, Rita Flynn and Michael Sturgess came into the room. Kevin Thornett explained the purpose of the inquiry and Harry's request to have the material examined. He asked Harry to leave the room while the team went about their work. Harry refused.

"There is no way this material is getting out of my sight until the team has examined it and come to their conclusions. I promise I will stand back and not touch anything, but I want to be certain this material is examined properly."

Kevin glared at Harry who was unmoved. At last Kevin relented. "You can stay, providing you keep out of the way and not interfere with the team."

"Thank you. That's all I ask."

Rita stepped towards Harry. "Okay, I'm going to take your prints. Put out your hands and stretch your fingers. Come on, you know the routine."

"But, Rita, you already have my prints on record."

Rita leaned over and spoke quietly. "Are you going to cooperate or do I have to remove your fingers with a blunt knife and take them back to the lab?"

Harry burst out laughing. "Okay, okay, I give in. Take my prints."

Rita smiled. "It works every time, Harry."

Harry turned to Michael Sturgess. "Could you take photos of all those slips? I want a copy for my records."

"I don't have a camera."

Tony walked to the door. "I'll get one from the desk."

Michael put plain paper on the table and asked Harry to write his normal signature three times. He pulled out a magnifying glass and compared his signatures with those on the bank slips.

"What do you think, Michael?" asked Harry stretching to get a closer look.

"On first glance you could say they were written by the same person, but I need to have a better look at some of the features."

"What are the features that tell you if it is a forgery?"

"It's not difficult to forge a signature. With a bit of practice you can get quite good at it. But a forger leaves certain signs that can be picked up by an expert graphologist."

"How do you do that?"

"Many forgers use the upside down method. They take a sample of your signature and copy it upside down and back to front. It's surprising how much easier and more accurate that is."

"So how does an expert like you tell the difference?"

"The pressure on the nib is different at the start of a down stroke from the finish. That results in a minute variation in the depth and width of the line from top to bottom. That's different if you are copying upside down. Here comes Tony with a camera."

Michael switched on the lights and opened the curtains before taking several photos of the slips. He spent the next half-hour studying the papers, drawing lines in his notebook and adding notes. He liked working alone, so Harry sat back and watched in awe.

As Michael turned away from the table Harry leaned forward and watched him studying the photos and taking notes. "When you get back to SIB, Michael, can you get George Black to make copies of all those photos? I'll pick them up later. I don't want them lost."

When Michael finished photographing, Rita stepped to the table and dusted the slips. The few fingerprints on the paper were not clear but she took images of them for later analysis.

Harry looked across the room where Kevin was sitting quietly watching the activity. "Kevin, could you give Michael that passbook so he can photograph the pages and note the signatures on each entry?"

"Here you are, Michael; but you must give it back to me before you leave," said Kevin.

Harry pointed at the pass book on the table. "Michael, could you please try to make out the name of the bank teller who signed each of those entries? Those signatures don't look anything like those of the usual teller I go to."

"What's his name?" asked Kevin.

"I go to the same teller most of the time. Tomorrow I'll bring in my pass book I use at that bank for you to look at. His name is Andrew Fogarty. Go talk to him. He'll tell you that I rarely go to anyone else."

Michael chimed in. "The signature is a bit of a scrawl but I think it is J McGill. The J, M and G are quite distinct but the other letters are blurred. I'll work on it more later."

Harry asked Rita to dust the passbook for prints.

As Tony and the team left, Kevin sat back at the table. "Talk to me, Harry about the cases you have been working on lately."

Harry took out his notebook and worked through everything that had happened since the attempt on his life at New Year. Kevin asked numerous questions to tease out each situation. He questioned why Harry was involved in all of those investigations and why he had gone off on a folly of his own to Leeton and the Hawkesbury Valley.

Harry emphasised the seriousness of his investigations. He highlighted the death of Stumpy Baxter, his mechanic, as well as Knuckles Elliott, Scarface Fisher and Billy Knobbs, and the disappearance of Bomber Earl. He tried to show how those events were probably tied to his attempted murder by shooting and car bombing.

Kevin asked questions about the influx of Melbourne criminals into Sydney and how that had changed the criminal landscape in the city.

Without breaching confidences from people like Sandy Blight, Harry summarised the situation.

"But surely, Harry, the shooting of Scarface Fisher closed that case involving your attempted murder?"

"I don't believe so, Kevin. And this charade with these bank deposits convinces me more and more that it's not over. Someone wants me out of the way and will do anything to achieve it. I believe that person is worried that I'm getting close to linking him to those murders and the attempt on my life."

"I think you're a bit paranoid, Harry; but enough for today. Be here first thing in the morning."

Chapter 56
Thursday

Harry woke in a lather of sweat. It was so humid that he felt he was lying under a hot wet blanket. There was not a breath of fresh air in the flat. A lone mosquito buzzed in his ear searching for a good landing spot to feed on his rich blood. Harry got out of bed to go to the sink to swallow two glasses of lukewarm water and moistened his parched mouth and throat. His tongue felt like a doormat after a dust storm.

Harry's frustration was reaching boiling point. He had so many loose ends; each just beyond his reach. He felt that he was close to a solution but had to suffer the indignity of being accused of corruption that was designed to take him off the case. Cooperation with the inquiry into the allegations conflicted with his need to get on with his investigations. There were too many dead bodies. He needed to get on with the job before someone else landed in the mortuary.

Harry knew that Tony and the SIB team would have given priority to the analysis of the bank documents yesterday, but he couldn't bear to wait around for the results. He dressed in his army disposal gear, put on his tanker hood and goggles, kick-started his bike and rode to the SIB centre in Redfern.

"My God," said Rita laughing as she saw Harry walking through the door. "You look like a sex-crazed possum that's been feeding on the weed. What the hell are you doing here? Didn't you listen to Twain when he told you that you were suspended? Get out of here. Go home. Go play Monopoly. Go straight to gaol. Do not pass Go. Do not collect two hundred."

Harry laughed. "Thanks for the warm welcome, Rita. You're the best thing that's happened today. I feel almost normal again. Tony and Michael; can I talk to you for a minute?"

"Oh damn," said Rita as she tossed her head sideways and walked away. "And here I thought that you came to take me away for the day for a romantic picnic on the beach or up in the mountains."

Harry chuckled and tapped her lightly on the arm. "That will have to wait for another day, Rita."

Rita snorted and giggled. "Yeah, yeah; promises, promises. That's all I get."

Tony called them into the interview room where he and Michael were examining the evidence from the day before. The passbook and deposit slips were on the table. "Michael, would you like to start and tell us what you've found?"

"Thanks, Tony. I believe that the teller at the bank who signed these papers is named J McGill. The signatures on the slips could easily pass as Harry's, and the average person would not know the difference, but I believe they are most likely forgeries."

Harry pointed at Michael's notes and scribbles. "What are the characteristics that tell you that? Could you show us?"

Michael took a large magnifying glass and pointed to the capital letters. He talked about the different down strokes. He then put the glass over Harry's signatures and outlined the differences. He also showed the differences in the stroke made on the small 'a' in Taylor. The 'a' on the documents had a slight backward slope. Harry was having difficulty picking up the minor differences but was relieved Michael showed that the signatures were different to his. Michael was convinced the differences were sufficient to say the signatures were not made by Harry.

At that moment, Jock Burns came into the room and saw Harry. "Well, here you are. Everyone was wondering where you were."

Harry looked up. "Well, tell everyone it's none of their business. I'm on suspension. But hey, Jock, it's good to see you. Sit down and listen to this."

Rita stepped to the table and displayed various prints. "Now, the ones on the right are Harry's. The ones in the middle are from the deposit slips and the ones on the left are from the passbook. None of the prints from the slips or passbook belong to Harry."

Harry sat back with a sigh. "Thank goodness. That's great work, Rita. That deserves a hamburger with the lot from Theo's Greek Café around the corner at lunch."

Rita tossed her head to shake the hair from her eyes and with a look of mock shock she looked at Harry. "Hah. Is that all I get? Well, you know what you can do with your burger; and I hope it hurts."

Harry burst out laughing, relieving the tension in the room. "Okay, Princess, I suppose it'll have to be fish and chips."

Tony broke in. "Okay, you two, let's get down to business. We'll get these reports through to Kevin Thornett this morning, but it certainly looks as though this will clear you of those allegations. The worry for you is working out who set you up."

Harry nodded. "Okay, Jock, let's go. We have work to do at the bank. Thanks, Tony. Thanks team. That's lifted a big burden from my shoulders. We must go now."

Rita slapped her thigh. "What about my fish and chips?"

"Sorry, Rita. Tony said it's not lunchtime, yet."

Rita threw the blackboard duster at him as he and Jock left the room.

Out in the car park, Harry directed Jock to drive to the Bank of New South Wales in Redfern. On arrival they asked to speak to the manager.

"Mr Auderley, thank you for seeing us. I'm Detective Senior Constable Harry Taylor and this is Detective Jock Burns."

The manager looked at Harry. "You don't look like a detective. Could I see your identification?"

Harry reached into his pocket but realised he handed in his badge yesterday. Jock saw his dilemma. "Mr Auderley, Detective Taylor is on a special mission today and is not in regular uniform. I can assure you that he is who he says he is. Here is my badge."

"Okay, what can I do for you?"

Harry put the photos on the desk. "We have reason to believe an employee of this bank altered documents to falsely show that a police officer was corrupt. Do you have a teller named McGill?"

"We have two tellers."

"I know Andrew Fogarty because I have an account in this bank and he's the man who always serves me. Who is the other teller?"

"That's John McGill."

"Look at the writing on those documents there. Are those his signatures?"

"It appears to be his, but I'd need to check more closely."

"Please ask Mr McGill to come in here."

When the teller entered, Harry asked him to stand near the desk. "Do you recognise either or both of us?"

"I'm not sure. I don't know who you are, and I don't know your friend."

"Look at the photo of the passbook. Is that your signature on those entries?"

McGill looked at the photos. "Yes. They are mine."

"And the deposit slips there?"

"Yes."

"The person owning that pass book made a number of entries with you. Describe that person."

McGill looked at Harry. "He was about your age and about five foot ten. He was maybe a little heavier than you."

Harry waited for a moment. "Surely, Mr McGill, if you made that many entries with that person you'd recognise him easily, here or in the street. Let's say that I opened an account with you and came back twenty times to make a deposit, with some of those deposits being large amounts. Would you recognise me in the street?"

"Probably yes."

Harry waited again until McGill shifted his stance. "Was I the person who deposited that money?"

"I don't think so; but I'm not sure."

"Where do you live, Mr McGill?"

"Elizabeth Street, Waterloo."

Harry leaned forward, put his elbows on the table and rested his chin on the bridge of his arched fingers. "Well, that is handy to work, here. And, of course, it's also handy to your relatives around the corner in Kensington Street. I can see the family resemblance."

"I don't know what you mean."

"Oh yes you do. You're related to Barry McGill. You can't mistake that florid freckled complexion and sandy-red hair. You even stand like him."

"I don't know who you're taking about."

Harry turned to the manager. "I'm sorry, Mr Auderley but we need to take Mr McGill to headquarters for further questioning."

Jock took McGill in the car while Harry rode his bike. Harry asked Jack Tomlinson to get Kevin Thornett to come to the interview room. Ten minutes later the inspector came in.

"What are you doing here, Harry? You're suspended until further notice. I haven't got the report back from SIB yet."

"It's okay, sir. You did ask me to be back here this morning. The report is on its way. It clearly shows that the signatures on the passbook and deposit slips were forged; and not by me."

"How do you know that?"

"I called into SIB this morning. None of the fingerprints are mine and I had nothing to do with those deposits. Jock and I went to the bank where we found the teller who processed the deposits. He is John McGill and he happens to be a close relative, and possibly a brother, of Barry McGill who, as you know, is also known as Shooter McGill, and is a renowned hit man for the big crime bosses in this city."

Jock spoke up. "We have Mr McGill in the cells waiting further questioning."

"Being a relative doesn't make him guilty," said Kevin.

Harry spread the copies of photos on the desk. "Look at these, Sir. Michael Sturgess, the handwriting and forgery specialist, is convinced that the signatures are not mine. Rita Flynn said that none of the fingerprints are mine. McGill couldn't identify me as the person who made the deposits even though he processed at least twenty of them with some of them being large amounts. I'm innocent and I have to get on with these investigations."

The inspector walked to the door. "I'll talk to the chief superintendent about this."

"Thank you, sir."

When Kevin came back, Harry asked Jack Tomlinson to bring in the prisoner. McGill sat at the desk but folded his arms in a defensive manner and stared at Harry.

Harry opened the questions. "John, is Barry McGill your brother?"

"No, he's a cousin; but I don't have anything to do with him."

"You have already admitted that it was you who processed the deposits in the account we showed you this morning. Who was the person who made those deposits?"

"Mr Harry Taylor."

"Let's try again, John. I'm Harry Taylor and I made no such deposits and scientific analysis proves that. So who made those deposits?"

"The person who made those deposits, called himself Harry Taylor."

"What if I talk to your cousin, Barry, and mention that we have discussed this matter with you?"

McGill froze. His eyes dilated. He wiped the hair back from his face. He said nothing.

Harry waited a good two minutes. "I don't think Barry would be happy with you, John. And I wouldn't like to see Barry unhappy. He can get quite nasty when he's upset."

"Look, it wasn't Barry who got me to do it. It was a friend of his. I've never met him before and he didn't tell me who he was. He promised me one hundred pounds if I set up the bank account and made the deposits under your name."

"Describe that man."

McGill gave a description that best fitted Tom Lebovich, but it could not be proof positive that he was the man.

Harry looked him in the eye and waited. "I'm going to get Detective Burns to take you back to the bank and inform your manager that you had no part in these forgeries, and that you had merely set up an account and took the deposits as per bank policy. For the moment you will act normally as a bank teller. If you mention this to anyone, I'll tell Barry of your involvement. Is that clear?"

"Yes. Does that mean you're not charging me?"

"For the moment, yes. But if you don't do as you're told all hell will break loose. Is that clear?"

"Thank you."

Harry turned. "Come back here, Jock after you've dropped him off."

Chapter 57
Thursday

Inspector Thornett stood up and paced the room. "You've just let a man go back to work when he's admitted being involved in a conspiracy to pervert the course of justice. What are you doing?"

"That fish is too small to put on the plate at the moment. I'll deal with him later," said Harry. "I want the big sharks. He's just part of the bait. I'm prepared to wait for the big ones to come closer before I tug on the line."

"Are you sure you're not playing with fire, Harry?"

"I've been in the line of fire for the last five weeks. It's me they're trying to take out. I need to get to whoever is behind all this."

Kevin pointed at the desk. "Pick up all that material and we'll go and see the chief."

As Kevin and Harry walked into the office, Allan Twain spun on his heel and poked his forefinger into Harry's chest and angrily shouted. "What the hell do you think you're up to. I gave you a direct order to stand down. You're on suspension. Now I hear that you have been out to the SIB poking your nose in there."

Harry took hold of the chief's wrist with both hands and slowly but firmly pushed the arm away, his eyes locked onto Twain's. He spoke slowly but with a quiet authority that commanded respect. "Sir, you should know better than try to assault me like that. I suggest that you sit down at your desk so that the inspector and I can bring you up to date with this investigation."

Twain pulled his hand away sharply, spun around and strode to his seat. "Well, get on with it. I don't have time to waste on people like you."

Kevin interrupted. "Excuse me, sir, I think you should look at these photos. I'm still waiting on the report from SIB which I'll bring to you the moment it arrives. The evidence here clearly indicates that Detective Taylor was not the person who deposited those amounts in that bank account."

Twain thumped the desk. "Well, I don't believe it. And do you know why I don't believe it? It's because I received another complaint about Detective Taylor only twenty minutes ago. He's been laundering money at the races to hide the fact that he's taking bribes from well-known criminals from Melbourne."

Harry stepped back, stunned. "That's absolute nonsense. I don't go to the races. So, it couldn't be me. Who told you that story?"

"Did you or did you not go to the races at Randwick last Saturday?"

"Yes, but that was for Bob Crow's birthday. You were there, so you know that."

"At the end of the last race did you go to see the bookmaker Charlie Bennett?"

"Yes, as a matter of fact I did. I won ten shillings on the last race and went to collect my winnings."

"Did you collect a parcel from Charlie's penciller, Graham Sayers?"

"I don't know who you're talking about. I collected my ten shillings and went home."

"We have evidence that you laundered money through Sayers and Bennett after the last race on Saturday, and some of that coincides with the deposits you made into that bank account during the week."

Kevin Thornett coughed to get attention. "Excuse me but could someone explain what this is all about?"

Allan Twain responded. "Criminals who make money illegally use the races to launder it so that they can legally claim that their new-found wealth is a result of winnings at the races; and it is hard to prove otherwise. They have the betting tickets to prove it."

"I still don't understand."

Twain pushed his hand forward. "After the last race the criminal goes to a bookmaker and hands him one thousand pounds. The bookmaker hands him back nine hundred together with a ticket to prove that he won that nine hundred on the last race winner. At the time they do it they already know which horse won the race."

"But it's costing him money to do that," said Kevin.

"That's right. The bookie gets one hundred pounds as his fee for laundering the money. The criminal doesn't mind because he now has proof that the other nine hundred came from winnings at the races, and the penciller notes it all in the books to show it's legal."

"Who is this penciller bloke?" asked Kevin.

"Every bookie has a penciller. He sits behind the bookie at the races and records all the bets, the prices, the winnings and losses. He's like an accountant."

"What's he got to do with the laundering?"

"After the last race they work out how much the criminal would have to put down at the going price to get that amount of winnings. He notes that in his records. It all looks legal. Not all bookies and pencillers are involved."

Harry interrupted. "But all I did was to collect my ten shillings. I don't know these men."

"Well, Mr Sayers is very clear that he recorded those winnings to you. I'm going to ask Inspector Thornett to continue this investigation, and you will remain suspended until this matter has concluded. You'll keep the inspector informed of your whereabouts at all times."

Harry strode out of the office and ran into Jock who had just returned. "Jock, come with me now."

They went to the interview room. Harry explained what had just happened. "While I'm talking to Kevin Thornett, I want you to look up the car licences of both the bookmaker and his penciller. I want to know where they live and where they work."

Jock left as Kevin walked in. "Let's start, Harry with your knowledge of the race meeting."

"Last Friday, Charlie Rockwell invited us all to the races on Saturday to celebrate Bob Crow's birthday. There were lots of people there including politicians, the top brass, lawyers, magistrates and some prominent criminals. At one stage we were advised by a crime boss to bet on a certain horse. It was obvious that the race was rigged."

"What's this about the last race?"

Harry cleared his throat. "We know the top criminals use that scam the chief talked about to launder money at the races so they can explain their wealth and avoid taxation. It's hard to prove otherwise."

"But the Chief said that you were involved."

"Obviously someone is getting worried that I'm getting too close to the truth, and they'll do anything to take me out of the scene. They tried to kill me twice and that didn't work, so now they are trying to set me up for corruption so that I'll be sacked."

"The chief mentioned that you were working for the Melbourne crime bosses."

"Up till now, everyone has been saying the problem is due to the influx of the Melbourne blokes and that it was them who organised the attempt on my life. I believe now it is more likely to be the Sydney lot who are calling the tune on this. For some unknown reason they think I'm taking bribes from Melbourne to protect them, and that I turn a blind eye to their activities in the suburban hotels."

"What would have been your next step in the investigation, Harry?"

"Please understand, Kevin, that I don't want to discuss my moves with anyone at the moment. All I ask is for you to give me three days to look into a few matters and get back to you."

Kevin sat back scratching his chin and shaking his head. "But you've been suspended."

"If I don't come back with answers to you in three days, you can sack me."

Kevin paused before answering. "If you let me down, you'll never work again. Do you understand that? Now get out of here."

"Thanks, Sir. I won't let you down."

Harry dashed out and found Jock in the interview room. "What have you got for me, Jock?"

"The bookmaker, Charlie Bennett, lives in Coogee, and the penciller, Graham Sayers, lives at Marrickville."

"Do you have addresses?"

"Better than that. I know that Sayers is a mathematics teacher at Saint John's Catholic College at Kogarah. He does pencilling for Bennett on the weekend and at the Harold Park trots on Friday nights."

"So, he does this for extra money and maybe to pick up some extra cash when a race is rigged and he knows the sure thing to win. If we leave now we might pick him up before he finishes at school this afternoon. Let's go."

They arrived at the school just before three-thirty. They identified themselves to the secretary and to Principal, Brother Aloysius.

"I'm not certain this is correct procedure, but I'll call Mr Sayers and let him decide," said the principal.

As he was still in his casual gear, Harry suggested to Jock that he take the lead. When Sayers came in, Jock commenced the questioning. "Mr Sayers, do you know why we are here?"

"No."

"Do you know either of us?"

"No. Never seen you before. Why are you here? What is this all about?"

"Look carefully at us again. Take your time. Do you recognise either of us?"

Sayers looked from one to the other. He looked at Brother Aloysius. "Brother, what is this all about?"

"These men wish to ask you some questions. If you don't want me here, I'll leave."

"No. Please stay. This is a mystery to me. I don't know these men."

Jock waited while Sayers looked back and forth between them. "Let us introduce ourselves, Mr Sayers. I am Detective Burns and this is Detective Taylor. Do you recognise us now?"

"I can't say that I do. I've never seen you before."

Jock turned to the principal. "Brother, could you record that, after ten minutes of careful examination, Mr Sayers failed to recognise either of us. He claims to have never seen or heard of us before."

Jock waited while Brother Aloysius got a notebook and recorded those matters. "Mr Sayers, if you have never seen us before nor have any knowledge of us, why did you lodge a complaint to police headquarters this morning claiming that Detective Taylor laundered money through you and Mr Bennett after the last race at Randwick last Saturday?"

"I did no such thing."

"Do you do pencilling for the bookmaker Charlie Bennett?"

Sayers looked embarrassed, his eyes flicking back and forth from the principal to Jock. Harry sat back not saying a word. "Mr Bennett is a friend of mine and I help him sometimes with his calculations."

Jock waited until he saw the perspiration under Sayers' armpits. "Does Brother Aloysius know of your second job?"

"It's not another job. I just help my friend in my spare time."

"Mr Sayers, stop the bullshit. I'm quickly losing my patience. You work for Bennett every Saturday at the races and every Friday night at the trots. That's a job. You get paid to do it."

"Charlie gives me a bit of cash occasionally to pay for petrol."

"A complaint with your name on it arrived on the chief superintendent's table this morning claiming that Detective Taylor laundered money through you after the last race at Randwick. You are aware of that practice with criminals and bookmakers. You record it all."

"I don't know what you are talking about."

"Mr Sayers, you will accompany us back to headquarters. Thank you, Brother, for your assistance. We will be in touch later."

They drove back along the Princes Highway towards the city but, at Tempe, Jock turned off the highway into Kendrick Park. Harry spoke for the first time. "Graham, let me put it this way. If you don't cooperate with us you'll go to gaol and you'll lose your job. You have been assisting criminals launder money at the races. We believe also that you, together with Charlie Bennett and some well-known criminals, are involved in race fixing."

"That's not true."

"I suspect you have a young family and a big mortgage on your house. If you cooperate with us we might be able to let you keep your job with no penalty. I want you to walk to that public toilet over there and back and think about it before you give us your answer. Take your time."

When he came back, Sayers said that he had heard a complaint had been made suggesting that he and Charlie had been involved. Under more persistent questioning he admitted that money laundering had taken place and that Charlie had asked him on occasions to add figures after the last race. He named major crime figures, a judge, two politicians, some lawyers and some police officers from the CIB. Harry and Jock drove him back to Kogarah.

"If you put all of that in writing and sign it, I will inform your principal it was a case of mistaken identity and that you were not involved in these matters. You will go about your life as normal. If you say anything to anyone about our discussions this afternoon, including Charlie Bennett, you will be looking at life in Long Bay Gaol. Do you understand?"

"I promise." Sayers let out a long, low breath. His head lowered half-way to his lap. He was totally exhausted.

Chapter 58
Friday

At seven o'clock in the morning Harry made a call to Jock's mother's house.

"Hello, Mrs Burns, would young Jock be out of bed yet?"

"Oh sure, Harry. He's out on his early morning run. He'll be back home for breakfast soon. I have his rolled oats, milk and molasses ready for him when he comes in the door. He has to keep up his strength."

"Mrs Burns, you spoil him. No wonder he doesn't want to leave home."

"Well, he's the only one I've got left and he's worth spoiling. Now what can I do for you, young Harry?"

"Could you ask him to pick me up at eight o'clock?"

Harry dressed in a suit and tie. He wanted to give the impression he was still on duty; not like yesterday when he was in casual battle dress. Jock arrived on time.

"How was your oats and molasses, Jock? How can you eat that rubbish on an empty stomach?"

"My mother has served me oats and molasses every morning of my life. She said a man has to have a solid breakfast to get through the day. Now, what have you got planned for us this morning?"

"I've decided to go into the lion's den and see what's happening there. We are going to pay a visit to Darkie Moffitt who is a standover man for the big boys from Melbourne."

"Why him?"

"Darkie came up from Melbourne last year to help the southerners set up, but he originally came from Sydney. I booked him twice for assault and robbery before the war. He lived with his mother at Rockdale. His father was a brutal man who spent most of his time inside and was killed in a fight in Grafton Gaol."

"What's the plan?"

"Let's call in on him and play it by ear."

Harry and Jock drove to Lennox Street, Rockdale. They stopped outside a small, neat, white weatherboard house with a red-tiled roof. When the door opened, a short, stocky man with jet black hair, slicked back with brilliantine, stood in the hallway, a stunned look on his face.

"Hello, Darkie, good to see you again," said Harry. "May we come in? We just want to talk."

"I don't s'pose I've got a choice, have I?" Darkie stepped back to allow Harry and Jock into the house and closed the door.

"Is your mum at home, Darkie?"

"No. Me mum died just before Christmas, so it's just me and my girlfriend here now."

"Where's your girlfriend?"

"She works down at the pub in Marrickville."

"Would that be at the Fitzroy with Angus McLean?"

"Yes. How did you know?"

Harry pointed to the kitchen table. "Let's sit here, Darkie. We need to have a talk. We know you're working for the big Melbourne boys and there's a lot of aggro happening between you lot and the Sydney blokes. We want to hear your side of the story."

"Why me?"

"Because you used to work for Tony Stavros and Whispers Durante before you went to Melbourne, and they are not happy with you now. There have been two attempts on my life. Knuckles Elliott, Scarface Fisher and Billy Knobbs have been killed. Bomber Earl has disappeared and my mechanic, Stumpy Baxter, was blown up in my car. There's been a fire-bombing at the Fitzroy and a drive-by shooting at the Elegant Lady. Now you start talking and let us know what's going on."

"Well, you bastards murdered Fisher, didn't you?"

"What do you mean?" asked Harry.

"All that story about Scarface coming out of that building shooting at the police was all bullshit."

"What are you talking about?"

"Scarface never carried a gun. Those bastards planted a gun on him. What they didn't know was that Scarface was left-handed and they planted the gun in his right hand. It was a set up. He wasn't the one who shot at you. He wasn't a shooter."

"Well, if he wasn't the shooter, then you must be the next in line to do that job because you and I know that you carry guns and have pistol-whipped many people. I suspect that you've gotten rid of some people who didn't pay up or who threatened your boss."

Jock noticed Darkie slowly open the drawer at the side of the table. Jock moved like lightning with a karate chop to Darkie's wrist and wrestled him to the floor. Harry responded with cuffs. They found a fully loaded Enfield revolver in the drawer. Harry wrapped it in his handkerchief.

After they restrained Darkie, Harry resumed his questioning. "Now, Darkie, you are about to be charged with the attempted murder of two police officers. We suspect that you were the person who took a shot at me on New Year's morning and organised the bombing of my car. We know now that you were involved in the theft of arms and explosives from Holsworthy army camp, and you are a suspect in the drive-by shooting of the Elegant Lady nightclub."

"This is a fuckin' set-up. You bastards are being paid by Durante and Stavros to get rid of us. Wait till my lawyer hears about this."

Harry and Jock sat back and waited for Darkie to finish his tirade of abuse. When he finished he was in a lather of sweat; spit dribbled from the corner of his mouth and his eyes were inflamed with anger. He kept kicking back at the leg of the chair with his heel.

"Now, Darkie, you have a choice. You can tell us the truth about all these matters or you'll be going to gaol for the rest of your life. What's it going to be?"

"You bastards. You're no better than your mates."

"What do you mean, Darkie?"

"You know what I mean or you wouldn't be here otherwise. You're workin' for them."

Harry got up and walked around the table to the sink, poured a glass of water and placed it in front of Darkie. He removed the handcuffs. "Now, have a drink, calm down and explain yourself."

"Well you know what I mean. Your mates in the CIB are behind this."

"Explain yourself, Darkie and do it quickly because I'm getting very impatient with you. Either you tell us the whole truth here now, or you're going away for the term of your natural."

"They didn't have to shoot Scarface. He had nothing to do with your shooting. They did that to get you off the track."

"What about the other matters?"

Darkie scratched his crotch. "Who do you think organised the police rush to Kogarah on the day of the armoured car robbery? That was Tank Sherman. He got all the police cars to block the roads near Kogarah so that Bomber Earl and Lebovich could do the job at North Rocks without interference."

"So what went wrong?"

"Bomber got greedy and tried to take all the loot and make a deal with Splinter Woods and Billy Stenson from Melbourne."

"What happened to him?"

"I don't know. There are lots of rumours but no proof. I heard he took a sky dive and went for a long swim towards New Zealand."

Harry tapped Darkie on the head. "What about the other things? Keep talking."

"What's in it for me?"

"That depends on what you tell us."

"What do you mean?"

"If you tell us everything, we might just put you away for the Holsworthy job, possession of illegal weapons and drug trading. If you don't, then you'll do life for attempted murder of police officers together with all the other matters. What's it to be?"

"Does that mean if I talk you'll let me go now?"

"No. It will be necessary to keep you under guard for your own protection until we investigate all of these matters. If word gets out that you've talked, we won't be able to protect you. I'm going to put you in the cell at Redfern Police Station until further notice. Now start talking."

For the next two hours Darkie explained how he had been an associate of Tony Pantano, Tom Lebovich, Bluey Ricketts and Barry McGill before he moved to Melbourne. He outlined how Durante, Stavros, Walsh and Travener were protected by senior members of the CIB.

Darkie sat forward, his hands spread out. "Mate, I used to be the delivery man from the mob to the senior police and some politicians and others in the high positions in the government and society. I did it mostly on a Saturday night at the casino, upstairs in the Elegant Lady. I covered each envelope containing money with a newspaper and slide it in front of each of the recipients.

Jock tapped the table. "Why did you go to Melbourne?"

"Things were getting too hot up here, and Splinter Woods made me a better offer."

Harry stood up. "Okay, Darkie, let's wrap it up for now. We'll take you back to Redfern. You won't speak to anyone until I say so. Let's go."

Harry and Jock drove back to Redfern where they put Darkie in a cell with instructions to the desk staff not to allow any visitors to the cell and no phone calls out.

As they walked out Jock turned to Harry. "What now, boss?"

"We have to move quickly. We can't hold Darkie indefinitely and I've got to get back to Thornett within three days with answers. Let's go and see Sandy Blight again. I think he knows more than he's telling us."

They stopped the car at the gate to the wharves. Jock showed his badge and asked the gate keeper to tell Sandy to come out to the car. Five minutes later Sandy got in the back seat.

"Bloody hell, you two, do you want to get me killed? Why did you come here with all my mates looking on?"

"It's okay, Sandy," said Jock. "I told the gatekeeper we were investigating a car accident, so stop worrying."

Harry turned around. "The other day when we were talking, you said the problem we have is that members of our own police force are involved in all this trouble with me and the Melbourne mob. What did you mean by that?"

"It's as clear as the freckle on your bum, Harry, but you can't see it because you're lookin' in the wrong direction. Look in the bloody mirror, mate and you'll see it."

"What the hell are you talking about, Sandy. For God's sake, spit it out."

For the next half-hour Sandy outlined how senior members of the CIB were in control of much of the big crime in Sydney and how they coordinated with the crime bosses; Whispers Durante, Tony Stavros, Rosie Travener and Squeaky Walsh. In return for their protection the crime bosses gave valuable information to the CIB so that they could wrap up cases against their competitors. It meant that the CIB received the good publicity for cleaning up the city of big crime.

"Are you saying those police officers control all the action?" asked Jock.

"Not all, mate. There's a group of politicians, judges, lawyers and other police in the suburbs involved in this mess as well. They're all scratching each other's backs. They're the fucking crims, mate."

Sandy confirmed what Darkie said earlier about the passing of bribe money over at the casinos. He outlined how all of this was linked to the drug scene at the markets through Romano and Gabor.

"But the big boys and the CIB don't do the dirty work," said Harry.

"No, mate. That's done by bastards like Lebovich, Pantano, Ricketts and McGill."

"What about the Melbourne mob? And why am I a target?"

"The Sydney blokes will do anything to get rid of the southerners and they think you're working with them; and that's why you have to be put down."

"Thanks, Sandy. We'll let you go now. As you walk through the gate put your licence back in your wallet. Tell the gatekeeper that we thought that you didn't have a licence when the other driver ran into you."

Jock dropped Harry off at Town Hall station.

"Be at headquarters early tomorrow morning," said Harry. "We have a lot of work to do."

Before he went home Harry walked to headquarters where he met Kevin Thornett. He asked if he could arrange with the Deputy Commissioner, Murray Fredericks, to meet them tomorrow morning. He gave little detail but emphasised that it must not, under any circumstances, be discussed with anyone else. He phoned Tony Jacobs and arranged for him and George Black to be there as well.

Chapter 59
Saturday

The cold early morning shower did little to relieve the tension in Harry's shoulders and neck. It had been a hot, humid night and Harry had too many things on his mind. He had tossed and turned throughout the night. It was a highly critical time of the operation and his whole career depended on what would happen in the next forty-eight hours. There were too many uncertainties. He could not depend on support from the chief super. He didn't know who he could trust at headquarters. All members of the CIB were now under suspicion.

He had confidence in Jock Burns and Tony Jacobs and his team, but was worried about involving them in the plan he hoped to put into place. All he had was a lot of hearsay and suspicion that wouldn't last five minutes in a court of law. With so little hard evidence it was hard to believe that Thornett and Fredericks would give him the green light to go ahead; but try he must. He had to act quickly before this got out of control.

A piece of toast and Vegemite with a cup of tea was all Harry had for breakfast before he rushed off to catch the train to the city. As he entered headquarters, Jimmy Wilkins on the desk, thinking Harry was back on duty, called out to him. "Hey, Harry, get yourself down to The Rocks straight away. There's been a shooting. The local police are there now."

"When did this happen?"

"Half an hour ago."

"When Jock comes in, send him down there. Contact Tony Jacobs and his team to go there instead of coming here."

Harry took a car and, on arriving next to the police wagon, he knew that the action had taken place at the boarding house where Sandy Blight lived. As he walked in the door he was met by the same angry wrinkled little man he had met there before.

"Get out of 'ere, you fuckin' bastard. Look what ya did to me mate, Sandy. Now he's dead because of you."

Harry edged past him. "Excuse me. Just step aside until I see what's happened here. I'll speak to you later."

"I'm not gunna speak to you. I don't want to end up like Sandy there. Look what happened to him because he spoke to you. You bastards should be shot on sight. You're all shitbags."

Harry looked up. "Constable, take this man out to the kitchen. I'll speak to him when I'm finished here."

Harry bent over to examine the body lying in the hallway. It was Sandy. He was lying on his back with a single bullet hole in the centre of his forehead. At that moment Tony Jacobs and his team arrived.

"G'day, Tony. It's appears to be a clear-cut case. One shot, instant death. Could you go over the site while I talk to the other residents here?"

"I thought you were under suspension," said Tony.

Harry smiled. "You should know, Tony that we good cops are always on duty."

"Do you still want us at headquarters?"

"After I finish here I've got a meeting with the top brass. Everything depends on how I go with them. I'll give you a call when I want you."

Harry walked to the kitchen where the constable and three other men were seated at the table. As soon as he appeared, the little man started screaming. "Get out of here ya stinkin' rotten bastard. You did this to Sandy. All he was doin' was talkin' to you. Now look what 'appened to him."

One of the others spoke up. "Come on, Jacko. Back off. We all know Harry is fair dinkum. Give him a break."

"I'll break his fuckin' neck. That's the only break I'll give 'im."

Harry walked around and sat next to Jacko. "Mate, I know how you feel. Sandy was my mate as well as yours. Now, you and I have to work together to get whoever did this to him. Tell me what happened this morning."

Jacko sat back sulking. Another man sat forward. "G'day, Harry. I'm Gazza. I've seen you here before and Sandy always said you were fair dinkum and his word's good enough for me."

"Who was first to the door after the shot?"

"I was," said Gazza. "I rushed to the door to see Sandy there on the floor. I looked outside and saw a car drive away quick like."

Harry spread his hands. "What sort of car was it?"

"It looked like a black Dodge coupé with whitewall tyres. It was a bit flash, if you get what I mean."

"Thanks, Gazza. That's the sort of information we need. Did Sandy say anything last night after he came home from work?"

"Yes," said Gazza. "he said that you had talked to him at the gates and when he went back to work, the others wanted to know what it was all about."

"What did Sandy tell them?"

"He said he told them that you were checking his car licence because he had been in an accident."

"Did they believe him?"

"Most of them did, but not the big boss of the gang. His name is Boris Weller, and he decides what comes in and goes out. They say he's connected to those bastards Lebovich and Bluey Ricketts. They control the drugs comin' in."

"What did Weller do?"

"I saw him abusing Sandy. He had him by the shirt-front and was screaming at him."

Harry stood up. He looked at Jacko and put his hand on his shoulder. "Jacko, I'll promise you that we'll get the bastards responsible for this."

Harry and Jock left and drove to headquarters.

***

Inspector Thornett was waiting for them in the office. Harry introduced Jock.

"Is the deputy commissioner in today, Kevin?"

"Yes. He's awaiting my call."

"Rather than repeat myself it would be better if he was here now. Could you call him?"

Five minutes later they got a call to go to the deputy's office. Murray Fredericks was a highly-respected officer and one clearly destined to take over after the current commissioner retired. He had a wide experience across most fields, as well as overseas as an advisor to the United Nations regarding the partition of Palestine. He had a calm, balanced, mature approach to dealing with problems and rarely rushed into doing things unless the circumstances demanded it. Harry felt he would get a good hearing.

Murray Fredericks looked up. "This best be good, Harry. I was supposed to be competing in the first round of my bowls singles championship this morning."

"My apologies, sir. I believe it is that important."

"Well, get on with it."

"I have reasons to believe that members of our Criminal Investigation Branch are corrupt and involved in the major crime scene in this city. They have been taking bribes from well-known criminals in this city and they have been protecting those criminals from prosecution. I believe their actions have led to recent killings, including an hour ago at The Rocks."

"Harry, you and I and Kevin here, as well as the chief superintendent, have all worked in CIB, and we know that much of our good intelligence comes from informants on the inside. It's an accepted practice that has been going on for as long as I have been in this Force."

"But Sir, it has gone well beyond that. Current evidence points to key figures in the branch going well beyond gathering intelligence to the point where they organise criminal activities. They determine which big jobs will happen and they select the criminals to do the job. When we do catch one of those criminals, we are told to back off because that person is involved in other matters relating to their operations."

"Give me an example."

"When Jock and I investigated the murder of Knuckles Elliott, we had evidence that Tom Lebovich was involved, but we were told by Sherman and Cross to back off."

Murray Fredericks poured himself a glass of water. "That doesn't indicate strong evidence."

Harry sat forward for emphasis. "We have stronger evidence that Sherman organised all police cars to rush to Kogarah on the pretence that there was a bank robbery, at the same time Bomber Earl and Tom Lebovich did that armed robbery at North Rocks. It was to take all police resources away from the robbery site allowing those two to get away."

"Why didn't you drag them in?"

"The CIB said that Lebovich wasn't involved. They blamed Bomber Earl and Billy Knobbs. Billy is now dead and Bomber has disappeared in suspicious circumstances."

Kevin Thornett pointed to Harry. "But all the intelligence points to the influx of the Melbourne gangs being the problem."

"Yes, that's true, but that's only half the story. The southerners are moving in and that is leading to a major turf war with the Sydney gangs. I believe that the attempts on my life are the result of rumours that I'm supporting the Melbourne boys and protecting them in the suburbs."

"Is that true?" asked Murray.

"Definitely not. I don't take bribes. Information from Darkie Moffitt and Sandy Blight yesterday suggests that the orders are coming from Sherman and Cross through the four big crime bosses in Sydney."

"Can you trust your sources, Harry?" asked Kevin.

"I can't depend on Sandy any more. He was shot an hour ago at The Rocks. He's dead."

"The way I see it, Harry is that you have a lot of suspicions, but little hard evidence that wouldn't even pass the pub test," said Murray.

"Not worth a pinch of salt," added Kevin.

"I agree," said Harry. "I need to get more evidence, so I'm asking you to give me permission to go ahead with my plan?"

"What is that plan?"

"I want to wire two of the CIB team and have them obtain the evidence I need to wrap up this case."

The inspector raised his arms. "You must be joking. They won't do that. You'll be committing suicide."

"Charlie Rockwell and Bob Crow are about to retire. I have evidence that both have taken bribes. They are only minor operators but they are involved. I want to provide them with wires and miniature cameras to get the evidence."

Murray Fredericks harrumphed. "There's no way any of them will rat on their mates; and especially Sherman and Cross."

"Yes they will," said Harry, "if we offer them immunity from prosecution, give them witness protection and a new life under a new identity. They don't want to risk gaol, a dishonourable dismissal and loss of superannuation."

"Why them?" asked Kevin.

"They have been very good officers for most of their career. They are corrupt but only in the minor league by comparison with the big boys. If we forgive them, for their minor indiscretions and protect them we can catch the big fish; but it will need your approval."

"How do you propose to go about this?"

"Jock and I will visit Charlie and Bob today. We will make them the offer."

"And if they refuse?"

"We'll lock them up for further discussions. They won't want to take it further for fear of losing their retirement entitlements."

Kevin stood up and walked around thinking. "If they agree, what will happen next?"

Harry explained how he had briefed Tony's team to be ready to fit Charlie and Bob with miniature cameras and wires and how they, together with Jock, would visit the Elegant Lady that night to record the transfer of bribes and record conversations about recent events.

"What do you think, Kevin?" asked Murray.

"It's extremely risky. I don't like it but Harry's got a point. There doesn't seem to be another way. We must put a stop to these senseless killings and drug wars and I've had my suspicions about Sherman and Cross for some time."

Murray looked at the ceiling. "I think I need to pass this by the commissioner and chief superintendent."

Harry coughed. "I'd prefer you didn't. This operation depends on the least number of people being involved; and I know that the chief is a close friend of Sherman. I don't want him warning Fred."

"I want you two to leave the room while I discuss this with Kevin."

Half an hour later, Harry and Jock were invited in again.

Murray paused before speaking. "I'm going to approve this operation but I'll make it clear that, if it fails, your careers are finished. Do you understand?"

"Perfectly clear," said Harry. "I wouldn't have expected anything less. Thank you. We'll keep you two posted every step of the way."

Chapter 60
Saturday

Harry phoned Tony Jacobs. He asked him to implement the first stage of the plan. George Black, the photography and sound expert, and Ross Oxford, an electrical and phone whiz, carried their tool kits to the Elegant Lady casino, dressed in overalls and boots. They told the security man they had received an urgent call from the manager to repair some lights upstairs. As it was too early for the manager to be on duty, the security man let them in and showed them in to the gambling casino upstairs.

George and Ross were very experienced and had worked on similar cases involving undercover operations. They set up hidden cameras in the low overhead lights and microphones in the private booths. They tapped all of the phones. They were in and out in forty minutes. They thanked the security man at the door as they left.

Harry asked Jimmy Wilkins to phone Bob Crow and Charlie Rockwell to demand that they come to headquarters immediately. The deputy commissioner wished to speak to them on an urgent matter.

Jimmy reported back. "They weren't happy. Bob said it was his day off and he was going to the races. Charlie told me to tell Fredericks to go jump in the lake because he had gone to the country to see his family."

Harry smiled. "Did you convince them, Jimmy?"

"I told them the deputy commissioner wanted to give them a special award in recognition of their outstanding service and they should dress in their best suits."

Harry laughed. "Jimmy, how do you sleep at night? Well done. Thanks."

When Charlie Rockwell came in, Harry escorted him to one of the interview rooms. Jock took Bob Crow to another room and asked him to wait for the deputy to arrive.

Charlie was not happy. "What the bloody hell are you doing here, Harry? What's going on? Where's the deputy commissioner? I was told he wanted to see me."

Harry sat at the desk. Jock came back in, closed the door and sat in the corner with notebook ready.

"Take a seat, Charlie. The deputy will be with us later, but I need to talk to you first."

"I smell a rat. What's this all about?"

"Charlie, you told me a couple of weeks ago that you were thinking of retiring. You've had enough. Is that still your plan?"

"Yes, I might have said that but I haven't made up my mind yet. Why do you ask?"

"Because I'm going to put an offer to you; one that I'm sure you won't be able to refuse."

"And what's that?"

"You're going to retire now on the condition that you give us vital information about some of your mates."

Charlie jumped up and moved towards the door. Jock stepped in front of him and led him back to the seat.

"What the fucking hell are you two doing? Do you want me killed?"

"Calm down, Charlie," said Harry. "Let's work through this slowly so that there is no misunderstanding."

"There's no way I'm going to rat on my mates. That's the lowest level of scumbag that anyone can be. What do you take me for? We police support our mates no matter what. You know the drill."

"Let me put it to you this way, Charlie. If you don't cooperate with us you're going down for bribery and murder for starters. It means you'll probably die in gaol."

"What the fuck are you two playing at? Get Allan Twain in here now and let's put a stop to this nonsense."

"Twain is not in charge of this operation. The deputy commissioner is. And we have his full backing. How many times have you shared in the bribe money that the crime bosses gave to Fred Sherman and Joe Cross?"

"What are you talking about?"

"Charlie, we know Fred gets a parcel each week from the big crime bosses and we know he shares some with his mates. We know, on occasions, that has included you."

"You don't have any proof that I take bribes, so you don't have a case. I'm leaving."

Jock stood up between Charlie and the door. Charlie reluctantly sat down again.

Harry continued. "Let's look at another matter. You, Bob, Fred and Joe went to Rosebery and murdered Scarface Fisher."

"That wasn't murder. That was self-defence."

Harry leaned forward and reached across the desk. "Charlie, that was cold-blooded murder. You know that, because you were the next closest person to Fred when it happened. Fisher didn't fire a shot. He didn't have a weapon. And, to make it worse, Fisher was not the man who took a shot at me and wasn't responsible for the bomb in my car. Your mate Lebovich was."

Charlie was sweating profusely. Beads of perspiration were running down his face and dripping off his bulbous nose. He banged his fist on the table. "Scarface came out shooting at Fred who fired back and killed him. He got what he deserved."

"No, Charlie. When Scarface came out of that house he was unarmed. He's never been a shooter. He never carried a gun."

"That's a lie. When he fell down he had a revolver in his hand."

"No, Charlie. He didn't have a gun in his hand. Fred put it there when he got to the verandah."

"You can't prove that."

"Oh yes I can. I have an independent witness in a neighbour who saw the shooting. You stupid people didn't do your homework. Not only was Scarface not a shooter, but he was also left-handed. Fred put the revolver in his right hand."

Charlie sat back without a word. The perspiration ran down his face to his collar. He took out a hanky to wipe his forehead. Harry paused before continuing.

"You and I know that Tom Lebovich was involved in the murder of Knuckles Elliott and Billy Knobbs, and he was with Bomber Earl in that North Rocks robbery, and yet you four have been protecting him. You knew that Fred was going to organise the diversion of cars to Kogarah. That makes you an accessory to those crimes. You're looking at life in gaol."

"I had nothing to do with it."

"Charlie, I'm going to get a pot of tea for us, but while I'm out I want you to think of what it will be like in Long Bay, Grafton or

Goulburn Gaols where you'll have to share a cell with some of those blokes you have put away over the years. Think about it."

Harry took his time. He returned with a pot, three mugs and a plate of Milk Arrowroot biscuits. He filled the mugs and said nothing as he chewed on a biscuit. Charlie finally broke the silence.

"You rotten bastards. You scum. How can you stoop so low to do this to us?"

"Very easy, Charlie. In the last five weeks I have had two attempts on my life and I've had my investigations cut short in order to protect you lot and your criminal mates. And you're behind it. My informant was shot dead this morning by one of your mates. Now you start talking because I'm running out of patience."

"I want to go to the toilet."

"Follow him, Jock and make certain he comes back here, because he's not leaving this building until he gives me an answer."

When he came back, Charlie looked at Harry with a look that was now more anxious than angry. "You said you had an offer."

Harry waited while he sipped his tea and finished another biscuit. "Well, that depends on whether you're willing to cooperate."

"What have I got to do?"

Harry explained how Tony's team were going to set him up with a miniature camera attached to a wire and switch in his trouser pocket, and a recording device that would fit in his inside suit pocket. He would go to the Elegant Lady casino that night and mix with Fred and Joe to come away with evidence of money being handed over. He also had to get them talking about the murders and the armoured van robbery.

Charlie took a deep breath, sat back and looked at the ceiling. "And what's in it for me?"

"If you cooperate fully— and I mean fully, no slip ups, no leaks— we'll let you retire gracefully without a conviction."

"Don't bullshit me, Harry. You don't have the authority to do that."

"You're right, Charlie but the deputy commissioner has, and he's waiting for your answer. What's it to be?"

"If I do this and retire I'll be dead in no time. That's not an option."

Harry tapped the desk. "Here's the deal. You do this and we'll give you an honourable retirement and we'll give you witness protection and a new identity. We'll move you to another place where nobody knows you."

"I don't have much choice, do I? But where would I go?"

"You've been separated from your wife for years but you have a son in New Zealand. Is that correct?"

"Yes, in Dunedin."

"Well, we can get you settled in Oamaru, Invercargill or Christchurch with a new name. You'll be close enough there."

"Can I have some time to think about it?"

Harry stood up. "Yes. I'm about to talk to Bob Crow and offer him the same deal. If he agrees, you will work as a team tonight. When I come back I want an answer. I can't wait any longer. Don't leave this room."

Harry asked a constable to guard the door as he and Jock moved to the next interview room where Bob Crow was waiting.

That interview was almost a repeat of the one with Charlie. There were the same angry outbursts, threats, panic attacks, attempts at staged walkouts, time outs and calm reflections.

"You'll never get away with this, Harry. They'll get you, mate. Believe me. They're bigger than you and me and the whole bloody police force put together."

"That might be so, Bob, but that's my worry, not yours. Now what's it to be? Where do you want to go?"

"I don't know. I've spent most of my life in Sydney."

"Didn't you once tell me that your wife's family came from Spain?"

"Yes."

"Well, let's set you two lovebirds up with a new identity in Spain. You'll find it nice and relaxed and cheaper to live there than here. Sit back in the sun. Do you agree to that?"

"I don't have a choice, do I? Okay, let's get it over and done with."

Harry phoned through to the deputy's office where Murray Fredericks and Kevin Thornett were waiting for the outcome of Harry's interviews. Harry and Jock then escorted Bob and Charlie to the deputy's office.

Murray Fredericks put Bob and Charlie through an hour of solid questioning to ensure that they knew exactly what they were agreeing to, and that they understood the dangers involved in what they were about to do that night. Only then did they give the go-ahead for the plan.

Following the deputy commissioner's approval, Harry took Bob and Charlie back to the interview room and called in Tony's team. George Black and Ross Oxford wired Bob and Charlie and showed them how to operate the camera from their side pockets, and how to set the recorder in motion. They took them through at least ten rehearsals before they were convinced that it would work with the minimum risk of exposure.

Harry kept them in that room until nightfall with only escorted visits to the toilet. He sent Jock out to get some pies and a pot of tea. He couldn't afford anyone else being involved. Everything depended on the tightness, silence and the small size of the team. He stared out the window while he raised and lowered his right arm, firmly tapping his left middle finger onto the desk. It was his way of controlling his nerves.

Chapter 61
Saturday

At eight o'clock the team took two cars to Bourke Street, Woolloomooloo. Harry arranged for George Black to accompany Bob and Charlie into the nightclub. George was a character in his own right and a good storyteller. He would blend perfectly into the casino atmosphere and he would be there if any hitch with the cameras or recorders occurred. Harry asked Jock to accompany them as well. Bob and Charlie were to introduce George and Jock as good prospects to join the CIB team.

Harry wouldn't go inside as that would be too obvious. He put on his tanker hood, took off his coat and tie and sat in the second car outside. His request to have Rita Flynn sit with him in the car so that it was less conspicuous as a surveillance operation was approved by Tony. Rita jumped at the opportunity to be involved in a real live operation. Their car was parked on the dark side of a narrow lane near the casino where he had a good view of the entrance. Their job was to take note of everyone who entered and exited the club.

The arrangement was for Bob, Charlie, Jock and George to remain in the club until two in the morning, or until Sherman and Cross left. After that, they were to go back to the SIB with Harry and Rita to debrief and allow George time to develop the film.

Early in the evening a number of well-dressed people entered the club. Harry didn't recognise them. The men were dressed in dinner suits or tuxedos, and the women were glamorous in their finest and best. Harry assumed that most of them were going to the ground floor dining section of the night club to celebrate a birthday or engagement or just to have a good night out. Harry could hear a piano playing in the background. At nine o'clock a singer entertained the guests.

The downstairs area was the legal part of the building and was what the general population saw as the public face of exciting downtown Sydney. For most ladies, an invitation to the nightclub for fine dining, with starched linen cloths, silver cutlery and crystal wine glasses, was an opportunity never to be missed, and an indication that the man with them was either very serious, or rich, or both. The white gloved waiters and the entertainment from the latest touring American singer were an added bonus.

But that was just the facade. Harry was not interested in the rich folk coming and going from their Rolls and Bentleys, or the young women who came out later and danced down the street with excitement after a couple of Pimm's or gin-and-tonics as they looked for the next thrill. He was only interested in those who were there for the upstairs action; the gambling, corruption, drugs and call girls. He wound down the window to let in some fresh air. The humidity and heat on this summer's night was stifling.

Rita nudged Harry. "I don't see why you didn't take me to the club tonight, Harry. Any other gentleman would have done the right thing. All I get is a car full of mosquitoes and sweat."

Harry laughed. "Stop complaining. You should be so lucky. I gave you a meat pie with sauce before we came here. Besides, I couldn't take you in there like that, dressed in slacks without your diamonds and pearls and with your hair all untidy."

Rita punched him on the arm. "You men. You're all alike. Not a sensitive bone in your bodies."

"Well, we haven't got time for sensitivities because the real customers are starting to arrive. Look over there."

A long white Lincoln Continental limousine pulled up at the door. Whispers Durante, with two young attractive girls, alighted and entered the building. The top-hatted doorman escorted them inside. Shortly after, a black Dodge coupé with whitewalled tyres pulled up. Harry recognised Tom Lebovich with his distinctive limp.

From then on there was a procession of well-known identities: at least three politicians including a current minister, a well-known judge, the conductor of the Symphony Orchestra, two prominent lawyers, the head of a well-known pastoral company, an interstate attorney-general and a number of other well-to-do men about town.

Rita was stunned as she saw the parade of identities entering the club. She got out of the car and watched as they were escorted to the lift to take them to the illegal gambling casino upstairs. When she got back in the car she grabbed Harry's sleeve and gasped. "Those people run this country and they are in an illegal casino as if they are going to the local café for a milkshake. Some of those politicians in there get up in parliament and preach morals and the sins of the flesh as if they are all so pure and innocent and then come here for a night of debauchery."

"Welcome to the real world, Rita. But look over there now. There's Fred Sherman and Joe Cross. They got a taxi here. I hope Bob and Charlie play their part or we're all dead."

Fred struggled to get his coat on. He was hot and sweaty and out of breath. Joe helped by hitching the shoulders up and straightening the back before they went in.

Among the other arrivals, Harry noticed Bluey Ricketts, Tony Stavros, Tony Pantano and Shooter McGill. Present in the upstairs casino tonight would be the hardcore criminals in this city mixing with the upper echelons of government, law enforcement and society. What a paradox, thought Rita.

Rita pointed at them through the windscreen. "How the hell can they get away with that?"

"It's all about power, money and influence, Rita. You and I will never have to worry about it unless we get sucked in with the corruption like some of our colleagues."

Harry looked up and noticed one of the security men from the club walking in their direction. He got out of the car and walked slowly towards him.

"Hey you two," shouted the man as he flexed his muscles for effect. "What the fuck are you doing here?"

Harry raised his hands in defence. "Sorry, mate. We don't mean to cause no trouble but me sheila just told me she's pregnant and we're trying to think of how we're gunna tell her parents. Her old man is a real bastard."

The muscles subsided. "Aah jeez, mate. That's no good. Youse can stay there for a while but don't be too long. It can get a bit rough around here at this time of night. Best of luck mate." He walked away.

Back in the car Rita gave him another thump on the arm. "Bloody hell, Harry, now you tell me I'm pregnant and I didn't feel a thing. Is that what it's like? Is this going to be the next virgin birth?"

They sat back and giggled, trying not to make too much sound as they enjoyed the moment.

It was a long boring wait. Harry and Rita amused themselves comparing the well-to-do going upstairs to the casino with the homeless and low life wandering the streets of down town Woolloomooloo.

At about two o'clock Harry pointed to the door of the club. Fred Sherman and Joe Cross came out, got into a cab and drove off. "Look. The others are starting to come out. There's Jock and Bob and, a little further back, George and Charlie."

"Are you going to pick up Fred and Joe now?"

"No. Let's get back to the SIB and check out what they got tonight. We need hard evidence first. Those other two can wait."

When they arrived back at SIB the others were there standing around the kitchen sink.

Harry pointed to Jock. "Sorry, mate but I want you to take Bob and Charlie to the safe house now. I already have officers there to look after them. Drop them and come back here."

"But I want to go home to get my things," said Bob.

"Neither of you are going anywhere near your houses. From this moment on, you are what you've never been. This is the start of your new life. Say goodbye to everything you ever did and everyone you ever knew. Bob, your wife is already at the safe house waiting for you."

"What if I say no?" asked Charlie.

"It's a free world, Charlie. You can say whatever you like but, if you refuse to go, I can arrange alternate accommodation at Long Bay. I can get you into a cell with Slasher Millthorpe. You do remember him, don't you? I'm sure he'd love to see you again."

"You bastard, Harry. Okay, it seems like I don't have a choice."

"Charlie, go and live the rest of your life in peace. You don't have family here now so go to New Zealand and start a new life. You've earned it. Now go with Jock."

When Jock left, Harry looked to George. "How did things go in there?"

"There were a few hairy moments. Charlie is a bit old and he's not used to things like miniature cameras and recorders. I had to take him to the toilets a couple of times to remind him but it all went okay in the end."

"Can you develop those photos now?"

"I've already started. I'll get them to you as soon as possible."

Twenty minutes later Jock returned. He, Rita, Harry and Tony sat down to analyse the night's activities. They were joined later by George and Ross Oxford. Ross started by playing some tapes. Some of the dialogue was indistinct because of other voices nearby or because Bob or Charlie were scratching their chests near the microphone. Harry and Jock took notes as they listened.

Some time later George came in with his photos. He laid them out on the table in the order they were taken. They all studied them closely.

"What do you think, Harry? Do you have enough to go on?" asked Tony.

"Yes. We have clear evidence of bribe money being passed over and we have enough sound bites to tie Fred and Joe with Lebovich, Pantano, and possibly Stavros, to major crimes. I don't have enough on Durante or McGill yet but I can tie Lebovich to the attempt on my life, the killing of Elliott and the North Rocks job."

"But is this enough to convince a court?"

"It will be after I work with Charlie and Bob tomorrow and get their signed statutory declarations. They can tie all the other pieces together plus the fact that Sherman and Cross organised and pulled off the murder of Scarface Fisher and organised the North Rocks job. I'll even be able to tie them to the attempt on my life. When we get details of their hidden bank accounts we will have a solid case."

"Why didn't you get Charlie and Bob to write their statements tonight?"

"They are older and they've just been through the biggest upheaval in their life. They're going to be sleeping in a strange place tonight, under guard. I'll let them have a sleep and a good late breakfast before we get their statements."

"What will you do if they change their minds?" asked Ross.

"They know that if they don't cooperate, they are heading for gaol for the rest of their life. With time to think overnight I'm sure they'll cooperate."

"What about Sherman and Cross? When will you pick them up?" asked Tony.

"From what you have shown me here tonight I'm convinced that they are totally unaware of what we just pulled off. I'll leave them until I have Bob and Charlie's statements. Then I have to get a final go-ahead from Murray Fredericks, the deputy commissioner."

Tony bit on another biscuit. "Do you see any difficulty from him?"

"No. Murray, in my opinion, will be the next commissioner after the boss retires. If he can show that he's cleaning out corrupt officers in the Force, the public will love it and the Premier will have no option but to make him the next chief."

"What about Allan Twain? I thought he was in the pocket of the Premier. I bet he wants that job more than Fredericks."

"Yes, he desperately wants it and will kill to get it, but if Fredericks pulls this off he will shoe it in."

"Do you know where Cross and Sherman live?"

"I know that Fred is at Strathfield and I think Joe is at Dover Heights."

"Best check that out," said Tony. "The rumour is that Joe is having it off with Fred's estranged wife, Gloria; and she lives at Coogee."

Harry shook his head. "My God, there's no honour among these bastards. Do you mean to say that Joe works with Fred during the day and bangs his wife at night? I bet Fred doesn't know."

"If he did, it would be a very short friendship," said Tony. "Just be very careful, Harry."

"Thanks for your help; and thank the team for me too."

Tony tapped him on the shoulder. "Better you than me, Harry. You're playing with fire, mate. Be careful you don't get burned."

"I'm going home. I'll see you in the morning."

***

It was early Sunday morning. Harry hadn't slept all night but he still had important tasks to complete. He had arranged for a shorthand typist to transcribe the important lines from the tapes to print, and while she completed that, he spent two hours with Bob and Charlie. They presented damning evidence that was later added to their statements. At eleven o'clock he called the Deputy Commissioner who agreed to meet him at headquarters with Kevin Thornett.

In the deputy's office, Jock and Harry laid out the evidence on his desk, including the statutory declarations from Bob and Charlie obtained that morning. Murray Fredericks and Kevin Thornett took their time to examine it and asked numerous questions. After a long session Murray looked at Harry.

"Congratulations, Harry. Well done. What's your plan from here?"

"I have Bob and Charlie in a safe house and in lockdown. They won't go anywhere until we finalise everything else. I won't move on the others until tonight. I'll wait until Joe Cross is home tonight and move in on him. He will be held in isolation. I'll do the same with Fred Sherman early tomorrow morning. I've selected some of the best officers to bring in Lebovich, Pantano and Stavros during the night. They also will be kept in isolation and will have no contact with the others until we bring them all in."

Kevin Thornett stood up and paced the room. "What if someone talks? What happens if some of the very important people there last night get a whiff of what's going on? Could someone like Durante or McGill get some of their friends in high places to throw it all back on us?"

Harry looked up at Kevin. "I'd only have to mention that *The Sunday Mirror* was interested in the story for them to back off."

Murray Fredericks walked to the window. "How confident are you, Harry that your operations tonight and tomorrow morning will go off without a hitch? Remember that you're dealing with two of the toughest men in this country. They're not going to take it sitting down."

"We have some really great officers in this police force and I've selected the best of them for this operation. I've already briefed them. They're ready to go when you give us the go ahead."

Murray paused and then pointed to the door. "You and Jock go and have some lunch. Come back here when you've finished."

One hour later they got the green light. They were ready for the final moves.

Chapter 62
Sunday

That afternoon Harry contacted his team and told them to be prepared for his next call. After leaving headquarters he checked out Joe Cross' house in Dover Heights but found no sign of life. He drove to Coogee where he located a house on the high side of Wolseley Road where Gloria Sherman, the estranged wife of Fred Sherman lived. Parked in front was a red 1946 Triumph Roadster, owned by Joe,. He carefully studied the layout of the house.

From the front, the orange-brick, red-tiled house sat high on a steeply sloping block. A single garage with a flat roof was cut into the embankment from street level. A verandah with a balustrade stretched across the front of the house. The ground level had a front door and two windows. From what he could see, Harry guessed they were the lounge and dining rooms. The upstairs windows were covered with Venetian blinds but Harry could see bedroom wardrobes through the larger of the two.

This was going to be a risky venture. Harry was anxious about his plan to take Joe in this house after dark. If he waited for night, when they were in bed, then entry at the lower level would give Joe enough warning to be prepared for the raid. Joe was known in the service as a shoot-em-up and take-em-down man. He didn't ask questions. If he was cornered he would shoot his way out. Harry didn't want to place his team in unnecessary danger. He wanted to improve the odds for his team. Entry at the ground floor level was too dangerous.

Walking around the house in daylight to look at the back was too risky so he went to the next corner, drove up the hill in Rainbow Street and found a spot where he could observe the rear of the house. The backyard was large and sloped upwards to the back fence. There was only one door and one window on the back wall and they led directly into the upstairs level. There was no lane across the back. The best chance at surprise was to go in through that back door. That gave them direct access to the upstairs hallway that led to the main bedroom at the front of the house.

It was risky but it was better than downstairs. The difficulty was getting easy access to that back door. He drove up Garnet Street that took him to the houses directly behind Gloria's. He noticed an older couple in the garden. Their house had a wide driveway down the side leading to a detached garage. This would give his team a way over the back fence to Gloria's back door. But he didn't want to put the old couple in danger.

Harry walked over to the fence. He was thankful that Kevin Thornett had given back his badge. He introduced himself to the couple.

"Hello there. I'm Harry Taylor. I was just admiring your beautiful garden. You should be very proud of it."

They looked up at the stranger. "Hello, I'm Bob Sampson, and this is my wife, Norma. Yes, we love our garden and now that we're retired, we have time to look after it."

Harry took his badge from his pocket and held it out for the couple to see. "Bob and Norma, I'm a detective with the New South Wales Police and I have to let you know that we are planning a secret operation here in your street tonight. We don't want to scare you but it will be important that you leave your home now and stay away until tomorrow morning."

"Oh my goodness," gasped Norma. "It's not something we've done?"

"No," Harry reassured. "It's just that we don't want to put you in any danger."

"We could go to our son's place but he doesn't have much room," said Bob.

"No, Bob," said Harry. "I'll take you to the Tattersall's Hotel in town and give you a free night of luxury for being such good citizens. I want you to go and pack a bag and I'll drive you there now."

"Is it to do with that nasty man in number sixty-two?" asked Norma.

"I can't discuss it with you; and the less you know the better."

Harry drove them into the city and booked them into the hotel. He returned to their house and took his time observing the house in Wolseley Street. He now had his plan.

***

At nine o'clock Sunday night, Harry assembled his team at Grant Reserve near Coogee beach. There were two detectives, Jock Burns together with Archie Harris from the Redfern station and two constables he knew and trusted from the Strathfield unit, Mark Clout and Don Irvine. He gave each of them a map of the nearby streets and a diagram of the house. He explained the situation in Garnet Street in regard to the old couple's home.

He asked the team to drive or walk around Wolseley, Rainbow and Garnet Streets to get a feeling for the layout. Half an hour later they gathered again at the reserve. Harry outlined the plan. He explained that there were no lights on downstairs and the only light on upstairs appeared to be in the main bedroom. Joe's car was still out front.

"One hour after the lights go out in the bedroom upstairs, Jock and I will go through the Garnet Street property, over the back fence and down to the back door. Jock will pick the lock and we will proceed down the corridor to the main bedroom. I want Archie to enter the front door with Mark and secure the lower level and the stairs. Don will go to the side door and cover any escape there."

"Do you see any problem, Harry?" asked Don.

"I want everyone to be extra careful. Joe will have his side-arm and I wouldn't be surprised if he has other weapons in the house. When you hear Jock and me shouting upstairs, break in and secure your areas."

Harry and Jock waited for ten minutes to allow the others to get into position. Jock picked the lock. The squeak of the door as it opened was loud. They stood still. There was no other sound. They moved quietly along the corridor to the bedroom. He was thankful it was carpeted.

As they reached the door a bedside light came on. Harry rushed in, his revolver out in front. Joe was rolling out of bed groping for his trousers on the floor and searching for his weapon. Harry stomped on his hand. Jock rushed to the other side of the bed with his gun pointed squarely at Gloria's face. She screamed.

Archie came rushing up the stairs. He dived on top of Joe as Harry removed the gun. They put him in cuffs. Don and Mark came in and covered the lower level and the stairs. Harry asked Archie to take

Gloria downstairs to the lounge room and hold her there. They pushed Joe back on the bed.

"Joe Cross," said Harry. "I'm charging you with a number of offences including murder, conspiracy to murder, corruption, bribery and other offences that we will detail when we get back to headquarters."

Joe sat on the side of the bed in his underpants, hair ruffled, his face screwed up with anger.

"Who the fucking hell do you think you are to pull a stunt like this? You're dead, Harry. You won't last the day."

"And who do you think is going to do the job this time, Joe? The last blokes you sent to kill me are in gaol. We picked them up earlier tonight."

"What are you talking about?"

"We have Stavros, Lebovich and Pantano in the cells now and we have Durante and McGill under twenty-four hour surveillance. You already got rid of Billy Knobbs and Bomber Earl, so they can't help you. I doubt that the Melbourne mob such as Nobby Clark and Darkie Moffitt will help you. So, you're left high and dry, Joe."

"Wait till I call Fred and Allan Twain. They'll have me out in no time and then you'll know who's in control."

"For your information, Joe, we have Fred in lockdown, and Allan Twain is not in charge of this operation. The Deputy Commissioner, Murray Fredericks, is in control and has approved this operation."

"Get me a phone. I'll call Bob Crow and Charlie Rockwell. They'll take care of it."

Harry passed Joe his trousers and shirt. "Jock will help you into these but Bob and Charlie won't be here to help. They have provided statutory declarations that will stand up in court proving your involvement in the murder of Scarface Fisher and the North Rocks robbery, as well as many charges relating to bribery and corruption. You're going down for life, Joe."

Joe glared at Harry. "I should have done the fucking job myself. Then we wouldn't be going through all this nonsense."

"Yes, Joe. You're right. If you had come to my side window at New Year and taken that shot at me, I wouldn't be here now locking you up for life. That was your biggest mistake. You wouldn't have missed. You are too practised with a gun. You have a proven record."

"Fuck you, Harry. You never fitted in. You could have been on clover if you had stuck with us but you were never a team man. You always wanted to go off by yourself and do it your way. I hope you rot in hell."

"Thanks for those kind words, Joe. Where you're going you'll have plenty of time to think about them. By the way, I have the best team in this state. They're here tonight. You can say hello to them as you go out."

"Where do you want him, Harry?" asked Jock.

"Take him to the wagon. I'll go downstairs and talk to Gloria."

As Harry walked into the lounge room, Gloria let blast with fury. As a former champion swimmer and hockey player she still had the body of a fit athlete, and she had a temper to match. She had wrinkles around her eyes, but Harry believed she was still capable of swinging a solid punch.

"You're dead, Harry Taylor. You're not going to get away with this. Wait 'til I call Fred. He'll have us out of here in no time."

"I find it interesting, Gloria, that here you are in bed banging away with Fred's best mate and yet you want him to come and rescue you. When he finds out what you two have been up to, you're the one in trouble. Besides, I can tell you that Fred will be joining you shortly, but not here."

Gloria tried desperately to get up from the couch but the cuffs prevented her from getting leverage. "What do you want, Harry?'

"I want the truth, Gloria and I mean the whole truth."

"What do you mean?"

"You know as well as I do that Fred has been involved in a number of illegal activities over many years."

"That's a bloody lie. How could you say that? Fred is the most highly-decorated policeman in this country. He has numerous awards and commendations for bravery. He's been responsible for bringing in the worst criminals in this state. He's a hero, not a weak piss-ant like you. Go ask the commissioner and the Premier of the state; they'll tell you. If you do anything to him all hell will break loose on you. So, watch it, scumbag."

Harry sat back and watched her face. "Now that you've got that off your chest, let's talk about the real world. Fred has been receiving substantial bribes from well-known criminals for many years. We have the proof and he's going to gaol for that and many other charges including murder."

"You're a stinking rotten liar. You have no proof."

Harry put a piece of paper on the coffee table. On it was a list of various properties in Sydney and on the Central Coast, together with a number of bank accounts in Fred's name as well as others in Gloria's maiden name and those of her children. At the bottom was a list of cars and power boats.

Harry coughed. "Could you please explain how Fred acquired all these properties and possessions from his meagre policeman's salary?"

"He was lucky at gambling. I've never seen someone as lucky; and he studied the form every week."

"Good try, Gloria, but we already know about the rigged races and the laundering of money after the last race with the bookmaker, Charlie Bennett. That will be added to the list of charges."

"You bastard, Harry. I never trusted you and neither did Fred or Joe."

"Well that makes me very happy, Gloria because I don't want to go where they're going. Now let's work out what we will do with you."

"You've got nothing on me. I haven't done anything wrong so release me now or I'll have your nuts for breakfast."

"Try again, Gloria. You've been mixed up in this all of your married life. You opened accounts in false names to hide those monies. You provided alibis for Fred and Joe to cover up some of their illegal activities. The two of you acquired many properties including this one and the big one in Strathfield. Just those two cost a fortune. The way I see it, Gloria, is that you look like going into the State Reformatory for Women at Long Bay for a very long time. Think about that while I check on the rest of the team."

Harry asked Archie to take off her cuffs and allow her to get dressed. He walked out and went to the kitchen. He talked to the others in the team and filled them in about his conversations with Joe and Gloria.

"How's Gloria taking it, Harry?" asked Archie.

"She's fighting fit to kill me, so I've left her to think about her options."

Half an hour later Harry returned to the lounge room.

"Now, Gloria, I'm going to make you an offer. You will provide us with a list of all the bank accounts in all the names, real and fake. You will list all property. You will provide us with a statutory declaration of your knowledge of Fred and Joe's involvement in various criminal activities, including their attempts on my life, the North Rocks robbery, their murder of Scarface Fisher and other matters. If you do, we will provide you with a new identity as a protected witness in a new location. If you don't, you're going to Long Bay for a long time. It's your choice."

"You bastard, Taylor. You don't give a woman a chance."

"Your husband and Joe didn't give me a chance. And neither did they give Elliott, Fisher, Earl, Knobbs and Sandy Blight a chance. Whose side are you on, Gloria?"

"What happens to all our assets?"

"Almost all of your assets have been acquired by illegal means. They will be confiscated and the proceeds will go into state coffers to help the poor. We will leave you with a bank account sufficient to provide for basic needs at your new secure location well away from here."

Gloria sat back and fumed, white hot anger on her face. After a few minutes she shouted. "Okay, okay, where do I sign these fucking papers?"

Harry turned away. "Archie, get her to fill out a full stat dec, even if it takes her all night to get it right and complete. After that, take her to the other safe house. We'll finalise her testimony tomorrow. Thanks, team. I'll see you first thing in the morning."

Chapter 63
Monday

The large, well-maintained red brick Federation house stood on the corner of Cooper Street, Strathfield, an exquisite dwelling in a select part of town. In the carport, next to the double garage, was a shiny new 1947 Ford Super Deluxe Convertible. Parked off street around the corner was a trailer topped with a 1938, 19-foot racing boat with an inbuilt V8 motor. There was no way a detective's salary could afford such a grand dwelling in such a prime location, together with three expensive vehicles and a prize motorboat, let alone all the other properties, bank accounts and possessions. The owner could only acquire such wealth through inheritance or by unlawful means.

It was four-thirty in the morning. After an overnight shower, the early morning light reflected from the wet surface of the road. An eastern grey honeyeater cackled in a nearby grevillea bush as it savoured the sweet nectar of the flowers. An early morning train tooted as it left Strathfield station for the city. A light came on in the house around the corner. All else in the street was quiet.

Harry gathered his team behind a large wattle tree across the street from the garage. He handed each of them a diagram of the house showing all rooms, doors and windows. As they studied the plan he pointed across the street to the front entry door in the centre of the building with the lounge room window opening onto the wrap-around verandah. Projecting forward on the left was a sitting room and an office. Behind those rooms was the main bedroom.

Mark and Don, the constables from Strathfield station, were very nervous. They were on the operation last night at Coogee, but this was of greater importance and magnitude. The man inside was the best-known policeman in the state; and probably in Australia. Archie and Jock, the two detectives, had been in many a tight spot before and were better prepared for most eventualities. They had also been at the rough end of verbal abuse from Fred Sherman and had no sense of loyalty to him. Tension and anxiety sweated in the early morning air.

Harry gathered the team in close. He spoke clearly but quietly with a command that gave confidence to the others. "We received good information from Fred's estranged wife, Gloria last night. Neither she nor her two sons will be in the house this morning. We know Fred is in there and we suspect he is with his girlfriend. We have disconnected the phone to the house."

Archie Harris half-raised a hand. "What do you want us to do with her?"

"Take her in. I don't expect to charge her but we need to get her bank and other details to check if she has been receiving benefits from Fred's gravy train."

"Okay, Harry, how do you want to do this?" asked Jock, standing like a solid block of granite, sledgehammer in hand.

"Alright, everyone listen up. Mark, I want you to go around the corner, through the side gate and around to the back door. We won't move until you're in position."

"Do you want me to stand guard outside?"

"No," said Harry. "When you hear us go in, smash the glass on the door, reach in, unlock it and go up the corridor towards the main bedroom. Block that corridor."

"What will us others do, Harry?" asked Don.

"Right, this is what will happen. Jock will smash in the front door with his sledgehammer and he and I will go straight for the bedroom. Don, I want you to stay at the front door to block anybody coming out that way. Archie will move into the lounge room to stop any exit through the side door onto the verandah. There are bars on the windows, so they will not try to escape that way. Check your weapons now. This man is dangerous and he will use any force to protect himself. Don't be afraid to use yours if you have to. Carry your weapon in one hand and the torch in the other, but don't switch on your light until you are inside. Any questions?"

"Do you expect any problems, Harry?" asked Jock, tucking his revolver into his belt to give himself a two handed grip on the hammer.

"You can expect that Fred will have a weapon beside his bed. He knows he has many enemies and will be prepared for any eventuality. Stay low when we go into that bedroom. If he shoots he will aim at the door opening at chest level. Okay, Mark, off you go. Let's get this over with before it gets too light. The sun will be fully above the horizon in an hour.”

Mark walked around the corner keeping his head below the hedge line, through the side gate and on to the back door. He signalled to the group as he disappeared behind the house. Harry waited another minute.

“Be very quiet until we smash that door, then shout your heads off to create panic and confusion for those inside. Let’s go.”

They went through the gate near the carport and walked across the grass to reduce noise. With one well-aimed swing Jock smashed the lock and an equally accurate kick opened the door. Archie moved to the right into the lounge room while Harry and Jock bent low through the doorway to the bedroom on the left.

“Police, police,” shouted Harry. “Don’t move. Freeze. Stay where you are.”

A naked woman, lying on the bed, screamed, grabbing the sheet and hauling it up. Harry rose slowly, shone his torch around and realised that there was no other person in the room.

Fred was not there. Harry was stunned. Thoughts ran quickly through his mind. Was he ever here tonight? Did he hear us coming and escape? Did we botch this operation? We might not get another chance. Fred’s no fool. Given any chance, he’ll be in charge as he always has been, and when that happens, someone will get hurt or be killed.

As Harry rushed from the bedroom he turned to the left to see Mark on his knees with Fred behind him applying a throttle hold. He had taken Mark’s gun and was holding it to the constable’s head. He had all of the aces.

Fred was in his fifties and had a paunch from overindulgence, but he was still a very fit, strong man. But more than fitness, he was a tough, brutal man who had never hesitated in killing a man when he felt so inclined. He had played first grade rugby league football in the forwards in his younger days, and was known for his take-no-prisoners approach. His cauliflower ears and twisted nose were testimony to the toughness he took into every match. In those days he would rather have a fight than a feed.

He’d carried that same approach into his police work throughout his working life and that is why he lived up to his nickname of ‘Sherman Tank’; or just ‘The Tank’. He had numerous awards for bravery for bringing in the top criminals. A number died in their confrontations with

Fred. The senior officers, media and the public promoted him as the 'top cop' who wouldn't take a backward step in getting the worst criminals off the street.

"Put that gun down," said Harry, standing firm in the hallway, arms outstretched, revolver pointing at Fred's head. "You're coming with us."

"You fucking little upstart prick. You think because you got a couple of medals in the war you can do anything. Well, you've got another think coming, Harry. I've dealt with more killers in my life than you've had breakfasts, and each of them would outshoot you blindfolded. So don't think you can take me down."

Fred was naked except for a brief pair of underpants. Harry could see the strength of his arms tightening around Mark's throat. Mark was struggling for breath.

"Let him go, Fred. You are surrounded. Put the gun down now. Don't make it hard on yourself."

"You blokes will never learn Harry. I heard cars pulling up in the street so I got up to go to the bathroom and, as I was coming out, who should walk in the back door past the bathroom, but this young pup here. It was like taking a doll from a kid." His knee was in Mark's back.

"I'll say it slowly, Fred. Let him go and put down that gun."

"There's no way you shitbags are taking me anywhere. I'm taking this kid with me and, if you do anything stupid, I'll kill him. Just think, Harry. What will you say to his parents tonight? How will you explain how your stupidity and incompetence killed their son? Come on, Harry, tell me how you will do it. You're supposed to be the smart young cop. While you're thinking about it, I'm taking him out the back and around to the car. I'm warning you, Harry. Don't any of you try to stop me."

Harry decided to change tack. "Okay, Fred, you've got the upper hand. But before you go, tell me why you ordered the contract on me? What did I do to you to deserve that?"

Tapping the barrel of the revolver to his forehead Fred replied. "Up here for thinking, Harry. You always refused to be part of my team. You thought that your shit didn't stink. You could have come back to the CIB and worked in my team and you would now be well off. You wanted to do it your way. Well, I can tell you, sonny boy, there is only one way, and that's my way. Get that through your thick skull."

Harry moved a step closer but stopped as Fred tightened his grip on Mark's neck. "But why have me shot? I didn't do anything to hurt you."

"You were interfering with my organisation. You had to go. You see, Harry, there are two types of people in this world: those with me and those against; and there are very few of them left."

Harry spread his legs and knees, pushed his hands and shoulders forward, clamped his left hand firmly over his right wrist and sighted along the barrel of his revolver directly into Fred's eyes. "You're not leaving here without us, Fred. We are all heavily armed. If you harm young Mark there, you'll finish up with more holes in you than a kitchen sieve, and photographs of your bullet-ridden naked body will appear on the front page of every newspaper in the country this afternoon. The Australian population will be able to see you for what you really are; nothing better than the criminals you have exterminated in the past. Now, put down that gun, let go of the constable and raise your arms."

Fred took a deep breath and dragged Mark to his feet but kept a firm hold on his neck. He was like a lion holding a limp gazelle. "No way. If you or any of your men try anything stupid, this bloke gets it first and you get it second. That stupid Lebovich missed you in your shed, but I won't miss; and you know that I can do it. This bloke's body will protect me until I get you. The others will be easy meat."

Fred shuffled slowly backwards towards the door, dragging Mark with him. He held the barrel of the revolver firmly against Mark's temple. Harry advanced, keeping pace with him.

"Tell all of your men to come into the hall where I can see them, Harry. Tell them to drop their weapons."

"No, Fred. That's not the way we are going to handle this. You are no longer in charge and your mates are running a mile to get away from you. They don't want to go down with you. They'll grab their cash and run like hell. They'll claim that they never knew you and had nothing to do with the corruption or the killings. You're on your own now, Fred. So, let's do this the easy way. Drop the weapon."

As Fred pushed his leg back through the back door opening, feeling for the outside step, a hand flashed behind his head, grasped his right wrist and snapped it back with force. A shot rang out and Mark dropped to the floor. As Fred staggered backwards, Jock's knee hit him in the small of his back. Fred screamed and fell to the ground, his head landing on the concrete step. Jock rammed his size-twelve boot down on his neck. He twisted Fred's arm with such force that the shoulder was about to pop. He secured the wrists behind his back with the cuffs.

Harry rushed down the corridor, quickly followed by Archie. Don escorted the girlfriend, loosely covered in a sheet, into the lounge room.

"Mark, are you okay?" shouted Harry, kneeling down to check him out.

Mark was gasping for air, coughing and spluttering, eyes and nose streaming. He couldn't speak. Archie ran into the kitchen to get a towel and some water. Harry checked Mark's body but found no wound. The gunshot had missed him.

Lights came on in the neighbouring houses. Dogs were barking. A man looked over the side fence.

"Hey, you. What the hell is going on? Who are you?" the neighbour shouted.

Jock, with his foot still firmly on Fred's neck shouted in his strong Scottish brogue that could easily be heard at Strathfield Railway Station some blocks away. "Get the hell back inside. This is a police operation. Move, move, move, now."

The man rushed to his door, pushing his wife back inside in the same movement. In the other houses, curtains could be seen pulled back a few inches to allow the neighbours a nervous glance at what was going on. This certainly was not what was expected in a prime location like Strathfield.

"Thanks, Jock," stammered Mark, as he regained his breath. "You saved my life, mate. I owe you one."

"No problems, mate. But I might need more than a wee dram when we finish up here."

"Mate, you can drink the bar dry. It's all on me." Mark got to his feet and patted Jock on the shoulder.

Harry stepped forward. "Mark. Go into the bathroom and freshen up. When you finish I want you to help Don interrogate the girlfriend in the lounge room. If necessary take her back to her place and do a search. I want bank books, cheques, statements and anything else that might make her an accessory to corruption or murder. I suspect she is just a one-night-stand for Fred, but check it out. When you finish, come back here and let me know."

Jock pulled on the handcuffs behind Fred's back until he stood up. "Where do you want this scumbag, Harry?"

"Take him to the kitchen, Jock. We'll interview him in there."

With his other hand, Jock grabbed the waistband of Fred's briefs and frogmarched him into the kitchen, pushing him down onto the hard chair. Fred squirmed on the chair, shoulders jutting forward and back as he tried to get comfortable, jaw jutting out and teeth clenched in defiance, his steely grey eyes riveted on Harry's face. He had never been in this situation before. He was always the one in control.

Harry sat down at the table, taking his time to find a pen and notebook. Jock drew up a chair behind Fred.

"Detective Senior Sergeant Fred Sherman," began Harry in a more formal tone. "I am charging you, among other things, with murder, conspiracy to murder, assault with a deadly weapon, corruption and bribery. You do not have to say anything but if you do not..."

"Cut out all this bullshit, Harry," shouted Fred, trying to push the table with his chest towards Harry. "You know as well as me that this won't stick. The top brass won't let it happen. Who the hell do you think has been looking after our team all these years? You'll be the one who gets the axe one way or another. I'll make certain of that."

Harry ignored the barbed threats. "We have clear evidence that you personally shot and killed Tommy Scarface Fisher. At that time Fisher was unarmed and had made no attempt to cause you or your partners, any harm. It was a clear case of cold-blooded murder."

"Well, that won't stick," snarled Fred. "The police enquiry clearly established that Tommy was carrying a weapon and had fired shots at us before we took him out. They even awarded me a bravery medal for my actions there. It's in there in the bedroom in the top drawer. You go and ask Joe. He'll tell you the truth."

Harry placed his left elbow on the table with his hand clamped around his chin. He reached forward with the other hand halfway across the table, closing his fist, slowly, his eyes focused unblinkingly on Fred. He waited until he saw the perspiration appear on Fred's forehead. "We have already followed your good advice and we have talked to Detective Cross, as well as Bob Crow and Charlie Rockwell. They have confirmed our evidence and identified you as the person who killed Scarface in cold blood."

Fred tried to get up. Jock slapped him hard on the shoulder and he fell back. "Joe and I have worked together for years. I know that he would never say that, because it's not true."

"We also have evidence from a neighbour who saw Scarface come out of the house in Lever Street, Rosebery. He will swear in court that Scarface had no gun. He saw you fire shots in the air from the second revolver, wipe it and drop it next to Scarface after you shot him. You then placed it in his right hand. The trouble is, Fred, Fisher wasn't a shooter, and he was left-handed." Harry sat back to let that sink in.

"He's a bloody liar. How much did you pay him to say that?"

Harry stood up, walked to the cupboard, got out two glasses, filled them with water from the tap and handed one to Jock. He drank the other one himself. "Now, Fred; let's deal with the attempted murder of myself. We are holding Tom Lebovich. He has admitted that he was the shooter, but it was you who paid Whispers Durante two thousand pounds to get him to do the job. Joe Cross also confirmed that you took out that contract on me."

"What a lot of fucking bullshit. You bastards are trying to stitch me up with these charges to get rid of me. If you think you're going to try to take over my place in the CIB, think again. None of my team will work with you, Harry."

"It would be the last place I'd want to work, Fred. You have corrupted almost everyone in that team and we have the evidence to put you away for a long time just on that charge alone."

Fred snorted, threw back his head and laughed out loud. "Nobody in the CIB talks unless I say so. You're really desperate now, Harry. That shows you what a piss-poor detective you have always been, and will always be in the future. You couldn't find your prick unless someone pointed it out to you."

Harry paused again. "When we leave here, Fred, we are taking you to Central Street Station. You will hear audio tapes and see photographs of you receiving bribe money in the Elegant Lady casino on Saturday night. That money was delivered to you from well-known criminals. You get that money each week and distribute some of it to your mates, including to some in senior positions in the Force. We also know of similar bribes going to senior politicians, lawyers and judges."

"Pull the other leg, Harry. Nobody would dare try a stunt like that."

"Well, Fred, let me tell you that your friends Bob and Charlie fully cooperated with us and will stand up in court to confirm the evidence. Your estranged wife, Gloria has also cooperated with this inquiry. We have closed all of the bank accounts in false names including in your wife's maiden name, your son's two Christian names and your dead mother's name."

Fred banged his forehead on the table. "That money was won at the races and is legal. It's not illegal to have different accounts. There is no way you can touch that. Being lucky with the horses is not a crime."

"We have clear evidence of you paying the bookmaker, Charlie Bennett, to write out winning tickets after the last race each week. Two weeks ago he got one hundred pounds to write a ticket for the horse that won. That allowed you to launder one thousand pounds of illegal money. You're going down for the lot, Fred."

Fred gritted his teeth, sat back and kicked the leg of the desk. "There's no bloody way you'll get me into court, Harry. And do you want to know why? Because a number of very senior politicians and the key men in the Office of the Director of Public Prosecutions will make certain the case does not proceed. It will be declared a no case to answer. And then the newspapers will scream blue murder that their bravest and most successful policeman has been falsely accused by a jealous officer wanting his position."

Harry smiled. "Good try, Fred. I'm now informing you that at least one senior politician and some senior public servants will be charged today with corruption. They will be in court before the day is out."

Fred slumped back in the chair. His head dropped. It took some time before he regained his composure. He shook his head from side to side before looking again at Harry. "Mate, can we do a deal? I can set you up for life, guaranteed."

"Fred, I'll do a deal with you. With all of those crimes, you know from experience that you will be going to a maximum security for life. This is my deal: either you go to solitary confinement for life or we'll put you in the main arena with the other prisoners. In solitary, you will be confined to your cell for most of the day and you'll die of boredom. In the open section you will be surrounded by all those blokes you have put away for life. They're a very nasty bunch and have got nothing to lose. I'm sure they will welcome you with open arms. There's a lot of payback coming to you Fred. Make your choice."

Fred spat on the table in front of Harry.

Harry stood and pointed at Fred. "Jock, get that horrible creature out of my sight."

Harry went to the back door and walked into the yard. The large bright yellow sun was rising above the horizon. The magpies and butcher birds were warbling and whistling their songs. A white butterfly landed on a petunia, busily sucking the nectar from the flower. Harry stopped and took time to breathe in the fresh morning air; deep breaths to clear his lungs of the stench he had just witnessed. He walked slowly around the spacious property feeling the tension drain from his weary body.

This would be a bright new day.

9 780648 895404